Split Second

David Baldacci is the internationally acclaimed author of eighteen bestselling novels. With his books published in at least 45 languages, and with over 90 million copies in print, he is one of the world's favourite storytellers. His family foundation, the Wish You Well Foundation, a non-profit organization, works to eliminate illiteracy across America. Still a resident of his native Virginia, he invites you to visit him at www.DavidBaldacci.com, and his foundation at www.WishYouWellFoundation.org, and to look into its programme to spread books across America at www.FeedingBodyandMind.com.

DAVID BALDACCI

Split Second

PAN BOOKS

First published 2003 by Warner Books, Inc., New York

First published in Great Britain 2003 by Macmillan

This paperback edition published 2010 by Pan Books
an imprint of Pan Macmillan, a division of Macmillan Publishers Limited
Pan Macmillan, 20 New Wharf Road, London N1 9RR,
Basingstoke and Oxford
Associated companies throughout the world
www.panmacmillan.com

ISBN 978-1-4472-1055-9

1 3 5 7 9 8 6 4 2

A CIP catalogue record for this book is available from
the British Library.

Printed and bound by CPI Group (UK) Ltd, Croydon, CR0 4YY

To my father, the greatest inspiration
a son could have

Prologue

It only took a split second, although to Secret Service agent Sean King it seemed like the longest split second ever.

They were on the campaign trail at a nondescript hotel meet-and-greet in a place so far out you almost had to use a satellite phone to reach the boonies. Standing behind his protectee, King scanned the crowd while his ear mike buzzed sporadically with unremarkable information. It was muggy in the large room filled with excited people waving "Elect Clyde Ritter" pennants. There were more than a few infants being thrust toward the smiling candidate. King hated this because the babies could so easily shield a gun until it was too late. Yet the little ones just kept coming and Clyde kissed them all, and ulcers seemed to form in King's belly as he observed this potentially dangerous spectacle.

The crowd drew closer, right up to the velvet rope stanchions that had been placed as a line in the sand. In response, King moved closer to Ritter. The palm of his outstretched hand rested lightly on the candidate's sweaty, coatless back, so that he could pull him down in an instant if something happened. He couldn't very well stand in front of the man, for the candidate belonged to the *people*. Ritter's routine never varied: shake hands, wave, smile, nail a sound bite in time for the six o'clock news, then pucker up and kiss a fat baby. And all the time King silently watched the crowd, keeping his hand on Ritter's soaked shirt and looking for threats.

Someone called out from the rear of the space. Ritter answered the jibe back with his own bit of humor, and the crowd laughed good-naturedly, or at least most did. There were people here who hated Ritter and all he stood for. Faces didn't lie, not for those trained to read them, and King could read a face as well as he could shoot a gun. That's what he spent all his working life doing: reading the hearts and souls of men and women through their eyes, their physical tics.

He keyed on two men in particular, ten feet away, on the right. They looked like potential trouble, although each wore a short-sleeved shirt and tight pants with no place to conceal a weapon, which dropped them several pegs on the danger meter. Assassins tended to favor bulky clothing and small handguns. Still, he mumbled a few words into his mike, telling others of his concern. Then his gaze flitted to the clock on the back of the wall. It was 10:32 in the morning. A few more minutes and they'd be on to the next town, where the handshakes, sound bites, baby kisses and face reading would continue.

King's gaze had turned in the direction of the new sound, and then the new sight, something totally unexpected. Standing facing the crowd and behind the hard-politicking Ritter, he was the only one in the room who could see it. His attention stayed there for one beat, two beats, three beats, far too long. Yet who could blame him for not being able to pull his gaze away from *that*? Everyone, as it turned out, including himself.

King heard the *bang,* like the sound of a dropped book. He could feel the moisture on his hand where it had touched Ritter's back. And now the moisture wasn't just sweat. His hand stung where the slug had come out the body and taken a chunk off his middle finger before hitting the wall behind him. As Ritter dropped, King felt like a comet flying hell-bent and still taking a billion light-years to get where it's actually going.

Shrieks from the crowd poured out and then seemed to dissolve into one long, soulless moan.

Faces stretched into images one only saw in carnival fun houses. Then the blur hit him like the force of an exploding grenade as feet moved and bodies gyrated and the screams came at him from all directions. People pushed, pulled and ducked to get out of the way. He remembered thinking: there's no greater chaos than when swift, violent death knocks on the door of an unsuspecting crowd.

And now presidential candidate Clyde Ritter was lying by his feet on the hardwood floor shot right through the heart. King's gaze left the newly deceased and turned toward the shooter, a tall, handsome man in a tweed jacket and wearing glasses. The killer's Smith & Wesson .44 was still pointing at the spot where Ritter had been standing, as though waiting for the target to get back up so he could be shot all over again. The mass of panicked people held back the guards who were fighting to get through, so that King and the killer were the only ones at the party.

King pointed his pistol at the chest of the assassin. He gave no warning, called out not one constitutional right accorded the assassin under American jurisprudence. His duty now clear, he fired once, and then again, though the first time was enough. It dropped the man right where he stood. The assassin never said a word, as though he'd expected to die for what he'd done, and accepted the terms stoically like a good martyr should. And all martyrs left behind people like King, the ones who were blamed for letting it happen in the first place. Three men had actually died that day, and King had been one of them.

Sean Ignatius King, born August 1, 1960, died September 26, 1996, in a place he'd never even heard of until the final day of his life. And yet he had it far worse than the others who had fallen. They went tidily into their coffins and were forever mourned by those who loved them – or at least loved what they stood for. The soon-to-be-ex-Secret Service agent King had no such luck. After his death his unlikely burden was to keep right on living.

1

EIGHT YEARS LATER

The motorcade streamed into the tree-shaded parking lot, where it disgorged numerous people who looked hot, tired and genuinely unhappy. The miniature army marched toward the ugly white brick building. The structure had been many things in its time and currently housed a decrepit funeral home that was thriving solely because there was no other such facility within thirty miles and the dead, of course, had to go somewhere. Appropriately somber gentlemen in black suits stood next to hearses of the same color. A few bereaved trickled out the door, sobbing quietly into handkerchiefs. An old man in a tattered suit that was too large for him and wearing a battered, oily Stetson sat on a bench outside the front entrance, whittling. It was just that sort of a place, rural to the hilt, stock car racing and bluegrass ballads forever.

The old fellow looked up curiously as the procession passed by with a tall, distinguished-looking man ceremoniously in the middle. The elderly gent just shook his head and grinned at this spectacle, showing the few tobacco-stained teeth he had left. Then he took a nip of refreshment from a flask pulled from his pocket and returned to his artful wood carving.

The woman, in her early thirties and dressed in a black pantsuit, was in step behind the tall man. In the past her heavy pistol in the belt holster had scraped uncomfortably against her side, causing a scab. As a solution she'd sewn an extra layer of cloth into her blouses at that spot and learned to live with any lingering irritation. She'd overheard some of her men joke that all female agents should wear double shoulder holsters because it gave them a buxom look without expensive breast enhancement. Yes, testosterone was alive and well in her world.

Secret Service agent Michelle Maxwell was on the extreme fast track. She was not yet at the White House detail, guarding the president of the United States, but she was close. Barely nine years in the Service, and she was already a protection detail leader. Most agents spent a decade in the field doing investigative work before even graduating to protection detail as shift agents, yet Michelle Maxwell was used to getting to places before other folks.

This was her big preview before almost certain

reassignment to the White House, and she was worried. This was an unscheduled stop, and that meant no advance team and limited backup. Yet because it was a last-minute change in plan, the plus side was no one could know they were going to be there.

They reached the entrance, and Michelle put a firm hand on the tall man's arm and told him to wait while they scoped things out.

The place was quiet, smelled of death and despair in quiet pockets of misery centered on coffins in each of the viewing rooms. She posted agents at various key points along the man's path: "giving feet" as it was called in Service parlance. Properly done, the simple act of having a professional with a gun and communication capability standing in a doorway could work wonders.

She spoke into her walkie-talkie, and the tall man, John Bruno, was brought in. She led him down the hallway as gazes from the viewing rooms wandered to them. A politician and his entourage on the campaign trail were like a herd of elephants: they could travel nowhere lightly. They stomped the earth until it hurt with the weight of the guards, chiefs of staff, spokespersons, speechwriters, publicity folks, gofers and others. It was a spectacle that if it didn't make you laugh would at least cause you considerable worry about the future of the country.

John Bruno was running for the office of president of the United States, and he had absolutely no chance of winning. Looking far younger than his fifty-six years, he was an independent candidate who'd used the support of a small but strident percentage of the electorate fed up with just about everything mainstream to qualify for each state's national ballot. Thus, he'd been given Secret Service protection, though not at the staffing level of a bona fide contender. It was Michelle Maxwell's job to keep him alive until the election. She was counting the days.

Bruno was a former iron-balls prosecutor, and he'd made a great number of enemies, only some of whom were currently behind bars. His political planks were fairly simple. He'd tell you he wanted government off the backs of the people and free enterprise to rule. As for the poor and weak, those not up to the task of unfettered competition, well, in all other species the weak died and the strong prevailed, and why should it be any different for us? Largely because of that position, the man had no chance of winning. Although America loved its tough guys, they weren't ready to vote for leaders who exhibited no compassion for the downtrodden

and miserable, for on any given day they might con-
stitute a majority.

The trouble started when Bruno entered the
room trailed by his chief of staff, two aides, Michelle
and three of her men. The widow sitting in front of
her husband's coffin looked up sharply. Michelle
couldn't see her expression through the veil the
woman was wearing but assumed her look was one
of surprise at seeing this herd of interlopers invading
hallowed ground. The old woman got up and
retreated to a corner, visibly shaking.

The candidate whirled on Michelle. "He was a
dear friend of mine," Bruno snapped, "and I am not
going to parade in with an army. Get out," he added
tersely.

"I'll stay," she fired back. "Just me."

He shook his head. They'd had many such stand-
offs. He knew that his candidacy was a hopeless long
shot, and that just made him try even harder. The
pace had been brutal, the protection logistics a nightmare.

"No, this is private!" he growled. Bruno looked
over at the quivering woman in the corner. "My
God, you're scaring her to death. This is repugnant."

Michelle went back one more time to the well.
He refused yet again, leading them all out of the
room, berating them as he did. What the hell could

happen to him in a funeral home? Was the eighty-year-old widow going to jump him? Was the dead man going to come back to life? Michelle sensed that her protectee was really upset because she was costing him valuable campaign time. Yet it wasn't her idea to come here. However, Bruno was in no mood to hear that.

No chance to win, and the man acted like he was king of the hill. Of course, on election day the voters, including Michelle, would kick his butt right out the door.

As a compromise Michelle asked for two minutes to sweep the room. This was granted, and her men moved quickly to do so while she silently fumed, telling herself that she had to save her ammo for the really important battles.

Her men came out 120 seconds later and reported everything okay. Only one door in and out. No windows. Old lady and dead guy the only occupants. It was cool. Not perfect, but okay. Michelle nodded at her candidate. Bruno could have his private face time, and then they could get out of here.

Inside the viewing room, Bruno closed the door behind him and walked over to the open coffin. There was another coffin against the far wall; it was also open, but empty. The deceased's coffin was resting on a raised platform with a white skirting that was surrounded waist-high with an assortment of beautiful flowers. Bruno paid his respects to the body lying there, murmuring, "So long, Bill," as he turned to the widow, who'd returned to her chair. He knelt in front of her, gently held one of her hands.

"I'm so sorry, Mildred, so very sorry. He was a good man."

The bereaved looked up at him from behind the veil, smiled and then looked down again. Bruno's expression changed and he looked around, though the only other occupant of the room was in no condition to eavesdrop. "Now, you mentioned something else you wanted to talk about. In private."

"Yes," the widow said in a very low voice.

"I'm afraid I don't have much time, Mildred. What is it?"

In answer she placed a hand on his cheek, and then her fingers touched his neck. Bruno grimaced as he felt the sharp prick against his skin, and then he slipped to the floor unconscious.

2

Michelle paced in the hallway, checking her watch and listening to the somber music wafting over the sound system. If you weren't sad, depressed or perhaps even suicidal before coming in here, you would be after five minutes of listening to this brain-numbing tripe, she concluded. She was livid that Bruno had closed the door, but she had let it go. You weren't supposed to let a protectee out of your sight, but the realities of life sometimes trumped the rule book. Still, she looked at one of her men and asked for the fifth time, "You're absolutely sure it's clean?" He nodded.

After waiting a bit more she went over to the door and knocked. "Mr. Bruno? We need to get going, sir." There was no answer, and Michelle let out an inaudible sigh. She knew that the other agents in her detail, all of them her senior in years with the Service, were watching her intently to see how she'd handle herself. Only seven percent of the approximately 2,400 field agents were women, with very few in positions of authority. Yes, it was not easy.

She knocked again. "Sir?" Another few moments passed, and Michelle felt her stomach muscles start to tighten. She tried the doorknob and looked up in disbelief. "It's locked."

Another agent stared at her, equally perplexed. "Well, he must have locked it, then."

"Mr. Bruno, are you all right?" She paused. "Sir, either acknowledge me or we are coming in."

"Just a minute!" That was Bruno's voice; it was unmistakable.

"Okay, sir, but we need to get going."

Two more minutes went by, and she shook her head and knocked on the door again. No response. "Sir, we're already late." She glanced at Bruno's chief of staff, Fred Dickers. "Fred, you care to try?"

Dickers and she had long ago reached a mutual understanding. Basically living together twenty hours a day, the detail leader and chief of staff had to get along, at least mostly, for things to work. They still didn't see eye-to-eye on everything, nor would they ever, but on this issue they were in agreement.

Dickers nodded and called out, "John, it's Fred. We really need to get going. We're way off schedule." He knocked on the door. "John? Do you hear me?"

Again Michelle's stomach muscles tightened.

Something wasn't right here. She motioned Dickers away from the door and knocked again. "Mr. Bruno, why did you lock the door, sir?" No answer. A bead of sweat broke on Michelle's forehead. She hesitated for an instant, thinking rapidly, and then suddenly yelled though the door, "Sir, your wife is on the phone. There's been a serious accident involving one of your kids."

The response was chilling.

"Just a minute!"

She barked at the other agents with her, "Take it down. Take it down!"

They put their shoulders to the door, once and then twice, and then it gave way and they swarmed into the room.

A room that was empty except for a dead man.

3

A funeral procession had started off. There were only about a dozen cars in the column as it headed out along the treelined drive. Before the last car disappeared down the road, Michelle and her team had burst out the front door of the funeral home and spread out in all directions.

"Lock this whole area down," she shouted at the agents stationed by Bruno's motorcade. They raced to carry out her orders. She spoke into her walkie-talkie. "I need reinforcements. From where I don't care, just get them. Now! And get the FBI on the horn." Her gaze fixed on the rear end of the last car in the funeral procession. Heads would roll over this. Her head would roll. Right now, though, all she wanted was to get John Bruno back, preferably living.

She saw reporters and photographers pouring out of the media trucks. Despite the nice photo op it would have made and Fred Dickers's entreaties that he should allow it, Bruno had shown some backbone and refused their request to come inside the funeral home. They hadn't taken the news well. Now they were erupting with full journalistic force as they sensed a story of far greater magnitude than a candidate's visit to pay his last respects to an old friend.

Before they could get to her, Michelle grabbed the arm of a uniformed officer who had come running up, apparently awaiting instructions.

"Are you security here?" she asked.

He nodded, his eyes wide, his face pale; he looked like he might either faint or wet his trousers.

She pointed down the road. "Whose funeral procession is that?"

"Harvey Killebrew's; they're taking him to Memorial Gardens."

"I want you to stop it."

The man looked dumbly at her. "Stop it?"

"Somebody has been kidnapped. And that" – she pointed at the procession – "would be a great way to get him out of the area, don't you think?"

"Okay," he said slowly. "Yeah."

"Then I want you to search every vehicle, in particular the hearse. Got it?"

"The hearse? But, ma'am, Harvey's in there."

Michelle looked at his uniform. He was a rent-a-cop, but she didn't have the luxury of being picky.

She eyed his name tag and said in a very quiet tone, "Officer Simmons? Officer Simmons, how long have you been . . . uh, in the security business?"

"About a month, ma'am. But I'm weapon-certified. Been hunting since I was eight years old. Shoot the wings off a mosquito."

"That's great." A month. He actually looked greener than that. "Okay, Simmons, listen carefully. My thinking is that the person is probably unconscious. And a hearse would be a great way to transport an unconscious person, don't you agree?" He nodded, apparently finally getting her point. Her face turned to a scowl and her voice to the crack of a pistol. "Now move your ass and stop that procession and search those vehicles."

Simmons went off at a dead run. Michelle ordered several of her men to follow him to oversee and help with the operation and instructed other agents to begin a thorough search of the funeral home. It was just possible that Bruno was hidden somewhere inside. She then pushed her way through the reporters and photographers and set up her command center inside the funeral home. From there she got back on the horn, consulted local maps and coordinated more efforts, establishing a one-mile perimeter with the funeral home as its center. Then she made the call she didn't want to make but had to. She phoned her superiors and said the words that would forever remain attached to her name and wrecked career at the Secret Service.

"This is Agent Michelle Maxwell, detail leader for John Bruno. I'm reporting that we – that *I've* lost the protectee. Apparently John Bruno has been kidnapped. The search is ongoing, and local law enforcement and the FBI have been contacted." She could feel the ax already descending upon her neck.

She joined her team of men who were tearing the funeral home apart from top to bottom looking for Bruno. Doing all of this without disturbing the crime scene was problematic at best. They couldn't interfere with the investigation to follow, but they had to search for the missing candidate.

Inside the viewing room where Bruno had disappeared, Michelle looked at one of the agents who'd scoped the room out before the candidate entered it. "How the hell could this have happened?" she demanded.

He was a veteran with the Service, a good agent. He shook his head in disbelief. "The place was clean, Mick. Clean."

Michelle often went by "Mick" at work. It made her seem more like one of the boys, which she'd grudgingly conceded was not such a bad thing.

"Did you check out the widow, question her?"

He looked at her skeptically. "What, give an old woman the third degree with her husband lying in a coffin five feet away? We looked in her purse, but I didn't think a body cavity search was really appropriate." He added, "We had two minutes to do it. You tell me anyone who could have done a proper job in two minutes."

Michelle stiffened as the meaning of the man's words became clear. Everyone would be looking to cover his butt and federal pension over this one. Stupid now when you looked at it: giving them only two minutes. She checked the doorknob. It had been rigged to lock when closed.

A coffin five feet away? She looked over at the copper-colored box. The funeral director was called for. He was paler now than even a mortician should be. Michelle asked him if the body was indeed that of Bill Martin. Yes, the man said.

"And you're sure the woman in here was Martin's widow."

"What woman would that be?" he asked.

"There was a woman dressed all in black, with a veil, sitting in this room."

"I don't know if it was Mrs. Martin or not. I didn't see her come in."

"I'll need Mrs. Martin's phone number. And nobody who works here can leave – not until the

FBI has arrived and completed its investigation. Understood?"

If possible, the man grew even paler. "The FBI?"

Michelle dismissed him, and then her gaze fell on the coffin and the floor in front of it. She bent down to pick up some rose petals that had fallen there. As she did so, she was eye level with the skirting that ran around the coffin. She reached over the flowers and carefully drew aside the fabric, exposing wood paneling. Michelle tapped on the wood. It was hollow. Using gloves, she and another agent lifted out one of the wood sections, revealing a space that could easily have concealed someone. Michelle could only shake her head. She'd blown this all around.

One of her men came up to her with a device in a plastic bag. "Some sort of digital recorder," he reported.

"That's how they generated Bruno's voice?" she said.

"Must have gotten a snippet of him from somewhere and used it to keep us at bay while they made their getaway. They must have thought the phrase 'Just a minute' would handle most queries from us. You tripped them up with your remark about Bruno's kids. There must be a wireless bug around here somewhere too."

21

Michelle read his thoughts. "Because they'd have to be able to hear us to make the recorded voice answer when I called out."

"Right." He pointed at the far wall where a section of the upholstered wall covering had been pulled back. "There's a door there. A passageway runs behind that wall."

"So there's their exit." She handed him the plastic bag. "Put it back exactly where you got it. I don't need a lesson from the FBI on maintaining the integrity of a crime scene."

"There must have been a struggle. I'm surprised we didn't hear anything," said the agent.

"How could we, with that death music bellowing everywhere?" she snapped.

She and the agent went down the passageway. The empty coffin on a rolling table had been left at a doorway here that opened onto the back of the building. They returned to the viewing room, and the funeral home director was called back in and shown the hidden doorway

He looked perplexed. "I didn't even know that was there."

"What?" Michelle said incredulously.

"We've only been operating this business for a couple of years. That's when the only funeral home in the area went out of business. We couldn't use that building because it had been condemned. This place was a lot of things before it was a funeral home. The current owners did minimal improvements. In fact, these viewing rooms went fairly unchanged. I had no idea there was a door or passageway there."

"Well, somebody certainly did," she said bluntly. "There's a door at the end of that hall that opens to the rear of the building. Are you telling me you didn't know about that either?"

He said, "That part of the facility is used for storage and is accessed by entrances inside the building."

"Did you see any vehicle parked out there earlier?"

"No, but then I don't go around there."

"Anybody else see anything?"

"I'll have to check."

"No, I'll check."

"I can assure you this is a very respectable establishment."

"You have secret hallways and exit doors you know nothing about. Aren't you worried about security?"

He looked at her blankly and then shook his head. "This isn't some big city. There's never any serious crime."

"Well, that streak was just broken. Do you have Mrs. Martin's phone number?"

He handed it over and she was called. There was no answer.

Alone for now, Michelle stood in the middle of the room. All those years of work, all that time proving she could do the job – it was all down the drain. She didn't even have the consolation of having hurled her body in front of a would-be assassin's bullet. Michelle Maxwell was now part of history. And she knew she was also history with the Secret Service. Her career was over.

4

The funeral procession was stopped and each car was searched, as was the hearse. It *was* Harvey Killebrew, devoted father, grandfather and husband, lying in there when they opened the casket. Virtually all the mourners were elderly and obviously frightened by all the men with guns, and there didn't seem to be a kidnapper within the bunch, but still the agents directed all the cars and the hearse back to the funeral home.

Rent-a-Cop Simmons approached a Secret Service agent who was climbing into his sedan to lead the caravan back to the funeral home. "What next, sir?"

"Okay, what I need is this road watched. Anyone trying to come out, you stop. Anyone coming in, you stop and check for appropriate credentials. We'll get you some relief as soon as we can. Until then, here is where you'll be. Got it?"

Simmons looked very nervous. "This is really big, isn't it?"

"Sonny, this is the biggest thing you'll ever have happen in your entire life. Let's just hope it turns out okay. But I kind of doubt that."

Another agent, Neal Richards, ran up and said, "I'll stay, Charlie. Probably not a good idea to leave him here all by himself."

Charlie glanced at his colleague and said, "Sure you don't want to come back and join the party, Neal?"

Richards smiled grimly and said, "I don't want to be within a mile of Michelle Maxwell right now. I'll stay with the kid."

Richards climbed into the vehicle next to Simmons, who maneuvered his van so that it blocked the road. They watched as the caravan of agents and mourners passed out of sight, and scanned the countryside in all directions. There was no sign of anyone. Simmons kept his hand firmly on the butt of his gun, his black leather glove crinkling as he squeezed the pistol grip. He reached over and turned up the volume on his police scanner and then looked nervously at the veteran agent.

He said in a loud voice, "I know you probably can't tell me, but what the hell happened back there?"

Richards didn't bother to look at him. "You're right, I can't tell you."

Simmons said, "I grew up here, know every inch of the place. If I was trying to get somebody outta here, there's a dirt lane about a half mile down the road. You cut through there and go out the other side, you're five miles away before you even know it."

Richards now glanced at him and said slowly, "Is that right?" He leaned toward Simmons and reached inside his coat pocket. The next moment Secret Service agent Neal Richards was lying facedown on the seat, a small red hole in the center of his back, the stick of gum he had pulled from his pocket still clenched in his hand. Simmons looked in the back of the van, where the woman was taking the suppressor off her small-caliber pistol. She had been secreted in a small area under the van floor's false bottom. The chatter from the police scanner had covered the slight noise she made coming out. She said, "Low-caliber dumdum, wanted to keep it in the body. Less mess."

Simmons smiled. "Like the man said, this *is* really big." He pulled out the dead agent's wireless mike and power pack and threw them deep into the woods. He drove off in the opposite direction of the funeral home. Eight hundred yards down the road he turned onto a weed-covered dirt lane. They pushed Agent Richards's body out there in an overgrown ravine adjacent to the road. Simmons had been telling the agent the truth: this road was the perfect escape route. Another hundred yards and two bends in the road brought them to an abandoned barn, its roof starting to fall in, its doors open. He drove directly into the space, got out and shut the barn doors. Parked inside was a white pickup truck

The woman emerged from the back of the van. She looked nothing like an elderly widow now. She was young, blond-haired, slender yet muscular and agile, dressed in jeans and a white tank shirt. She had used many names over her brief life and currently went by "Tasha." As dangerous as Simmons was, Tasha was even more lethal. She had that essential trait of a polished killer: she possessed no conscience.

Simmons took off his uniform, revealing jeans and a T-shirt. Next he pulled out a makeup kit from the rear of the van and removed the wig, matching sideburns and eyebrows and other parts of his facial disguise. He had been hidden in the hollow platform under Bill Martin's casket; after helping to carry John Bruno out, he assumed the role of "Officer Simmons."

From the van they lifted a large box containing

Bruno. The box was marked as containing communication equipment in case anyone had bothered to look. A large tool case was situated against the back of the white pickup's rear window. They took Bruno and placed him inside the tool case and locked it. There were vents in the sides and top of the case, and its interior had been padded.

Next they loaded bales of hay that were stacked in a corner of the barn into the bed of the truck; that mostly concealed the tool case. They jumped into the cab of the truck, donned John Deere caps and pulled out of the barn, taking another weed-infested dirt road back to the main drag about two miles farther down.

They passed a stream of police cars, black sedans and SUVs heading, no doubt, to the crime scene. One young cop even smiled at the pretty woman in the passenger side of the truck cab as he sped by. Tasha gave him a flirty look and waved back. The pair drove on with their kidnapped presidential candidate safely unconscious in the back.

Two miles ahead of them was the elderly man who'd sat by the entrance to the funeral home when John Bruno and his entourage passed by. His whittling done, he'd escaped Maxwell's lockdown by a few minutes. He drove alone in his ancient, muffler-rattling Buick Impala. He'd just received the news from his colleagues. Bruno was safely tucked away, and the only casualty had been one Secret Service agent unlucky enough to pair up with a man he undoubtedly believed was harmless.

After all this time and work, it had finally begun. He could only smile.

5

The red Ford Explorer pulled to a stop near a large cedar log structure shrouded in deep woods. The place was intricately constructed and far closer to a lodge in scale than a single-family cabin, though only one person lived there. The man got out and stretched his limbs. It was still early, and the sun had just begun its ascent.

Sean King went up the wide hand-hewn timber steps and unlocked the door to his home. He stopped in the spacious kitchen to make coffee. As it percolated, he looked around the interior, appraising each mitered corner, the placement of each log, the proportion of window space to wall. He'd pretty much built the place himself over a four-year period while he lived in a small trailer on the perimeter of the fifteen-acre spread about thirty-five miles west of Charlottesville in the Blue Ridge Mountains.

The interior was furnished with leather chairs and overstuffed couches, wooden tables, Oriental rugs, copper lighting fixtures, plain bookshelves filled with an eclectic assortment of volumes, oil and pastel paintings, mostly done by local artists, and other items one collects or inherits in the course of a lifetime. And at forty-four years old King had lived at least two lives thus far. He had no desire to reinvent himself yet again.

He went upstairs, made his way along the catwalk that ran the length of the house, and entered his bedroom. Like the rest of the place, it was very organized, things neatly arranged and not an inch of wasted space.

He stripped off his police deputy's uniform and climbed into the shower and let the sweat of a night's work wash away. He shaved, washed his hair and let the hot water loosen up the surgical scar on his middle finger. He had long ago learned to live with this small souvenir of his days as a Secret Service agent.

If he were with the Service now, instead of living in a beautiful log house in the middle of lovely central Virginia, he'd probably be packed into a town house in some stultifying cookie-cutter bedroom community outside the Washington Beltway and still married to his ex-wife. He also wouldn't be getting ready to go to his thriving law practice. He certainly wouldn't be a volunteer deputy police officer one night a week for his rural community. He'd be about to hop on another plane, watch politicians smile, kiss babies and lie, waiting patiently for the moment when someone tried to kill his guy. What a gig that was, and it included all the frequent flier miles and Tums he wanted!

He changed into a suit and tie, combed his hair, drank his coffee in the sunroom off the kitchen and read the newspaper. The front page was dominated by reports of the kidnapping of John Bruno and the subsequent FBI investigation. King read the main story and related articles carefully, absorbing all relevant details. He clicked on the TV, found the all-news channel and watched as the newsperson reported on the death of Neal Richards, veteran Secret Service agent. He'd left behind a wife and four kids.

It was undeniably tragic, sad, all of that, but at least the Service took care of the survivors. Neal Richards's family would have their full support. That couldn't take away the loss, but it was something.

The reporter then said that the FBI had no comment. "Of course not," King said to himself; they never commented on anything, and yet eventually somebody would let slip to somebody who would run to a friend at the *Post* or the *Times* and then everybody would know. Yet what they knew was usually wrong! However, the media beast had an insatiable appetite, and no organization could afford to totally starve it, not even the FBI.

He sat up and stared at the image of the woman on the TV standing near a group of folks at a podium. This was the Secret Service part of the story, King instantly sensed. He knew the breed well. The woman looked professional, calm, with a relaxed alertness so familiar to King. And something else was in her expression that he couldn't quite read. There was belly fire, for all of them had some measure of that. Yet there was something more: subtle defiance perhaps?

The Service was assisting the FBI in every way, one of the men said, and they were, of course, also conducting their own internal investigation. The Service's Inspection Division would be handling this investigation, King knew, because they had been all over his butt after the Ritter assassination. Reading the bureaucratic doublespeak, King knew this meant that blame had already been assessed and would be made public as soon as the relevant parties had signed off on the appropriate spin to put on the awful news. Then the press conference was over, and the woman was walking away and getting into a black sedan. She was not speaking to reporters on orders from the Service, the voiceover said, and the narrator also helpfully identified her as Michelle Maxwell, head of the security detail that had lost John Bruno.

So why parade her in front of the press? wondered King. Why wave red meat in front of a caged beast? He almost immediately answered his own question: to give a face to the coming blame. The Service was often very good about protecting its own, and agents had screwed up before, been given administrative leave and then reassigned. However, there might be some political pressure on this one that was screaming out for a head to fall. "Here she is, folks," they might have said. "Go get her, although we still have to do our official investigation, but don't let that stop you." And now King understood the look of subtle defiance in the woman's features. She knew exactly what was going on. The lady was attending her own hanging and not liking it.

King sipped his coffee, munched on a piece of toast and said to her and the TV, "Well, you can be as pissed off as you want, but you can also just kiss your ass good-bye, Michelle."

Next a picture of Michelle Maxwell appeared on the screen while some more background information on the woman was given. A high school all-American in basketball *and* track and a heavyweight academic as well, she'd gone on to graduate from Georgetown in three years, with criminal justice as her major. If that wasn't high-octane enough, during college she'd turned her considerable athletic talents to another sport and had won a silver medal at the Olympics in women's rowing: a scholar athlete, what could be more inspiring? After a year as a police officer in her native Tennessee she'd joined the Service, ferociously worked her way up the ladder at double-quick time and was currently enjoying the wonderful status of a scapegoat.

And a handsome scapegoat she was, King thought, and then caught himself. Handsome? And yet there *were* masculine qualities about her, the forceful, almost swaggering way in which she walked, the impressive spread of shoulders – no doubt all that rowing – the jawline that seemed to promise extreme obstinacy at frequent intervals. And yet the feminine side was certainly there. She was over five-nine and, despite the broad shoulders, slender, but she had nice, subtle curves too. The hair was black, straight and shoulder-length, regulation enough for the Service but still stylish. The cheek-bones were high and firm, the eyes green, luminous and intelligent – clearly those eyes missed very little. In the Secret Service such X-ray vision was a necessity.

The overall look was not that of a classic beauty, but Michelle was probably the girl who was always faster and smarter than all the boys. In high school she likely had every male gunning to be the first to steal her virginity. From the look of the woman, though, he doubted any had succeeded on anything other than Maxwell's terms.

Well, he said silently to the TV screen, there is life after the Service. You can start over and re-create yourself. You can be reasonably happy against all the odds. But you never do forget. Sorry, Michelle Maxwell, I speak from experience on that one too.

He checked his watch. Time to go to his real job drafting wills and leases and charging by the hour. Not nearly as exciting as his old occupation, yet at this stage of his life Sean King was very much into boring routine. He'd had enough excitement to last him several lifetimes.

6

King backed his Lexus convertible, top down, out of the garage and headed off to work for the second time in eight hours. The drive took him through winding roads, fabulous views, the occasional wild-life sighting and not much traffic, at least until he hit the road into town, where the automobile volume picked up some. His law office was located on the appropriately named Main Street, the only avenue of consequence in the downtown area of Wrightsburg, a small and relatively new township halfway between the far larger municipalities of Charlottesville and Lynchburg.

He parked in the lot behind the two-story white brick town home that housed King & Baxter, Attorneys and Counselors-at-Law, as the shingle hanging outside proudly proclaimed. He'd gone to law school thirty minutes away at the University of Virginia before dropping out after two years and opting for a career in the Secret Service. At the time, he wanted more adventure than a stack of lawbooks and the Socratic method could provide. Well, he'd had his share of adventure.

After the dust settled from the Clyde Ritter killing, he'd left the Secret Service, finished his degree and opened a solo practice in Wrightsburg. It had now expanded to a two-lawyer firm, and King's life was finally clicking on all cylinders. He was a respected counselor and friend to many of the most prominent in the area. He gave back to the community as a volunteer deputy police officer and in other ways as well. One of the most eligible bachelors in the area, he dated when he wanted and didn't when he didn't. He had a wide assortment of friends, though few who were intimates. He liked his work, enjoyed his free time and didn't let much rattle him. His life was marching itself off in carefully constructed and unspectacular measure. He was perfectly fine with that.

As he got out of the Lexus, he saw the woman and contemplated ducking back inside, but she'd already spotted him and rushed over

"Hello, Susan," he said as he pulled his briefcase out of the passenger seat

"You look tired," she said. "I don't know how you do it."

"Do what?"

"Busy lawyer by day, police officer by night."

"Volunteer deputy police officer, Susan, and only one night a week. In fact, the most exhilarating thing to happen last night was swerving my truck to miss hitting a possum."

"I bet when you were with the Secret Service, you went days without sleep. How exciting, if exhausting."

"Not exactly," he said, and started to head to his office. She followed.

Susan Whitehead was in her early forties, divorced, attractive, rich and apparently dead set on making him her fourth husband. King had handled her last divorce, knew firsthand the number of impossibly annoying quirks the woman had, how vindictive she could be, and his sympathies lay entirely with poor husband number three. He was a timid, reclusive man so smashed under the iron fist of his wife that he'd finally gone off on a four-day drinking, gambling and sex spree in Las Vegas that had been the beginning of the end. He was now a poorer but no doubt happier soul. King had no interest at all in replacing him

"I'm having a small dinner party on Saturday and was hoping you could come."

He mentally checked his calendar, found Saturday night free and said, without missing a beat, "I'm sorry, I've got plans, thanks anyway. Maybe another time."

"You have a lot of plans, Sean," she said coyly. "I'm really hoping that I fit into them at some point."

"Susan, it's not good for an attorney and client to become personally involved."

"But I'm not your client anymore."

"Still, a bad idea. Trust me on that one." He reached the front door and unlocked it before adding, "And you have a great day." He went inside, hoping she wouldn't follow. He waited a few seconds in the foyer of the building, breathed a sigh of relief when she didn't charge in, and headed up the stairs to his office. He was almost always the first in. His partner, Phil Baxter, was the litigation arm of the two-person firm, while King handled all the other areas: wills, trusts, real estate, business deals, the steady moneymakers. There was a lot of wealth secreted in the quiet nooks and crannies around Wrightsburg. Movie stars, business tycoons, writers and other enriched souls called this area home. They loved it for its beauty, solitude, privacy and local amenities in the form of good restaurants, shopping, a thriving cultural community and a world-class university down the road in Charlottesville.

Phil was not an early riser – court did not open

until ten – but he worked very late, the opposite of King. By five o'clock King was usually back home, puttering in his workshop or fishing or boating on the lake that his house backed up to, while Baxter labored on. The two consequently made a nice match.

He opened the door and went in. The receptionist/secretary wouldn't be there yet. It was not quite eight.

The chair lying on its side was the first thing that caught his eye, and after that the items that were supposed to be on the receptionist's desktop but were now strewn across the floor. His hand went instinctively to his holstered gun, only he had no holster or gun. All he had was a really kick-ass codicil to a will he'd drafted that would intimidate only the future heirs. He picked up a heavy paperweight from the floor and peered around. The next sight froze him.

There was blood on the floor by the door leading into Baxter's office. He moved forward, holding the paperweight ready; with his other hand he pulled out his cell phone, dialed 911 and spoke quietly and clearly to the dispatcher. He reached out his hand to the doorknob, thought better of it and pulled a handkerchief out of his pocket so no prints would be smeared. He slowly eased the door open, his muscles tensed, ready for an attack, yet his instincts told him that the place was empty. He looked into the darkened space and used his elbow to flick on the light.

The body was lying on its side directly in front of King; a single gunshot wound to the center of the chest, exiting out the back. It wasn't Phil Baxter. It was another man – very well known to him, though. And this person's violent death was about to shatter Sean King's peaceful existence.

He let out the breath he'd been holding in, and it all hit him in a blinding instant. "Here we go again," he muttered.

7

The man was sitting in his Buick and watched as the police cars pulled up in front of King's law building and the uniformed officers raced inside. His appearance had changed much since he'd sat playing the role of an old man whittling in front of the funeral home while John Bruno was being carried away. The suit he'd worn that day was two sizes too large, to make him look small and emaciated; the dirty teeth, whiskered face, moonshine flask, whittling and a wad of chew in the mouth were all carefully designed to draw the eye to him. And the observer would come away with an indelible impression of who and what he was. And that conclusion would be absolutely incorrect, which was the whole point really.

He was younger now, perhaps by more than thirty years. Like King, he had re-created himself. He munched on a buttered bagel, sipped his black coffee and quietly pondered King's reaction to the discovery of the body in his office. Shocked at first and then perhaps angry, but not surprised – no, not really surprised when one thought about it.

As he considered this, he turned on the radio, which was always set to the local news channel, and he got the eight o'clock report, which started off with the abduction of John Bruno, the lead story for just about every news service worldwide. It had even chased the Middle East and professional football from the minds of many Americans, at least temporarily.

The man licked his fingers clean of butter and sesame seeds as he listened. The story had to do with Michelle Maxwell, the Secret Service detail leader. She'd been officially placed on administrative leave, which, he knew, meant she was one foot from the professional grave.

So the woman was out of the game, at least officially. Yet unofficially? That was why he'd memorized Maxwell's every feature as she passed by him that day. It wasn't out of the question that he'd confront her again at some point. He already knew her complete background, but the more information, the more intelligence, the better. She was a woman who might sit home and grow bitter, or one who'd charge forward and take risks. From the little he'd seen of her, he thought the latter more likely.

He refocused on the scene unfolding in front of him now. Some of the townsfolk, just showing up for work or opening their shops, were wandering toward the lawyer's office as yet another police car and then a crime scene van pulled into the small parking lot. This was clearly something new for the respectable little metropolis of Wrightsburg. The men in uniform hardly seemed to know what to do. It was all so heartening to the man as he munched on his bagel. He'd waited so long for all of this; he intended to enjoy it. And there was much more to come.

He noted once again the woman standing outside the office. He'd seen Susan Whitehead when she approached King in the parking lot. A girlfriend? A would-be lover was probably more accurate, the man deduced from the encounter he'd witnessed. He raised his camera and took a couple of shots of her. He waited for King to come out for air, but that was probably not going to happen. King had covered much ground in his rounds as a deputy. So many back roads to traverse, lonely roads they were too. Anything could be out there, in the thick woods, waiting for you. And yet where was one really safe these days?

Inside a zippered bag in his trunk was a very special item that had to go to a special place. In fact, now was the perfect opportunity to do so.

After tossing the remains of his breakfast in a garbage can on the sidewalk he put the rusted Buick in gear and drove off, muffler rattling. He pulled down the street, glancing once in the direction of King's office and flippantly gave a thumbs-up sign. As he passed by Susan Whitehead, who was staring at King's office, he thought, Maybe I'll be seeing you. Sooner rather than later.

The Buick disappeared down the road, leaving a stricken Wrightsburg in its wake.

Round one was now officially over. He could hardly wait for round two.

8

Walter Bishop, a man very high up in the Secret Service, paced in front of Michelle Maxwell, who sat at a small table and watched. They were in a small conference room deep inside a government building in Washington filled with people reeling from recent events.

Over his shoulder he said, "You should feel relieved you're only being placed on admin leave, Maxwell."

"Oh, yes, I'm thrilled you've taken my gun and badge. I'm not stupid, Walter. Judgment has already been passed. I'm gone."

"The investigation is ongoing – in fact, it's just beginning."

"Right. All those years of my life, down the toilet."

He whirled and snapped, "A presidential candidate was kidnapped right under your nose – a first in the agency's history. Congratulations. You're lucky you're not in front of a firing squad. In some other countries you would be."

"Walter, don't you think I feel that too? It's killing me."

"Interesting choice of words. Neal Richards was a fine agent."

"I know that too," she snapped back. "Do you think I knew that this rent-a-cop was in on it? There is no one in the Service who feels worse than I do about Neal."

"You never should have allowed Bruno in that room alone. If you'd simply followed standard procedures, this never would have happened. At the very least that door should have been open far enough for you to see your man. You never, ever take your eyeballs off your protectee; you know that. That's Protection Detail 101."

Michelle shook her head. "Sometimes, on the job, in the middle of all the things we have to put up with, you strike compromises, to keep everybody happy."

"It's not our job to keep people happy. It's our job to keep them safe!"

"Are you telling me this is the first time a judgment call was made in the field to let a protectee in a room without an agent?"

"No, I'm saying this is the first time that call was

made and something like this happened. It's strict liability, Michelle. No excuses will avail. Bruno's political party is up in arms. Some nuts are actually saying the Service was paid off to knock Bruno out of the race."

"That's absurd."

"I know it is and you know it is, but you get enough people saying it, well, then the public starts believing it."

Michelle had perched on the edge of her seat during this exchange. Now she sat back and looked calmly at the man.

"Just so we're clear, I accept full responsibility for what happened, and none of my men should be affected. They were following orders. It was my call and I blew it."

"Good of you to say. I'll see what I can do about that." He paused and added, "I suppose you wouldn't consider resigning."

"No, Walter, I really wouldn't. And just so you know, I'm hiring an attorney."

"Of course, you are. This is America. Here any screwup can hire a lawyer and actually get money for being incompetent. You must be so proud."

Michelle suddenly had to blink back tears at this stinging rebuke, yet part of her thought she deserved it. "I'm just protecting myself, Walter, just like you would if you were in my position."

"Right. Of course." The man put his hands in his pockets and glanced toward the door in a show of dismissing her.

Michelle rose. "Can I ask one favor?"

"Certainly you can ask. Although you have un- believable balls to do so."

"You're not the first person to notice that," she said coolly. He waited expectantly, without reply- ing. "I want to know how the investigation is going."

"The FBI is handling all of that."

"I know, but they must be keeping the Service informed."

"They are, and that information is for Service personnel only."

"Meaning I'm not?"

"You know, Michelle, I had my doubts when the Service started actively recruiting women. I mean you spend money to train an agent, and then, poof, she gets married, has babies and retires. All that training, money, time, down the drain."

Michelle couldn't believe she was listening to this, but she remained silent.

"But when you came on board, I thought, now

this gal has what it takes. You were the poster woman for the Service. The best and the brightest."

"And with it came high expectations."

"Every agent here has high expectations thrust upon them, nothing less than perfection." He paused and added, "I know that your record was spotless before this. I know that you were moving up rapidly. I know that you're a good agent, but you messed up, we lost a protectee and an agent lost his life. It's not necessarily fair but there you are. It wasn't really fair for them either." He paused again, and his eyes took on a faraway look. "You may stay with the Service in some capacity. But you'll never, ever forget what happened. It'll be with you every minute of every day for the rest of your life. And that will hurt you far worse than anything the Service could do to you. Trust me."

"You sound pretty sure about that."

"I was with Bobby Kennedy at the Ambassador Hotel. I was a rookie cop in L.A. assigned to do local backup for the Secret Service when RFK came through. I just stood there and watched a man who should have gone on to be president bleed to death on the floor. Every day since then I've wondered what I could have done differently that would have prevented it from happening. It was one of the major reasons I joined the Service years later. I guess I wanted to make up for it somehow." His gaze caught hers. "I never did make up for it. And, no, you never forget."

9

With the press staking out her townhouse in suburban Virginia, Michelle checked into a hotel in D.C. She used the breathing space to snatch a quick, informative lunch with a girlfriend who happened to be an FBI agent. The Secret Service and the Bureau didn't always see eye-to-eye. Indeed, in federal law enforcement circles the Bureau was the eight-hundred-pound gorilla in relation to all the other agencies. However, Michelle liked to remind her FBI buddies that their agency had been founded with seven former Secret Service agents.

Both women were also members of WIFLE, or Women in Federal Law Enforcement. It was a support network with conventions and annual meetings, and though her male colleagues loved to rib her about it, WIFLE had been a great tool for Michelle as she confronted issues at work related to her gender. Her friend was clearly nervous about meeting with Michelle, but Michelle had helped her earn an Olympic silver medal, thereby securing a bond that almost nothing could break.

Over Caesar salads and iced tea Michelle was given the results of the investigation thus far. Simmons was a member of the security service that had guarded the funeral home, although he wasn't supposed to be on duty that day. In fact, the funeral home was only patrolled at night. Simmons – of course, that wasn't his real name – had disappeared. The paper trail at the company was useless. None of Simmons's information checked out: stolen Social Security number, fake driver's license and references, the works, all expertly done. He'd been employed there less than a month. Thus far, Simmons was a major dead end.

"When he came running up, I thought he was just some green rent-a-cop, so I commandeered him and put him into action. We didn't even search his van. Bruno was obviously hidden in the back somewhere. I played right into his hands. Gave him a perfect opportunity to kill one of my men." In her misery Michelle put her face in her hands. With an effort she recovered, pushed a forkful of lettuce in her mouth and chewed so hard her teeth hurt.

"Before they pulled the plug on me, I found out that they got the slug out of Neal Richards. It was a dumdum. Probably never get a ballistic match, even if we lay our hands on the probable weapon that fired it."

Her friend agreed and then told Michelle that the van had been discovered in an abandoned barn. It was being run for prints and other microscopic indicators, but nothing had turned up thus far.

Mildred Martin, wife of the deceased, had been found at her home, working quietly in her garden. She had been planning to go and see her husband later that night with friends and family. She hadn't called John Bruno and asked him to come to the funeral home. Her husband had been Bruno's law supervisor, and they'd been close. If the candidate wanted to come and see her dead husband, he could have; it was simple as that, she told investigators.

"Yet why did Bruno scramble his schedule and go to see Martin at the funeral home at the last minute?" asked Michelle. "It was just dropped on us out of the blue."

"According to his staff, he received a call from Mildred Martin that morning asking him to come and see her husband at the funeral home. And according to Dickers, Bruno's chief of staff, Bruno was agitated after getting the call."

"Well, a close friend of his had died."

"But Dickers also says Bruno already knew that Martin was dead."

"So you think there's more to it?"

"Well, she picked a time when there weren't that many people at the funeral home. And a few things Bruno said after the call led Dickers to believe there was more to the meeting than simply paying last respects."

"So that may be why he pushed me so hard to leave them alone in there?"

Her friend nodded. "Well, depending on what the widow had to say, I suppose Bruno would want it to be private."

"But Mildred Martin said she didn't call."

"Somebody impersonated her, Michelle."

"And if Bruno hadn't come?" She answered her own question. "Then they would have just left. And if I'd gone in with him, they wouldn't have tried it, and Neal Richards . . ." Her voice trailed off. "What else do you have?"

"Our thinking is that this had been planned for some time. I mean, they had to coordinate a lot of different things, and they executed it to perfection."

"They must have had inside sources on Bruno's campaign. How else would they know his schedule?"

"Well, one way was his campaign's official Web site. The event he was going to when he took a detour to the funeral home had been scheduled for quite some time."

"Damn it, I told them not to post his schedule on the Web. Do you know that a waitress at one of the hotels where we stayed knew more about Bruno's itinerary than we did, because she'd overheard Bruno and his staff talking about it? They don't bother to tell us until the last minute."

"Frankly, with all that, I don't know how you do your job."

Michelle looked at her sharply. "And having Bruno's mentor conveniently die? I mean, that started the whole chain of events."

The woman was already nodding. "Bill Martin was elderly, had terminal cancer in its late stages and died in bed during the night. Under those circumstances no report was filed with the medical examiner, and no autopsy was conducted. The attending physician signed the death certificate. However, after what happened, his body was posted, and toxicology tests were run on the postmortem samples."

"And they found what?"

"Large amounts of Roxanol, liquid morphine, which he was taking for pain, and over a liter of embalming fluid, among other things. No gastric contents because those had been drained during the embalming. No smoking gun really."

Michelle eyed her friend closely. "And yet you don't look convinced."

Her friend finally shrugged. "Embalming fluid gets into all major vessels, cavities, solid organs, so it's tough to be accurate. But under the circumstances the medical examiner took a sampling of the middle brain, where typically the embalming fluid doesn't penetrate, and she found a spike of methanol."

"Methanol! But that's a compound of embalming fluid, isn't it? What if the embalming fluid did get in there?"

"That's a concern. And in case you didn't know, there are differences in embalming fluids. High-budget embalming fluids have less methanol but more formaldehyde. Low-budget ones, like Martin's, have higher levels of pure methanol. Added to that is that methanol is found in lots of things, like wine and liquor. Martin was reportedly a heavy drinker. That might account for the spike, the M.E. couldn't be sure. Bottom line, though, for a man as terminally ill as Bill Martin it wouldn't have taken a large dose of methanol to kill him."

She took out a file and flipped through it. "The autopsy also found organ damage, shrunken mucous membranes, stomach lining torn, all markers for methanol poisoning. And yet he had cancer throughout his body and had undergone radiation and chemotherapy. All in all the M.E. had a mess on her hands. The probable cause of death was circulatory failure, but there are lots of reasons a very elderly man with a terminal illness would have died from circulatory failure."

"Yet killing someone with methanol, knowing he'd probably be embalmed without an autopsy, that's pretty ingenious," said Michelle.

"Actually that's pretty damn scary."

"But he must have been murdered," said Michelle. "They couldn't just wait around hoping Martin would die on his own and then have his body at the funeral home precisely when Bruno was passing through." She paused. "List of suspects?"

"I really can't say. It's an ongoing investigation, and I've already told you more than I should have. I might have to pass a polygraph on this, you know."

When the check came, Michelle was quick to grab it. As they walked out together, her friend said, "So what are you going to do? Lie low? Look for another position?"

"The 'lying low' part, yes; the 'looking for another job,' not yet."

"So what, then?"

"I'm not ready to give up my career at the Service without a fight."

Her friend eyed her warily. "I know that look. What are you thinking?"

"I'm thinking you're FBI, and it's better that you don't know. Like you said, you might have to pass a polygraph."

10

The worst day of Sean King's life had been September 26, 1996, the day Clyde Ritter died while then Secret Service agent King was focusing on something else. Unfortunately the second worst day of his life happened to be right now. His office had been filled with police, federal agents and technical crews asking lots of questions and not getting lots of answers. Amid all this forensic foraging they'd taken fingerprint samples from King, Phil Baxter and their secretary; for elimination purposes, they said. That could cut both ways, King well knew.

The local press had arrived too. Fortunately he knew them personally and gave vague answers that they accepted with little comment. The national press would be coming very soon, because there was something extremely newsworthy about the murdered man. King had suspected it, and those suspicions were confirmed when a contingent of folks from the U.S. Marshals Service showed up on his doorstep.

The dead man, Howard Jennings, had been employed at King's law practice as a title searcher, proofreader, overseer of trust account records and a gofer, sort of a jack-of-all-trades. His office was on the lower level of the law building. He was quiet, hardworking, and kept to himself. There was nothing whatsoever remarkable about what the man did for a living. However, he was very special in one respect.

Jennings was a member of WITSEC, the program more popularly known as witness protection. Forty-eight years old with a degree in accounting, Jennings (that, of course, wasn't his real name) had once been gainfully employed as a bean counter for a criminal organization operating in the Midwest. These folks specialized in racketeering, extortion and money laundering and used arson, beatings, disfigurements and the occasional homicide to get their point across. The matter had attracted great national attention because of the lethality of the organization's methods and the complexities of the case.

Jennings had quickly seen the light and helped send a slew of very dangerous folks to penitentiaries. Yet some of the most deadly had escaped the federal net; hence his enrollment in WITSEC.

Now he was a corpse and King's headache was just beginning. As a former federal agent with high-level clearances, King had dealt with WITSEC in some joint efforts between the Secret Service and the U.S. Marshals. When Jennings interviewed with him, his background check and other due diligence made King suspect that Jennings was in the program. He didn't know for certain, of course; it wasn't like the Marshals Service would confide in him about the identity of one of its people, but he had his suspicions, suspicions that he'd never shared with anyone. It had to do with Jennings's paucity of references and work background, something that would occur when one has wiped out his former life.

King was not a suspect in Jennings's murder, he was told, which, of course, meant that he was probably near the top of the list. If he informed the investigators that he believed Jennings was WITSEC, he might very well find himself in front of a grand jury. He decided to play dumb for now.

He spent the rest of the day calming down his partner. Baxter was a big, burly former UVA football player who'd spent a couple of years in the NFL riding the bench before going on to become an aggressive and highly competent trial lawyer. However, the ex-jock was not used to corpses in his office. That was a form of "sudden death" he wasn't very comfortable with. King, on the other hand, had spent years at the Secret Service working counterfeiting and fraud involving very dangerous gangs. And he'd killed men as well. Thus he was better equipped to deal with a murder than his partner was.

King had sent his receptionist, Mona Hall, home for the day. Mona was a frail, nervous type, so the sight of blood and body would not have set well with her. However, she was also a confirmed and accomplished gossip, and King had no doubt that the local phone exchange was being burned up with wild speculation about the homicidal goings-on at the offices of King & Baxter. In a quiet community such as Wrightsburg, that could lead the topics of conversation for months if not years to come.

With the building now shut down by the feds and under around-the-clock security, King & Baxter had to move its legal operations temporarily to its partners' homes. That evening the two lawyers carried out boxes, files and other work to their cars. As beefy Phil Baxter drove off in his equally large SUV, King leaned against the hood of his car and stared up at his office. With lights ablaze, the investigators were still going hard and heavy in there, scrutinizing the place for any clue as to who had put a bullet into the chest of Howard Jennings. King took in the mountain vistas behind the building. Up there was his home, a place he'd built out of the ruin of one life. It had been good therapy for him. Now?

He drove home, wondering what the next morning would bring. He ate a bowl of soup in the kitchen while he watched the local news. There were pictures of him on the screen, references to his career at the Secret Service, including his disgraced exit, his law career in Wrightsburg and assorted speculation about the dead Howard Jennings. He switched off the television and tried to focus on some work he'd brought home. However, his attention kept wandering, and he finally just sat in his den surrounded by his world of lawbooks and boring documents and stared into space. With a jolt he came out of his musings.

He changed into shorts and a sweater, grabbed a bottle of red wine and a plastic glass and went down to the covered dock behind his house. There he boarded the twenty-foot jet boat he kept there along with a fourteen-foot sailboat and a Sea-Doo personal watercraft or PWC, which was akin to a motorcycle on water, plus a kayak and a canoe. About a half mile across at its widest point, and perhaps eight miles long with numerous coves and inlets, the lake was very popular with recreational boaters and fishermen; stripers, bluegill and catfish filled the deep, clear waters. The summer was over now, the renters and seasonal residents gone.

His vessels were on power lifts, and he lowered the jet boat into the water, fired it up and turned on the running lights. He hit the throttle and went out about two miles, breathing in the brisk air, letting it wash over him. He entered an uninhabited cove, cut the engine, dropped anchor, poured a glass of wine and contemplated his now grim-looking future.

When news spread that a person in the WITSEC program had been murdered in his law office, King would once more be in the national spotlight, something he was dreading. The last time, one tabloid went off the deep end, running a story actually claiming he'd been bribed by a violent, radical political group to look the other way while Clyde Ritter was gunned down. Well, the libel laws were still alive and well in the United States, and he'd sued and won a large settlement. He'd used this "windfall" to build his house and start life anew. Yet the cash hadn't come close to erasing what had happened. How could it?

He sat up on the boat's gunwale, kicked off his shoes, stripped off his clothes and dove into the dark water, stayed under for a bit and then came up sucking oxygen. The lake was actually warmer than the outside air.

His career as a Secret Service agent really came crashing down when a video of the assassination, taken by a local TV news crew covering the Ritter event, was released to the public. It clearly showed him looking away from Ritter far longer than he should have. It showed the assassin drawing his gun, pointing it, firing, killing Ritter, and all the while King had been staring off, as though in a trance. The clip even showed children in the crowd reacting to the gun before King realized what was going on.

The media had chosen to excoriate King, no doubt fueled by the outcry of Ritter's people and not wanting to appear biased against an unpopular candidate.

He could recall most of the headlines: "Agent Lets Eyes Wander While Candidate Dies"; "Veteran Agent Blows It"; "Asleep at His Post." Or the one that read, "So That's Why They Wear the Shades," which under different circumstances might have actually made him chuckle. Worst of all, though, he'd been largely shunned by his fellow agents.

His marriage had fallen apart under the strain. Actually it had started to fall apart long before that. King had been gone far more than he was home, sometimes leaving on an hour's notice, with no fixed return date. Under those pressing circumstances he'd forgiven his wife's first affair and even the second. The third time, however, they separated. And when she quickly agreed to a divorce after his world fell in, well, he couldn't say he'd spent a lot of time crying about it.

And yet he'd survived it all and rebuilt his life. And now?

He slowly climbed back on board the jet boat, wrapped a towel he kept in the boat around his middle and drove back. Instead of going to his dock, he cut the engine and running lights and pulled into a small cove a few hundred yards down from his place. King quietly dropped the small mushroom anchor in the water to keep his boat from drifting into the muddy bank. Up near the rear of his house a beam of light was arcing back and forth. He had visitors. Perhaps it was the media sniffing around. Or perhaps, he thought, Howard Jennings's killer had come looking for another score.

11

King quietly waded to shore, put his clothes back on and was now squatting in the darkness behind some bushes. The light still swung back and forth as someone moved through the area that ringed the eastern perimeter of his property. King made his way toward the front of his house shielded by a wall of trees. There was a blue BMW convertible parked in the driveway that he didn't recognize. He was about to go over to it when he decided the best course of action was to get some hardware. With a nice big pistol in hand, he'd feel a lot better about things.

He slipped inside the dark house, got the gun and went back out a side door. The arc of light had disappeared now, and that had him worried. He knelt down and listened. The sharp *crack* of a fallen branch reached his ears. It had come from his right, barely ten feet away; then came a footstep and then another. He braced himself, his pistol ready, safety off.

He launched himself, hitting the person low and hard and landing on top of him, King's pistol right in his face.

Only it wasn't a him. It was a her! And she had a pistol out too. It was pointed at him, the barrels of the two guns almost touching.

"What in the hell are you doing here?" he said angrily when he saw who it was.

"If you'd get off me, I might have the breath to tell you," she snapped.

He took his time climbing off, and when she reached a hand out for him to assist her, he ignored it.

She was wearing a skirt, blouse and short jacket. The skirt had slid up to nearly her crotch during the collision. As she struggled to regain her feet, she tugged it back down.

"Are you in the habit of mugging all your visitors?" she said testily as she put her gun back in the waist clip and brushed herself off.

"Most of my visitors don't go sneaking around my property."

"Nobody answered the front door."

"Then you go away and call another time. Or didn't your mother teach you?"

She folded her arms across her chest. "It's been a long time, Sean."

"Has it? I hadn't noticed. I've been kind of busy with my new life."

She looked around. "I can see that. Nice place."

"What are you doing here, Joan?"

"Came to see an old friend who's in trouble."

"Really? Who's that?"

She smiled demurely. "Murder in your office. That's trouble, isn't it?"

"Sure it is. I was talking about the 'old friend' part."

She nodded toward the house. "I've driven a long way. I've heard about the southern hospitality around here. Care to show me some?"

Instead, he contemplated firing a round over her head. Yet the only way he would find out what Joan Dillinger was up to was to play along. "What sort of hospitality?"

"Well, it's almost nine o'clock and I haven't had dinner. Let's start with that and then go from there," she said.

"You show up unannounced after all these years and expect me to cook you dinner? You've got some guts."

"That shouldn't surprise you by now, should it?"

★

As he fixed the meal, Joan explored the main level of his home, carrying the gin and tonic he'd given her. She perched on the counter in the kitchen while he worked away. "How's the finger?" she asked.

"It only hurts when I'm seriously ticked off. Sort of like a mood ring. And just so you know, it's throbbing like hell right now."

She ignored the barb. "This place is spectacular. I heard that you built it yourself."

"Gave me something to do."

"I didn't know you were a carpenter."

"I worked my way through school building things for people who could afford it. Then I decided what the hell, I'd do it for myself."

They ate at the table off the kitchen that had a commanding view of the lake. With the meal they drank a bottle of merlot he'd fetched from his wine cellar. Under different circumstances it would have been a very romantic setting.

After dinner they carried their wineglasses into the family room, with its cathedral ceiling and walls of window. When he saw she was shivering some, King turned on the gas fireplace and tossed her a throw blanket. They sat across from each other on leather couches. Joan kicked off her heels and curled her legs up under her and then placed the blanket over them. She raised her glass to him. "Dinner was fabulous." She breathed in the wine's bouquet. "And I see you've added sommelier to your list of credentials."

"Okay, your belly's full, you're suitably buzzed. Why are you here?"

"When something extraordinary entailing a major criminal investigation happens to a former agent, everybody's interested."

"And they sent you to see me?"

"I'm at a level where I can send myself."

"So this is unofficial on your part? Or are you just here to spy for the Service?"

"I'd characterize it as unofficial. I'd like to hear your side of things."

King cradled his glass, fighting an urge to throw it at her. "I don't have a side of things. The man worked for me for a short time. He was killed. Today I found out he was in witness protection. I don't know who killed him. End of story."

She didn't respond but just stared into the fire. She finally rose, padded over to the fireplace and knelt in front of it, running her hand along the stone facade.

"Carpenter *and* stonemason?"

"I subbed that out. I know my limitations."

"That's refreshing. Most men I know won't admit to having any."

"Thanks. But I still want to know why you're here."

"It has nothing to do with the Service and everything to do with you and me."

"There is no 'you and me.'"

"Well, there was. We worked together at the Service for years. We slept together. Given different circumstances we might have moved on to a more permanent arrangement. And I would like to think that if you heard that a man who happened to be in witness protection had been murdered at a place where I worked and my past was being dredged up again, you might come and see how I was coping."

"I think you'd be wrong about that."

"Well, that's why I'm here. I wanted to make sure you were all right."

"I'm glad my miserable situation afforded you this wonderful opportunity to exhibit your compassionate nature."

"Sarcasm really doesn't suit you, Sean."

"It's late, and it's a long drive back to D.C."

"You're right. It's too long a drive actually." She added, "Looks like you have lots of room." She rose and sat down next to him, uncomfortably close.

"You look fit enough to qualify for the FBI's Hostage Rescue," she said, running an admiring eye over his trim six-foot-one-inch frame.

He shook his head. "I'm an old man for that stuff. Bad knees, bum shoulder and all."

She sighed and looked away, tucking some stray hairs behind her ear. "I just turned forty."

"Consider the alternative. It's not the end of the world."

"Not for a man. Forty and unmarried for a woman, it's not so pleasant."

"You look great. Great for thirty, great for forty. And you've got your career."

"Didn't think I'd last that long."

"You lasted longer than me."

She put her wineglass down and turned to him. "But I shouldn't have." There followed an uncomfortable silence.

"It was years ago," he finally said. "Water under the bridge."

"Obviously not. I see the way you're looking at me."

"What did you expect?"

She picked up her wine again and finished it in one long sip. "You actually have no idea how hard this was for me to come here. I changed my mind about ten times. Took an hour to decide what to wear. It was more nerve-racking than securing a presidential inauguration."

He had never known her to talk this way. She

was always the ultraconfident one. Bantering with the boys like she was not only one of them but the ringleader to boot.

"I'm sorry, Sean. I'm not sure I ever said that I was sorry."

"Bottom line, it was my fault. Case closed."

"That's very kind of you."

"I just don't have the time or energy to hold a grudge. It's not that important to me."

Slipping into her heels, she rose and put on her jacket. "You're right, it is late and I should be going. I'm sorry if I interrupted your *wonderful* life. And I apologize for being so concerned about you that I came here to see how you were doing."

King started to speak, hesitated, and then as she headed toward the door, he let out a sigh and said, "You've had too much to drink to drive these back roads at night. The guest room's at the top of the stairs, on the right. There are pajamas in the bureau, and your own bath, and whoever gets up first makes the coffee."

She turned back. "Are you sure? You don't have to do this."

"Trust me, I know that. I *shouldn't* be doing this. I'll see you in the morning."

She looked at him with an expression that said,

"Are you absolutely sure you won't come see me *before* the morning?"

He turned and headed away. "Where are you going?" she asked.

"I've got some work to do. Sleep tight."

Joan went outside and got her overnight bag out of the car. When she came back in, he was nowhere around. The master bedroom looked to be at the far end of the hall. She slipped across and peeked inside. It was dark. And empty. She slowly went to her room and closed the door.

12

Michelle Maxwell's arms and legs moved with maximum efficiency, at least as she judged herself by the far lower standards of these post-Olympic days. Her scull cut through the waters of the Potomac as the sun rose and the already heavy air held the promise of a less chilly day. It was here at George-town that she'd begun her rowing career. Her muscular thighs and shoulders were burning with the effort she was expending. She'd passed every other scull, kayak, canoe and comparable vessel on the water, including one that had a five-horsepower engine.

She pulled her scull up to one of the boathouses that sat on the banks in Georgetown, bent over and took deep, long breaths, the endorphins coursing through her blood providing a pleasant high. A half hour later she was in her Land Cruiser heading back to the hotel she'd moved to near Tysons Corner, Virginia. It was still early and traffic was light –

relatively light, that is, for a region that routinely saw clogged highways as early as 5:00 a.m. She showered and put on a T-shirt and boxers. With no uncomfortable shoes or stockings, and no holster chafing her, it felt great. She stretched, rubbed her tired limbs down and then ordered room service and threw on a robe before her breakfast was delivered. While having pancakes, orange juice and coffee, she channel-surfed the TV, looking for more news on the Bruno disappearance. Ironic that she was the lead agent in the field that day and was now getting her news on the investigation from CNN. She stopped surfing when she saw a man on TV who looked familiar. He was in Wrightsburg, Virginia, surrounded by news crews and obviously not enjoying it.

It took her a few moments to place him, and then she got it. The man was Sean King. She'd joined the Service a year or so before the Ritter assassination. Michelle had never known what became of Sean King, and had no reason to want to know. But now, as she listened to the details of Howard Jennings's murder, she began to want to know more. Part of it was purely physical. King was a very good-looking man: tall and well built with close-cropped black hair now heavily graying at the temples. He must be in his mid-forties now, she calculated. He had the sort of face that looked better with lines; it gave him an attraction that he probably never had in his twenties or thirties, when he was probably too pretty-boy-looking. Yet it wasn't his handsome features that intrigued her the most. As she listened to the sketchy details leading to Jennings's death, there was something about the murder, something she couldn't quite put her finger on.

She opened the copy of the *Washington Post* that had been delivered to her room and, scanning the pages, found a short but informative article about the slaying. The account also contained facts about King's past, the Ritter fiasco and its aftermath. As she read the account and then looked at the man on the screen, she felt a sudden, visceral connection to him. They'd both made mistakes on the job, and it had cost them greatly. It appeared King had rebuilt his life pretty dramatically. Michelle wondered if she'd be anywhere near as triumphant in reconstructing her world.

She had a sudden inspiration and phoned a confidant of hers at the Service. The young man wasn't an agent. He was in administrative support. Every field agent needed to cultivate strong ties to the admin staff, for those were the folks who really knew how to cut through the red tape that plagued most government agencies. He was a huge admirer of Michelle's and would have somersaulted down the hall if she had condescended to have coffee with him. Well, she did so condescend. The price was, he had to bring her copies of certain records and other materials. He waffled at first – he didn't want to get in trouble, he said – but she soon persuaded him otherwise. She also got him to agree to slow-walk her admin leave papers such that she would have access to the Secret Service database using her name and password for at least another week or so.

They met at a small café downtown where she got the records from him. She gave the young man a hug that she let linger just long enough for her to be quite certain that he would continue to do her bidding. When she joined the Service, she had not handed in her membership in the female ranks. At one level it was just another tool. In fact, used judiciously, it was far more powerful even than her ·357·

As she was getting back into her truck, a voice called out. She turned to see an agent she had leap-frogged over in climbing the career ladder. The look on his face was clear. He was here to gloat.

"Who would have thought?" he began inno-cently. "Your star was shooting straight up. I still can't understand how you let it happen, Mick. I mean, leaving the guy alone in a room you hadn't really swept. What the hell were you thinking?"

"I guess I wasn't thinking, Steve."

He slapped her on the arm, a little harder than he needed to. "Hey, don't worry, they're not going to let their superstar woman fall. You'll get reassigned, maybe guarding Lady Bird down in Texas. Or maybe the Fords. That way you get six months in Palm Springs and six in Vail and a sweet per diem. Of course, if it were one of us poor slobs, they'd cut our heads off and forget about us. But who said life was fair?"

"You might be surprised. I might not be with the Service when this is all over."

He smiled broadly. "Well, maybe life is fair after all. Hey, you take care." He turned to leave.

"Oh, Steve?" He turned back. "I trust you got the memo that they're doing a computer sweep on everybody's laptop next week. You might want to get that porno stuff off – you know, from that site you keep checking from the office? That might blow your clearances. And who knows, maybe even your wife might find out. And while we're on the subject, are big boobs and a tight ass really worth the risk? I mean isn't that, like, so sixteen-year-old?"

Steve's smile disappeared; he extended his middle finger to her and stalked off.

Michelle couldn't stop smiling all the way back to the hotel.

13

Michelle spread out the documents on her bed, going over them meticulously and making notes along the way. It became apparent that King had had a spotless record and a long list of commendations in his career at the Service – at least until that fateful day when his attention wandered and Clyde Ritter paid the ultimate price.

During his stint working counterfeiting early on in his career, King had even been wounded when a bust went down badly. He killed two men after taking a round in his shoulder. And years later he killed Ritter's assassin, albeit a few seconds too late. That made a total of three men he'd gunned down in the line of duty. Michelle had fired thousands of rounds in training, but even in her brief stint as a police officer in Tennessee she'd never shot anyone for real. She often wondered what that would feel like, whether it would change you, making you either too reckless or too careful to do your job properly.

Clyde Ritter's assassin was a professor at Atticus College. Professor Arnold Ramsey was not a prior known threat and had no ties to any radical political organization, although it was later learned he was an outspoken critic of Ritter. He left behind a wife and daughter. Some legacy to leave behind for the kid, Michelle thought. What was she supposed to do when talking about her family? *Hi, my dad was a political assassin, like John Wilkes Booth and Lee Harvey Oswald. He was shot to death by the Secret Service. So what does your dad do?* No one else had been arrested in connection with the assassination. The official conclusion was that Ramsey acted alone.

Finished for now with the paper trail, she picked up the video that was part of the official record. She popped it into the VCR underneath the TV and turned it on. She sat back and watched as the scene from the hotel meet-and-greet during the Ritter campaign materialized on the TV. This video had been taken by a local television crew filming the Ritter event. It had put the final nail in King's coffin. Despite taking great pains to make sure such a mistake was never repeated, the Service had chosen not to show this video to its recruits. Perhaps out of embarrassment, Michelle thought.

She stiffened when she saw the confident-looking Clyde Ritter and his entourage enter the packed room. She knew little about Ritter other than that he had started life as a TV minister and made a considerable fortune. Thousands of people from across the country had sent him money, in amounts large and small. There'd been claims that numerous wealthy older women, mostly widows, had given him their life savings in exchange for his promise they'd go to heaven. Yet there was no hard evidence of that, and the furor died down. After leaving the quasi-religious life he ran for and was elected to Congress from a southern state, though she didn't know which one. He had a dubious voting record on racial and other issues of civil liberties, and his brand of religion was over the top. Yet he was beloved in his state, and there were enough voters in the country dissatisfied with the direction of the major party platforms that Ritter had run for president, as an independent. That grand ambition had ended with a bullet in his heart.

Next to Ritter was his campaign manager. Michelle had looked him up in the file too. He was Sidney Morse. The son of a prominent California attorney and an heiress mother, Sidney Morse had been, strangely enough, a playwright and stage director before turning his considerable artistic talents to the political arena. He earned a national reputation managing large political campaigns, turning them into media-driven extravaganzas with emphasis on sound bites and perception over any kind of substance, and his win rate was astonishingly high. That probably said more for the gullibility of the modern voter than the high standards of the modern candidate, Michelle thought.

Morse became a troubleshooter for hire, crossing the political aisle when the money and situation were right. He joined the cause when Ritter's campaign really started to take off and the candidate needed a more seasoned helmsman. Morse had the reputation for being brilliant, crafty and, when called for, ruthless. All sides agreed that he helped Ritter run a damn near perfect campaign. And from all accounts he enjoyed the hell out of rocking the establishment with his third-party juggernaut. However, Morse had been a political outcast after Ritter's assassination, and his life had been in a downward spiral. Over a year ago Morse, his mind gone, had been committed to a state mental institution where he'd probably live out the rest of his life.

Michelle stiffened again when she saw Sean King directly behind the candidate. She mentally counted off the agents in the room. There weren't that many, she realized. She'd had three times that number on her Bruno detail. King was the only agent anywhere near Ritter. She wondered who'd come up with that lousy plan.

As an avid student of her agency's history, Michelle knew that the Secret Service's mission had evolved over time. It had taken the tragic deaths of three presidents, Lincoln, Garfield and McKinley, for Congress to act substantively on the issue of presidential security. Teddy Roosevelt received the first real dose of Secret Service protection after McKinley was gunned down, although things were far less sophisticated back then. As late as the 1940s Harry Truman, Franklin Roosevelt's newly elected vice president, didn't even have a Secret Service agent assigned to him until one of Truman's aides argued convincingly that a person who was a single heartbeat away from becoming the most powerful man in the world was damn well entitled to at least one professional lawman with a gun watching over him.

As the meet-and-greet went on, she watched Agent King do all the right things, his gaze constantly moving. The Secret Service drilled that practice into you. Once, the Service had competed with other federal law enforcement agencies to see which of them was best at telling when someone was lying. The Service had won hands-down. To Michelle the reason was obvious. An agent on protection detail spent most of his or her time trying to divine the innermost thoughts and motives of people solely from their exteriors.

And then the moment came. King seemed riveted by something to his right. So enthralled was Michelle at speculating on what he could have been looking at that she didn't see Ramsey pull his weapon and fire. She jumped when the sound came and realized that, like King, her attention had also wandered. She rewound the tape and watched Ramsey slip his hand into his coat pocket, partially hiding the movement behind a Ritter sign he was holding with his other hand. You couldn't see the gun clearly until Ramsey pointed it at the candidate and fired. King recoiled, presumably as the bullet exited Ritter and hit him in the hand. As Ritter collapsed, the crowd burst into complete hysteria. The cameraman filming the video had apparently dropped to his knees, and Michelle saw torsos and legs running helter-skelter. Other agents and security personnel were pushed back against the sides of the room by the mad rush of frightened people. It only took seconds and seemed like forever to her. And then the cameraman must have stood again, because Sean King returned to the screen.

Blood streaming down his hand, King had his gun out, pointed directly at Ramsey, who still held his own weapon. It is a normal human reaction to flinch, panic and fall to the ground, immobile, when a shot is fired. Training at the Service was designed to override this instinct. When an unknown fired a shot, you moved! You grabbed the protectee and got the hell out of there as fast as you could, often physically carrying the person in the process. King did not do that, principally because, Michelle assumed, he had a man in front of him holding a gun.

King fired once, twice, calmly it seemed; he didn't say a word that Michelle could tell. And then as Ramsey fell, King simply stood there, looking down at the dead candidate as other agents finally dashed forward and grabbed Ritter and, their training still working, rushed off with him, leaving King behind to face the music.

Michelle would have given anything to know what the man was thinking right at that moment.

She rewound the tape and watched it again. The *bang* came as Ramsey fired. But there had been a sound before that. She rewound the tape again and listened intently. There it was, like a *beep* or a *clang*, or a *ding*. That was it. A *ding*! It was coming from the direction where King was staring. And she seemed to hear a slight hush or whooshing sound.

She thought rapidly, a ding in a hotel almost

always meant that an elevator car had arrived. And the whooshing sound could have been the elevator doors opening. The diagram of the room where Ritter was shot showed a bank of elevators. If an elevator door had opened, had it revealed anything to Sean King? And if so, why hadn't he said? And why hadn't anyone else seen something? Lastly, why hadn't anyone picked up on what she had just noted after having watched the tape a couple of times? But why was she so interested in Sean King and his plight from eight years ago? And yet she *was* interested. After days of tedium she wanted to *do* something. She needed action. Impulsively Michelle packed her bag and checked out of the hotel.

14

Like Michelle Maxwell, King had also risen early and was also out on the water. He was, however, in a kayak, not a scull, and was going considerably slower than Michelle. The lake was ripple-free at this hour, and the quietest it would be all day. This was the perfect place to think, and he needed to do a lot of that. Yet it wasn't to be.

He heard his name being called and looked up. She was standing on the rear deck of his house, calling out to him and holding up a cup of what he assumed was coffee. Joan was wearing the pajamas he kept in the guest bedroom. He took his time paddling back in and then walked slowly up to the house where she met him at the back door.

She smiled. "Apparently you were the first up, but no coffee was on. That's okay, I live to provide suitable backup."

He accepted the coffee from her and sat at the table after she insisted on making him breakfast. He watched her prancing barefoot around his kitchen in the pajamas, apparently playing the role of the happy vixen housewife with aplomb. He remembered that Joan, though one of the toughest agents the Service had ever produced, could be as feminine as any woman, and in private moments she could be downright sexually explosive.

"Still prefer scrambled?"

"That's fine," he answered.

"Bagel, no butter?"

"Yep."

"God, you're so predictable."

I guess so, he thought. He ventured a question of his own. "Any news on Jennings's death, or am I not cleared for it?"

She stopped cracking eggs. "That's FBI territory, you know that."

"Agencies talk to each other."

"Not any more than they used to, really, and that was never a lot."

"So you know nothing." He said this in an accusatory manner.

She didn't answer, and instead scrambled the eggs, toasted the bagel and presented the meal complete with silverware, napkin and more coffee. She sat across from him and sipped orange juice while he ate.

"Not having anything?" he asked.

"I'm watching my figure. Apparently I'm the only one here doing that."

Was it his imagination, or did her foot graze his leg underneath the table?

"What did you expect? After eight years we just jump back into the sack?"

She tipped her head back and laughed. "In an occasional fantasy, yes."

"You're crazy, you know that? I mean certifiable." He was not joking.

"And I had such a normal childhood. Maybe I'm just a sucker for a man in shades packing heat."

Okay, that time it was clear. Her foot *had* touched his leg. He was sure of that because it was still there and currently heading toward certain private areas of his person.

She leaned forward. Her gaze was not soulful; it was predatory. Clearly she wanted him, here, now, on the kitchen table in the middle of his "predictable scrambled eggs." She stood and slid off the pajama bottoms, revealing flimsy white panties. Next she slowly and deliberately undid the pajama top as though challenging him to stop her at each button. He didn't. He just watched as the pajama top opened. She wore no bra. Joan dropped the pajama top in his lap and with one hand swept the dishes off the table and onto the floor.

"It's been way too long, Sean. So let's just do something about it." She climbed up on the table in front of him and lay on her back, her thighs spread. Joan smiled as he stood, towering over her in her glorious, pandering near-nakedness.

"You going mainstream on me?" he asked.

"What do you mean?"

He glanced at the light fixture on the ceiling. "You didn't go for the three-pointer with your underwear."

"Oh, but the day's still young, Mr. King."

Her smile disappeared as King picked up the pajama top and laid it delicately over her private parts.

"I'm going to get dressed. I'd appreciate if you'd clean up this mess."

As he walked away, he heard her laughing. By the time he got to the top of the stairs, she called out, "You've finally grown up, Sean, I'm so impressed." He shook his head and wondered what insane asylum she had escaped from.

"Thanks for breakfast," he called back.

★

As King was coming back downstairs after showering and dressing, there was a knock at the door. He glanced out the window and was surprised to see a police car, a U.S. Marshals van and a black SUV. He answered the door.

He knew Todd Williams, the police chief, since Sean was one of Todd's volunteer deputies. Todd looked distraught as one of two FBI agents stepped forward and flashed his credentials like he was brandishing a switchblade.

"Sean King? We understand that you have a pistol registered to you."

King nodded. "I'm a volunteer deputy. The public likes to see us armed in case we have to shoot any bad guys. So?"

"So we'd like to see it. In fact, we'd like to take it."

King glanced sharply at Williams, who looked at him and shrugged and then took a huge, symbolic step backward.

"You have a warrant?" King asked.

"You're a former federal agent. We hoped you'd cooperate."

"I'm also a lawyer, and we're not a real cooperative breed."

"It's up to you. I've got the paper right here."

King had pulled that same trick before as a fed. His "search warrant" was often a photocopy of a *New York Times* crossword puzzle neatly folded. "Show it to me," he demanded.

The warrant was produced and it was for real. They wanted his service revolver.

"Can I ask why?"

"You can ask," said the agent.

Now the deputy U.S. marshal stepped forward. He was about fifty, stood about six-five and was built like a professional boxer, with broad shoulders, long arms and huge hands.

"Let's just cut the cute shit, okay?" he said to the agent before looking at King. "They want to match it against the slug taken out of Jennings. I'm assuming you don't have a problem with that."

"You think I shot Howard Jennings in my office and used my own service revolver to do it? What, as a matter of convenience, or because I'm too cheap to spring for another gun?"

"Just eliminating possibilities," said the man pleasantly. "You know the drill. Being a Secret Service agent and all."

"Was. Was a Secret Service agent." He turned. "I'll get the gun."

The big man put a hand on King's shoulder. "No. Just show them where it is."

"So let them in my house and they can go merrily along picking up evidence to build a case against me?"

"An innocent man has nothing to hide," the deputy marshal shot back. "Besides, they won't peek, Scout's honor."

An FBI agent followed King inside. As they walked down the hall, the agent looked in surprise at the mess in the kitchen.

"My dog is kind of wild," explained King.

The man nodded. "I got a black Lab named Trigger. What's yours?"

"Pit bull bitch named Joan."

They went to his den, where King opened the lockbox and then motioned the agent to inspect the contents. The man bagged the pistol, handed him a receipt for the weapon and followed King back outside.

"Sorry about this, Sean," said Todd. "I know it's all a crock." The good police chief didn't sound like he meant it, King noted.

As the men pulled off in their vehicles, Joan came down the stairs, fully dressed.

"What did they want?"

"Collecting for the policemen's ball."

"Uh-huh. Are you a suspect or what?"

"They took my gun."

"You have an alibi, right?"

"I was on patrol. I saw nobody and nobody saw me."

"Too bad I wasn't here earlier. I could have given you a hell of an alibi if you had just played your cards right." She raised her right hand and placed her other on an imaginary Bible. "Your Honor, Mr. King is innocent because at the time of said murder, yours truly was getting seriously banged on the kitchen table by the said Mr. King."

"Maybe in your dreams."

"It has been in my dreams. But now I think I'm too late."

"Joan, do me a great favor: get out of my house."

She stepped back, her eyes searching his. "You're not honestly worried about it, are you? The ballistics won't match and that'll be it."

"You think so?"

"I'm assuming you had your gun with you while you were on patrol."

"Of course, I did. My slingshot's broken."

"Jokes. You always made stupid jokes when you were the most nervous."

"A guy is dead, Joan, in my office, dead. None of this is really funny."

"Unless you murdered the man, I don't see how your gun could have done it." He didn't answer and she said, "Is there something you haven't told the police?"

"I didn't kill Jennings, if that's what you're thinking."

"I wasn't thinking it. I know you too well."

"Well, people change, they really do."

She picked up her bag. "Would it be all right if I came to visit you again?" She added quickly, "If I swear not to do that." She glanced over at the trashed kitchen table.

"Why did you do it?" he asked.

"Eight years ago I lost something important to me. This morning I tried to get it all back, using a method that turned out to be embarrassingly stupid."

"What's the point of our seeing each other again?"

"I actually have something I want to ask you."

"So ask."

"Not now. Another time. I'll be in touch."

After she left, he started to pick up the kitchen. In a few minutes everything was clean and back in order. If only he could do the same thing to his life. However, he had a feeling that a lot more things were going to be broken before this was over.

15

Michelle took a short puddle-jumper flight to North Carolina. Because she didn't have her credentials and badge anymore but did have her weapons permit, she had had to check her gun and a small knife she always carried into the cargo hold, retrieving them only after the plane landed. The blanket policy of confiscating all weapons that had been enacted after 9/11 had been relaxed somewhat, although without her badge it was not that easy. Michelle rented a car and drove about an hour to the small town of Bowlington, fifty miles east of the Tennessee border and in the shadow of the Great Smoky Mountains. However, there wasn't much of a town left anymore, she soon discovered. Textile manufacturing had driven the area in its heyday, she was told by an old-timer at the gas station where she stopped.

"They make all that stuff in China or Taiwan for peanuts now, not the good old U.S. of A.," lamented the man. "What we got left here, not much." He punctuated the comment by spitting some tobacco chew into a mason jar, rang up her soda and handed back her change. He asked her what she'd come here for, but she was noncommittal. "Just passing through."

"Well, ma'am, just so you know, there ain't much to pass through to."

She got in her car and drove through the mostly deserted and impoverished town. She saw lots of old people either sitting on their sagging front porches or creeping across their small, ragged yards. As she pulled up to the place, Michelle wondered why eight years ago Clyde Ritter had seen fit to stop here on his campaign trail. He probably could have scrounged up more votes in a cemetery.

Situated a few miles outside of the town proper, the Fairmount Hotel had not only seen better days, it seemed about one wavering support beam from tumbling down. The structure was eight stories high and encircled by a six-foot-high chain-link fence. The architecture of the place was a very mixed bag. The building was over a hundred years old and seemed to be Gothic in some parts with fake turrets and balustrades and towers, and Mediterranean in other respects with stucco walls and a red tile roof. Its ugliness could not be overexaggerated, Michelle decided. Even the term "white elephant" hardly seemed to do it justice.

There were No Trespassing signs on the fence, but she didn't see any security guard hut or any security guard making rounds. Off to the side of the hotel she found a gap in the fence. However, before slipping through here, she decided to reconnoiter the area, her Secret Service training kicking in.

The land was fairly flat all around except near the rear of the building where it sloped down to the fence. Michelle eyeballed the angle of the slope to the fence and smiled. She had won state championships in the high and long jumps two years in a row. With a little juice in her veins and a decent tailwind and using that slope, she might be able to jump the damn fence. Ten years ago she probably would have tried, just for fun. She continued her walk and then decided to move a little ways into the woods. When she heard rushing water, she moved farther into the dense trees.

In a few minutes she located the source of the sound. She went to the edge of the cliff and peered down. It was about a thirty-foot drop to the water. The river was not very wide, but it moved fast and looked fairly deep. There were a couple of thin ledges jutting out from the cliff, and small boulders clung to the sides there as well. As she watched, one broke loose and plummeted down, smacking the surface of the water, and then was quickly carried away by the rush of the river. She had a sudden chill watching this spectacle; she'd never liked heights very much and turned and walked back into the fading sunlight.

After slipping through the gap in the fence, Michelle made her way to the massive front entrance; however, it was locked and chained. Moving on, she found a large window farther down the left side that had been broken out, and she stepped through there. She had assumed the electricity was shut off, and so she had brought a flashlight. She clicked on her beam and started looking around. She walked through rooms that were filled with dust, dampness, mold and also vermin, from the sounds of scurrying feet. She also saw overturned tables, cigarette butts, empty liquor bottles and discarded condoms. The abandoned hotel apparently now served as a night-club of sorts for the slim under-seventy crowd left in Bowlington.

She'd brought with her a copy of the Fairmount's floor plan, which was included in the files her friend had given her. Using this document, she made her way to the lobby and from there to the interior room where Clyde Ritter had been shot to death. It was paneled in mahogany now, with gaudy chandeliers and burgundy carpeting. When she shut the door behind her, it became so quiet and still that Michelle was glad to feel her pistol riding on her belt clip. The .357 she'd turned in had been replaced by a sleek SIG nine-millimeter. Every federal agent had a personal backup.

Her reason for being here was not simply to satisfy her own morbid curiosity. There were some interesting parallels that intrigued her. Bruno's kidnapping had also occurred in an obscure rural town, not too far from here. It had taken place in an old building, albeit a funeral home as opposed to a hotel. There had to have been some inside source relating to the plot against Bruno, she was sure of that. And with what she had discovered so far about the Ritter killing, she was becoming convinced that an insider had played a role there as well. Maybe what she learned here could help with her own dilemma; at least she hoped so. It beat sitting in a hotel room moping.

Michelle perched on a small table in the corner and consulted her file, which had a detailed diagram of the location of all the players on that fateful day. She walked over and placed herself in the spot where Sean King had stood, Clyde Ritter just in front of him. Her gaze moved around the room, and she noted where one Secret Service agent had been stationed, and then another and yet another. The crowd had been behind a rope, and Ritter had been leaning over it exchanging greetings. Various members of Ritter's campaign team had been strewn around the space. Sidney Morse had been on the other side of the rope across from Ritter. She'd also seen Morse on the video. He had run screaming like everyone else. Doug Denby, Ritter's chief of staff, had been over by the door. The assassin, Arnold Ramsey, had been in the back of the room but had slowly made his way forward until he was standing in front of his victim. He'd been carrying an FOC, "Friend of Clyde," sign and, to Michelle's trained eye when she watched the video, he hadn't appeared to be dangerous.

Michelle glanced to the right and saw a bank of elevators. She imagined herself to be Sean King for a moment more, and she gazed right and left, sweeping the room in precise grids, pretending to speak into her throat mike, one hand out, as though touching the back of Ritter's sweaty shirt. Then she glanced, as King had, to the right and kept her gaze there for as long as he had; she counted the seconds off in her head. The only thing of note in that direction was the bank of elevators. The *ding* she'd heard had to have come from there.

The banging noise startled her so badly that she

drew her pistol and pointed it at all corners of the room. She was breathing so hard and shaking so badly that she sat down on the floor suddenly sick to her stomach. She realized quickly that a banging sound was not to be unexpected in an abandoned hotel: It could have been a falling ceiling tile, or perhaps a squirrel had gotten inside and run into something. Still, the timing was abysmal. She had to marvel at King's ability to endure the same surprise and, while wounded, retain enough presence of mind to pull his weapon and gun down an armed man. Would *she* have been able to ignore the pain in her hand, the chaos all around, and fire? Now that she'd partially experienced the situation for herself, her respect for him rose several notches.

She pulled herself together, looked at the elevator bank and then at her file. She had read more of the official record on the flight down, and had learned that this set of elevators had been turned off, secured by the Secret Service during Ritter's event. Presumably there would have been no *ding* to be heard. And yet she'd heard one. And King's attention *had* been riveted on this spot, or at least in this direction. Although he later claimed it was just a matter of his focus wandering, she wondered if it was more than that. She looked at a photo of the room at the time of the assassination. The carpeting had been put in afterward. The floor back then was wood. She rose, pulled out her knife and, eyeballing the spot, cut up the carpet. After she pulled back the rug and exposed a four-by-four square, she shone her light at the exposed spot.

The dark stains were still there. Blood was almost impossible to get out of wood; obviously the hotel had opted to just carpet over it. King's and Clyde Ritter's blood, she thought to herself; it was mixed together for all time. She next went over to the wall beyond where King had stood. The bullet that killed Clyde Ritter and wounded King had lodged here, although it had long since been dug out. The upholstered walls that were present at the time of the Ritter assassination had been replaced with the thick mahogany paneling. Again, this was a cover-up of sorts, as though the hotel owners could wipe away what had occurred. It hadn't worked, since the hotel closed down soon after Ritter's death.

She entered the enclosed office area through a doorway behind the front desk. Large file cabinets were stacked against one wall, and there were still papers, pens and other office items on the desks, as though the place had been abandoned in the middle of the day. She went to the file cabinets and was surprised to see that they were filled. She started sifting through them. Although the hotel undoubtedly had computers at the time of Ritter's assassination, they also apparently kept backup records on paper. That made things a little easier. Using her flashlight, she found the materials for 1996 and then those for the day Ritter had been there. In fact, the only records here were for 1996 and early 1997. Michelle surmised that the hotel had shut down shortly after the assassination and no one had bothered to clear anything out. If the hotel records had been confiscated during the subsequent investigation, they had been returned.

The Ritter party had stayed over one night at the Fairmount. King had checked into the hotel along with Ritter's entourage. The records showed King had occupied room 304.

She made her way up the main staircase to the third floor. She didn't have a passkey, but she did have her lockpick kit and the door quickly yielded. The things a trained federal agent could do. She went inside, looked around and found nothing except what one would expect to find in such a place: a mess. She saw that there was a connecting door into the next room, 302. She went through and saw a room exactly like the one she'd just left.

Downstairs she was about to leave when a thought struck her. She went back to the office area and looked for the employee files. Unfortunately here she struck out. Thinking for a bit, she then checked her floor plan of the hotel, located the main housekeeping supply section and headed there. This room was large and filled with shelves, empty counters and a desk. Michelle looked through the desk and then checked a large file cabinet back against one wall. Here she found what she wanted: a clipboard with names and addresses of housekeeping employees on moldy, curled paper. She took the list with her and went back to the office to look for a phone book, but the only one she found was far out-of-date and therefore probably useless. Emerging into the darkness outside, she was surprised to realize she'd spent over two hours inside the hotel.

She checked into a motel and used the phone book in her room to check the names and addresses of the maids on the employee list against the phone book. She found three that still lived in the area — at the same addresses they had back then. She began calling. There was no answer at the first, and she left a message. At the other two the phone was picked up by the former maids. Michelle identified herself as a documentary filmmaker working on a project about political assassinations and conducting interviews with people familiar with the Ritter murder. Both women, surprisingly enough, said they'd be very happy to be part of such a film. Perhaps not so surprising, she reflected, for what else was there to do here? Michelle made appointments with both for the following day. Then she grabbed a quick dinner at a country-western roadside diner where three cowboy-hat-wearing dudes hit on her in the span of ten minutes. Vastly fed up by the time the third fellow made his pitch, she munched her cheese-burger with one hand, showed her gun with the other and watched as the would-be suitor fled. *Oh, to be so popular.* After dinner she spent a couple of hours in her room going over the questions she'd ask the women the next day. As she was doing so, the other former maid called back and also agreed to speak with her. As Michelle drifted off to sleep, she wondered where she was really heading with all this.

Outside Michelle's motel room, the old Buick, its muffler still rattling and its exhaust still noxious, pulled to a stop. The driver cut off the engine and sat there, his gaze fixed on the door to Michelle's room. So intense was his concentration that it appeared the man could see right through the walls, perhaps right into the mind of the young Secret Service agent.

Tomorrow promised to be an interesting day. He

hadn't anticipated that Michelle Maxwell would come here to perform her own sort of investigation. Yet now that she had, it would have to be dealt with, delicately. He'd carefully constructed his list of targets and had no desire to add to that number injudiciously. However, plans did change as situations developed; whether Maxwell became a target remained to be seen.

There was a lot left to do, and a young inquisitive Secret Service agent could become a serious source of trouble. He debated whether to kill her right now, actually reaching down to the floorboard for his favored weapon of murder. As his fingers curled around the hard metal, he brooded on the matter further, and then his grip relaxed.

Too little preparation and too many potential complications would flow from her death right now. That was just not his way. So Michelle Maxwell would get to live another day. He put the Buick in gear and drove off.

16

The first two former Fairmont Hotel maids whom Michelle interviewed were not helpful. The assassination was the biggest thing that had ever happened in the town and in their lives, and in their discussions with "filmmaker" Michelle both women were prone to conjure all sorts of outlandish theories without being able to offer anything in the way of solid facts. Michelle listened politely and then left.

The third home she went to was a modest structure but neat, set back from the road. Loretta Baldwin was waiting for Michelle on the wide porch. Baldwin was a slender African American of sixty-plus years with high, pointed cheekbones, an expressive mouth and steel-rimmed spectacles that magnified her darting and energetic brown eyes. She sat ramrod straight in her chair and had a way of looking one over without seeming to that any Secret Service agent would be proud of, Michelle observed. Her hands were long and heavily veined. When the two women shook hands, there was such strength in the older woman's grip that it took the athletic Michelle by surprise. Michelle sat in the rocker next to Loretta's and accepted the glass of iced tea the woman offered.

"This film you doing, sweetie, we talking big or small?"

"It's a documentary, so small."

"So I guess no juicy part for me."

"Well, if your interview makes the cut, then yes, you'll be in it. We'll come back and film you at that point. I'm just doing preliminary research now."

"No, honey, I mean is this a *paid* engagement?"

"Oh, no, no it's not. Limited budget."

"Too bad. Not too many jobs 'round here, you see."

"I expect not."

"Not used to be that way."

"Like when the hotel was open?"

Baldwin nodded and rocked slowly in the gathering breeze. The weather had turned chilly, and Michelle wished more for a hot cup of coffee than a glass of iced tea.

"Who you talked to so far?" When Michelle told her, Baldwin smiled and then chuckled. "Them gals have no clue, you understand me, no clue about nothing. Did little Miss Julie tell you she was there when Martin Luther King Jr. was shot?"

"Yes, she mentioned that. She actually looked a little young for that."

"I'll say. She knows Martin Luther King like I know the pope."

"So what can you tell me about that day at the hotel?"

"A day like any other. Except we knew he was coming, of course. I mean Clyde Ritter. I knew about him, from the TV and all, and I read my newspaper, every day I do. The man's thinking was more in line with George Wallace before he found the light, but he seemed to be doing okay, which tells you all you need to know about this country." Then she stared at Michelle, a look of mirth in her eye. "Is your memory that good? Or maybe I ain't saying nothing you think is important enough to write down."

Michelle started and then pulled out a notepad and began scribbling. She also set a small recorder down on the table next to the woman. "Do you mind?"

"Hell no. Anybody sues me I ain't got no money. See, that's the poor person's best insurance policy: no assets."

"What were you doing that day?"

"Just like any other day, cleaning rooms."

"Which floor did you have?"

"*Floors.* Always had people calling in sick. Most time I had two floors all by myself. Had it that day, second and third. By the time I finished, seemed like it was time to start over again."

Michelle tensed at this. King had stayed on the third floor. "So you weren't on the main floor when the shooting occurred?"

"Now, did I say that?"

Michelle looked confused. "But you said you were cleaning."

"Is there a law against coming down and seeing what all the hoopla was about?"

"Were you in the room where the shooting happened?"

"I was right outside the door. There was a supply closet down that hall, and I had to get some things, you understand." Michelle nodded. "Management didn't like us maids to show ourselves in the main area, you see. Like they don't want the guests to know we're even there. Now, how do they think the place stays clean, you see my point?" Yes, Michelle said, she did. "Well, the room where Ritter was shot was called the Stonewall Jackson Room. It's not like down here we have us any Abraham Lincoln or Ulysses S. Grant rooms."

"I can understand that."

"Well, I poked my head in and I saw that man shaking hands and talking real slick and smooth and his eyes would hold anybody's he was talking to. I read where he was a TV preacher too. I could see how that man could get dollars and votes, yes indeed. He just had that way. But from a person of color's perspective I think Clyde Ritter was right at home in the Stonewall Jackson Room and was probably sleeping in the Jefferson Davis Penthouse Suite and loving that too, and damn if he was going to get my vote."

"I can understand that too. Besides Ritter, did you notice anyone else?"

"I remember a police officer blocking the doorway. I had to kind of look around him. I could see Ritter like I said, and there was the man behind him, real close."

"Secret Service. Agent Sean King."

Baldwin stared hard at her. "That's right. You say that like you know the man."

"Never met him. But I've been doing a lot of research."

Baldwin ran her gaze up and down Michelle, a scrutiny that made the younger woman finally blush. "You got no ring on your finger. What, are you telling me there ain't any eligible men that would appreciate a beautiful young thing like you?"

Michelle smiled. "I keep really crazy hours. Guys don't like that."

"Hell, honey, men don't like nothing but a meal and their beer in front of them when they want it, nobody questioning the stupid things they do, all the free time in the world and a warm body to do the sex thing when they feel like it, and no talking after."

"I see you have them pretty well figured out."

"Like it takes a lot of deep thinking?" She fell silent for a moment. "Yep, a real nice-looking man. When he fired that gun, though, he wasn't real nice-looking."

Michelle tensed again. "You saw that?"

"Yep. All hell broke loose when Ritter got shot. You wouldn't believe it. The policeman in front of me, he turned to see what was going on, but he got knocked down and people tripped over him. I just froze. I've heard guns go off, fired 'em myself growing up, to scare off critters and trespassers and such. But this was different. Then I saw King shoot Ramsey. Next I seen them run off with Ritter, but that man was dead, anybody could see that. And I watched that King fellow stand there just looking down, like, like . . ."

"Like he'd just seen his life end too," Michelle suggested.

"Just like that. How'd you know?"

"I know someone who had a similar experience. Did you by chance hear a sound before Ritter was shot, something that might have distracted Agent King?" Michelle didn't want to mention that that sound could have been the *ding* of an elevator car because she didn't want to influence Baldwin's recollection.

The old woman thought about this and then shook her head. "No, I can't say that I did. There was lots of noise. I tell you what I did do. I ran down the hallway and hid in the supply closet. I was so scared I didn't come out for an hour."

"But before all that you maybe cleaned the third floor?"

Baldwin looked over at her. "Why don't you ask me what you want to ask me and save us both a lot of time?"

"Okay, did you clean Agent King's room?"

She nodded. "They had all checked out before the event. But I got people's names down on my list. Yes, I cleaned his room before all the shooting started, and let me tell you it needed cleaning." She looked pointedly at Michelle.

"Why, was he a real slob?"

"No, but there was just a lot of activity in that room the night before, I guess." She raised an eyebrow as she said this.

"Activity?" asked Michelle.

"Activity."

Michelle had been perched on the edge of her rocker. Now she sat back. "I see."

"Looked like a couple of wild animals had gone through that room. Even found a pair of black lace panties on top of the ceiling light fixture. Don't know how they got there, and I don't want to know."

"Any idea who the other animal was?"

"No, but it seems to me you don't look too far away, you see my point?"

Michelle's eyes narrowed as she thought about this. "Yes, I think I do," she said. "So you didn't notice anyone getting off the elevator when all this happened?"

Baldwin looked at her strangely. "Trust me, honey, I wasn't paying attention to no elevators."

She looked at her notes. "So I see the hotel is closed now."

"Shut down not all that long after Ritter was shot. Bad publicity and all. Bad for me, ain't had a steady job like that since."

"I see they have a fence up."

Baldwin shrugged. "Folks who want to take a

piece of the place, boys doing drugs and dragging their girlfriends in there for you know what."

"So any plans to reopen it?"

Baldwin snorted loudly. "Knock it down more than likely."

"Any idea who owns it now?"

"Nope. It's just some big old empty pile of nothing. Sort of like this town."

Michelle asked her a few more questions and then thanked her and took her leave, but not before giving Loretta Baldwin some money for helping.

"Let me know when it's going to air. I'll watch it on the TV."

"When and if it does, you'll be the first to know," Michelle replied.

Michelle got back in her car and drove off. She now had another stop to make.

As she pulled off, she heard the rattle of a muffler about to fall off and looked up in time to see an ancient, rust-eaten Buick slowly pull down the street past her, the driver barely visible. Her only thought about it was that the car certainly symbolized this town, in that they were both falling apart.

The Buick driver looked over at Michelle without seeming to. As soon as Michelle pulled off, the man glanced over at a smiling Loretta Baldwin counting her money and rocking in her chair. He'd captured their entire conversation using a sound amplifier recorder hidden in the antenna of his car, and he'd also taken pictures of the two women using his long-range camera lens. Their discussion had been very interesting, so very enlightening on a personal level. So Loretta the maid had been in the supply closet on that day. Who would have thought it, after all these years? And yet he had to put that aside for now. He slowly turned the car around and followed Michelle. He felt certain she was going back to the hotel. And after hearing her conversation with Loretta Baldwin, he understood why.

17

King was at his office desk going over a file when there were footsteps outside his door. Neither his partner nor his secretary was coming in today, so he rose and, armed with a letter opener, went swiftly over to the door and opened it.

The men staring back at him looked grim. There was Todd Williams, the Wrightsburg chief of police, the same big uniformed U.S. marshal and two gents who flashed FBI credentials. King brought them all into the small conference room adjacent to his office.

The marshal leaned forward in his chair. His name was Jefferson Parks, he said, and he did not go by "Jeff," he told King firmly, but by "Jefferson," although he preferred simply "*Deputy* Marshal Parks." "U.S. *marshals* are political appointees. The deputies do the real work," he said.

He held up a pistol in a plastic evidence bag. "This is the pistol that was taken from your home," he said in a flat, low voice.

"If you say so."

"It *is* your pistol. Chain of custody intact."

King glanced at Williams, who nodded his head.

"Okay," said King. "And you want to give it back to me because . . .?"

"Oh, we're not giving it back," said one of the FBI agents.

Parks continued, "We dug the bullet that killed Jennings out of the wall of your partner's office. It was jacketed, so there was little projectile deformity. We also found the shell casing. The shot that killed Howard Jennings was fired from your gun. Pinprick, land, groove and even shell ejector mark. A perfect match."

"And I'm telling you that's impossible!"

"Why?"

"Let me ask you a question. What was the time of Jennings's death?"

"Medical examiner says between 1:00 and 2:00 a.m. the night before you found him in your office," replied Parks.

"At that time I was making my patrol rounds. And that pistol was in my holster."

One of the FBI agents perked up. "Do we take that as a confession?"

King's look made it clear what he thought of that comment.

Parks considered this and said, "We've been checking your movements that night. Your vehicle was seen on Main Street around the time Jennings was killed."

"I probably was there. My rounds include the town area, so it would be logical that someone saw my truck then. But you don't have a witness that saw me at my office, because I wasn't there."

One of the FBI agents was about to respond until Parks put a big hand on his arm.

"That's not something we have to discuss with you at the moment," said Parks. "But we do have a positive on the ballistics, and with your background you know that's as good as a fingerprint."

"No, not quite as good as a print. It doesn't place me at the crime scene."

"On the contrary, we have your gun at the scene, and we have you nearby the scene. That's pretty strong evidence."

"Circumstantial evidence," countered King.

"And there have been convictions on a lot less," shot back Parks.

"We should have done a trace metal test when they took the gun from you," said one of the FBI agents.

"Wouldn't have done any good," said King. "I handled my gun the night before you came, so there would have been microscopic traces in my skin from the metal."

"Convenient," said the agent.

Parks's gaze was on King. "May I ask why you were handling your gun? You weren't on duty."

"I thought there was a prowler around my house."

"Was there?"

"No. Just an old acquaintance."

Parks looked at him strangely, but apparently decided against pursuing the matter.

"Care to tell me my motive?" asked King.

"The man works for you. Maybe he was stealing, or maybe he found out you were stealing from clients and tried to blackmail you. You arrange to meet him and kill him."

"Nice theory, only he wasn't stealing from me, and I wasn't stealing from my clients because I don't have direct access to any of their funds. Check it out."

"Oh, we will but that's just two possibilities. Another might be that you somehow found out Jennings was WITSEC, and you let that slip to the wrong people."

"And they killed him with *my* gun that was in *my* holster?"

"Or you did it to pocket the fee."

"So now I'm a hit man."

"Did you know Jennings was WITSEC?"

King hesitated an instant too long, at least to his thinking. "No."

"Care to take a polygraph on that?"

"I don't have to answer that."

"Just trying to help you out," said Parks. "I mean you've already admitted having the murder weapon on you at the time Jennings was killed."

"Just so you know, you haven't advised me of my rights, so I doubt anything I've said to you is admissible anyway."

"You're not under arrest. You haven't been charged," pointed out one of the FBI agents. "So we're under no obligation to read you anything."

Parks said, "And if called to testify, we can merely repeat what you said in our presence."

"Hearsay," said King. "And I don't really think you can get it in under an exception, because it's prejudicial. I'd get a mistrial in a heartbeat."

"You don't practice criminal law, do you?" said Parks.

"No, why?"

"Because what you just said was a crock of shit."

King didn't look as confident now. Parks pressed on.

"So are you retracting your statement that the gun was with you at that time?"

"Am I under arrest?"

"It might depend on how you answer my question."

King rose. "From now on, all discussions will be with my *criminal* defense attorney present."

Parks rose too, and for a moment King had the feeling that the big man was going to come across the table and throttle him. Yet he just smiled and handed the bagged gun to one of the FBI agents.

"I'm sure we'll be seeing you," he said pleasantly. "Just don't make any travel plans for outside the area; that won't make me happy."

As they were leaving, King pulled Williams aside.

"Todd, why is Parks running the show? The FBI takes a backseat to no one."

"The dead guy was in witness protection. Parks is really high up at the Marshals Service. I think he was actually the one who placed Jennings in this area. And he's ticked off that he's dead. I guess he pulled some strings in D.C." Todd looked uncomfortable and his voice dropped. "Look, not for one instant do I believe you're mixed up in this . . ."

"And you were about to say *but*?"

Todd looked even more uncomfortable. "But I think it would be best . . ."

"If I suspend my duties as a deputy pending the outcome of all this?"

"I appreciate your understanding."

After Todd left, King sat at his desk. What was bothering him was that he hadn't been arrested on the spot. In truth, they had enough to charge him. And how had the gun he'd been holstering on that night been used to kill Jennings? King could think of two scenarios, and when the other thought struck him he almost put his fist through the wall. How could he have been so stupid? *Joan Dillinger.*

He picked up the phone and called an old friend in Washington. The man was still employed by the Secret Service and had remained on King's side throughout the Ritter ordeal. After some personal and professional chitchat King asked him how Joan Dillinger was doing.

"Don't really know."

"Oh, I thought you two worked closely together."

"Well, we did until she left."

"Left? Left the Washington field office?"

"No, the Service."

King almost dropped the phone. "Joan is no longer with the Secret Service?"

"She left about a year ago. Went into private

security consulting. And she's making a boatload of cash, from what I've heard. And probably needs every penny. You know Joan likes to live well."

"You got a number for her up there?" King wrote the information down.

His friend continued, "I guess you've heard about our troubles. It's really too bad. Maxwell was good, a real supercharged model."

"I saw her on TV. I'm reading scapegoat, am I right? I'm sort of an expert."

"Comparing what she did to your situation is apples and oranges. Maxwell made a huge error in judgment. She was detail leader, you were just one of the grunts."

"Come on, how many bedrooms have we stood outside of while the guy was in there having serious carnal knowledge with a woman who wasn't his wife? And it's not like we ever searched those ladies for weapons. And I don't remember us going to the mat to stand next to the damn bed."

"But nothing bad happened."

"No thanks to us."

"Okay, I'm not going to get into it any further, because I have to watch my blood pressure. So you gonna hook up with Joan?"

"Oh, I have a feeling I'm going to see her real soon."

18

Michelle slipped back inside the Fairmount and went directly to the hotel office again. King had occupied room 304. Loretta Baldwin had hinted that she should not look too far from there, so she checked the occupant for room 302. Michelle remembered there was a connecting door.

"Damn," she said when she saw the name on the registration card. J. Dillinger had been in room 302. Could that be Joan Dillinger? She'd met Dillinger briefly a couple of times. The woman had moved higher in the agency than almost any of her gender had previously and then abruptly quit. Michelle remembered being intimidated by the lady, something she was definitely not used to. Joan Dillinger had a reputation for being more cool under pressure, more tenacious, more ballsy than anyone else, man or woman. Ambitious as hell, she'd left the Service to grab the brass ring of private-sector consulting.

But while she was at the Service she was someone Michelle had looked up to.

And yet was Joan Dillinger the other half of the wild animal act Loretta Baldwin had described? Was the iron lady whom Michelle admired the same woman whose black lace panties ended up on the overhead light? Was King's mental lapse in guarding Clyde Ritter due to sheer physical exhaustion from a night of sex with Joan that was so explosive it had sent her flimsy underwear skyward? She felt certain it was Joan because on the index card used for registration, her address, like King's, was the Secret Service headquarters in Washington.

Michelle put both index cards in her bag and went to the Stonewall Jackson Room. There she looked at the doorway from where Loretta Baldwin witnessed the first assassination of a politician campaigning for the U.S. presidency in almost thirty years. She stood where Loretta had and closed the door. It was again so quiet in here that she could hear her own pounding heartbeat.

As soon as she left the room and went back into the lobby, this sensation stopped. Normal sounds returned, and she could no longer hear the jarring thumps of her heart. She was beginning to wonder if the Stonewall Jackson Room was haunted, perhaps by a very upset Clyde Ritter. She went down the hallway and found the supply closet where Loretta said she'd hidden. It was fairly large and had shelves lining three of the walls.

Michelle went up the stairs to the third floor, shining her light around in wide arcs. She reached room 302 and went in. She tried to envision Joan Dillinger knocking softly on the door to King's room and being admitted. Maybe after a few drinks and some Secret Service gossip, Joan's panties had hit the overhead light, and they'd created their own personal highlight reel.

She went out into the hall and walked back toward the stairwell. She stopped and looked at the large garbage chute that was set up at one window. Obviously somebody had started doing some work here and then just as obviously stopped. She leaned out the window, her eyes adjusting to the daylight. Down below, the chute ended in a Dumpster. It was filled with debris, mostly old mattresses, curtains and carpeting, all of which looked thoroughly rotted.

She walked back to the lobby level and then paused. The stairs kept going down to the basement level. There couldn't be anything down there of interest, and as those low-budget horror films teach, you never, ever venture into the basement. Well, unless you were an armed Secret Service agent. She took out her pistol and made her way down. Here the hallway carpet was torn up and the air filled with mildew and rot. She passed a spot and came back. She pushed open the small door and shone her light in. It was a dumbwaiter, a large one. She couldn't tell if it connected to all eight floors or not. The Fairmount, she'd learned, was a very old hotel, and this might have been the way laundry or other bulky items were moved up and down. There were buttons on the wall next to the dumbwaiter to turn it on and off, so it had been powered by electricity, and a rope on pulleys inside the shaft was doubtless used as a backup in case the power supply was interrupted.

She kept going down the hall until it stopped at a wall of debris that had collapsed from the floor above. The place was literally falling apart. They better hurry up with the wrecking ball, or else they wouldn't need it.

Michelle needed fresh air and sunlight. She jogged up the stairs. The light hit her right in the eyes. The voice barked in her ear.

"Freeze. Hotel security. I'm armed and prepared to use my weapon."

Michelle held up her gun and flashlight. "I'm a Secret Service agent." She said this so automatically that she forgot she didn't have the badge or creds anymore.

"Secret Service? Right, and I'm Marshal Matt Dillon."

"Can you take the flashlight out of my eyes?" she asked.

"Put your gun on the floor," said the voice. "Nice and easy."

"I'm doing it," said Michelle. "Just don't accidentally pull the trigger and shoot me in the process."

As she straightened back up, the light moved away from her eyes.

"What are you doing here? This is private property."

"It is?" she said innocently.

"There's a fence and signs up, lady."

"Well, I guess I came in another way."

"What's the Secret Service doing down here? You got something to show that to be true, by the way?"

"Can we go outside in the light? I feel like I've been spelunking on dry land for about six hours."

"Okay, but don't pick up your gun. I'll get it."

They walked outside, where Michelle got a better look at the man. He was middle-aged with short grayish hair, medium height and trim, and wearing a rent-a-cop uniform.

He stared at her while he held his pistol in his left hand and slid her pistol into his waistband with his other. "Okay, you were going to show me your badge. But even if you are Secret Service, you still got no business here."

"Do you remember about eight years ago a politician named Clyde Ritter was killed at this hotel?"

"Remember? Lady, I've lived here my whole life. It's the only exciting thing that's ever happened in this damn place."

"Well, I came down to check it out. I'm relatively new to the Service, and this is one of the scenarios we study at the training center – things to avoid, of course. I guess I was just curious, wanted to see for myself. I came all the way from Washington, and I saw that it was closed up, but I didn't think a quick peek would hurt."

"I guess I can see that. Now, your badge?"

Michelle thought for a moment. As her hand reached up to touch her chin, it nudged a tiny bit of metal on the way. She took off her lapel pin with the Secret Service insignia and held it out. The lapel pins were worn to allow agents to be identifiable to each other. The colors were constantly changed to prevent successful forging. It was such a routine for her that even on suspension she rose each morning and put one on.

The guard took the lapel pin and studied it before handing it back.

"I left my badge and creds back at the motel where I'm staying," she explained.

"Okay, I suppose it's all right. You sure don't look like the riffraff who break into boarded-up hotels." He started to hand back her gun and then stopped. "But first, how's about you open your bag?"

"Why?"

"So I can see what's in it, that's why."

She very reluctantly handed her bag over. As he looked through it, Michelle said, "So who owns the place?"

"They don't tell folks like me that. I just walk the walk and keep people out."

"Is there somebody here twenty-four seven?"

"Hell if I know, I just pull my shift."

"So what are they going to do with this place, knock it down?"

"Beats me. They wait much longer, it'll fall down." He pulled the hotel index cards out of her bag and looked at them. "You mind telling me what you're doing with these?"

She tried to look as innocent as possible. "Oh, those? Well, I happen to know both of those people. They were here when the shooting happened. I . . . I just thought they might like to have them, sort of as souvenirs," she added lamely.

He just stared at her and then said, "Souvenirs?

Damn, you federal people are weird." He dropped the cards back into the bag and handed it and her gun back.

As Michelle returned to her car, the security guard watched her go. He waited a few more minutes and then went into the hotel. When he came out ten minutes later, his appearance had drastically changed. Michelle Maxwell was very quick on her feet, he judged. She might very well make his list if she kept up this sort of activity. That's why he'd come here and dressed as a security guard, to see what she'd found. Certainly those names on the cards had been interesting but hardly surprising: Sean King and J. Dillinger. What a delightful pair. Buick Man climbed into his car and drove off.

19

"Deputy Marshal Parks, what can I do for you today? How about I cop to a couple of misdemeanors, do community service, and let's call it a day?" King was sitting on his front porch watching the lawman climb out of his car and then head up the steps. The big man was dressed in jeans and a blue windbreaker that, ironically, read "FBI" and a baseball cap with the initials "DEA."

In response to King's look, Parks said, "I started doing this when I was a D.C. cop way back in the seventies. I get this stuff from every agency there is. One of the few perks we in law enforcement have. For my money, DEA has the nicest stuff." He sat down in a rocking chair next to King and rubbed his knees.

"When I was young, it was pretty cool being so big, a star football and basketball player in high school with the pleasant duty of nailing all the cheerleaders. I even carried the pigskin to pay for college."

"Where was that?"

"Notre Dame. I never started, but I played in pretty much every game. Tight end. Better blocker than receiver. Only had one career touchdown but it was sweet."

"That's impressive."

Parks shrugged. "Now that I'm not so young, it's not so cool anymore. It's just a big pain in the ass. Or the knees or the hips or the shoulders – take your anatomical pick."

"So how'd you like being a cop in our nation's capital?"

"I like being a marshal a lot better. Those were weird times. Lots of shit going on."

King held up his bottle of beer. "You off duty enough to have one?"

"No, but I'll enjoy a smoke. Got to combat this fresh, bracing mountain air somehow. Nasty stuff. Don't know how you folks stand it."

Parks pulled a cigarillo from his shirt pocket and coaxed it to life with a mother-of-pearl lighter, then snapped the lid shut. "You got a nice place here."

"Thanks." King watched him carefully. If Parks was heading up the investigation of Howard Jennings's death along with his other duties, he was a busy person, and his being here had to have a purpose.

"Nice law practice, nice home, nice little town. Nice guy who works hard and gives back to his community."

"Please, I'll start blushing."

Parks nodded. "Of course, nice successful people kill other people all the time in this country, so that doesn't mean shit to me. Personally I don't like nice guys all that much. Mark 'em as pantywaists."

"I wasn't always so nice. And it wouldn't take too much of an effort for me to revert to my old asshole ways. In fact, I feel an explosion coming on."

"That's encouraging, but don't try to get on my good side."

"And how nice can I really be? My gun was the murder weapon."

"Yes, it was."

"Would you care to hear my theory on that?"

Parks eyed his watch. "Sure, if you can spare a second and fetch me one of those brews. Funny thing, I just went off duty."

King did and handed the bottle to him. The marshal sat back in his chair and propped his size fourteens up on the railing and took a swig in between cigar puffs.

"Your theory on the gun?" he prompted as he watched the sun setting.

"I had it with me at the time Jennings was killed. According to you, that same gun killed Jennings."

"Seems pretty straightforward so far," Parks said. "In fact, I can handcuff you right now if you want."

"Well, since I didn't kill Jennings, it seems pretty clear that I didn't really have my gun with me."

Parks shot him a glance. "You changing your story?"

"No. On the six days I don't use it I keep my gun in a lockbox. I live alone, so I don't always lock the box up."

"Pretty stupid."

"Trust me, after this it goes in an underground vault."

"Go on."

"Theory number one, someone takes my gun and leaves a substitute in its place, which I take with me that night. This same person uses my gun to kill Jennings, then puts it back in my box, retrieving the substitute. Theory number two, a substitute gun is used to kill Jennings, and that substitute is placed in my lockbox and becomes the one the ballistics test was run on."

"The serial numbers on the gun we ran matched the one registered to you."

"Then it's my first scenario."

"So you're saying somebody took your gun way

back when, because they would have had to do that to make an exact replica, and then did this substitution to make it look like your gun killed Jennings?"

"That's what I'm saying."

"Are you telling me a former lawman doesn't know his own weapon?"

"It's a mass-produced nine-millimeter, Marshal. It's not some fancy-ass museum piece with diamond studs. I got the gun when I became a deputy. I wear it once a week, never take it out of its holster and then forget about it. Whoever copied it knew what they were doing, though, because it seemed just like mine, weight distribution and feel of the grip."

"And why go to all this trouble to pin it on you?"

"Well, murderers often try to pin it on someone else, don't they? I mean that's sort of the point. Jennings worked for me. Maybe they thought folks would think what you said earlier, that I killed Jennings because I caught him stealing or he caught me stealing. Motive, gun match, no alibi. Lethal injection here I come."

Parks put his feet on the floor and sat forward. "Very interesting. Now, let me give you a theory in return. Jennings had lots of guys looking to kill him. That's why he was in the program. So maybe you knew he was WITSEC and ratted him out for a chunk of cash. Then whoever hired you paid you back by using your gun and stiffing you in the form of a frame. How's that?" Parks eyed him steadily.

"Actually that one works too," conceded King.

"Uh-huh." Parks drained his beer, stubbed out his cigarillo and stood. "How are the media hounds?"

"Not as bad as I would have thought. Most haven't discovered my house yet. When they do, I'll just chain off the road at the bottom of the hill, post signs and start shooting trespassers."

"Now, there's my kind of asshole."

"I told you I had it in me."

Parks headed down the stairs to his car.

King called to him. "So how come I'm not under arrest?"

Parks opened the car door. "Well, primarily because I think your theory number one has some validity. Maybe you *were* carrying a substitution weapon while your gun was used to kill Jennings."

"I actually didn't think you'd accept my theory that easily."

"Oh, I'm not saying you didn't have Jennings killed and did the gun substitution yourself. Although my favorite scenario still has you ratting him out and the actual triggerman framing you for it." He looked down at the ground for a second. "No witness in the history of WITSEC who stayed in the program and followed the rules has ever been

killed. That was a great sales point to potential witnesses. Now we can't claim that anymore. And it
happened on my watch. I placed Jennings here, and
I feel responsible for his death. So just so you know,
if you did set him up, I'll personally select the prison
you'll be going to, and it'll be one where you'll
scream for the death penalty about three hours after
you check in, asshole or not." Parks opened his car
door and touched the brim of his DEA baseball cap.
"Now, you have a real nice evening."

20

The next day King left Wrightsburg early, fought northern Virginia morning rush hour traffic and arrived in Reston, Virginia, around ten. The ten-story office building was relatively new and now about half-leased. A dot-com company had rented the entire space several years ago and despite having no products or profits, decorated it lavishly and then, astonishingly, ran out of money. The area was very nice with shops and restaurants at the nearby Reston Town Center. Well-dressed consumers slipped in and out of pricey stores. People struggled to get where they needed to go on the congested roads. It all had a high-energy, upscale feel to it. Yet King simply wanted to accomplish what he'd come to do, then retreat to the bucolic environs of the Blue Ridge.

The top floor of the building was now occupied by a firm known simply as the Agency, a name it had actually trademarked for commercial use, probably much to the chagrin of the CIA. The Agency was one of the premier investigative and security firms in the country. King rode up in the private elevator, waving to a surveillance camera that was eyeballing him, and was met in a small waiting room off the main lobby by someone who looked armed and ready to use his weapon. King was searched and had to step through a metal detector before he was allowed to proceed to the lobby. It was tastefully appointed and had no one in it other than a watchful woman at the front desk who took his name and dialed her phone.

He was escorted back by a stylishly dressed young man with broad shoulders and curly dark hair, wearing a headset and displaying an arrogant manner. He opened the door and motioned King through and then left, closing the door behind him. King looked around the office. It was a four-window corner unit, the glass all heavily tinted and reflecting from the outside, though on the top floor the only things capable of peeping in would be birds, or folks in dangerously low-flying planes. The whole feel of the place was quiet, understated yet undeniably prosperous.

When a side door opened and she walked in, King didn't know whether to say hello or knock the woman over her desk and strangle her.

"I'm very touched that you'd brave the traffic to

come and see me," said Joan. She was dressed in a dark pantsuit that was flattering to her figure, not that many clothing choices wouldn't be. Yet the sleek cut of the suit and her three-inch spikes gave her the impression of height she really didn't have.

"Thanks for seeing me."

"Only fair considering how much of *me* you've seen recently. But I really was very surprised to hear from you."

"Well, now we're even. Because I can't tell you what a shock it was to find out you weren't with the Service anymore."

"I didn't tell you that when I came to your house?"

"No, Joan, that one you somehow forgot to mention."

She sat down on a small leather sofa set against one wall and motioned for him to join her. On the table in front of her was a coffee service. While King sat, she poured.

"You can hold the eggs, toasted bagel. And lace panties," he added. He was very surprised when the woman reddened at his remark.

"I'm really trying very hard to block that out of my mind," she said quietly.

He took a sip of coffee and looked around. "Wow,

look at this place. At the Service did we even have desks?"

"No, because we didn't need them. We were either driving really fast in cars . . ."

"Or pushing till our feet gave out," he finished for her. "Pushing" was Secret Service shorthand for being on duty, usually standing at a post to secure it.

She sat back and looked around her office. "It is nice, but I'm not really here that much. I'm usually on a plane somewhere."

"At least you get to fly commercial or private. Military transport is hard on the back, butt and stomach. We flew enough of those."

"You remember going on *Air Force One*?" she asked.

"Anyone who has never forgets."

"I miss that part."

"But you make a lot more money."

"I guess you do too."

He shifted his weight and balanced his cup in the palm of his hand. "I know you're busy, so I'll get down to it. A U.S. deputy marshal named Jefferson Parks came to see me. He's heading up the investigation on Howard Jennings, the murdered WITSEC. He was the one who came for my gun while you were there."

Joan looked interested. "Jefferson Parks?"

"You know him?"

"Name sounds very familiar. So they took your gun. And ballistics cleared you?"

"Actually no. It was a match. My gun killed Howard Jennings."

King had thought over this phrasing very carefully on the drive up, because he wanted to test the woman's response to it. She almost spilled her coffee. Either she had really boned up on her acting skills or it was a sincere reaction.

"That can't be right," she said.

"That's what *I* said. But fortunately the marshal and I saw eye-to-eye on the method that someone *could* have used to make my gun the murder weapon while I thought I had it on me."

"How?"

King briefly explained his substitution theory. He'd thought about withholding it from her but decided it didn't really matter, and he wanted her reaction to this as well, mostly for the follow-up statement he was going to make.

Joan thought about this, longer than King felt was really necessary.

"That would take a lot of planning and skill," she finally said.

"And access to my house. They would have had to get the gun back in my box before the posse showed up to take it, you know, the morning that *you* were there."

He finished his coffee and poured himself another cup while she stewed on this. He offered to freshen hers but she declined.

"So you came here to tell me that, what, you think I framed you?" said Joan stiffly.

"I'm just telling you that someone did, and I just told you how I think they did it."

"You could have told me that over the phone."

"Yes, I could, but you paid me a visit, and I wanted to return the honor. At least I called first."

"I didn't set you up, Sean."

"Then all my troubles are over. I'll call Parks and tell him the good news."

"You know, you can be a real smart-ass."

He put down his coffee cup and drew very close to her. "Let me just lay it out for you. I've got a dead man in my office, and my gun killed him. I've got no alibi and a pretty damn sharp marshal who, while maybe he buys my theory on a frame, is by no means convinced of my innocence. And this man would shed no tears if I'm locked up for the rest of my life or given some toxic bug juice to transport me to the hereafter. And then you come to visit me out of the blue and somehow forget to tell me that you're no longer with the Secret Service. You make a big deal of apologizing, acting all nice, with the result that I let you stay overnight. You try your best to seduce me on my kitchen table for a reason I still can't fathom, but I can't believe only has to do with you wanting to scratch an eight-year-old itch. You're alone in my house while I'm out on the lake, and my gun mysteriously turns out to be the murder weapon after it's picked up on that very same morning. Now, Joan, maybe I am more suspicious than my neighbor, but I'd have to be on life support and breathing through a frigging tube not to be a little paranoid about that sequence of events."

She eyed him with maddening calm. "I didn't take your gun. I know nothing about anyone who might have. I have no proof of that. You just have my word."

"Again, that's such a relief."

"I never told you that I was still with the Service. You just assumed."

"You never said you weren't!" he snapped.

"You never asked!" She added, "And that wasn't my best."

King looked confused. "What?"

"You said I did my best to seduce you. Just for the record, that wasn't my best."

Both sat back now, seemingly out of words or breath or both.

153

"Okay," he said, "whatever game you're playing with me, you just go ahead and play it. I'm not going down for Jennings's murder, because I didn't do it."

"Neither did I, and I'm not trying to frame you. What motive would I have?"

King said, "Well, if I knew that, I wouldn't be here, would I?" He rose. "Thanks for the coffee. Next time hold the cyanide, it gives me gas."

"As I told you before, I came to see you for a very particular purpose." He stared at her. "But I didn't get around to it. I guess seeing you after all those years made more of an impact than I thought it would."

"So what was the purpose?"

"To make you a proposition." She quickly added, "A *business* proposition."

"Like what?"

"Like John Bruno," she replied.

His eyes narrowed. "What do you have to do with a missing presidential candidate?"

"Thanks to me, the firm was hired by Bruno's party to find out what happened to him. In lieu of our standard rate I negotiated another arrangement. Our out-of-pocket expenses are covered, but we accepted a much lower daily rate. However, it comes with a potentially lucrative bonus."

"What, like a finder's fee, no pun intended."

"A multimillion-dollar one to be exact. And since I brought in the account, under the firm's policy of getting to eat what you kill, I personally get sixty percent."

"How exactly did you manage that?"

"Well, as you know I had a pretty good career at the Service. And in the time I've been here I've brought several very high-profile cases to a successful conclusion, including the return of a Fortune 500 executive who was kidnapped."

"Congratulations. Funny I never heard about it."

"Well, we like to keep a low profile to the public. To those who are in the know, however, we're a major player."

"Millions, huh? I didn't think third-party candidates had that kind of war chest."

"A large part of it is special liability insurance, and Bruno's wife has family money. His campaign was also very well funded. And since they have no candidate to expend money on, they want to pay me, and I have no problem with that."

"But Bruno's case is an ongoing federal investigation."

"So what? The FBI doesn't have a monopoly on solving crimes. And Bruno's people flatly don't trust the government. In case you haven't been reading your newspaper, some of them think their candidate was set up by the Service."

"They said the same thing about me and Ritter, and it's as crazy now as it was then," said King.

"But it presents a wonderful opportunity for us."

"Us? And what exactly is my part in all this?"

"If you help me find Bruno, I'll pay you forty percent of what I get; it'll be seven figures to you."

"I'm not rich, but I really don't need the money, Joan."

"But I do. I left the Service before I did my twenty-five years, so I'm sort of screwed on the pension. I've been here a year, making a lot more money, and I've socked most of it away, but I'm not enjoying myself. In my years at the Service I worked the equivalent of a forty-year career. I see in my future white beaches, a catamaran and exotic cocktails, and this score will allow me to do that. And maybe you don't need the money, but what you do need is something good to happen to you. Where the newspapers tout you as a hero instead of the fall guy."

"So you're now my P.R. person?"

"I think you need one, Sean."

"Why me? You've got all the resources of this place."

"Most of the experienced people are pissed that I landed the deal, and they won't work on it with me. The ones who are left are young, overeducated and street-stupid. Your fourth year in the Service you broke the largest counterfeit ring in the Northern Hemisphere working solo from the field office in Louisville, Kentucky, of all places. That's the sort of investigative talent I need. And it also helps matters that you live two hours from where Bruno was snatched."

He looked around. "I don't even work at this place."

"I can use anyone I want in the investigation."

He shook his head. "I haven't done this stuff in years."

"Like riding a bike." She sat forward and stared at him intently. "Like riding a bike, Sean. And I don't think I'd be making this proposition to you if I'd set you up to take a murder rap. I need you with me if I want the payoff. And I want the payoff."

"I have my law practice."

"Take a sabbatical. If we're going to find Bruno, it'll be sooner rather than later. Look at it this way. It's exciting. It's different. It might not be like old times. But maybe it'll be like new times." Her hand lightly touched his. Somehow it was a far more seductive gesture than the tacky stunt she'd pulled on his kitchen table.

"And maybe you can show me how to sail the catamaran, because I don't have a clue," said Joan quietly.

21

Loretta Baldwin lay in the bath and let the hot water take the chill off her bones. The bathroom was dark; she liked it that way, like a mother's womb, comforting. She chuckled; she had to, every time she thought of it. About that girl that had come by asking all those questions pretending to be making a film about Clyde Ritter, as if anyone would bother. The girl was probably some sort of police officer or private investigator, though why anyone would be digging up the Clyde Ritter mess was beyond her. Yet Loretta would take the money, every cent of it. Just like she had all these years. She'd told the truth, at least to the questions the girl had asked; she just hadn't asked the right ones. Like what Loretta had seen when she was hiding in the supply closet. What a nervous wreck she'd been getting it out of the hotel, yet no one really noticed her in the chaos. She was just one of the maids, invisible really. And she knew ways out of the hotel that not even the Secret Service had been aware of.

At first she thought to go to the police with what she'd found and seen, but then decided not to. Why get messed up in something like that? And she'd tired of spending her life cleaning up other people's messes. And what did she care about Clyde Ritter? A man like that was far better off in the grave, where he couldn't spread his poison.

So she had done it. Sent the note and photo to the person telling what she'd seen and what she now possessed, and arranging for money to come to her. And it had come and she hadn't broken her silence and the person she was blackmailing never knew her identity, right up to the end. She'd been real tricky, using a series of P.O. boxes, fake names and one close friend, now dead, to help her cover her tracks. She hadn't been greedy. It wasn't a whole lot of money, but with no steady work all these years the cash had come in real handy, let her keep her home, pay her bills, buy some nice things, help her family. Yes, it was all right.

And that girl had never thought to ask; yet how could she have known? And even if she had, Loretta would have lied, just like the girl had lied to her, because if she was a documentary filmmaker, Loretta was Lena Horne. That thought made her laugh so hard she started to choke.

After she settled back down, her thoughts grew more somber. The money was no longer coming, but there was nothing she could do about that now. All things had to end. But she hadn't been a spendthrift. She'd put some of the money away, knowing that her golden goose would not last forever. She could get by a while longer, and maybe by then another goose would present itself. That girl had given her money. That was a start. Loretta Baldwin was nothing if not optimistic.

The phone rang, startling her. Her bones thoroughly warmed, she opened her eyes and started to climb out of the bathtub. Maybe this was another golden goose calling right now.

She never made it to the phone.

"Remember me, Loretta?"

The man stood over her, a metal pole with a flattened end in his hands.

She would have screamed, but he pushed her under the water with the pole and held her there. For an elderly woman Loretta was fairly strong, but not nearly strong enough. Her eyes kept widening, her body jerking. She grabbed the pole, and water splashed all over the floor. Finally she had to take a breath and her lungs filled with water and it was over quickly after that.

He lifted the pole off and studied her features. Her shriveled body stayed at the bottom of the tub, her dead eyes staring at him. The phone had stopped ringing; the house was silent. He left the room for a minute, located Loretta's pocketbook and returned to the bathroom. He pulled out the money Michelle had given the woman, five twenties neatly tucked away in an inside compartment.

He hooked Loretta's body with the pole and lifted her out of the water. He opened her mouth with his gloved hand and then crammed the money inside. He clamped her jaw shut and let go. She settled back to the bottom, the ends of the twenty-dollar bills sticking out of her mouth. It wasn't a very attractive look, but it was so very fitting an end for a black-mailer, he thought.

He spent time going through her possessions, searching for the item of his she'd taken all those years ago, but it wasn't here. To still be denied after all this time? Perhaps Loretta had had the last laugh. And yet she was lying quite dead in the bottom of a tub of water with money stuffed in her mouth. So who was really laughing?

He took his pole and left the way he'd come.

The Buick started up and rattled off. That chapter

of his life, that loose end, was finally over. He'd have to drop Michelle Maxwell a thank-you note, perhaps among other things. He would never have known the woman's identity if the Secret Service agent hadn't come around asking questions. Loretta Baldwin had not been part of the original plan, only an opportunity that had fallen into his hands and was far too good to pass up.

He was finished with the little province of Bowlington for now. He wished Loretta Baldwin a nice eternity in hell for her crimes. He'd doubtlessly be joining her at some point, and who knew, maybe he'd kill her all over again.

Now, there was a thought!

22

King listlessly cast his line into the water and slowly reeled it back in. He was standing on his dock, the sun up barely an hour. The fish weren't biting, yet he didn't care. The spread of mountains seemed to be watching his uninspired efforts with a brooding focus.

Joan undoubtedly had several complex motives in making her offer. Which ones favored him to any degree other than the financial compensation? Probably none. Joan's schemes tended to only advance her interests. At least he knew where he stood with the woman.

With Jefferson Parks, King was less certain. The marshal seemed sincere, but that could simply be a facade; it often was with lawmen, King knew. He'd played that game in his investigative career at the Service. King didn't doubt that whoever had killed Howard Jennings would feel the full wrath of the big man. King just wanted to make certain that he didn't become that target.

The ripple of water gently touched one of the pilings on his dock, and he looked up to see its source. The scull slid across the lake's surface, the woman pulling hard on her paddles. She was close enough that King could see the muscled definition of her shoulders and arms revealed by her tank top shirt. As she slowed and coasted toward him, something about her looked very familiar.

She glanced around in surprise, as though unaware she was close to shore.

"Hello," she said, and waved.

He didn't wave back, only nodded. He cast his line again, purposely close to her.

"I hope I'm not interfering with your fishing," she said.

"That depends on how long you're going to stay."

She drew her knees up. She was wearing black Lycra shorts, and the thigh muscles were long and looked like cable under skin. She pulled her hair out of its ponytail and wiped her face with a towel.

She looked around. "Boy, it's beautiful here."

"That's why people come," he said warily. "And where exactly did you come from?" He was trying hard to place her.

She pointed south. "I drove over to the state park and put in there."

"That's seven miles by water!" he exclaimed. The woman wasn't even winded.

"I do this a lot."

Her scull drifted closer. And King finally recognized her. He could barely contain his astonishment.

"Would you like a cup of coffee, Agent Maxwell?"

She looked surprised for a moment and then seemed to sense that such a pretense was both unnecessary and even silly under the circumstances.

"If it's not too much trouble."

"One fallen agent to another, no trouble at all." He helped her dock the scull. She eyed the covered boat slips and the storage sheds attached to each. King's jet boat, kayak, Sea-Doo and other vessels were sparkling clean. Tools, ropes, gear and other items were neatly stacked, hung or otherwise arranged.

"A place for everything and everything in its place?" she said.

"I like it that way," replied King.

"I'm sort of a slob in my personal life."

"I'm very sorry to hear that."

They walked up to the house.

Inside he poured the coffee, and they sat at the kitchen table. Michelle had put on a Harvard sweat-shirt over her tank top and slipped on a pair of matching sweatpants.

"I thought you went to Georgetown?" said King.

"I got this sweat suit when we did some rowing on the Charles River in Boston while we were training for the Olympics."

"That's right. The Olympics. Busy woman."

"*I* like it that way."

"Not so busy now, though. I mean you have time for early morning water sports and paying visits to ex–Secret Service agents."

She smiled. "So you won't accept my being here as just a coincidence?"

"The real tip-off was the sweat suit. Sort of tells me you hoped to get out of your boat at some point before you got back to your car. On top of that, I doubt you would have rowed seven miles, Olympian or not, unless you knew I was home. I had several phone hang-ups this morning about thirty minutes apart. Let me guess, you have a cell phone in your scull."

"Once an investigator, always an investigator, I guess."

"I'm just glad I was home to greet you. I wouldn't have wanted you to wander around. I've had people doing that here lately, and I don't really care for it."

She lowered her cup. "I've been doing some wandering lately."

"Really? Good for you."

"Went down to North Carolina, a little place called Bowlington. I believe you've heard of it." He put down his cup too. "The Fairmount's still standing but it's closed up."

He said, "In my opinion they should just shoot it and put it out of its misery."

"I've always wondered about something. Maybe you can enlighten me?"

"I'll sure do what I can," King said sarcastically. "I mean I don't have much else to occupy my time, so by all means, let me help *you* out."

She ignored his tone. "The agent configuration with Ritter. You had low manpower, which I guess I understand. But the way you guys were laid out was a disaster. You were the only agent within ten feet of the man."

King took a sip of coffee and studied his hands.

"I know this is a huge imposition," Michelle said apologetically. "I just show up and start asking questions. Just tell me to leave and I will."

Finally King shrugged. "What the hell. You're getting a taste of what it's like with the Bruno kidnapping. That sort of makes us blood brothers, in a way."

"In a way."

"Meaning what?" he said testily. "That I screwed up more than you and you don't want to be lumped with me?"

"Actually I think I messed up a lot more than you did. I was detail leader. I let a protectee out of my sight. I didn't have anyone shooting. I didn't have to kill anyone while pandemonium was breaking out all around me. You lost your focus for a few seconds. Unforgivable in a Secret Service agent, probably, but I blew it all along the way. I think you shouldn't want to be lumped with *me*."

King's expression softened and his voice grew calmer. "We had barely half the usual complement of agents. That was partly Ritter's choice and partly the government. He was not well liked, and everyone knew he had no chance to win."

"But wouldn't Ritter want as much security as possible?"

"He didn't trust us," said King simply. "We were representatives of the administration, insiders. Even though he was a member of Congress, he was an outsider. Way outside with a screwball platform and radical supporters. He even thought we were spying on him, I swear to God. Consequently they kept us in the dark on everything. Changing schedules at the last minute without consulting us, it drove the detail leader, Bob Scott, crazy."

"I actually can relate. But that wasn't really reflected in the official record."

"Why would it be? They had their responsible parties. End of story."

"But that doesn't fully explain why the security layout was so poor that day."

"Ritter seemed to get along with me. Why, I don't know. Our politics were certainly not the same. But I was respectful, we joked some and I think to the degree he trusted any of us, he trusted me the most. Consequently, when I was on duty, I always covered his back. Other than that, he didn't like agents around him. He was convinced that the people loved him. That no one would want to hurt him. That false sense of security probably came from his days as a preacher. His campaign manager, guy named Sidney Morse – now, he was supersharp, and he didn't like that setup very much. He was a lot more realistic about things. He knew that there were people out there who might take a pop at his guy. Morse always wanted at least one agent right next to Ritter. But the rest of the guys were always strewn around the perimeter, way in the background."

"And pretty much useless when the shot was fired and the crowd panicked."

"You've seen the tape, I take it."

"Yes. Now, the layout of the agents wasn't your fault. I would have thought the detail leader would have pushed harder on that."

"Bob Scott was ex-army, fought in Vietnam, even was a POW. He was a good guy, but for my money he tended to pick the wrong battles to fight. He had a lot going on in his personal life at the time. His wife had filed for divorce a couple months before Ritter was killed. He wanted out of protection to go back into investigation. I think he regretted ever leaving the military. He fit in better in a uniform than a suit. Sometimes he'd even salute people and he always used military time, while as you know, the Service used the standard clock. He just preferred that life."

"Whatever happened to him?"

"Resigned from the Service. I took most of the heat, but as you found out, the buck stops with the detail leader. He'd pulled his time, so his pension was secure. I lost track of him. It's not like the guy would be sending me Christmas cards." He paused and then said, "He was also a bit of a barrel sucker."

"Gun-happy? Not so unusual for a former soldier. Most law enforcement agencies have their share of those."

"It was a little unhealthy with Bob. He was a real Second Amendment poster boy."

"Was he at the hotel when it happened?"

"Yes. Sometimes he'd go ahead with the advance team to the next city, but he decided to stay put in Bowlington. I'm not sure why. It was a real one-horse town."

"I saw Sidney Morse on the video; he was right by Ritter."

"Always was. Ritter had a bad habit of losing track of time, and Morse kept him on a tight leash."

"I heard Morse was quite a force."

"He was. When the campaign started, a guy named Doug Denby was Ritter's chief of staff and also his de facto campaign manager. When the campaign started gaining momentum, Ritter needed someone full-time who was really seasoned. Morse fit that bill. The whole campaign was energized when he showed up. He was a fat guy with a motor that never quit, really flamboyant and theatrical. Always munching candy bars with his left hand and talking on a cell phone with his right, barking orders, working the media. I don't think he ever slept. Denby played second fiddle to Sidney Morse. Hell, I think even Ritter was intimidated by him."

"How did Morse and Bob Scott get along?"

"They didn't see eye-to-eye on everything, but

that was okay. Like I said, Bob was going through a rough divorce, and Morse had a younger brother – Peter, I think his name was – who was involved in some bad stuff that was really stressing Sidney out too. So he and Scott had some common ground there. They got along pretty well. Now, Morse and Doug Denby didn't really get along. Doug was the issues guy, sort of an old-school southerner with views that maybe would have been in the mainstream fifty years ago. Morse was the flash, the guy from the West Coast, the showman, getting Ritter in the public eye, on all the talk shows, putting on quite a production. Real quickly the flash became more important than the issues on the campaign trail. Ritter couldn't win anyway, but he was a big ham, not so unusual for a TV preacher. So the more his face and name got out, the better he liked it. From what I could tell, the main strategy was to shake up the big boys – and they sure did that, thanks to Morse – and work deals with them later on. It got so that Ritter just did what Morse told him to do."

"I'm sure Denby didn't take that very well. What ever happened to him?"

"Who knows? Where do old chiefs of staff go? Anybody's guess."

"I take it since you had morning duty, you probably went to bed early the night before?"

King stared at her for a long moment. "After I was off duty, I hit the gym in the hotel with a couple of guys from my shift, had an early supper, and, yeah, I went to bed. Why are you interested in all this, Agent Maxwell?"

"Please, call me Michelle. I saw you on TV after Jennings was killed. I had heard of you at the Service. After what happened to me, I had an impulse to learn more about what happened to you. I felt a connection."

"Some connection."

"Who were the other agents assigned to Ritter?"

He looked sharply at her. "Why?"

She looked at him with an innocent expression. "Well, maybe I know some of them. I could go and talk to them. See how they dealt with what happened."

"I'm sure it's printed in some report somewhere. Go look it up."

"It would save me time if you'd just tell me."

"Yeah, it would, wouldn't it?"

"Okay, was Joan Dillinger one of the members of the protection detail?"

At this King rose and went over to the window, peering out for a few moments. When he looked back, he was scowling. "Are you wired? Either strip and show me you're not or you can just jump back in your scull and row your ass right out of my life."

"I'm not wired. But I will strip if you really think it's necessary. Or I could go jump in the lake. Electronics and water don't really go well together," she added pleasantly.

"What do you want from me?"

"I'd like an answer to my question. Was Joan assigned to the detail?"

"Yes! But on a different shift from mine."

"Was she at the hotel that day?"

"It seems to me that you already know the answer, so why are you asking?"

"I'll take that as a yes."

"Take it any way you want."

"Did you two spend the night together?"

"Next question and make it a good one, because it'll be your last."

"Okay, right before the shot was fired, who was on the elevator when it opened?"

"Don't know what you're talking about."

"Sure you do. I heard the *ding* of an elevator right before Ramsey fired his shot. It distracted you. Those elevators were supposed to have been closed off. Whoever or whatever was on that elevator when it opened took your complete attention. That's why Ramsey could get his shot off and you never saw it.

I've made some inquiries at the Service about it. People reviewing the video heard a sound too. It wasn't in the official record but I made some phone calls yesterday. They questioned you about it. You said you heard something but saw nothing. You explained it away as possibly a malfunction with the elevator. And they didn't push any further because they already had their responsible party. But I'm convinced you were looking at something. Or more to the point, some*one*."

In response King opened the door onto the rear deck and motioned her out.

She rose and put down her coffee cup. "Well, at least I got to ask my questions. Even if I didn't get them all answered."

As she was passing by him, she stopped. "You're right. You and I are now forever linked in history as two bad agents who screwed up. I'm not used to that. I've excelled at everything I've ever done. I'm betting you're the same way."

"Good-bye, Agent Maxwell. I wish you all the best."

"I'm sorry our first meeting had to be this way."

"First and hopefully last."

"Oh, one more thing. Although it was never covered in the official report, I'm sure you've already considered the possibility that the person on the elevator was used to distract you while Ramsey pulled his gun and fired."

King said nothing.

"You know, it's interesting," said Michelle as she looked around.

"You seem to find a lot interesting," he said curtly.

"This place," she said, pointing at the high ceilings, the glistening beams, the polished floors, everything neat and tidy. "It's beautiful. *Perfectly* beautiful."

"You're certainly not the first person to say so."

"Yes," she went on as though she hadn't heard him. "It's beautiful, and it should be cozy and warm." She turned and looked at him. "But it's not. It's very utilitarian, actually, isn't it? Items placed just so, almost like they were staged, staged by someone who felt the need to control it all and in doing so took all the soul out of it, or at least didn't put any of his own soul into it." She wrapped her arms around herself. "Yes, very cold." She looked away from him.

"I like it that way," he said tersely.

She glanced at him sharply. "Do you, Sean? Well, I bet you didn't used to."

He watched her long legs and energetic pace quickly cover the distance down to the dock. She put her scull in the water and very soon was merely a speck on the surface of the lake. It was only then that he slammed the door shut. As he was walking by the table, he saw it, stuck under her coffee cup. It was her Secret Service business card. On the back she had written in her home and cell phone numbers. His first impulse was to throw it away. Yet he didn't. He held on to it as he watched the speck grow smaller and smaller until she rounded a bend and Michelle Maxwell disappeared completely from view.

23

John Bruno was lying on a small cot staring at the ceiling, a twenty-five-watt bulb his only illumination. The light would stay on for an hour and then go off; then it would come on for ten minutes and then be extinguished; there was never any pattern. It was maddening and debilitating and designed to break down his spirit. It had done its job well.

Bruno was dressed in a drab gray jumpsuit and had many days' growth of beard on his face, for what sane jailer would provide a prisoner with a razor? Bathing was done by towel and bucket that appeared and disappeared while he was asleep; erratically timed meals were passed through a slot in the door. He'd never seen his captors and had no idea where he might be or how he'd gotten here. When he'd tried to talk to the unseen presence providing the food through the slot, he got no reply and had finally given up.

His food, he'd discovered, was often drugged and would send him into deep sleep or provoke occasional hallucinations. Yet if he didn't eat, he'd perish, so he ate. He was never allowed to leave his cell, and his exercise was restricted to ten paces across and ten paces back. He did push-ups and sit-ups on the cold floor to keep his strength. He had no idea if he was under surveillance, and it little mattered if he was. He'd contemplated early on some method of escape but had concluded escape was impossible. And to think it had all started with Mildred Martin, or rather an impersonator, in that funeral home. For the hundredth time he silently cursed himself for not following Michelle Maxwell's advice. And then, being the egomaniac he was, he cursed Maxwell for not being more forceful, for not insisting on accompanying him into that room.

How long he'd been here he didn't know. They'd taken all his personal belongings including his watch while he was unconscious. Why he'd been kidnapped he couldn't fathom. Whether it had to do with his candidacy or his former career as a prosecutor he didn't know. It had never occurred to him that it might be neither. He'd harbored hopes early on for a quick rescue, but he could no longer realistically keep that belief. The people who'd taken him clearly knew what they were doing. He'd fallen back on the slender hope of a miracle, and yet as the hours and days passed, that hope had begun to dim. He thought of his wife and children and his presidential campaign and was resigned that his life might end here, his body perhaps never found. He remained puzzled, though, about why they were keeping him alive.

He rolled over on his stomach, unable to face even the meager light anymore.

The person who sat in another cell at the end of the corridor had been here far longer than John Bruno. The despair in the eyes and the slouch in the body signaled there was no hope left. Eat, sit, sleep, and probably die at some point. That was the bleak future. The person shivered and wrapped a blanket closer around.

In another part of the large underground space a man was engaged in some interesting activities. In contrast to the despair of the prisoners, his energy level and hopes were very high indeed.

Round after round was fired into a human silhouette that hung on a target a good hundred feet away in the soundproofed room. Every shot was placed in the kill zone. He was certainly a marksman of enviable skill.

The man pressed a button, and the target flew down the motorized line toward him. He put up a fresh target and hit a button, and it flew to the farthest point available on the shooting range. He loaded a fresh magazine in his pistol, put on his eye and ear protectors, took aim and fired off fourteen rounds in less than twenty-five seconds. When the target was brought back this time, he finally smiled. Not one shot had gone astray – "throwing a round" in law enforcement parlance. He put his weapon away and left the shooting range.

The next room he entered was smaller than the shooting room and very different in configuration. Floor-to-ceiling shelves housed all manner of detonators, wiring for explosives, and other equipment used by those intent on blowing up something as efficiently and effectively as possible. In the center of the room was a large worktable, where he sat and began massaging wires, transistors, timers, detonators and C-4 plastic explosives into multiple devices designed for massive destruction. He brought to this task the same attention to detail that had been present at the shooting range.

He hummed while he worked.

An hour later he went to yet another room that

was set up completely unlike the first two. To the observer who could see only the interior of this space and not the ones housing guns, explosives and human chattel, there was nothing sinister or malign here. It was an artist's studio that lacked nothing for the creation of art in practically any medium, except for natural light. That was impossible in a place so many meters below ground. Yet the artificial light here was acceptable.

Neatly hanging on one wall were shelves holding heavy coats and boots, special helmets, thick gloves, red bubble lights, axes, oxygen tanks and other like equipment. The gear wouldn't be needed for a while yet, but it was good to be prepared. Rushing now could mean disaster. Patience was required. And yet he looked forward to the moment when it would all come together, when he could finally say that success was his. Yes, patience.

He settled himself down at a worktable and for the next two hours labored with deep concentration, painting, cutting, erecting and fine-tuning a series of works that would never grace the inside of a museum or, for that matter, any personal collection. Yet they were as important to him as the most distinguished masterpieces of any era. In a very sub-stantial way all this work was *his* masterpiece, and like many of the old masters' works, it had been years in the making.

He continued his labors, counting down to the time when his greatest achievement would finally be complete.

24

Michelle was on her laptop, surfing through the Secret Service's database and finding some interesting items. She was focused and absorbed, and yet when her cell phone rang, she sprang off the bed and grabbed it. The screen flashed "Caller ID Block," but she answered it anyway, hoping it was King. It was. His initial words were very welcome.

"Where do you want to meet?" she asked in answer to his query.

"Where are you staying?"

"At a quaint little B and B about four miles from you off Route 29."

"The Winchester?" he asked.

"That's it."

"Nice place. Hope you're enjoying yourself."

"I am now."

"There's an inn called the Sage Gentleman about a mile from where you are."

"I passed it on the way here. Looks very clubby."

"It is. I'll meet you for lunch. Twelve-thirty?"

"I wouldn't miss it. And, Sean, I appreciate your calling me."

"Don't thank me until you've heard what I have to say."

They met on the broad porch that encircled the old Victorian-style home. King was dressed in a sport coat, green turtleneck and beige slacks, Maxwell in a long pleated black skirt and white sweater. The stylish dress boots she was wearing brought her up to within an inch of King's height. Her dark hair fell across her shoulders, and she had even put on a bit of makeup, something she normally didn't do. Secret Service work did not lend itself to fashion pleasantries. However, because your protectee often attended formal events with well-dressed, wealthy people, an agent's wardrobe and grooming habits had to be up to the task, which wasn't always easy. Thus an old agency adage was: Dress like a million bucks on a blue-collar paycheck.

King pointed at the dark blue Toyota Land Cruiser with roof racks in the parking lot.

"Is that yours?"

She nodded. "I'm into active sports on my time

off, and that thing can go anywhere and carry anything I need."

"You're a Secret Service agent. When do you
have any time off?"

They sat at a table in the rear of the restaurant.
The place wasn't too full, and they were enjoying
about as much privacy as one could in a public place.

When the waiter came and asked if they were
ready to order, Michelle immediately said, "Yes, sir."

King smiled at this but said nothing until the
waiter departed.

"It took me years to get over that."

"Over what?" she asked.

"Calling everyone 'sir.' From waiters to
presidents."

She shrugged. "I guess I never realized I was
doing it."

"Why would you – it's ingrained. With a lot of
other things." He looked pensive. "One thing about
you has been puzzling me."

A tiny smile crept across her features. "Just one?
I'm disappointed."

"Why did a supersmart superjock like yourself
go into law enforcement? Not that there's anything
wrong with that. It just seems like you'd have other
opportunities."

"It was a genetic thing, I guess. My father,

brothers, uncles, male cousins are all cops. My dad's the police chief in Nashville. I wanted to be the first girl in my family to do it. I did a year's stint as a police officer in Tennessee and then decided to break the family mold and applied to the Service. I was accepted and the rest is history."

After the waiter brought their food, Michelle dug into hers while King quietly worked on his wine.

"I take it you've been here before," she said between bites.

King nodded as he finished off his glass of Bordeaux and started eating. "I bring clients, friends, other lawyers here. This area has quite a few places as good as if not better than this one. They're well hidden in the nooks and crannies hereabouts."

"Are you a trial lawyer?"

"No. Wills, trusts, business deals."

"Do you enjoy it?"

"It pays the light bill. It's not the most exciting job in the world, but you can't beat the views."

"It *is* pretty here. I can understand why you'd relocate to a place like this."

"It has its attractions and limitations. Here, sometimes you fall under the delusion that you're insulated from the stress and tribulations of the rest of the world."

"But they tend to follow you, don't they?"

"Second, you believe you can actually forget your past and start life anew."

"But you have."

"Had. Past tense."

She wiped her mouth with her napkin. "So why did you want to see me?"

He held up his empty glass of wine. "How about joining me? You're not on duty."

She hesitated and then nodded.

A minute later they had their drinks, and after they finished their meal King suggested they move to the small lounge situated off the dining area. There they sank into old leather chairs and breathed in the aromas of old cigar and pipe smoke augmented by the odors of ancient, leather-bound books on the worm-eaten walnut shelves that stood shoulder-to-shoulder along the walls. They had the room to themselves, and King held the glass up to the light coming in through the window and then sniffed it before taking a sip.

"Good stuff," said Michelle after she took a mouthful.

"Give it ten more years, and you'll never know you were drinking the same wine."

"I know nothing about it other than screw top or cork."

"Eight years ago I was the same way. Actually

beer was more my specialty. And it fit my wallet better too."

"So about the time you left the Service you switched from beer to wine?"

"Lots of changes took place in my life about then. A friend of mine was a closet sommelier, and he taught me all I know. We took a methodical approach, working through French wines and then Italian and even nudged around California whites, though he was quite the snob about that. For him, reds were where it was at."

"Hmmm, I wonder if you're the only wine connoisseur who's killed people? I mean they just don't seem to go together, do they?"

He lowered his glass and looked at her with an amused expression. "What, does a love of wine seem prissy to you? Do you know how much blood has been spilled over wine?"

"Do you mean while drinking it or talking about it?"

"Does it matter? Dead is dead, isn't it?"

"You would know that better than I do."

"If you think it's a simple matter of notching your gun after you do the deed, it's not."

"I never thought that. More like notching your soul?"

He put down his glass. "How about an information exchange?"

"I'm game, within reason."

"Quid pro quo. Relatively equal value."

"Judged by whom?"

"I'll make it easy. I'll go first."

Michelle sat back. "I'm curious. Why?"

"I guess we can put it down to the fact that you're as unwilling a participant in your nightmare as I was eight years ago in mine."

"Yes. You called us blood brothers."

"Joan Dillinger was at the hotel that night."

"In your room?"

King shook his head. "Your turn."

Michelle thought about this for a few moments. "Okay, I talked to one of the maids who was working at the hotel when Ritter was killed. Her name is Loretta Baldwin." King looked puzzled when she said this. "Loretta says she cleaned your room that morning. And she found a pair of black lace panties on the ceiling light fixture." She paused and then added with a perfectly straight face, "I'm assuming they weren't yours. You don't seem like the lace type."

"No. And black's not really my color in underwear."

"Weren't you married during that time?"

"Separated. My wife had an annoying habit of sleeping with other men when I was out of town, which was basically all the time. I think they even started bringing their own pajamas and toothbrushes. I was feeling really out of the loop."

"It's good you can joke about it now."

"If you had asked me eight years ago, I wouldn't have been so glib. Time doesn't really heal, it just makes you not give a crap."

"So you had, what, a fling with Joan Dillinger?"

"It actually seemed a little more than that back then. Stupid when you think about it. Joan's not that sort of woman."

Michelle leaned forward. "About the elevator—"

King interrupted. "Your turn again. I'm getting tired of reminding you."

Michelle sighed and sat back. "Okay, Dillinger's not at the Service anymore."

"Doesn't count. I already know that. What else?"

"Loretta Baldwin told me she hid in the supply closet down the hall from the room where Ritter died."

King looked interested. "Why?"

"She was scared to death and took off running. Everyone else was doing the same thing."

"Not everyone," King said dryly. "I stayed pretty much in the same place."

"Now, about the elevator."

"Why do you care about that?" he asked sharply.

"Because it seemed to captivate you! So much so that you didn't even know there was an assassin standing in front of you until he fired."

"I just zoned out."

"I don't think so. I heard the noise on the tape. And it sounded like an elevator car arriving. And I'm thinking that when those doors opened, whatever or whoever you saw grabbed your attention and didn't let it go until Ramsey fired." She paused and then added, "And since that elevator bank was locked off by the Secret Service, I'm guessing that it was a Secret Service agent who was on there, because who else could have done it without being stopped? And I'm betting that agent was Joan Dillinger. And I'm also betting that for some reason you're covering for her. Would you care to tell me that I'm wrong about all that?"

"Even if what you say is true, it doesn't matter. It was my screwup and Ritter died because of it. No excuses are good enough. You ought to know that by now."

"But if you were *purposefully* distracted, that's a different story."

"I wasn't."

"How do you know that? Why else would

someone have been on that elevator at the precise moment Ramsey chose to fire?" She answered her own question. "Because he knew that elevator car was going to come down, and he knew the person on it would be able to distract you, giving him the chance to kill Ritter, that's why. He was waiting for the elevator to come before he fired."

She sat back, her look not one so much of triumph, but of defiance, like she'd shown on TV during the press conference King had seen.

"That isn't possible. Just trust me. Call it the worst timing in the world, that's all."

"I'm sure you won't be too surprised if I don't take your word for it."

He sat there in silence, for so long, in fact, that Michelle finally rose. "Look, thanks for lunch and the wine lesson. But you can't tell me a smart guy like you doesn't look in the mirror every morning and wonder, what if?"

As she started to walk off, her cell phone rang. She answered it. "What? Yes, it is. Who? Uh, that's right, I did talk to her. How did you get this number? My card? Oh, that's right. I don't understand why you're calling." She listened for a bit more and then turned pale. "I didn't know. My God, I'm so sorry. When did it happen? I see. Right, thank you. Do you have a number where I can call you?"

She clicked off, pulled a pen and paper from her purse, wrote the number down and slowly sat in the leather chair next to King.

He eyed her quizzically. "Are you okay? You don't look okay."

"No, I'm *not* okay."

He leaned forward and put a steadying hand on her quivering shoulder. "What happened, Michelle? Who was that?"

"That woman I talked to who worked at the hotel."

"The maid, Loretta Baldwin?"

"That was her son. He found my name on a card I left there."

"Why, did something happen to Loretta?"

"She's dead."

"What happened?"

"She was murdered. I asked her all these questions about the Ritter killing, and now she's dead. I can't believe it's connected, but then I can't believe it's not either."

King jumped up so quickly it startled her badly.

"Is your truck filled with gas?" he asked.

"Yes," she said, looking confused. "Why?"

King seemed to be talking to himself. "I'll call my appointments for the rest of the day and let them know."

"Let them know? Let them know what?"

"That I won't be able to meet them. That I'm going somewhere."

"Where are you going?"

"No, not just me – you and me. We're going to Bowlington, North Carolina, to find out why Loretta Baldwin isn't living anymore."

He turned and headed to the door. Michelle didn't follow; she just sat there, bewildered.

King turned back. "What's the problem?"

"I'm not sure I want to go back there."

King came back and stood in front of her, his expression very stern. "You came to me out of the blue asking a lot of very personal questions. You wanted answers and I gave them to you. Okay, now I'm officially interested too." He paused and then barked out, "So let's go, Agent Maxwell. I don't have all day!"

She jumped to her feet. "Yes, sir," Michelle said automatically.

25

When he climbed into her truck, King quickly observed the interior of Michelle's vehicle and could not conceal his disgust. He picked up a power bar food wrapper off the floor by his foot that still had a hunk of stale "power chocolate" inside. The backseats were full of items haphazardly strewn around: water and snow skis, assorted oars and paddles, gym clothes, sneakers, dress shoes and a couple of skirts, jackets and blouses and a pair of pantyhose still in its packaging. There were warm-up suits, books, a northern Virginia yellow pages, empty soda and Gatorade cans and a Remington shotgun and a box of shells. And that was just what King could see. God only knew what else was lurking in here; the smell of rotten bananas was hammering his nostrils.

He looked over at Michelle. "Make a note to never, ever invite me to your place."

She glanced at him and smiled. "I told you I was a slob."

"Michelle, this is beyond a slob. This is a mobile garbage dump; this is total and complete anarchy on wheels."

"So philosophical. And call me Mick."

"You prefer 'Mick' to 'Michelle'? Michelle is an elegant, classy name. Mick sounds like a punch-drunk boxer-turned-doorman in uniform braids and fake medals."

"The Secret Service is still a guy's world. You go along to get along."

"Just drive them around in this truck one time, and you'll never be mistaken for anything but a guy, even if your name was Gwendolyn."

"Okay, I get the point. So what do you expect to find down there?"

"If I knew that, I probably wouldn't be going."

"Will you visit the hotel?"

"I'm not sure. I haven't been back since it happened."

"I can understand that. I'm not sure I could ever go back to that funeral home."

"Speaking of, anything new on the Bruno disappearance?"

"Nothing. No ransom request, no demands of any kind. Why would you go to all the trouble to kidnap John Bruno, including the murder of a Secret Service agent, and possibly the man he was going to pay his last respects to, and then do nothing with him?"

"Right, Bill Martin, the deceased. I thought he must have been killed."

She looked at him in surprise. "Why?"

"They couldn't very well plan this whole scheme and hope the guy croaked in accordance with their time schedule. And they couldn't exactly work it the other way. The guy dies, and then they scramble to put it all together in a couple of days, coincidentally right when Bruno is passing by. No, he had to be murdered too."

"I'm impressed with your analysis. I heard you were the real deal."

"I was in investigation a lot longer than I was a human shield. Every agent works so hard to get to protection and especially the presidential detail, and then once there they can't wait to get out of it and back to investigation."

"Why do you think that is?"

"Ungodly hours, in control of nothing in your life. Just standing around waiting for a shot to be fired. I pretty much hated it, but it's not like I had a choice."

"Were you assigned to POTUS?"

"Yes. Took me years of hard work to get there. I spent two years at the White House. It was great for the first year, and then after that, it wasn't so great. It was just constant travel, having to deal with some of the biggest egos in the world and being treated like you were a couple of notches below the White House gardener. I especially like the staff members who were all of about twelve years old and truly didn't know their ass from a hole in the ground busting our chops over everything they could think of. Ironically enough I was just coming off that assignment when they put me on Ritter's detail."

"Gee, that's heartening considering I've spent years of my life trying to get there too."

"I'm not saying don't go for it. Riding on *Air Force One* is a thrill. And having the president of the United States tell you you're doing a good job is damn nice too. I'm just saying don't believe all the hype. In many ways it's like any other protection gig. At least with investigation you get to actually arrest bad guys." He paused and looked out the window. "Speaking of investigation, Joan Dillinger recently came back into my life and made me an offer."

"What sort of offer?"

"To help her find John Bruno."

Michelle nearly drove off the road. "What!"

"Her firm's been hired by Bruno's people to find him."

"Excuse me, doesn't she know the FBI is on the case?"

"So? Bruno's folks can hire anyone they want."

"But why involve you?"

"She gave me an explanation that I don't really buy. So I don't know why."

"Are you going to do it?"

He looked at her. "What do you think? Should I?"

She glanced quickly at him. "Why ask me?"

"You seem to have your suspicions about the woman. If she was involved in Ritter's killing and now she's involved in another third-party candidate matter, don't you find that interesting? So should I or shouldn't I . . . *Mick*?"

"My first inclination would be no, you shouldn't."

"Why, because it might turn out to bite me in the butt?"

"Yes."

"And your second inclination, which I'm sure is a lot more self-serving and conniving than your first?"

She eyed him, saw his amused expression and smiled guiltily. "Okay, my second inclination would be for you to do it."

"Because then I'd have the inside track on the

investigation. And I could feed you everything I find out."

"Well, not everything. If you and Joan rekindle your romance, I don't really want to know the details about that."

"Not to worry. Black widows eat their mates. I barely escaped the first time."

26

A little over two hours after leaving Wrightsburg they arrived at Loretta's home. There were no police cars around, but yellow police tape was across the front door.

"I guess we can't go in," she said.

"Guess not. How about her son?"

She pulled the number from her purse and called. The man answered, and she arranged to meet him at a coffee shop in the small downtown area. As Michelle was about to drive away from Baldwin's house, King stopped her.

"Give me a sec." He jumped out of the truck and walked up and down the street, and then he went around the block and disappeared from Michelle's view. A few minutes later he came from around the rear of Baldwin's house and rejoined Michelle.

"What was that all about?" she asked.

"Nothing. Except Loretta Baldwin has a nice place."

As they drove to the downtown area, they passed several police cars parked at various intersections, the officers intently checking the occupants of each car. Overhead they saw a helicopter cutting back and forth.

"I wonder what's up?" Michelle said.

King turned on the radio and got a local news station. They found out that two men had escaped from a state penitentiary nearby and a massive police search was under way.

When they got to the coffee shop, Michelle was about to park and get out but then stopped.

"What is it?" asked King.

She pointed to a road off the main strip where two county cop cars were parked. "I don't think they're looking for the escaped cons. We're being set up."

"Okay, call the son again. Tell him you had nothing to do with his mother's murder, but if he wants to talk, he can do it over the phone."

Michelle sighed, put the truck in gear and drove off. When they reached a secluded enough spot she pulled off the road. She called Loretta's son and told him what King had asked her to say. "All I want to know is, how was she killed?"

"Why should I tell you?" replied the son. "You

visit my mama, and the next thing I know she's dead."

"If I planned on killing her, I wouldn't have left my name and phone number behind, would I?"

"I don't know, maybe you're into some freaky thrills."

"I came to talk to your mother about what she knew about the Ritter killing eight years ago. She told me she knew very little."

"Why you want to know about that?"

"I'm into American history. Are the cops with you right now?"

"What cops?"

"Don't bullshit me. Are they, yes or no?"

"No."

"Okay, I'll just assume you're lying about that. Here's what I think. I think my talking to your mother about the Ritter assassination might have led to someone killing her."

"Ritter? That's crazy. They killed the man who did that."

"Can you be sure he was acting alone?"

"How the hell *can* I be sure?"

"Exactly. So, again, how was your mother killed?"

There was silence on the other end of the phone.

Michelle decided to try a different angle. "I only met with your mother for a little while, but

I definitely liked what I saw. She was a real pistol who said what was on her mind. You have to respect that. She was a lifetime of wisdom rolled up into one very tough shell."

"Yes, she was," said the son. "And go to hell." He hung up.

"Damn," said Michelle. "I thought I had him."

"You do. He'll call back. Give him time, he has to ditch the cops."

"Sean, he just told me to go to hell."

"So he's not the most subtle person in the world. He's a guy. Just be patient. We're not multitaskers like you women; we can only do one thing at a time."

About thirty minutes later the phone rang.

Michelle looked at him. "How'd you know?"

"Guys are suckers for a good phone voice. And you said all the right things about his mother. We're suckers for our mothers too."

"Okay," said the son over the phone, "they found her in the bathtub, drowned."

"Drowned? So how do they know it wasn't an accident? Maybe she had a heart attack."

"There was money stuffed in her mouth, and the house had been ransacked. I don't call that a damn accident."

"House ransacked and money stuffed in her

mouth?" repeated Michelle, and King raised his eyebrows.

"Yep, a hundred bucks. Five twenties. I found her. I had called that night but she didn't answer. I live about forty miles away. I drove over. Damn! Seeing her like that." His voice broke off.

"I'm sorry. And I'm also sorry that I never even asked your name."

"Tony. Tony Baldwin."

"Tony, I'm sorry. I visited your mother to talk about the Ritter assassination. I was interested in how it happened. I found out she was there that day and still lived in Bowlington, and I went to visit her. I talked to two other former maids too. I can give you their names. That's all I did, I swear."

"Okay, I guess I believe you. So you got any idea who did this?"

"Not yet, but starting right now, finding out is my number one priority."

She thanked him, hung up and turned to King.

"Money stuffed in her mouth," he said thoughtfully.

"My money," said Michelle miserably. "I gave her that hundred dollars, five twenties, for answering my questions."

King rubbed his chin. "Okay, robbery wasn't a motive. They wouldn't have left the cash. But they searched the house. The person was looking for something."

"But the cash in her mouth. My God, that's gruesome."

"Maybe not so much gruesome as making a statement."

She looked at him curiously. "What sort of statement?"

"Maybe a fatal one, for both of them. Who would have thought it?"

"What are you talking about?"

"I can't tell you."

"Why the hell not?"

"Because I haven't finished thinking about it, that's why. It's just the way I do things."

Michelle threw up her hands in frustration. "God, you are so maddening."

"Thanks, I really work at it." King looked out the window for a while and then finally stirred. "Okay, this is a small town, and we're bound to attract suspicion, particularly with so many cops around. Let's head out and find a place to stay. We'll wait until late tonight before we hit it."

"Hit what?'

He looked at her. "I can be as nostalgic as the next person."

Michelle scowled. "Do lawyers always find it impossible to actually answer a question directly?"

"Okay, I think it's about time I paid the Fairmount Hotel a visit. Is that direct enough for you?"

27

They approached the hotel from the rear, careful to stay close to the thick tree line. The two were dressed identically and moved in tandem. They waited a bit at the edge of the trees, scanning the area ahead for signs of anyone. Satisfied, they moved out, quickly covering the ground between the forest and the fence surrounding the hotel. Scrambling over, they dropped on the other side. One of the pair pulled a pistol, and then they made their way down the rear face of the hotel. They found a side door that they forced open. In another moment they disappeared inside the dark space.

King and Michelle parked a good distance away from the Fairmount Hotel and covered the rest on foot. As they approached the building, they ducked back into the woods as the chopper, its searchlight racing over the ground, shot across overhead.

"This is actually exciting," said Michelle as they emerged from the trees and threaded their way to the hotel. "You know, sort of being on the other side of the badge for a change."

"Yeah, it's a thrill a minute. Just think, I could be at my house with a nice glass of Viognier in front of a blazing fire reading Proust instead of skipping merrily through the environs of Bowlington, North Carolina, while dodging police choppers."

"Please tell me you don't actually read Proust while drinking wine," she said.

"Well, only if there's nothing good on ESPN."

As they drew near to the hotel, King ran his gaze along the jumbled facade. "This place always struck me as something Frank Lloyd Wright might have designed if he'd been strung out on heroin."

"It is pretty ugly," agreed Michelle.

"Just so you understand Clyde Ritter's sense of aesthetics, he thought the Fairmount was beautiful."

The gap in the fence Michelle had used on her earlier visit had been sealed. So they were forced to go over the fence. King looked on a little enviously as Michelle clambered over with much greater ease than he would probably demonstrate. He was right. He almost fell on his face coming down the other side when his foot caught in one of the links. She helped him up without comment and led him down the side of the building. They entered through the same place she'd used on her first visit.

Inside she pulled out a flashlight, but King held up a warning hand. "Wait a minute. You said there was a guard."

"Yes, but I didn't see him around when we came through."

King looked at her strangely. "Actually as I recall, you said the second time you came you ran into the guard, but the first time there wasn't anyone."

"He could have been making his rounds on the other side. They probably just patrol the perimeter."

"Yeah, probably," said King. He nodded for her to turn on the flashlight, and they made their way toward the lobby.

"The Stonewall Jackson Room is just down this hall," she said.

"Oh, is it? I had no idea."

"I'm sorry, Sean. It was so long ago and I was just here."

"Forget it," he said. "I'm just being a jerk."

"Do you want to go there now?"

"Maybe later. There's something I want to check first."

"The closet Loretta Baldwin hid in?"

"Great minds really do think alike. The next thing you know you'll be drinking fine wine and reading thought-provoking literature. And maybe, just maybe, that might lead you actually to clean out your truck, if you find you have a spare year or two."

They went to the closet and pulled open the door. Taking the flashlight from Michelle, King went inside and looked around. He zeroed in on a small crevice in the very back, then turned to her.

"Loretta was small?"

"Almost skeletal."

"So she could have gotten back there with no problem. She didn't actually say where she was hiding in here?"

"No, but she could have just stood anywhere."

King shook his head. "If I was a terrified person in the middle of murder, mayhem and screaming, panicked people, and I ran into a closet to hide, I think I'd burrow in as deeply as possible. It's sort of instinctive, like pulling the covers over your head. She wouldn't have known at that point what the hell was going on. For all she knew, some guy with a gun would come running in here to hide too and—" He stopped and stared at the spot where Loretta might have hidden.

"What is it, Sean?"

He simply shook his head. "I'm not sure." He stepped back out of the closet and shut the door.

"Okay, where now?" asked Michelle.

213

He drew a long breath. "To the Stonewall Jackson Room."

When they arrived there, Michelle silently watched, shining the light along his path as King stepped off the room's parameters precisely, his gaze sweeping every point. Then he looked at the spot where he'd stood eight years before. Letting go of another deep breath, King walked over and seemed to take up his old post there, his hand creeping up on the imaginary back of a sweaty, coatless Clyde Ritter.

King was now firmly back in September 1996 as his gaze went to the imaginary people, the potential troublemakers, babies being kissed, the jibe from the back and Ritter's response to it. He even found himself mumbling into his mike, relaying intelligence. He glanced at the clock at the back, though there wasn't one there, and he couldn't have seen it in the darkness anyway. Only three more minutes and the meet-and-greet would be over. Amazing when you thought about it. If Ramsey had been late or Ritter had ended the event early, none of it would have happened. How different King's life would have been.

He wasn't quite aware of it, but his gaze was now on the elevator bank. He heard the *ding* over and over. In his mind's eye the doors opened over and over. It was as though he were being sucked into that vacuum.

The *bang* startled him badly, but his hand flew to his holster, and he pulled out his imaginary gun, his eyes going to the floor where Ritter's body was. Then he looked over at where Michelle was standing with the flashlight, having just slammed the door shut.

"Sorry," she said, "I just wanted to see your reaction. I guess I shouldn't have done it."

"No, you shouldn't have," he said firmly.

She came and stood beside him. "What were you thinking just now?"

"Would it surprise you if I told you I wasn't really sure?"

"Talk it out, then. It might be important."

He thought for a few moments. "Well, I remember staring at Arnold Ramsey. He had this expression on his face that was not the look of a man who'd just assassinated a presidential candidate. He didn't look scared or defiant, or angry or nuts."

"What *did* he look like?"

King stared at her. "He looked surprised, Michelle, as though he hadn't expected to kill Ritter."

"Okay, that truly makes no sense. He'd just shot the man. Do you remember anything else?"

"After they took away Ritter's body, I remember

Bobby Scott coming over to me, to check my injury."

"Under the circumstances that was pretty remarkable."

"Well, he didn't know what had happened. He just knew he had a wounded agent. All the crap hit later."

"Anything else?"

King studied the floor. "When they were taking me out later, Bobby and Sidney Morse were going toe-to-toe out in the corridor. There was another guy with them, someone I didn't recognize. Morse was about five-ten and two hundred fifty pounds of mostly blubber, and you had ex-marine-built-like-an-oak-tree Bobby Scott, and they were really going at it. It was quite a sight. Another time it might have made me laugh."

"What were they arguing about?"

"Ritter was dead and it was Scott's fault – I'm sure that's what Bobby was hearing from Morse."

"Did you see either of them after that?"

"I only saw Bobby at some official hearings that took place afterwards. We never spoke privately. I always thought about calling him up, telling him I was sorry for what had happened. But I never did."

"I read where Sidney Morse was committed to a mental institution."

"Yep. I don't think he really cared what Ritter's politics were. For Morse, it was all a show, a big production. He was in show business or something way back when. And I did overhear him telling someone that if he could propel a guy like Ritter to the national spotlight, it would make him – Morse – an icon."

Michelle looked around and shivered. "It's so quiet in here. It reminds me of a tomb."

"Well, in a way it is. Two men died here."

"I'm glad it wasn't three."

Wasn't it? King thought.

She drew a line on the floor with the beam from the flashlight. "The rope to hold back the crowds was right about here, wasn't it?" King nodded. "So it would have pretty much run from that wall to about a foot behind the edge of the wall for the elevator bank. And on the video I remember that it ran catty-cornered. Do you remember who placed the rope there?"

"It would have been the Service."

"So the detail leader, Bob Scott?"

"I doubt that Bobby got into those sorts of details."

"So how do you know the Service did it, for sure?"

He shrugged. "I guess I don't. I just knew Ritter and I were going to be behind that rope."

"Exactly." She handed the light to King and positioned herself where King had stood and looked over at the elevators. "Okay, with the rope there and you here, you'd be the only one in the room who could see the elevators. That seems prearranged. And, by the way, the elevator was certainly holding your attention again."

"Forget the elevator," he snapped. "Why the hell am I even here? Ritter was a jerk. Hell, I'm glad he's dead."

"He was still a presidential candidate, Sean. I didn't like John Bruno, but I guarded the man like he was the president of the United States."

He said curtly, "You don't need to lecture me on agency standards. I was guarding presidents while you were spending all your time rowing a boat for a hunk of metal."

Michelle said slowly, "Is staying up all night screwing another agent when you're posting the next day part of Secret Service protection standards? If it is, I must have missed that one in the manual."

"Yeah, it's right next to the rule about never leaving a protectee alone in a room. I guess you missed that one too," he shot back.

"I hope Joan was worth it."

"Loretta Baldwin told you about the panties on the ceiling light, so draw your own conclusion."

"That was a bad judgment call. I wouldn't have slept with you before a shift no matter how tempted I might have been. Not that I would have been."

"Thanks. That's good to know . . . *Mick*."

"In fact," Michelle continued boring in, "your being distracted I can accept a lot more than your sleeping around before going on duty."

"This is all really interesting. Now, do you want to check this place out, or do you want to continue dissecting my life decisions?"

"I tell you what, why don't we just leave?" she said abruptly. "I'm suddenly sick of the atmosphere here."

She strode off, and King, shaking his head wearily, slowly followed.

Outside the room, she was already out of sight. King called after her and shone the light and finally picked her out of the shadows. "Michelle, wait up. You'll kill yourself getting out of here without a light."

She stopped, her arms crossed over her chest, and scowled back at him. Then she stiffened, and her head snapped in the other direction. King saw a blur come from out of the darkness, and Michelle cried out. He rushed forward as the two men came into the beam of his flashlight and descended on Michelle.

"Watch out!" yelled King as he raced forward. Before he could get to them, a gun one of the men was brandishing went flying away, the result of a precise kick executed by Michelle. Next her left foot crunched the face of the other guy, and he flew against a wall and slumped down. Like a dancer practicing a carefully choreographed routine, she spun and dropped the other guy with a wicked snap kick to the kidney. Both men tried to get back up, but she laid one of them out with an elbow smash to the back of his neck, while King knocked the other one out with his flashlight.

Breathing hard, he looked over as Michelle searched in her bag. She produced two pairs of Tie-Tights and ingeniously bound the unconscious men together. The woman hadn't even broken a sweat. She looked up at King and his inquiring look.

"Black belt. Fourth-degree," she said.

"Of course," King said. He shone his light on the pair still dressed in their blue inmate jumpsuits. "Looks like our friends the escaped prisoners. Guess they couldn't find any new duds."

"I'll call it in, do the locals a favor. Anonymously, of course." She pulled out her phone.

"Hey, Michelle?"

"Yeah?"

"I just want you to know that I feel very safe with a big, strong woman around to protect me."

After she called the police, Michelle and King hustled to her Land Cruiser, getting to it about the time the chopper came soaring over on its way to the hotel. Michelle followed the path of the aircraft and then the swath its light cut through the woods. When she saw him, she gasped.

Revealed off on a side road was a truck, and sitting in the truck was a man, sharply exposed now by the light. And then in an instant the light was gone and so was the man. Michelle could hear the truck being started, and then it sped off.

Michelle jumped into her truck, screaming for King to follow.

"What is it?" he yelled, closing the door after him as she fumbled with her keys.

"There was a man in a truck. Didn't you see him?"

"No, I didn't."

"Didn't you hear his truck take off?"

"With that chopper going over? Who was it?"

"He looked different, because he must have been

wearing a disguise when I saw him the first time — and maybe he's wearing one now — but I could see his eyes clearly. The eyes don't lie. It was him, I could swear to it."

"Who!"

"Officer Simmons, the rent-a-cop at the funeral home, the man who kidnapped Bruno and killed Neal Richards."

King looked at her, bewildered. "Are you really sure?"

She put the truck in gear. "Sure enough." She turned the truck around and was about to head down the side road after the other vehicle when a number of police cars appeared and blocked their way.

Michelle slammed her fists against the steering wheel. "Damn it, what a time for the local cops to show."

As one of the car doors opened and the man got out, King shook his head and said, "It's not the locals, Michelle."

The man came over to the driver's side and motioned Michelle to put her window down. She did so, and he leaned in and looked first at her and then at King.

"You two mind stepping out of the vehicle?" said Jefferson Parks.

28

The interrogation went on for most of the night. The police refused to listen to Michelle's pleas to allow her to leave to try to find the man she had seen in the truck. They clearly had other priorities, and when she tried to explain about the man being the person who'd kidnapped John Bruno, their expressions grew very skeptical. "That'll keep," the sheriff said firmly.

She then spent a very unpleasant hour having her pride wounded by Walter Bishop of the Secret Service. After being told of her detainment by the North Carolina police, he'd flown down to read Michelle the riot act.

Bishop thundered, "I thought when I reminded you of how fortunate you were to still be with the Service that it would have made an impression on you. Now I find you're involved in things that don't concern you. I don't see how you could have messed up any more than you have." He looked at King.

"Oh, but I'm wrong about that, because now you're keeping company with one of the Service's legendary losers. You can start a club, the screwup club. You have the *king* of them right here. Isn't that right, Sean?"

King had loathed Bishop when he was at the Service, and Bishop had been one of the loudest voices in crucifying King. The intervening years hadn't mellowed the ex-agent's feelings one jot.

"Careful, Walt," said King. "I won a libel case and I can win a slander case, and the pleasure it would give me to pickle your teeny-weeny dick in a jar, I can't begin to tell you."

"I'll have your soul!" Bishop roared.

"I'm not with the Service anymore, so save the histrionics for somebody who actually cares, if you can find one."

"You can't talk to me that way!"

"I'd rather talk to a pile of horseshit than waste one minute of my life with a lightweight peckerhead like you!" King snapped back.

"I never let a presidential candidate die because my head was up my ass!"

"Your head's always been in your ass! At least I came up for air."

And the conversation pretty much went downhill from there. To such an extent, in fact, that just about everyone in the building, prisoners included, strained to listen.

Michelle had never heard anyone talk to Walter Bishop that way, and it was all she could do not to burst out laughing at some of the things coming out of King's mouth. It was as though he'd been saving up verbal ammo for the last eight years.

After Bishop stormed back to Washington, Jefferson Parks and the local sheriff joined Sean and Michelle as they sipped bad coffee from the vending machine.

"So what are you doing down here?" King said to Parks.

The deputy marshal was visibly upset. "I told you not to leave the jurisdiction. And then my men tell me you're not only in another state, but you're nosing around the town where Clyde Ritter bought it. And on top of that, I get a message that your partner over there" – he inclined his head at Michelle – "is mixed up in some murder involving a local woman. Now, one more time: you left the jurisdiction after I asked you not to because . . ."

King snapped, "I wasn't under arrest. And it's not like I jumped on a plane to Fiji with my retirement plan in cash. I went to North Carolina in a truck filled with sporting equipment and half-eaten power bars. Big deal!"

"And we were fortunate enough to be able to capture those convicts," said Michelle. "We did help you out there."

"I do appreciate that," said the sheriff, "but I'd also like to understand better your connection to Ms. Baldwin. We haven't had a murder down here, well, since Clyde Ritter, and I don't like it one bit."

Michelle explained once more her conversation with Loretta.

The sheriff rubbed his jaw and hitched at his pants. "Well, I just don't figure it. Loretta didn't seem to say anything to you that implicated anybody."

"Right." Michelle had fibbed a bit and left out the part about the black lace panties and the activity the night before in King's room, for which King gave her a grateful look. "So I'm not sure there is a connection to my meeting her. It might just be an enormous coincidence."

"And the money in her mouth, you said that was your cash?"

Michelle nodded. "At least I think so. I gave her a hundred dollars in twenties because she'd helped me." She paused and added, "I had nothing to do with her death."

The sheriff nodded. "We've already checked your alibi. People remembered seeing you up in Virginia at the time Loretta was killed."

"So what was the motive?" asked Parks. He held up his hands when they looked at him. "What you've just described is a motiveless crime. Unless the lady had some enemies you don't know about. Or maybe it's a random killer, but my gut tells me it isn't. Money in the mouth: this was personal."

The sheriff shook his head. "Loretta Baldwin was the last person who would have any enemies. I mean, okay, she had a sharp tongue, and the gossip that came out her mouth, it was eye-opening, though usually right on the money. But it was little stuff. Nothing anybody would murder her over."

"Well, you never know," said King. "What may seem little to you might be really important to someone else."

The sheriff nodded but looked unconvinced. "Maybe." He stood. "Okay, I've got your statements. You're free to go."

As they started to leave, Michelle went over to the sheriff.

"The Fairmount, do you know who owns it now?"

"Last I heard it was some Japanese company bought it, wanted to turn it into a country club with a golf course." He chuckled. "I guess they didn't do their homework. The hotel has a lot of land, but most of it is wetlands. And there's not more than a handful of folks around here who know what a golf club even looks like."

"Do you know the name of the security service that guards the hotel?"

He looked puzzled. "What security service?"

Michelle hid her surprise and rejoined King and Parks.

"So how'd you get down here so fast?" King asked him.

"My men were following you."

"Take my advice, that's a waste of resources."

"Yeah, it's been pretty damn boring so far."

Michelle said, "Marshal, there's something that happened tonight. It has nothing to do with the murder of Loretta Baldwin, but I believe it has something to do with John Bruno's disappearance."

"Bruno?" Parks looked puzzled. "How the hell does Bruno figure into this?"

Michelle told him about the man she'd seen.

He shook his head. "How can you be sure it was him? You barely caught a glimpse of a man in poor light."

"I'm a Secret Service agent. Reading and remembering faces is what I do."

Parks still looked skeptical. "Well, okay, then tell the FBI. It's their case. I'm just trying to find out who killed one of my witnesses." He glanced over at King. "And also trying to keep tabs on this fellow, and he's not making it easy," he growled.

"You want me to wait around until you collect enough evidence to hang me?"

"I have enough to arrest you right now if I wanted to. So don't tempt me." He glowered at them both. "So you two heading back to good old Virginia?"

King said, "Well, I've pretty much had my fill of good old Bowlington."

29

So I guess you don't believe me either."

It was early in the morning, and Michelle and King were driving back to Wrightsburg.

"About what?" King asked.

"Simmons! The man I saw in the truck."

"I believe you. You saw what you saw."

She looked at him, surprised. "Well, Parks clearly didn't, why do you?"

"Because a Secret Service agent never forgets a face."

She smiled. "I knew I liked having you around. And look, there's something else. There apparently isn't a security firm guarding the Fairmount. So the guy who stopped me was a fake."

King looked very concerned. "Michelle, it could have been the same guy who killed Loretta."

"I know. I dodged a bullet there."

"What did he look like?" Michelle described him.

"Sounds like a couple billion guys walking around. Nothing distinctive."

"That was probably intentional. So another dead end? That seems to be a recurring theme in this case."

Later that morning, they pulled onto the drive heading up to King's house. When they reached the top, King's face darkened.

"Oh, hell," he exclaimed as he looked up ahead. An annoyed-looking Joan Dillinger was pacing in front of his house.

Michelle had seen her too. "The esteemed Ms. Dillinger doesn't look very happy."

"I know you're suspicious of her, but play it cool. She's one sharp lady."

Michelle nodded.

King got out of the truck and walked up to Joan.

"I've been calling you," she said.

"I've been out of town," explained King.

She started when Michelle climbed out of the Land Cruiser.

Glancing suspiciously at King and then back at Michelle, she said, "You're Agent Maxwell?"

"Yes. We actually met a few years ago when you were still with the Service."

"Of course. And you've certainly made a splash in the papers recently."

"That's right," Michelle said. "Coverage I could do without."

"I'm sure. What a surprise to see you here," Joan said as she looked at King intently. "I didn't know you and Sean even knew each other."

"It's a recent thing," said King.

"Uh-huh." Joan touched Michelle on the elbow. "Michelle, would you excuse us? I have something to talk about with Sean that's very important."

"Oh, no problem. I'm pretty beat anyway."

"Sean has that effect on lots of women. In fact, he could even be considered hazardous to some people's health."

The two women engaged in a stare-down. "Thanks for the tip, but I can take care of myself," said Michelle.

"I'm sure. But given the right opponent, you could find yourself out of your league."

"Actually that's never happened to me."

"Me either. They say the first time is truly memorable."

"I'll keep that in mind. Maybe you should too."

"Good-bye, Michelle," said Joan. "And thanks so much for letting me take Sean off your hands," she added icily.

"Yeah, thanks, *Mick*," muttered King under his breath.

Michelle drove off, and King walked up the steps, with Joan marching right behind him. He could feel the white heat of her anger on the back of his neck. The condemned man going the last mile was the closest analogy he could come up with, and right now it seemed far too close.

Inside, Joan sat down at the kitchen table, while King put on some water for hot tea. Joan's expression brimmed with fury. "So would you care to tell me about you and Michelle Maxwell?"

"I already did. She's a recent phenomenon in my life."

"I don't believe in phenomena like that. She loses Bruno and then shows up on your doorstep.

"What do you care?"

"What do I care? Are you insane? I'm investigating Bruno's disappearance, and you pop up with the detail leader who's on suspension for losing him."

"She looked me up because we both lost presidential candidates, and she wanted to compare notes. That's it. Bruno really doesn't enter the equation."

"Excuse me for saying, but my bullshit meter is clanging so hard it's popping some springs."

"That's the truth, accept it or not." He held up an empty cup. "Tea?" he asked pleasantly. "You look like you could use some. I've got Earl Grey, pepper-mint or the old standby, Lipton."

"Screw the tea! Where were you and she coming from?" she demanded.

King kept his voice calm. "Oh, from about eight years ago."

"What!"

"Just taking a walk down memory lane."

"Eight years ago?" She looked at him incredu-lously. "Did you go to Bowlington?"

"Bingo. Sugar and cream?"

"What the hell did you go there for?"

"Sorry, I don't think you're cleared for it."

Joan slammed her fist on the table. "Cut the shit, Sean, and tell me!"

He stopped making the tea and stared at her. "It's none of your damn business unless you tell me you have some interest in the Ritter assassination that I don't know about."

She looked at him warily. "What the hell is that supposed to mean?"

"Why don't *you* tell *me* what it means?"

Joan sat back, took a deep breath and ran a hand through her tangled hair. "Does she know we spent the night together at the hotel?"

"It doesn't matter what she knows or doesn't know. This is between you and me."

"I still don't know where all this is going, Sean. Why are you raking all this up now?"

"Maybe I don't know why. And maybe I really don't care to know, so let's just drop the whole damn thing. Water under the bridge, right? Sleeping dogs lie, okay? Let asshole Ritter rest in peace, right?" He prepared the tea and handed her a cup. "Here, peppermint, drink it!"

"Sean—"

He grabbed her arm and leaned very close. "Drink your tea."

His very low voice and intense gaze seemed to calm her down. She picked up her cup and took a sip. "It's good, thank you."

"You're welcome. Now, about your Bruno offer. Suppose I say yes. What's the first step in our little partnership?"

Joan still looked very upset, but she took out a file from her briefcase and went over its contents. She took a deep, apparently cleansing breath and said, "We need facts. So I've put together a list of people to interview." She slid across a piece of paper that King looked at.

"And going to the crime scene and working the angle from there."

King was running his eye down the list. "Okay, pretty thorough. Everyone from Mrs. Bruno to Mrs.

Martin to Colonel Mustard and the butler." He stopped at one name on the list and looked up at her. "Sidney Morse?"

"He's supposedly at a mental institution in Ohio. Let's verify that. I'm assuming you'd recognize him?"

"I don't think I'll ever forget him. Theories going in?"

"Do I take all this interest as a yes?"

"Take it as a maybe. Theories?"

"Bruno had lots of enemies. He may already be dead."

"If so, the investigation is over before it started."

"No, my deal with Bruno's people is to find out what happened to him. I get the money whether he's found alive or not."

"Good negotiating. I see you haven't lost your edge."

"The work is just as hard if he's dead. In fact, it's more problematic if he's not alive. They pay me for results, whatever those results happen to be."

"Fine, understood. We were talking theories."

"One side has him kidnapped to throw the election their way. From what I can gather, Bruno's constituency might have been enough to swing the vote if he either withheld his support from or threw it to another party."

"Look, I really don't buy that a major political

party kidnapped Bruno. Maybe in another country, but not here."

"Agreed. It's pretty far-fetched."

King sipped his tea and said, "So let's get back to more conventional malfeasance, shall we?"

"They kidnapped him for money, and the ransom demand will be forthcoming."

"Or a gang he wreaked havoc on when he was a prosecutor took him."

"If so, we'll probably never find the body."

"Any likely suspects on that?"

Joan shook her head. "I thought there would be, but actually no. The three worst organizations he helped break up have no active members on the outside. He did prosecute some local gangs in Philly after he left D.C., but they tended to operate within a two-block radius with little sophistication beyond guns, knives and cell phones. They wouldn't have had the brains or resources to snatch Bruno right out from under the Secret Service."

"Okay, we rule out enemies from when he was a prosecutor and those for political gain, and we have left pure financial motivation. Was he worth enough to take that risk?"

"By himself, no. As I said before, his wife's family has money, but they're not Rockefellers either. They could pay a million dollars but not more than that."

"Well, it sounds like a lot, but a million bucks just doesn't go as far as it used to."

"Oh, how I'd love to find out," said Joan. She glanced at her file. "Bruno's political party has funds, but still, there are lots of other targets with far bigger payoffs."

"And ones that don't have the Secret Service guarding them."

"Exactly. It's like whoever took Bruno did it for—"

King broke in. "For the challenge? To show they could beat the Secret Service?"

"Yes."

"They must have had inside info. Somebody on Bruno's staff."

"I've got some possibilities. We'll have to check them out."

"Great. But right now I'm going to grab a quick shower."

I guess exploring your past is a dirty business," she said dryly.

"Boy, it sure can be," he shot back as he walked up the stairs.

She called after him. "Are you sure you want to leave me alone? I might hide a nuclear bomb in your sock drawer and get you into real trouble."

King went to his bedroom, flipped on the bathroom light, turned on the shower and started brushing his teeth. He turned to close the door, lest Joan get any weird ideas.

As he put his hand on the door and gave it a push, he sensed it was heavier than it should be. Far heavier, as though it had been weighted down with something. His adrenaline instantly surging, he eased it open with his hand and as it swung by, peered around curiously. The door's momentum, together with its increased weight, caused it to come around and close firmly. He didn't even hear the smack of the door against the jamb. His focus was entirely on the source of the extra weight.

He'd seen a lot of unsettling things in his life. Yet the sight of the Wrightsburg socialite and his former client Susan Whitehead hanging on the back of his bathroom door, her dead eyes staring at him, a large knife plunged right through her chest, almost dropped him to the floor.

30

An hour later King sat on his stairs as the investigative teams finished up and the body of Susan Whitehead was removed. Chief Williams came over to him. "We're done here, Sean. Looks like she was killed around five o'clock this morning. She goes for walks around then, I was told, and we're assuming she was taken at that time and killed immediately. That's why there wasn't any blood on the floor in your bathroom. She bled somewhere else. Anything you can tell me?"

"I wasn't here. I just got back from North Carolina."

"I don't mean that. I'm not implying that *you* killed Ms. Whitehead."

There was just enough emphasis on the word "you" for King to look up and say, "And I didn't have her killed either, if that's what you're so subtly implying."

"Just doing my job, Sean. I've got a damn crime

spree going on, and right now nobody's above suspicion. I hope you can understand that. I know that Ms. Whitehead is your client."

"*Was* my client. I handled her last divorce, that's it."

"Okay, I might as well ask you this because, well, there's been talk around town." King stared at him expectantly. "There's been talk that maybe you and Ms. Whitehead were, well, seeing each other. Were you?"

"No. She might have wanted a relationship, but I didn't."

Williams's brow furrowed. "Was it a problem for you? I mean I know how the woman could be. Pretty overwhelming."

"She wanted something between us and I didn't. Simple as that."

"And that's all, you're sure?"

"What exactly are you trying to do here? Build a case that I had the woman killed because, what, I didn't want to *date* her? Give me a break."

"I know it sounds crazy but, well, people do talk."

"Especially around here."

"And Ms. Whitehead was very prominent. Lots of friends."

"Lots of *paid* friends."

"I wouldn't go around saying that, Sean, I really

wouldn't." He held up the note that had been pinned to the chest of the unfortunate Whitehead. It had been placed in an evidence bag.

"Any ideas about this?"

King looked at the note and shrugged. "Only that it's from someone who was at the Ritter assassination or knows a lot about it. I'd give it to the FBI, if I were you."

"Thanks for the advice."

As Williams walked off, King rubbed his temples and contemplated taking a bath in pure bourbon and drinking half of it. The phone rang. It was his law partner, Phil Baxter.

"Yeah, it's true, Phil. She's dead, right here in my house. I know, it shocked the hell out of me. Look, I might need you to cover some things at the office for me. I . . . What's that?" King's expression darkened. "What are you talking about, Phil? You want to go solo? Can I ask why? I see. Sure, if that's what you want. You do what you have to do." He hung up.

Almost immediately his phone rang again. It was his secretary, Mona Hall, calling with her resignation. She was too scared to work for him anymore, she whined. Dead bodies kept turning up. And people were suggesting that King was somehow in on it, not that she ever believed that, but, well, where there's smoke . . .

After he hung up with Mona, a hand touched his shoulder. It was Joan.

"More trouble?"

"My law partner is hightailing it as fast as he can, and my secretary just joined him in the full retreat. Other than that, everything's fine."

"I'm sorry, Sean."

"Look, what can I expect? I've got dead bodies falling all around me. Hell, I'd be running too."

"I'm not running anywhere. In fact, I need your help more than ever."

"Well, it's nice to be wanted."

"I'm staying in the area for a couple of days while I set up interviews and do some background digging. Give me a call but make it soon. If you're not going to work with me, I have to move on. I have a private plane available. I want to help you through this, and I think work is the best way to do that."

"Why, Joan? Why do you want to help me?"

"Call it repayment of a debt long overdue."

"You don't owe me anything."

"I owe you more than you think. I see that quite clearly *now.*"

She gave him a peck on the cheek, turned and left.

The phone rang again and King snatched it up. "Yeah?" he said testily.

It was Michelle. "I heard. I'll be there in half an hour." He remained silent. "Sean, are you okay?"

He looked out the window as Joan drove off. "I'm fine."

King grabbed a quick shower in the guest bathroom and then took a seat at the desk in his study. His brow furrowed in concentration as he wrote down, from memory, the words from the note that had been found on Whitehead's body.

Déjà vu, Sir Kingman. Try to remember if you can where you were on the most important day of your life. I know you're a smart guy but a little rusty, so you probably want a hint. Here it is: 1032AM09261996. Talk about pushing a post. Talk about giving good feet. Look forward to seeing you soon.

Ten-thirty-two a.m. on September 26, 1996, was the exact time that Clyde Ritter had been killed. What could this mean? So intense was his concentration that he never even heard her come in.

"Sean, are you okay?"

He jumped up and yelled out. Michelle screamed and fell back.

"God, you startled me," she said.

"Startled *you*? Damn, woman, haven't you ever heard of knocking?"

"I did. I have been for the last five minutes, nobody answered." She looked at the piece of paper. "What is that?"

He calmed and said, "A note from somebody in my past."

"How far in your past?"

"Does the date September 26, 1996, ring a bell?"

It clearly did. After a little hesitation he handed her the note.

She finished reading and looked up at him. "Who could have left it?"

"The person who brought Susan Whitehead's body here and deposited it in my bathroom. They came as a package. I guess the person didn't want me to miss seeing the note."

"Was she killed here?"

"No. The police think she was grabbed early this morning, killed, and then her body was brought here."

She looked down at the piece of paper. "Do the police know about that?"

He nodded. "They have the original. I made this copy."

"Any thoughts on who wrote it?"

"Yes, but none that make a lot of sense."

"Was Joan still here when you found the body?"

"Yes, but she had nothing to do with it."

"I know, Sean. I wasn't implying that. How did you leave things with her?"

"I'm going to call her, tell her I'm thinking about the Bruno offer and I'll get back to her."

"So what now?"

"We go back to Bowlington."

Michelle looked surprised. "I thought you were done with the Fairmount Hotel."

"I am. But I want to know how an unemployed maid supported herself and who stuffed money in her mouth."

"But you don't know if that's connected to the Ritter killing."

"Oh, but I do. And the last question is the biggie." She looked at him expectantly. "Who did Loretta Baldwin see in that supply closet?"

31

I appreciate your meeting with me," said Joan.

Jefferson Parks sat down across from her in the small dining area of the inn where Joan was staying. He looked at her warily. "It's been a while."

She said, "Six years. The joint task force case in Michigan. The Secret Service and the U.S. Marshals were privileged to carry the bags of the FBI."

"As I recall, you broke the thing wide open and managed to let everybody know you had."

"Horn blowing should start at home, and I seem to have a knack for it. And if it had been a man, the credit would have come regardless."

"Come on, you really think that?"

"No, Jefferson, I really *know* that. Shall I cite you about a thousand examples? I have them right on the tip of my tongue."

"Along with about a ton of acid," muttered Parks under his breath. Out loud he said, "So you wanted to see me?"

"The Howard Jennings case?" said Joan.

"What about it?"

"I was just wondering about the status. Professional courtesy."

"I can't talk to you about an ongoing investigation. You know that."

"But you can tell me certain things that aren't confidential or that won't jeopardize your investigation, but as yet haven't made a public splash."

Parks shrugged. "I'm not sure I know what you mean."

"For instance, you haven't arrested Sean King, presumably because, despite certain circumstantial evidence that seems to implicate him, you don't believe he's guilty. And possibly you have facts that point in other directions. And he couldn't have killed Susan Whitehead because he wasn't here. In fact, I believe that *you* provided him with an alibi."

"How do you know that?"

"I'm an investigator, so I investigated," Joan said.

"The person who killed Howard Jennings and the one who killed Susan Whitehead needn't be the same. The crimes could be totally unrelated."

"I don't think so and neither do you. It seems to me that while the crimes are very different they are also very much the same."

Parks shook his head wearily. "I know you're real

smart and I'm real stupid, but the more you talk, the less I understand what the hell you're saying."

"Let's suppose that Jennings wasn't killed because he was in WITSEC. Let's suppose he was killed because he worked for Sean King."

"Why?"

She ignored his question. "Now Susan Whitehead was killed elsewhere and then brought to Sean's house. In neither case is the evidence strong enough to show that he killed the victim, and in fact, in Whitehead's case the proof is the other way entirely: he had an alibi."

"Which he didn't have with Jennings, and his gun was the murder weapon," countered the deputy marshal.

"Yes, he explained the gun substitution theory, which I take it you agree with."

"I'm not going to say one way or another. Here's one theory: Jennings was killed by his old partners in crime, and they tried to frame King for it. His gun, no real alibi, body in his office, a classic setup."

"Yet could they be sure?" wondered Joan.

"Sure of what?"

"Sure that Sean wouldn't have an alibi that night? He could have easily had an emergency call to go on while he was on duty, or someone that saw him at the time Jennings was killed."

Parks answered, "Unless they knew the pattern of his rounds and waited for him to reach the downtown area and then killed Jennings. He was seen around there at the time of the murder."

"Seen, yes, but, again, if he had met someone along the way or received a call at the time he was downtown, he has an alibi and the case goes away."

"So where does that leave us?" asked Parks.

"With your framers not really caring if Sean is arrested for the crime or not. And in my experience framers are rarely so sloppy. If they were careful enough to steal his gun, copy it down to the last detail, kill Jennings with it and then return it to Sean's house, they would have chosen a time and place for the killing that would have allowed Sean no possibility of an alibi. In short, I can't allow for such extraordinarily careful planning with the weapon and such carelessness with the alibi. Murderers are seldom so schizophrenic in their work."

"Well, King could have rigged this all himself, to throw us off."

"With the motive of ruining the nice life he's made for himself here?"

"Okay, I get your point, but why are you taking such a keen interest in all this?"

"Sean and I used to work together. I owe him,

shall we say. So if you're looking for your killer, I'd look elsewhere."

"You have any idea exactly where?"

Joan looked away. "I suppose everyone has ideas." And with that she abruptly ended the meeting.

After Parks left, Joan took the piece of paper out of her purse. She'd persuaded one of the county deputies to let her make a copy of the note found on Susan Whitehead's body while King and Chief Williams were occupied elsewhere. After reading through it she took from her wallet another piece of paper she'd kept all these years. She carefully unfolded it and stared at the few words written on it.

The note she was holding was one that she believed Sean had left for her in her room at the Fairmount Hotel on the morning Ritter was killed. After their vigorous night of lovemaking she slept in, and King went on duty. When she woke up, she saw the note and did precisely what it asked, even though the request carried some professional risk. After all, she was nothing if not a risk taker. At first she simply thought it bad timing, atrocious timing. Then she wondered what Sean had really been up to that morning. She said nothing back then for a simple reason: It would have ruined her career. Now this new development had thrown an entirely new angle on all of this.

The question was what to do about it.

32

As King and Michelle climbed into Michelle's Land Cruiser, he looked around in surprise.

"You cleaned out your truck."

She said nonchalantly, "Oh, I just picked up a few things here and there."

"Michelle, it's spotless and it smells good too."

She wrinkled her nose. "There were some old bananas. I don't know how they got in here."

"Did you do it because of the hard time I gave you?"

"Are you kidding? I just, you know, I had some time to kill."

"I appreciate it anyway." Something struck him. "What'd you do with all the stuff? You haven't been home."

She looked embarrassed. "You probably don't want to see my room at the inn."

"No, I probably don't."

They got to Bowlington and met Tony Baldwin. With his and the local sheriff's permission, they looked around Loretta Baldwin's home.

"What was your mother living on? Social Security?" King asked as he surveyed the nice interior.

"No, she was only sixty-one," said Tony.

"Did she work?" Tony shook his head as King looked around at the furniture and rugs, the neat little touches here and there. The kitchen had appliances far newer than the house, and a late-model Ford sedan was parked in the garage.

King stared at Tony. "So I give up. Were you supporting her, or did she have a rich relative who died?"

"I've got four kids. I barely make ends meet."

"Let me guess: did she send money to you?" Tony looked uncomfortable.

"Come on, Tony," said Michelle, "we're just trying to find out who did this to your mother."

"Okay, okay, yeah, she had some money. From where, I don't really know and didn't really want to ask. When you got a bunch of mouths to feed, you don't look a gift horse in the mouth, right?"

"She ever mention where it might be coming from?" Tony shook his head. King then said, "When was the first time you noticed this flow of money?"

"Not sure. I mean she sent me some cash for the first time years ago."

"How many years? Think carefully, it's important."

"Maybe six or seven or so."

"When did she stop working at the Fairmount?"

"It closed down pretty soon after Ritter got shot."

"Had she worked since?"

"Nothing steady and the last few years not at all. She'd done crap work all her life. It was time to take it easy," he said defensively.

"So your mother never said anything about where the money came from? Any friends or other family she might have spoken to about it?"

"I'm the closest family she has. Friends, I don't know. She had a real good friend, Oliver Jones, but he's dead now. She might have told him."

"Any way we can talk to his family?"

"Didn't have any. He outlived them all. Died about a year ago."

"Nothing else you can think of?"

Tony considered this and his expression changed. "Well, last Christmas Mama said something a little strange."

"What was it?"

"The last five or six years she'd always sent nice presents for the kids. Only last Christmas she didn't.

My little girl, Jewell, she asked her grammy how come she didn't send any presents, didn't she love them anymore? You know how kids are. Well, anyway, Mama said something like, 'Honey, all good things must come to an end,' something like that."

Michelle and King shared a significant glance. King said, "I suppose the police have searched the house pretty thoroughly."

"Top to bottom, didn't find nothing."

"No check stubs, deposit slips, old envelopes to show maybe where the money came from?"

"No, nothing like that. Mama didn't like banks. She dealt in cash only."

King had strolled to the window and was looking out at the backyard. "Looks like your mother was really into her garden."

Tony smiled. "She loved flowers. Put a lot of work into it when she could. I'd come up every week and help out. She'd sit out there for hours and just look at her flowers." Tony started to say something, then paused before asking, "You want to go look at 'em?" King started to shake his head, but Tony quickly added, "See, today's the day I usually came up to weed. I mean I know she's not around to see it anymore, but it was important to her."

Michelle smiled and said in a sympathetic tone, "I love gardens, Tony." She nudged King.

"Right. I'm into gardens too," said King without much enthusiasm.

While Tony Baldwin pulled at some weeds in one of the beds, Michelle and King walked around the yard and admired the flowers.

King said, "Loretta's secret cash flow started shortly after Ritter died."

"Right. So you're thinking blackmail?"

He nodded. "Although I'm wondering how Loretta was blackmailing someone simply because she might have seen him or her in the closet."

"Meaning they might have just come in there for the same reason she did, because they were scared?"

"Only there has to be more to it. Remember when we were looking in the closet, and I said that she had probably squeezed in the back. I thought so because for all she knew some guy might come in with a gun—" He broke off and suddenly looked at her wide-eyed.

"What are you saying? That maybe she *did* see someone come in with a gun?"

"Or with something. Why else would she have gotten suspicious? I mean there were probably lots of people running around trying to hide."

"But why a gun?"

"Why not? Some guy trying to stash a gun in a supply closet right after there's been an assassination makes more sense than trying to hide a pair of glasses or a bundle of cash. A gun is instantly incriminating. It would peg him as part of the assassination plot. Okay, let's say the guy has a gun on him. He's afraid to try to go outside with it, because he might get stopped and searched. So when all hell is breaking loose, he runs in and hides it in the closet, not knowing Loretta is in there. He might have planned to stash the gun in the closet all along. He might have intended to retrieve it later, or just let the police find it if it was clean of any incriminating evidence. So he stuffs the gun in between some towels or something and leaves. Loretta comes out from her hiding place and takes it. Maybe she thinks she'll bring it to the police but then changes her mind and goes down the blackmail highway. Since she works at the hotel, she could probably sneak out an exit no one is covering or else hide the gun and come back to get it later."

Michelle considered this line of reasoning. "Okay, so she has the gun and she's seen the guy, and if she doesn't know who he is, it's easy enough to find out. She contacts him anonymously, possibly with a picture of the gun and where she was when she saw him, and starts extracting payment. It works, Sean, as well as anything else."

"And that's why her house was ransacked. They were looking for the gun."

"You really think Loretta kept it here some-where?"

"You heard Tony: the woman didn't believe in banks. She was probably the sort who kept anything of importance right where she could lay her hands on it."

"So the big question is, where's the gun now? Maybe the killer found it."

"Maybe we take the house apart board by board."

"That doesn't make sense. Unless there's a secret compartment somewhere, hiding the gun in a wall doesn't make it real convenient to get to."

"That's true." King's gaze was absently roaming over the little garden. He stopped at one spot, passed it and then came back. He walked over to the row of hydrangea bushes. Six pink ones, and one in the middle of the group that was blue.

"Nice hydrangeas," he said to Tony.

He came over wiping off his hands on a rag. "Yeah, Mama loved those the most, probably even over the roses."

King looked curious. "Interesting. She ever say why?"

Tony looked puzzled. "Why what?"

"Why she liked hydrangeas over roses?"

"Sean, do you really think that's important?" asked Michelle.

Tony rubbed his chin. "Well, now that you mention it, she told me more than once that to her those hydrangeas were priceless."

King glanced sharply at Michelle and then stared at the blue hydrangea and exclaimed, "Damn!"

"What is it?" asked Michelle.

"The longest long shot in the world. But it might just be. Quick, Tony, do you have a shovel?"

"A shovel? Why?"

"I've always been curious about pink and blue hydrangeas."

"Nothing special about that. Some people think they're different bushes, but they're not really. I mean you can get yourself pink and blue ones, but you can also change pink to blue by raising the pH in the soil, make it more acidic, or blue to pink by making the soil more alkaline and lowering the pH. They got stuff to make it more acidic, aluminum sulfate, I think they call it. Or you can put some iron filings in the soil, tin cans, even rusty nails and such. That'll change the color from pink to blue too."

"I know, Tony. That's why I want the shovel."

Tony fetched the tool from the garage, and King started to dig around the blue hydrangea. It didn't take long before his shovel clinked against something hard. And a short time later he pulled out the object.

"Nice source of iron," said King as he held up the rusty pistol.

33

King and Michelle had stopped at a small diner for a quick bite after leaving poor Tony dumbstruck in his mother's garden.

Michelle said, "Okay, I'm officially impressed with both your detective *and* gardening skills."

"Lucky for us that iron is a component of steel, or else we never would have found the gun."

"I get the gun and blackmail part and why Loretta was murdered. But I still don't understand the point of stuffing the money in her mouth."

King fingered his coffee cup. "I once worked a joint task force with the FBI in L.A. Russian mobsters were extorting money from every business in a one-square-mile area and also running a financial scam, which was why we were involved. We had some snitches on the inside; some cash got to them from us – you fight fire with fire, right? Well, we found our snitches full of bullet holes in the trunk of a car with their mouths stapled shut. When we took the staples out, we found cash wadded up in there, probably the same cash we paid them. The message was clear: you talk, you die and you eat the betrayal money that caused your death."

"So the money in Loretta's mouth was symbolic? The ultimate hush money treatment?"

"That's how I read it."

"Wait a minute. Her son said that the money stopped coming about a year or so ago. But if the person was still around to kill Loretta, why did he stop paying? And why would she have accepted that? I mean why didn't she go to the police at that point?"

"Well, it'd been seven years or so. What was she going to tell the cops? That she had amnesia and had just remembered everything, and oh, by the way, here's the gun?"

"Well, maybe the person being blackmailed figured that out too, and that's why he stopped paying. Maybe he figured her leverage was gone."

"Whatever the case, apparently very recently some-one found out that Loretta was the blackmailer, and she paid with her life."

Michelle suddenly paled and she clutched his arm. "When I spoke with Loretta, she mentioned that she was in that supply closet, although she never said she saw anyone. You don't think?"

King picked up on her concern. "Someone might

have overheard her tell you, or she might have told someone else later."

"No, she was killed so soon after I spoke with her. It must have come from my conversation with her. But we were alone on that porch. Yet somebody must have heard. God, I'm probably the reason she's dead."

King gripped her hand. "No, you're not. The person who held her under the water in the bathtub is the reason she's dead."

Michelle closed her eyes and shook her head.

King said firmly, "Listen to me, I'm sorry about what happened to Loretta, but if she was blackmailing the person who killed her, that's a dangerous game she chose to play. She could have gone to the police and given them the gun years ago."

"That's what we should do."

"We will, although the serial numbers have been drilled out, and it's in pretty poor condition. Maybe the forensics boys at the FBI can pull something out of it. There's a satellite office in Charlottesville. We'll drop it off when we get back home."

"So what now?"

"If someone hid a gun in the supply closet of the Fairmount Hotel on the day Clyde Ritter was assassinated, what does that tell you?"

It suddenly hit her. "That maybe Arnold Ramsey *wasn't* working alone."

"That's right. And that's why we're going there right now."

"Where?"

"Atticus College. Where Arnold Ramsey was a professor."

34

The beautiful tree-lined, brick-paved streets and elegant ivy-covered buildings of tiny Atticus College did not seem like a place that could spawn a political assassin.

"I'd never heard of this school until Ritter was killed," said Michelle as she drove her Land Cruiser slowly down the main campus thoroughfare.

King nodded. "I hadn't realized how close it was to Bowlington." He looked at his watch. "It only took us thirty minutes to get here."

"What did Ramsey teach here?"

"Political science with a special emphasis on federal election laws, although his personal interest was radical political theory." Michelle looked at him in surprise.

He explained. "After Ritter was killed, I made it my business to get a Ph.D. in Arnold Ramsey." He glanced at Michelle. "You drop a guy, the least you can do is take the time to learn about him."

"That sounds a little callous, Sean."

"It's not meant to. I just wanted to know why a seemingly reputable college professor would kill a nut of a candidate who had no chance to win anyway and sacrifice his life in the process."

"I would think that would have been checked out pretty thoroughly."

"Not as thoroughly as if it had been a real bona fide candidate. Besides, I think everybody just wanted to get the whole mess over with."

"And the official investigation concluded that Ramsey acted alone."

"Based on what we've found, they apparently concluded incorrectly." He stared out the window. "I don't know, though, it's been a long time. I'm not sure we're going to find anything useful here."

"Well, we *are* here, so let's give it our best shot. We might spot something everybody else missed. Just like you did with the blue hydrangea."

"But we also might find out something that might be better left undiscovered."

"I don't ever think that's a good thing."

"You're always for the truth coming out?"

"Aren't you?"

King shrugged. "I'm a lawyer. Go ask a real human being."

They were directed from one person and one department to another until they found themselves sitting in the office of Thornton Jorst. He was medium height, trim, and appeared to be in his early fifties. A pair of thick eyeglasses and pale complexion gave him a very professorial air. He'd been a friend and colleague of the late Arnold Ramsey.

Jorst sat behind a cluttered desk piled high with opened books, reams of manuscript pages and a laptop symbolically covered with very low-tech legal pads and colored pens. The shelves that covered the walls of his office seemed to sag under the weight of the impressively thick works collected there. King was staring at the diplomas on the wall when Jorst held up a cigarette. "Do you mind? A professor's inner sanctum is one of the few places left where one can actually light up."

King and Michelle both nodded their assent.

"I was surprised to hear that the two of you were here asking about Arnold."

"We normally call ahead and make official appointments," said King.

"But we were in the area and decided the opportunity was too good to pass up," added Michelle.

"I'm sorry, I didn't get your names?"

"I'm Michelle Stewart and this is Tom Baxter."

Jorst eyed King. "Pardon me for saying so, but you look very familiar."

King smiled. "Everybody says that. I've just got that kind of average face."

Michelle said, "That's funny, I was going to say that I recognized you from somewhere, Dr. Jorst, but I just don't remember where."

"I'm on TV locally a fair amount, especially now with the elections drawing close," said Jorst quickly. "I like my anonymity, but having one's fifteen minutes of fame every now and then is good for the ego." He cleared his throat and said, "I understand that you're doing a documentary of some sort on Arnold?"

Michelle sat back and took on the air of a scholar herself. "Not just him, but on politically motivated assassinations in general, but with a special emphasis. The hypothesis is that there are quite marked distinctions between people who target politicians. Some do so because of pure mental imbalance or a perceived personal grievance against the target. And others strike because of deep philosophical beliefs, or even because they believe themselves to be doing good. They might even regard killing an elected official or candidate as an act of patriotism."

"And you want my opinion on which of these categories Arnold fell into?"

"Being a friend and colleague, you've doubtlessly given the matter a great deal of thought," said King.

Jorst eyed him keenly through the wisps of smoke. "Well, I can't say the issue of what drove Arnold to become an assassin hasn't intrigued me over the years. However, I can't claim he fits neatly into any ideological or motivational box either."

"Well, maybe if we look at his background and the time period that led up to his action, we might be able to get somewhere," suggested Michelle.

Jorst checked his watch.

"I'm sorry," said Michelle. "Do you have a class?"

"No, actually I'm on sabbatical. Trying to finish a new book. So fire away."

Michelle took out a pen and notebook. "Why don't we start with a little background on Ramsey?" she prompted.

Jorst leaned back in his chair and stared at the ceiling. "Arnold did the hat trick at Berkeley, B.A., M.A., Ph.D. All at the top of his class, by the way. He also somehow found time to participate in protests against the Vietnam War, burn his draft card, march in civil rights demonstrations, attend sit-ins and lie-ins, get arrested, risk his life, all of that. He had by far the best academic credentials of any professor this department has ever employed and quickly achieved tenure here."

"Was he popular with his students?" asked King.

"For the most part, I think he was. More popular than I am with mine." Jorst chuckled. "I'm a far tougher grader than my late, lamented colleague."

"I assume his political leanings were far different than Ritter's?" asked Michelle.

"Ninety-nine percent of America would have fallen into that category, and thank God for that. He was a TV preacher who sucked money out of deluded people all over the country. How could a man like that run for the White House? It made me ashamed of my country."

"Sounds like Ramsey's opinions rubbed off on you," said King.

Jorst coughed and attempted a chuckle. "I certainly agreed with Arnold's assessment of Clyde Ritter as presidential material. However, I differed with him drastically on the proper response to the man's candidacy."

"So Ramsey was vocal about his feelings?"

"Very." Jorst stubbed out his cigarette and immediately lit another. "I remember him stalking around my office and pounding his fist into the palm of his hand and decrying the state of a citizenry that

would allow a man like Clyde Ritter to gain pur-
chase in national politics."

"But he had to know that Ritter had no chance
of winning."

"That wasn't the issue. What wasn't nearly so
obvious was the deal-making that was going on
behind the scenes. Ritter had reached a critical mass
in the polls, and that had started to make both the
Republicans and the Democrats extremely nervous.
He'd easily reached poll levels that enabled him to
receive federal election funds and qualified him for
national debate time. And whatever you could say
about Ritter, he talked a good game. He was incredibly glib, and he connected with a certain element
of the voting population. And you also have to
understand that in addition to Ritter's own presidential campaign, he'd cobbled together an independent
party coalition that had numerous candidates running for various offices in many of the larger states.
That could have had disastrous consequences for the
major party candidates."

"How so?" King asked.

"In many elections around the country his slate
was splitting the traditional voting bases for the
major-party candidates, in effect giving him control
over the outcome of perhaps thirty percent of the

seats in play. Now, when you have that much leverage in the political arena, well . . ."

"You get to pretty much name your price?" suggested King.

Jorst nodded. "What Ritter's price would have been is anyone's guess. After his death the wind went completely out of his party. The major parties really dodged a bullet there. Excuse me, poor choice of words. But I really believe that Arnold thought if Ritter weren't stopped, he'd end up destroying everything America stood for."

"And that was clearly something Ramsey didn't want to see happen," said King.

"Obviously not, considering he shot the man," Jorst said dryly.

"Did he ever talk about doing something like that?"

"As I told the authorities back then, he didn't. Yes, he'd come in here and rant and rave about Ritter, but he certainly never made any threats or anything. I mean that's what freedom of speech is all about. He was entitled to his opinion."

"But not entitled to kill for it."

"I didn't even know he had a gun."

"Was he close with other professors here?" asked Michelle.

"Not really. Arnold intimidated many of them.

273

Schools like Atticus don't usually get such academic heavyweights."

"Friends outside the college?"

"None that I knew of."

"How about among his students?"

Jorst eyed King. "Excuse me, but this seems more like an investigation into Arnold personally, rather than a documentary on why he killed Clyde Ritter."

"Maybe it's a little of both," said Michelle quickly. "I mean it's difficult to understand motivation without understanding the man and how he went about his plan to assassinate Ritter."

Jorst considered this for a few moments and then shrugged. "Well, if he tried to recruit any student to help, I certainly never heard of it."

"He was married at the time of his death?" asked Michelle.

"Yes, but separated from his wife, Regina. They had one daughter, Kate." He rose and went over to a shelf containing numerous photos. He handed one to them.

"The Ramseys. In happier times," he commented.

King and Michelle looked at the three people in the photo.

"Regina Ramsey is very beautiful," remarked Michelle.

"Yes, she was."

King glanced up. "Was?"

"She's dead. Suicide. Not that long ago actually."

"I hadn't heard that," said King. "You said they were separated?"

"Yes. Regina was living in a small house nearby at the time of Arnold's death."

"Did they share custody of Kate?" asked Michelle.

"That's right. I don't know what the arrangements would have been if they'd divorced. Regina, of course, took full custody when Arnold died."

"Why were they separated?" asked Michelle.

"I don't know. Regina was beautiful and an extremely accomplished actress in her youth. She'd been a drama major in college, in fact. I believe she was going to make that her career, and then she met Arnold, fell in love, and that all changed. I'm sure she had many suitors, but Arnold was the man she loved. Part of me thinks she finally committed suicide because she could no longer live without him." He paused and added in a small voice, "I thought she was happy around that time. I guess she wasn't."

"But she apparently couldn't live *with* Ramsey either," commented King.

"Arnold had changed. His academic career had peaked. He'd lost his enthusiasm for teaching. He was very depressed. Perhaps that melancholy affected the marriage. But when Regina left him, his depression only worsened."

"So maybe in shooting Ritter he was trying to recapture his youth," Michelle said. "Change the world and go down as a martyr for the history books."

"Maybe. Unfortunately it cost him his life."

"What was the daughter's reaction to what her father did?"

"Kate was utterly devastated. I remember seeing her the day it happened. I will never forget the look of shock on that girl's face. And then a few days later she saw it on TV. That damn tape from the hotel. It showed everything: her father shooting Ritter and the Secret Service agent killing her father. I saw it too. It was horrific, and—" Jorst stopped talking and looked intently at King. His expression slowly hardened, and he finally rose from behind his desk. "You really haven't changed all that much, Agent King. Now, I'm not sure what's going on here, but I don't appreciate being lied to. And I want to know right now what your real purpose is in coming here and asking all these questions."

King and Michelle exchanged glances. King said, "Look, Dr. Jorst, without making a long explanation out of it, we've recently discovered evidence that strongly suggests Arnold Ramsey wasn't alone that day. That there was another assassin, or potential assassin, in the hotel."

"That's impossible. If that were true, it would have come to light before now."

"Maybe not," said Michelle. "Not if enough important people wanted it all to quietly go away. They had their killer."

"And they had the Secret Service agent who screwed up," added King.

Jorst sat back down. "I . . . I can't believe it. What new evidence?" he asked warily.

"We can't say right now," King told him. "But I wouldn't have come all the way down here if I didn't think it was worth checking out."

Jorst took out a handkerchief and wiped his face. "Well, I guess stranger things have happened. I mean, look at Kate Ramsey."

"What about Kate?" Michelle asked quickly.

"She attended college here at Atticus. I was one of her professors. You'd think this would be the last place she'd have wanted to come. She was brilliant like her father; she could have gone anywhere. But here is where she came."

"Where is she now?" asked King.

"She's doing postgraduate work in Richmond at Virginia Commonwealth University's Center for

Public Policy. They have a first-rate political science department. I wrote her a reference myself."

"Was it your feeling she hated her father for what he'd done?"

Jorst considered the question for a lengthy time before answering. "She loved her father. And yet she may have hated him in the sense that he'd gone away and left her, choosing his political beliefs, as it were, over his love for her. I'm not a psychiatrist but that's a layman's guess. Although she's turned out to be a chip off the old block."

"How do you mean?" asked Michelle.

"She marches in protests, writes letters, lobbies government and civic leaders and writes articles for alternative publications, all just like her father did."

"So she may have hated him for leaving her, but she's now emulating him?"

Appears to be that way."

"And her relationship with her mother?" asked King.

"Fairly good. Although she might have blamed her mother somewhat for what happened."

"In that she wasn't there for her husband? That if she had been, he might not have been driven to do what he did?" asked King.

"Yes."

"So you didn't see Regina Ramsey after her husband died?" asked Michelle.

"No, I did," he said quickly, and then hesitated. "Certainly at the funeral; and while Kate was a student here and some other times."

"What was the cause of death, do you remember?"

"An overdose of drugs."

"She never remarried?" inquired King.

Jorst turned a little pale. "No. No, she didn't." He recovered and noticed their inquisitive looks. "I'm sorry, this is all rather painful for me. These were my friends."

King studied the faces of the people in the photo some more. Kate Ramsey looked to be about ten in that picture. Her features were intelligent and loving. She stood between her parents, holding hands with both of them. A nice, loving family. On the surface anyway.

He handed the photo back. "Anything else you can think of that might help?"

"Not really."

Michelle gave him a card with her numbers on it. "Just in case something occurs to you," she explained.

Jorst looked at the card. "If what you say is true, that there was another assassin, what exactly was he supposed to do? Provide a backup in case Arnold missed his target?"

"Or," said King, "was somebody else supposed to die that day too?"

35

When they called the Center for Public Policy at VCU, King and Michelle were told that Kate Ramsey was away but was expected to return in a couple of days. They drove back to Wrightsburg, where King pulled into the parking lot of an upscale grocery store in the downtown area.

"I guess I owe you a fancy dinner and a nice bottle of wine," explained King, "after dragging you all over the place."

"Well, it was a lot more fun than standing in a doorway with a gun while a politician scrounges for votes."

"Good girl. You're learning." King suddenly stared out the window, obviously thinking about something.

"Okay, I know that look. What's going through that head of yours now?" asked Michelle.

"You remember Jorst kept saying that Atticus was lucky to have someone like Ramsey, that Berkeley scholars and national experts didn't just drop into schools like Atticus every day?"

"Right. So?"

"Well, I saw Jorst's diplomas in his office. He went to decent schools, but nothing even in the top twenty. And I'm guessing the other professors in the department weren't superstars like Ramsey, which was maybe why they were intimidated by him."

Michelle nodded thoughtfully. "So why did a brilliant Berkeley Ph.D. and national expert end up teaching at a place like Atticus?"

King looked at her. "Exactly. If I had to guess, it's because Ramsey had some skeletons in his closet. Maybe from his protesting days. Maybe that's why his wife finally left him."

"But wouldn't that have come out after he assassinated Ritter? They would have checked his background with a fine-tooth comb."

"Well, not if it was covered up well enough. And you're talking a long time before the assassination. And the sixties were a crazy time."

As they meandered through the grocery store aisles gathering items for dinner, Michelle noted the whispers and glances the well-heeled patrons were giving King. At the checkout counter King tapped the shoulder of the man in front of him who was doing his best to ignore King's presence.

"How's it going, Charles?"

The man turned and blanched. "Oh, Sean, yes, good. And you? I mean . . ." The man looked thoroughly embarrassed at his own question, yet Sean just kept smiling.

"Shitty, Charles, just shitty. But I'm sure I can count on you, right? Got you out of that nasty tax problem a few years ago, remember?"

"What, oh, I . . . oh, there's Martha out front waiting. Good-bye."

Charles hustled off and climbed into a Mercedes station wagon driven by a distinguished-looking white-haired woman whose mouth dropped open when her husband started telling her of his encounter. She drove off in a huff.

As King and Michelle headed out with their grocery bags, she said, "Sean, I'm sorry about all of this."

"Hey, the good life had to end sometime."

Back at King's house he fixed an elaborate dinner that started with a Caesar salad and crab cake appetizers and was followed by pork tenderloin in a mushroom and Vidalia onion sauce and a side serving of garlic mashed potatoes. For dessert they feasted on chocolate éclairs. They ate on the rear deck overlooking the lake.

"So you can cook, but are you available to rent for parties?" she joked.

"If the price is right," he answered.

Michelle held up her wineglass. "Nice stuff."

"It should be, it's right in its prime. I've had it in my cellar for seven years. One of my most cherished bottles."

"I'm honored."

Sean eyed the dock. "How about a spin on the lake later?"

"I'm always game for water activities."

"There are some swimsuits in the guest room."

"Sean, one thing you'll learn about me: I never go anywhere without sports gear."

With King driving the big red motorcycle-like Sea-Doo 4TEC and Michelle seated behind him, her arms wrapped around his waist, they went out about three miles, and then King dropped a small anchor into the shallow water of a cove. They sat on the Sea-Doo, and King looked around.

"Give it six weeks or so, and the colors here will be something to see," said King. "And I also love how the mountains look with the sun going down behind them."

"Okay, time for some exercise to work off that

meal." Michelle took off her life jacket, then stripped off her top and sweatpants. Underneath she wore dazzling red Lycra shorts and a matching workout top.

King found himself staring at her, openmouthed, the beautiful mountain vistas no longer engaging his attention.

"Problem?" asked Michelle as she glanced at him.

"No problem here," said King as he quickly looked away.

"Last one in." She dove into the water and came up. "Going to join me?"

He stripped down and dove in and came up next to her.

Michelle eyed the shoreline. "How far do you think that is?"

"About a hundred yards. Why?"

"I'm thinking about entering a triathlon."

"Gee, why am I not surprised?"

"I'll race you," she said.

"It won't be much of a race."

"Pretty cocky, huh?"

"No, I mean you'll kick my ass."

"How do you know that?"

"You're an Olympian, I'm a middle-aged attorney with bum knees and a bad wing where I got shot doing my public service stint. It'd be like racing your grandmother with lead weights on her feet."

"We'll see. You might surprise yourself. One-two-three-go!" She took off, her strokes cutting cleanly through the warm, flat water.

King swam after her and surprisingly made up the distance fairly easily. In fact, by the time they drew close to shore they were neck and neck. Michelle started laughing when he reached over and playfully grabbed her leg. They reached land in a tie. King lay on his back and sucked in air like there wasn't enough in the entire atmosphere to satisfy him.

"Well, I guess I did surprise myself," he said between gasps. Then he looked over at Michelle. She wasn't even breathing hard, and the truth struck him.

"You shit, you weren't even trying."

"Yes, I was. Well, I mean I had to allow for the age difference and all."

"Okay, that does it."

He jumped up and went after her as she raced screaming away. Yet she was laughing so hard King had no trouble running her down. He lifted her over his shoulder, carried the woman out into waist-deep water and ceremoniously dumped her. She came up sputtering and still laughing.

"What was that for?"

"To show you that while I may be over forty, I ain't dead."

Back at the dock as he was raising the Sea-Doo up on its lift he asked, "So how did you go from basketball and track to Olympic rowing?"

"I liked track better than basketball, but I missed the team element. In college a friend of mine was a rower, and I got into it through him. Seems like I had a natural talent for it. Out on the water my motor never seemed to quit; I was like a machine. And I loved the high you got from leaving everything you had out on those oars. I was the youngest member of my team. When I first tried out, no one gave me much of a chance. I guess I proved them wrong."

"I think you've probably spent a good part of your life doing that. Particularly in the Secret Service."

"It hasn't all been wine and roses."

"I'm not that familiar with the sport. What was your rowing event called?"

"Fours with coxswain, meaning four women pulling for all they're worth and a coxswain calling out the strokes. The focus is absolutely complete."

"What was it like to be in the Olympics?"

"The most exhilarating *and* most nerve-racking time of my life. I was so stressed I threw up before our first heat. But when we took the silver and came within a hair of the gold, there was no greater feeling in the world. I was still basically a kid and felt like I'd reached the pinnacle of my life."

"Still feel that way?"

She smiled. "No. I'm hoping the best is yet ahead for me."

They showered and changed into dry clothes. When Michelle came down, King was going over some notes at the kitchen table.

"Interesting reading?" she asked as she combed out her wet hair.

He looked up. "Our interview with Jorst. I'm wondering if he knows more than he's telling. And I'm also wondering what we might learn from Kate Ramsey."

"If she'll talk to us."

"Right." He yawned. "We'll think about it tomorrow. Long day."

Michelle looked at her watch. "It is late. I guess I better be going."

"Look, why don't you just stay here tonight? You can stay in the guest room where you just showered," he added quickly.

"I have my own place. You don't have to feel sorry for me. I'm a big girl."

"I do feel sorry for you because all the junk that was in your truck is now in your room at the inn. Something might be alive in there. It might come and get you in the middle of the night." He smiled and then said quietly, "Stay here."

She graced him with her own smile and a look in her eyes that seemed very suggestive. Although that might have just been the wine he'd had.

"Thanks, Sean. I'm actually pretty whipped. Good night."

He watched her go slowly up the stairs. The long, muscular legs slid into the nice, firm butt, and then her body continued into the Olympic shoulders and up the long neck and, well . . . Hell! As she disappeared into the guest room, he let out a sigh and tried desperately not to think about what he was so desperately thinking about.

He went around to all the doors and windows and made sure they were locked. He was planning on having an alarm company come out and wire his house. He'd never thought he'd need that here. Half the time he didn't even lock his doors. Boy, that had changed.

He paused at the top of the stairs and looked toward the guest room door. Inside, a beautiful young woman was lying in bed. Unless he was seriously mistaken, if he opened that door and went in, he'd probably be allowed to stay the night. Then again, with the way his luck was running, if he opened the door, Michelle might just shoot him in the balls. He stood there for a few moments more, thinking. Did he really want to start something with this woman? With all that was going on? The answer, as much as he didn't want to accept it, was pretty clear. He trudged down the hall to his own room.

Outside near the bottom of the road leading up to King's house, the old Buick, lights out, stopped, and the engine was cut off. The rattling muffler had been fixed because the driver no longer desired to be noticed. The car door opened, and the man climbed out and looked through the trees at the silhouette of the darkened house. The rear doors on the Buick opened, and two more people emerged: it was "Officer Simmons" and his homicidal female companion, Tasha. Simmons looked a little nervous while Tasha seemed ready for adventure. The Buick Man just appeared focused. He glanced at his companions and nodded. Then all three moved toward the house.

36

King awoke from a dead sleep as the hand went over his mouth. He saw the gun first and the face second.

Michelle put a finger to her lips and whispered in his ear. "I heard some noises. I think someone's in the house."

King pulled on his clothes and pointed out the door with a questioning look.

"I think at the rear of the house, lower level. Any idea who it could be?"

"Yeah, maybe somebody's bringing me another dead body."

"Anything of value in the house?"

He started to shake his head and then stopped. "Shit. The gun from Loretta's backyard. It's in my lockbox in the study."

"You really think . . .?"

"Yeah, I really do." He picked up the phone to call the police but put it back down.

"Don't tell me," she said. "It's dead?"

"Where's your cell phone?"

She shook her head. "I think I left it in my truck."

They slipped down the stairs listening for any more sounds that might pinpoint where the intruder was. It was dark and quiet. The person could have been anywhere, watching, waiting to pounce.

King looked at Michelle and whispered, "Nervous?"

"It *is* a little creepy. What do *you* do when it gets dicey?"

"Go get a bigger gun than the other guy has."

The *bang* came from the direction of the staircase leading to the lower level.

Michelle looked at him. "Okay, I say no confrontation. We don't know how many or how well armed."

"Agreed. But we have to get the gun. You have your car keys?"

She held them up. "Way ahead of you."

"I'll drive. We'll call the cops once we're out of here."

With her covering him, King slipped into his study, got the lockbox and made sure the gun was inside. They went quietly out the front door.

They climbed into the Land Cruiser's front seat, and King put the key in the ignition.

The blow struck him from behind, and he fell against the horn, which started blaring.

"Sea—" yelled Michelle, but her voice was cut off, along with most of her wind, when the leathery garrote went around her neck and ripped into her skin.

She desperately tried to dig her fingers under the leather, but it had already sunk in too deeply. Very quickly her lungs were bursting, her eyes bulging in their sockets; her brain felt like it was on fire. From the corner of her eye she saw King slumped against the steering wheel, the blood running down his neck. Then she felt the rope twist and tighten and a hand reached over the front seat and grabbed the rusty gun. The rear truck door opened and then closed, and footsteps moved away, leaving her to die.

The garrote kept tightening, and Michelle put her feet up against the dashboard to try to arch her body, to get some leverage and separation from the person who was doing his best to kill her. She dropped back down, her breath nearly gone. The sound of the horn was exploding in her ears; the sight of the unconscious and bloodied King only added to her hopelessness. She arched again and slammed her head into the face of the person strangling her. She heard him cry out, and the rope loosened, but only a bit. Next she reached back, trying to seize hair to pull, skin to tear or eyeballs to gouge. She was finally able to grip her attacker's hair and pulled as hard as she could, but the pressure on her throat kept up. She scratched and clawed at the face, and then her head was ripped back, almost pulling her over the seat. She thought her spine had cracked, and Michelle went limp and slid forward.

She could feel the breath of the person who was killing her, exerting every ounce of strength to finish her off. Tears of desperation and agony slid down her face.

The breath was right in her ear. "Just die," he hissed. "Just die!"

His mocking tone suddenly revitalized her. With her last bit of energy Michelle's fingers closed around her gun. She pointed it backward, against the seat, her index finger finding the slender bit of metal. She barely had any strength left, and yet she found the small reserve of will she needed to do it. She just prayed her aim was true. She wouldn't get a second chance.

The gun fired, and the bullet ripped through the seat. She heard the impact with flesh and next the grunt, and the garrote immediately loosened and then fell away. Free, Michelle sucked in huge amounts of air. Dizzy and sick to her stomach, she pushed open the truck door and fell out onto the ground.

She heard the rear door open. The man climbed out, holding his bloodied side. She raised her gun, but he kicked the door fully open and it slammed into her, knocking her down. Beyond furious now, Michelle bounced back up and aimed her pistol even as he turned and ran.

However, before she could fire, she dropped to her knees and was violently sick to her stomach. When she looked up, her vision was so blurred, her head pounding so hard, that there seemed to be three men running away. She fired six shots; all were placed in a tight bunch at what she thought was the real flesh and blood of the man who had done his best to murder her.

All six missed by a wide margin. She'd picked the wrong image to shoot.

The footsteps hurried away, and a short time later a car started up and raced off, spewing gravel and dirt.

With a final gasp Michelle dropped to the ground.

37

The blaring truck horn finally attracted the attention of a passing deputy who discovered the unconscious King and Michelle. They were taken to UVA Hospital in Charlottesville. King recovered first. His head wound was bloody, but his skull proved hard enough and he'd suffered no serious damage. Michelle's recovery would take a little longer, and she was sedated while her injuries were worked on. When she woke, King was sitting next to her, his head bandaged.

"God, you look awful," she said in a weak voice.

"That's all I get after sitting in this damn chair for hours waiting for the princess to awaken? "God, you look awful?""

"I'm sorry. It's really wonderful to see your face. I wasn't sure you were alive."

He studied the marks on her swollen neck. "Whoever it was did a number on you. Did you see anybody?"

"No. It was a man, that's all." She added, "I shot him."

"You did what?"

"Shot him, through the seat."

"Where'd you hit him?"

"In the side, I think."

"The police are waiting to take a statement. I've already given them mine. The FBI and Deputy Marshal Parks are here too. I filled them in on finding the gun and my theory about Loretta blackmailing someone."

"I'm afraid I can't tell them much."

"There must have been at least two of them: one to flush us out of the house and the other waiting in your truck. They were counting that I'd grab the gun. Saved them from looking for it. Someone must have been tailing us when we were at Loretta's house. They could have seen us discover the gun, and decided to get it back."

"There were three of them, then, because there were two in the car." She paused and then said, "They got the gun, didn't they?"

"Yes. Stupid when you think about it. We should have taken it right to the FBI, but we didn't and that's that." He sighed and put a hand on her shoulder. "That was a close one, Michelle, way too close."

"I fought as hard as I could."

"I know you did. You're the only reason I'm alive. I owe you."

Before Michelle could answer, the door opened and a young man came in. "Agent Maxwell?" He held out credentials that identified him as Secret Service. "As soon as you're discharged from the hospital, and have talked to the police, you're to accompany me back to Washington."

"Why?" asked King.

The man ignored him. "The doctors say you're lucky to be alive."

"I don't think luck had much to do with it," King pointed out.

"Why am I going back to Washington?" Michelle asked.

"As of right now, you're being reassigned to a desk at the Washington field office."

"Walter Bishop's handiwork," said King.

"I really can't say."

"I know. That's why *I* said it."

"I'll be here when you're ready to go." The man nodded curtly at King and left.

"Well, it was fun while it lasted," said King.

She reached out and took his hand, squeezing it. "Hey, I'll be back. I'm not going to let you have a good time all by yourself."

"Just rest for now, okay?" She nodded. "Sean?" He looked at her. "About last night, the swim and everything. It was fun. I think we both needed that. Maybe we can do it again someday."

"Hell yes, I loved dumping your butt in the water."

King was walking down the hallway after leaving Michelle when a woman stepped in front of him. Joan looked both anxious and upset. "I just heard. You're okay?" She looked at his bandaged head.

"I'm fine."

"Agent Maxwell?"

"Fine too. Thanks for asking."

"You're sure you're all right."

"I'm fine, Joan!"

"Okay, okay, calm down." She motioned to some chairs in an empty room off the main corridor. They sat, and Joan looked at him, a serious expression on her face.

"I heard you discovered a gun at that woman's home."

"How the hell did you find that out? I just told the cops."

"I'm in the private sector, but I didn't turn in my investigative skills when I left the Service. Is it true?"

He hesitated. "Yeah, I found a gun."

"And where do you think it came from?"

"I have my theories. But I'm not in a sharing mood."

"Well, let me jump right in with one of mine. This woman was a maid at the Fairmount Hotel, she had a gun hidden in her garden and she meets a violent death with money stuffed in her mouth. She was blackmailing the person who was the owner of that gun. And that person may have been involved in Ritter's assassination."

He stared at the woman in amazement. "Who the hell are your sources?"

"Sorry, I've used up my sharing spirit too. So you get the gun, lose the gun, and you're almost killed in the process."

"Michelle actually got it a lot worse than I did. They just knocked me out. Apparently they did their best to kill her."

She looked at him strangely when he said that. "Do you think this has anything to do with Bruno's disappearance?" she asked abruptly.

He looked surprised. "How could it? Just because Ritter and Bruno were both presidential candidates? That's quite a stretch."

"Maybe so. But things that look complex tend to have very simple cores."

"Thanks for the detective lesson. I'll sure remember that one."

"Maybe you need some basic lessons. You're the one running around with the woman who let Bruno be kidnapped."

"She didn't let Bruno be kidnapped any more than I let Clyde Ritter get shot."

"The fact is, I'm investigating Bruno's disappearance, and at this juncture I can't assume anyone is above suspicion, including your lady friend Michelle."

"Great, and she's not my 'lady friend.' "

"Okay, what exactly is she?"

"I'm just following up some stuff, and she's helping me."

"Wonderful. I'm glad you've teamed up with someone, since it appears you've blown me off completely. Is Maxwell also offering a million-dollar payday if you crack the case, or just a kick-ass adventure between the sheets?"

He eyed her closely. "Don't tell me you're jealous."

"Maybe I am, Sean. But regardless, I think I at least deserve an answer to my offer."

King glanced in the direction of Michelle's room but turned back when Joan put a hand on his arm.

"I need to get going on this. And you never

know, we might just find out the *real* truth about Clyde Ritter."

He stared defiantly at her. "Yeah, we just might," he shot back.

"So you're in? I need to know. Right now."

After a moment he nodded. "I'm in."

38

They flew via private plane to Dayton, Ohio, and then drove to a state mental facility that was about thirty minutes north. Joan had called ahead and gotten the necessary approvals to visit Sidney Morse.

"It wasn't as difficult as I would have thought," she told King on the drive there. "Although when I told the woman whom I wanted to see, she laughed. Said we could come if we wanted, but it wouldn't do us much good."

"How long has Morse been there?" King asked.

"About a year or so. He was committed by his family. Or rather his brother, Peter Morse. I guess that's all the family he had left."

"I thought Peter Morse was in trouble with the police. And wasn't he a druggie?"

" '*Was*' being the operative word. He never went to prison, probably due to his brother's influence. He apparently cleaned up his act and when his older brother went nuts, put him in the state mental hospital."

"Why in Ohio?"

"It seems that prior to being committed, Sidney was living with his brother here. I guess he was so far gone he couldn't live by himself."

King shook his head. "Talk about your reversal of fortune. In less than ten years the guy goes from king of the hill to permanent residence in a nuthouse."

A little while later King and Joan were sitting in a small room at the bleak institution. The sounds of wails and cries and sobbing filtered down the hallways. People whose minds had long since left them were hunched over in wheelchairs in the corridors. In a recreation room off the main reception area a small group of patients watched a show on TV. Nurses, doctors and attendants slowly moved up and down the halls in their scrubs, their energy seemingly sapped by the depressing surroundings.

King and Joan both stood as the man was wheeled into the room by one of the attendants. The young man nodded to them. "Okay, here's Sid."

The young man knelt down in front of Morse and patted him on the shoulder. "Okay, Sid, these people want to talk to you, okay, you hear me? It's cool, just talk." The attendant grinned when he said this.

He stood and Joan said, "Um, is there anything we should know, anything to avoid?"

The man smiled, showing a row of crooked teeth. "Not with Sid. It really doesn't matter."

King hadn't been able to take his gaze off the wreck of a man who eight years ago had nearly pulled off one of the most impressive feats in American politics. Morse had lost some weight but was still chubby. His hair had been shaved off, although he had a short beard shot with gray. King had remembered his eyes being laser sharp, missing nothing. Now those eyes were clearly lifeless. It *was* Sidney Morse, but just barely, only the shell really.

He said, "So what's the diagnosis?"

"That he ain't never leaving here, that's what," said the attendant, who introduced himself as Carl. "His mind's totally gone. Cracked out and ain't coming back. Look, I'll be down the hall. You can just come get me when you're done." Carl walked off.

Joan glanced at King. "I can't believe it's him," she said. "I know his rep and career took a big hit after Ritter was killed, but you'd think it wouldn't come to *this.*"

"Maybe it happened in stages. And I guess a lot can happen in eight years. I mean look at me. He was shattered after the Ritter debacle. Nobody wanted him. He grew depressed. And maybe his younger brother introduced a very vulnerable Sidney to some heavy drugs while they were living together. I recall during the campaign that Sidney said his brother's drug habit had gotten him into a lot of trouble. He said his brother was pretty creative in coming up with ways to get the cash to support his habit. Quite the con man."

King knelt in front of Morse. "Sidney, Sidney, do you remember me? I'm Sean King. Agent Sean King," he added.

There was no reaction. A bit of spittle oozed out of the man's mouth and clung to his lip. King glanced at Joan. "His father was a well-known lawyer," he said, "and his mother was some kind of heiress. I wonder where all that money went?"

"Maybe it's used to support him here."

"No, this is a state institution. It's not some fancy private place."

"Well, maybe his brother has control of it. I guess they each inherited and now he has both shares. And who cares about the Morse brothers? I'm here to find John Bruno."

King turned to look back at Morse. The man

hadn't moved. "God, look at those knife marks on his face."

"Self-mutilation. Sometimes that goes with being unbalanced."

King rose, shaking his head.

"Hey, have you played the game with him?" said a high-pitched voice.

They both turned and looked at the short, skinny man standing behind them holding a ragged stuffed rabbit. His features were so tiny he looked like a leprechaun. He wore a ratty bathrobe and apparently little else. Joan averted her gaze.

"The game," said the man, who looked at them with a childlike expression. "Have you played it yet?"

"What, with him?" asked King, pointing to Morse.

"I'm Buddy," said the man, "and this is Buddy too," he said, holding up the ragged rabbit.

"Nice to meet you, Buddy," said King. He looked at the rabbit. "And you too, Buddy. So you know Sid?"

Buddy nodded vigorously. "Play the game."

"The game, right, why don't you show me? Can you do that?"

Again Buddy nodded his head, and smiled. He ran to the corner of the room where there was a box of stuff. He pulled out a tennis ball and came back to them.

He stood in front of Morse and held up the ball. "Okay, I'm pitching the . . ."

Buddy's focus seemed to wander, and he just stood there holding the ball and his rabbit with his mouth wide open and his eyes expressionless.

King prompted, "The ball. You're pitching the *ball*, Buddy."

Buddy came back to life. "Okay, I'm pitching the ball." He made a great show of a major league windup that exposed far more of his anatomy than either King or Joan cared to see. As he let the ball go, however, it was in a slow, underhand style.

It was heading right for Morse's head. A second before it hit him, Morse's right hand shot up and caught the ball. Then the hand dropped, the ball still clenched there. Buddy hopped round and then took a bow. "The game," he said.

He went over to Morse and tried to get the ball back, but Morse's fingers remained clenched around it. Buddy turned to them with a pathetic expression. "He never gives it back. He's mean! Mean, mean, mean!"

Carl popped his head in. "Everything cool? Oh, hey, Buddy."

"He won't give the ball back," Buddy cried out.

"No problem. Calm down." Carl strode over, took the ball out of Morse's hand and gave it back to Buddy. Buddy turned to King and held out the ball. "Your turn!"

King looked at Carl, who smiled and said, "It's okay. It's just a reflex action. Docs here have a long name for it, but that's the only thing Sid does. The others get a big kick out of it."

King shrugged and gently tossed the ball to Morse, who caught it again.

"So, does anyone ever visit Sid?" Joan asked Carl.

"Brother used to when he first got here, but he ain't been around for a long time now. I guess Sid was some big deal years ago 'cause we had some reporters come by when he was admitted. But that didn't last long after they saw what shape he was in. Now nobody comes. He just sits in that chair."

"And catches the ball," added Joan.

"Right."

As they were leaving, Buddy came racing up after Joan and King. He had the tennis ball in his hand. "You can have this if you want to. I have lots of others."

King took the ball. "Thanks, Buddy."

Buddy held up his rabbit. "Thank Buddy too."

"Thanks, Buddy."

He looked at Joan and held up the rabbit even higher. "Kiss Buddy?"

King nudged Joan with his elbow. "Go ahead, he's cute."

"What, I don't even get dinner first?"

Joan pecked the rabbit on the cheek. Then she said, "So are you good friends with Sidney? I mean Sid."

Buddy nodded so hard his chin hit his chest.

"His room's right next to mine. Wanna see?"

King looked at Joan. "We're here."

"In for a dime, in for a dollar," she replied with a shrug.

Buddy took Joan's hand and led them down a hallway. King and Joan weren't sure they were supposed to be in this area without an attendant, but no one stopped them.

Buddy halted in front of one room and slapped the door. "This is my room! Wanna see? It's cool."

"Sure," said Joan. "Maybe you have some more Buddys in there."

Buddy opened the door and then immediately closed it. "I don't like people looking at my stuff," he said, staring at them anxiously.

King let out a long, exasperated sigh. "Okay, Buddy, your house, your rules."

"Is this Sid's room?" Joan was pointing to the door to the left of Buddy's.

"Nope, this one." Buddy opened the door to the right.

"Is this okay, Buddy?" asked King. "Can we go in?"

"Is this okay, Buddy? Can we go in?" Buddy repeated, looking at the two with a big smile.

Joan was scanning the hallway and saw no one watching. "I think it's okay, Buddy. Why don't you keep watch outside?" She slipped inside, and King followed and closed the door. A suddenly panicked-looking Buddy stood by the door.

Inside they looked around the Spartan quarters. "Sidney Morse's fall was long and complete," commented Joan.

"They often are," King said distractedly as he examined the place. The smell of urine was very strong in here. King wondered how often the sheets were changed. There was a small table in the corner. On it were several photographs, all without frames. King picked them up. "I guess no sharp objects in the room like glass and metal."

"Morse doesn't look capable of suicide, or anything else for that matter."

"You never know, he could swallow that tennis ball and choke to death." King examined the pictures. There was one of two young men in their teens. One held a baseball bat. He said, "The Morse brothers. They look to be around high school age." He held up another photo. "And I guess these are their parents."

Joan joined him and looked at the photos. "Their mother was pretty homely."

"Homely but rich. That makes a big difference to a lot of people."

"The dad was very handsome."

"As I said, the prominent lawyer."

Joan took the photo and held it up. "Both boys took after their father. Sidney was chunky even back then but nice-looking. Peter was good-looking too . . . nice build, with the same eyes as his brother." She studied the confident way he held the baseball bat. "He was probably a jock in high school who hit his peak at eighteen and went rapidly downhill from there. Drugs and bad news."

"Wouldn't be the first time."

"How old would Peter be now?"

"A little younger than Sidney, so early fifties maybe."

She gazed at Peter's face. "Sort of a Ted Bundy type. Good looking and charming, and he'll slit your throat the minute you let your guard down."

"Reminds me of some women I've known."

There was a small box in the corner. King went over and sifted through the contents. They included a number of old, yellowed newspaper clippings. Most chronicled Sidney Morse's career.

Joan was peering over his shoulder. "Nice of his brother to bring this scrapbook of sorts along. Even if Sidney can't read it." King didn't answer. He kept going through the pages.

King held up one very curled newspaper article. "This talks about Morse's early career staging plays. I remember him telling me about it. He really put together these elaborate productions. I don't think any of them made any money, though."

"Not that he probably cared. The son of a rich mom can afford to dally like that."

"Well, he gave it up at some point and started to really work for a living. Although you could say he ran Ritter's campaign like a stage production."

"Anything else before we officially rule Sidney Morse a complete and total dead end?" she asked.

"Shouldn't we look under the bed?" asked King.

Joan eyed him disdainfully. "That's a boy job."

King sighed and cautiously peered under the bed. He rose quickly.

"Well?" she asked.

"You don't want to know. Let's get out of here."

As they left the room, Buddy was right there waiting.

"Thanks for your help, Buddy," Joan said. "You've been a real peach."

He looked at Joan excitedly. "Kiss Buddy?"

"I already did, Buddy," she reminded him politely.

Buddy suddenly looked ready to cry. "No, *this* Buddy." He pointed to himself.

Joan's mouth dropped, and she glanced at King, obviously looking for help.

"Sorry, that's a girl job," he said, grinning.

Joan gazed at the pitiful Buddy, swore under her breath and then suddenly grabbed him and planted a big one right on the little man's lips.

She turned, wiped her face and muttered to King, "The things I do for a million bucks." Then she stalked out.

"Bye, Buddy," said King, and he left.

A very happy Buddy waved frantically and said, "Bye, Buddy."

39

The private plane landed in Philadelphia, and thirty minutes later King and Joan were nearing the home of John and Catherine Bruno in an affluent suburb, along the city's famed Main Line. As they passed the brick-and-ivy-clad homes and stately grounds, King looked over at Joan. "So, old money here?"

"Strictly from the wife's side. John Bruno grew up poor in Queens, and then his family moved to Washington, D.C. He went to law school at Georgetown and started working as a prosecutor in D.C. right after graduation."

"Have you met Mrs. Bruno?"

"No. I wanted you with me. First impressions, you know."

A Hispanic maid in a starched uniform complete with frilly apron and subservient demeanor showed them into the large living room. The woman almost curtsied as she left. King shook his head at this antiquated spectacle and then refocused when the small woman entered the room.

Catherine Bruno would have made an excellent first lady, was his preliminary opinion. In her mid-forties she was petite, refined, dignified, sophisticated, the very essence of blue blood and good manners. His second opinion was that she was far too full of herself. This was bolstered by the woman's habit of looking over your shoulder when she spoke to you. As though she couldn't waste her precious eyesight on anything below aristocracy. She never even asked King why his head was bandaged.

Joan, however, made the woman focus very quickly. She'd always had that way about her, sort of like a tornado in a can. King had to suppress a smile as his partner bored in.

Joan said, "Time is not on our side, Mrs. Bruno. The police and the FBI have done all the right things, but their results have been negligible. The longer your husband remains missing, the less chance there is of getting him back alive."

The haughty eyes came back to terra firma. "Well, that's why you were hired by John's people, wasn't it? To get him back safe?"

"Precisely. I have a number of inquiries going, but I need your help."

"I've told the police all I know. Ask them."

"I'd prefer to hear it from you."

"Why?"

"Because depending on your answers, I might have follow-up questions that the police didn't think to ask."

And, King thought to himself, we want to see for ourselves if you're lying your little stuck-up ass off.

"All right, go ahead." She looked so put off by the whole process that King suddenly suspected her of having an affair, the recovery of her husband being the last thing she wanted.

"Did you support your husband's political campaign?" Joan asked.

"What kind of question is that?"

"The kind we'd like an answer to," Joan said pleasantly. "You see, what we're trying to narrow down are motives, potential suspects and promising lines of investigation."

"And what does my support of John's political career have to do with that?"

"Well, if you were supporting his political ambitions, then you might have access to names, private discussions with your husband, things that might have concerned him from that part of his life.

317

If, however, you weren't in the loop, we'll have to look elsewhere."

"Oh, well, I can't say I was delighted that John was pursuing a political career. I mean he had no chance; we all knew that. And my family . . ."

"Didn't approve?" coaxed King.

"We're not a *political* family. We have a spotless reputation. It practically gave my mother a heart attack when I married a criminal prosecutor who grew up on the wrong side of the tracks and was over ten years my senior. But I love John. Still, you have to balance things and it hasn't been easy. These sorts of things aren't exactly looked upon with favor among my circle. So I can't say I was his political intimate. However, he had a sterling reputation as a lawyer. He prosecuted some of the toughest cases in Washington and later in Philadelphia, where we met. That gave him a national reputation. Being around all those politicians in D.C., I suppose he got the itch to jump into the fray, even after we moved to Philadelphia. I didn't agree with his political ambition, but I'm his wife, so I supported him publicly."

Joan and King posed the standard questions, to which Catherine Bruno gave standard and mostly unhelpful answers.

"So you can think of no one who'd wish to harm your husband?" Joan asked.

"Aside from those he prosecuted, no. He's had death threats and the like but nothing recently. After he left the U.S. Attorney's Office in Philadelphia, he spent a few years in private practice before plunging into the political arena."

Joan stopped writing notes. "What firm was he with?"

"The Philadelphia office of a Washington-based firm, Dobson, Tyler and Reed. They're in downtown Philadelphia on Market Street. A very well respected establishment."

"What sort of work did he do there?"

"John didn't talk about business with me. And I never encouraged it. It didn't interest me."

"But presumably it was trial work."

"My husband was happiest when he had a stage to perform on. So, yes, I'd say trial work."

"And he voiced no special concerns to you?"

"He thought the campaign was going reasonably well. He had no delusions of winning. He was only making a statement."

"After the election what was he going to do?"

"We never really discussed it. I always assumed he'd go back to Dobson, Tyler."

"Can you tell us anything about his relationship with Bill Martin?"

"He mentioned his name every now and then, but that was really before my time."

"And you have no idea why Bill Martin's widow would want to meet with your husband?"

"None. As I said, that relationship was really before our marriage."

"First marriages for you both?"

"His first, not mine," was all she offered.

"And you have children?"

"Three. It's been very hard on them. And me. I just want John back." She started to sniffle, as though on cue, and Joan pulled out a tissue and handed it to her.

"We all do," said Joan, doubtlessly thinking of the millions of dollars it would earn her. "And I won't stop until I accomplish that goal. Thank you. We'll be in touch."

They left and headed back to the airport.

So what do you think?" asked Joan while they were in the car. "Is your nose twitching?"

"First impression: a snobby wench who knows more than she's telling us. But what she's *not* telling could have nothing to do with Bruno's kidnapping."

"Or it could have everything to do with it."

"She doesn't seem thrilled with this political gig, but what spouse really is? She's got three children, and we have no reason to believe she doesn't love them or her husband. She's got all the money. She gains nothing by having him kidnapped. She'd be paying part of the ransom."

"But if there's no ransom, she pays nothing. She's single again and free to marry someone of her own class who's not in the dirty world of politics."

"That's true," he agreed. "We just don't know enough yet."

"We'll get there." Joan opened her file and looked at it. As she was reading, she said, "The attack on you and Maxwell took place around two in the morning. Here I was thinking I was special, only to find that you invite all sorts of women to spend the night."

"Just like you, she slept in the guest room."

"And where did *you* sleep?"

He ignored her. "Who's next on the list?"

Joan closed her file. "I'd like to hit this law firm – Dobson, Tyler – while we're in town, but we'll need time to check it out first. So it's on to Mildred Martin."

"What do we have on her?"

"Devoted to her husband, who worked with

Bruno in D.C. Some of my preliminary digging *suggested* that the young John Bruno played fast and loose as a prosecutor in D.C. and left Martin holding the bag."

"So the widow Martin would be no fan of Bruno's?"

"Right. Bill Martin had terminal lung cancer. It had also spread to his bones. He had, at most, a month. But that didn't work in somebody's time-table, so they had to help him along." She flipped open a file. "I was able to get the autopsy results on Martin. The embalming fluid had spread every-where, even to the vitreous fluid, which otherwise is a pretty good place to spot poison because it doesn't turn to jelly like blood does upon death."

"Vitreous? That's eyeball fluid?" asked King.

She nodded. "There *was* a spike in the methanol level in the midbrain sample they took."

"Well, if the guy was a heavy drinker, that's not unusual. Methanol is in whiskey and wine."

"Right again. I just note it because the M.E. did. However, methanol is also a component of embalm-ing fluid."

"And if they knew there wouldn't be an autopsy and the body gets embalmed . . ."

Joan finished for him. "The embalming process

could mask the methanol presence or at least confuse the M.E. when an autopsy is actually performed."

"Perfect murder?"

"No such thing with us on the case," said Joan with a smile.

"So what do you think Mildred can tell us?"

"If Bruno changed his schedule to meet with someone calling herself Mildred Martin, then he must have thought the real Mildred had something important to tell him. From what I know of John Bruno, he does nothing that doesn't help him."

"Or maybe hurt him. And what makes you think she'll tell *us*?"

"Because after checking her out, I've found she's also a hard drinker and a sucker for a handsome man who shows her some attention. I hope you get the hint. And if you can manage it, take off the bandage – you have such nice hair."

"And what's your part?"

She smiled sweetly. "The heartless bitch. A role I've perfected."

40

After they landed, King and Joan rented a car and drove to Mildred Martin's house, arriving in the early evening. It was a modest place and in the sort of neighborhood that people who didn't have a lot of money retired to. It was about five miles from the funeral home where Bruno had been kidnapped.

They rang the bell and knocked on the door, but no one answered.

"I don't understand. I called ahead," said Joan.

"Let's check around back. You said she's a drinker. She could be back there getting wasted."

In the small backyard they found Mildred Martin sitting at a wicker table on a lumpy, moss-covered brick patio, having a drink, smoking a cigarette and admiring her garden. She was about seventy-five, had the heavily wrinkled face of a lifelong smoker and sun worshiper and wore a lightweight print dress and sandals in the warm, breezy air. Her hair was dyed. Other than the gray roots, the primary color was a sort of orange. The smell of citronella filled the air from a bucket of the substance that sat lighted under the table.

After introductions were made, Mildred said, "I like sitting back here. Even with the damn mosquitoes. This time of year the garden can really shine."

"We appreciate your seeing us," said King politely. He'd followed Joan's instructions and removed his head bandage.

Mildred waved them to seats at the table and held up her glass. "I'm a gin girl and hate to drink alone. What can I get you?" Her voice was deep and gravelly, permanently engraved with decades of liquor and cigarettes.

"Screwdriver," said Joan with a quick glance at King. "I just love those."

"Scotch and soda," said King. "Can I help you?"

She laughed heartily. "Oh, if I were forty years younger, yes you could." With an impish smile she walked a little unsteadily to the house.

"She seems to have finished her mourning period," commented King.

"They were married forty-six years and by all accounts had a good relationship. Her husband was about eighty, in poor health and suffering great pain. Maybe there's not much to grieve about."

"Bill Martin was Bruno's mentor. How so?"

"Bruno worked for Martin when he first started as a criminal prosecutor in Washington. Martin taught Bruno the ropes."

"At the U.S. Attorney's Office?" asked King.

"That's right," she said.

King looked around. "Well, the Martins don't seem to be all that well off."

"Public service doesn't pay very well, we all know that. And Bill Martin didn't marry an heiress. They moved down here after he retired. Mildred grew up here."

"Well, nostalgia aside, it's not the sort of place I'd want to come rushing back to."

Mildred returned with their drinks on a tray and sat down. "Now, I guess you want to get down to brass tacks. I've already talked to the police. I really know nothing about any of this."

"We understand, Mrs. Martin," said King, "but we wanted to meet and talk with you personally."

"Lucky me. And please call me Millie. Mrs. Martin is my mother-in-law, and she's been dead for thirty years."

"Okay, Millie, we know you've talked to the police, and we know that they did an autopsy on your husband's body."

"God, that was a complete waste of time."

"Why's that?" Joan said sharply.

Mildred eyed her keenly. "Because no one poisoned him. He was an old man with terminal cancer who died peacefully in his own bed. If I can't drop in my garden, I'd prefer to go that way too."

"You know about the phone call to Bruno?"

"Yes, and I've already told the police I didn't place it. They checked my phone records. I guess they didn't believe me."

Joan leaned forward. "Yes, but the point is that Bruno was reportedly very agitated after getting the call. Can you explain why?"

"If I didn't make the call, how should I know? Unfortunately mind reading isn't among my repertoire. If it were, I'd be rich."

Joan persisted. "Look at it this way, Millie. Bruno and your husband were once close but no longer really were. Yet he gets a phone call, which he thinks is from you, asking to meet, and he gets agitated. The person calling would have had to say something plausible for that to happen, something that Bruno would logically associate with you or your husband."

"Well, perhaps it's as simple as the person's having told him Bill was dead. I hope that would have upset him. After all, they were friends."

Joan shook her head. "No. Bruno already knew. That's been confirmed. He wasn't planning on coming to the funeral home until he got the phone call."

Martin rolled her eyes. "Well, that's not surprising."

"Why do you say that?" asked King.

"I won't beat around the bush. I wasn't John Bruno's biggest fan, although Bill worshiped the ground he walked on. Bill was almost twenty-five years older and acted as a mentor. Now, I'm not saying Bruno wasn't good at what he did, but let's put it this way: John Bruno always did what was in the best interests of John Bruno and everybody else be damned. As an example, he's twenty minutes from the body of his *mentor* and doesn't have the decency to stop his campaigning to come and pay his respects. Until, that is, he gets a phone call, allegedly from me? Well, that's all you need to know about John Bruno."

"I take it you wouldn't have voted for him for president," said King, smiling.

Martin laughed a deep, throaty laugh and put her hand on top of his. "Oh, honey, you're so damn cute I could just put you on my shelf and look at you all day." After she said this, she didn't remove her hand.

"You should get to know him first," said Joan dryly.

"I can hardly wait."

Joan said, "Did your dislike for John Bruno start at any particular time?"

Martin picked up her empty glass and crunched on an ice cube. "What do you mean by that?"

Joan looked down at some notes in front of her. "Around the time that your husband headed the U.S. Attorney's Office in Washington there were some irregularities resulting in a number of convictions being overturned and other prosecutions derailed. It was a pretty nasty business all around."

She lit another cigarette. "It was a long time ago. I don't really remember."

"I'm sure that if you think about it, it'll come back to you," suggested Joan firmly. "Perhaps you could refrain from any more drink? This is really very, very important."

"Hey," said King, "lay off. She's doing us a favor. She doesn't have to tell us anything."

Martin's hand returned to King's. "Thank you, honey."

Joan rose. "I tell you what: why don't you finish questioning her while I go have a cigarette and admire the *lovely* garden." She picked up Mildred's pack of cigarettes. "Mind if I poach one?"

"Go ahead, honey, why should I die alone?"

"Why indeed, *honey*?"

Joan stalked off, and King looked at Martin in an embarrassed fashion. "She can be a little abrupt."

"Abrupt? She's a cobra in heels and lipstick. Do you really work for her?"

"Yes. I'm actually learning a lot."

Mildred glared at Joan, who was tapping cigarette ash on a rose vine. "Just remember to keep your hand on your zipper when she's around, or you might wake up one morning missing something really important."

"I'll keep that in mind. Now, what she was talking about, the things in your husband's office, I could tell you had some definite thoughts about that, didn't you? In fact, your husband eventually resigned because of those irregularities, didn't he?"

Martin held her chin high, though her voice quivered. "He took the blame, because he was the boss and he was honorable. There aren't many men like Bill Martin anymore. Like old Harry Truman, the buck stopped with him. Either rightly or wrongly."

"Meaning he shouldered the blame though it really wasn't his fault?"

"I need another drink before I break another crown with all this damn ice," she said, starting to rise.

"You thought it was Bruno's fault, didn't you? He left D.C. before the hammer fell, ruined your husband's career and went on to head up the U.S. Attorney's Office in Philadelphia. And there he garnered a bunch of high-profile convictions and rode that to a lucrative private practice and eventually to a run for the White House."

"I see you've done your homework."

"But your husband remained an admirer, so he didn't share your belief, did he?"

She sat back down. "Bill was a good lawyer and an exceptionally bad judge of character. I have to hand it to Bruno; he said and did all the right things. Do you know that he called here to tell Bill he was running for president?"

King looked at her in surprise. "Really? When was that?"

"Couple of months ago. I answered the phone. Could have knocked me over with a stick hearing his voice. I wanted to give him a piece of my mind, but I didn't. I held my tongue. We chatted like two old friends. He told me all the great things he'd done, his wonderful life in Philadelphia society. It made me want to throw up. Then I gave the phone to Bill, and they talked for a while. All Bruno wanted to do was gloat and rub it in. Let Bill know he'd risen so much further than Bill ever had."

"I just assumed Bruno hadn't had any contact with either of you for years."

"Well, it was just the one phone call, and a damn irritating one at that."

"Did Bill say anything on the phone that might have led to Bruno's coming to see him at the funeral home?"

"No. Bill hardly talked at all. He was pretty weak even at that point. And I certainly didn't say anything to Bruno that would get him all agitated. Although I wanted to, believe me."

"About the stuff at the U.S. Attorney's Office?"

"Among other things."

"Did you ever have any proof?"

"Bruno was a lawyer, he covered his tracks well. His shit never stunk. He was long gone before it all came out."

"Well, I guess you're not really sorry he disappeared."

"John Bruno can go to hell. In fact, I hope he's already there."

King leaned forward, and this time he put his hand on top of hers. "Millie, this is really important. Despite your husband's autopsy being inconclusive, there is evidence that suggests he might have been poisoned, perhaps with methanol. You see, that method of poisoning would have been disguised in the embalming process. His death and his body's being at that funeral home started this whole thing rolling. Whoever took Bruno couldn't have left that to chance. Your husband had to be there at a certain time, meaning he had to die on a certain date."

"That's what the FBI said, but I'm telling you that no one could have been poisoning Bill. I would have known about it. I was with him every day."

"Just you? Your husband was very ill before he died. Did you have any help? Anyone who came by? Any medication that he took?"

"Yes. And the FBI took it all to analyze and found nothing. I ate the same food, drank the same water. And I'm fine."

King sat back and sighed. "Someone imperson-ated you at the funeral home."

"So I heard. Well, I look good in black; it goes well with my new hair color." She looked at King's half-empty glass. "Would you like another?" He shook his head. She said, "Bill was a Scotch man too, right up to the end. It was one of the few pleasures he had left. Kept his own stash of twenty-five-year-old Macallan's." She chuckled. "He had some every night. I'd just pour a shot in his feeding tube using a big syringe. Eating he could have cared less about, but he looked forward to his Scotch even through his belly, and the man made it to eighty, not bad."

"I bet you keep a good supply on hand."

She smiled. "At our age, what's left?"

King looked down at his glass. "How about you? Ever drink Scotch?"

"Never touch the stuff. Like I said, gin is my game. Scotch is too much like paint thinner. If you want to clear your sinuses out, by all means drink the stuff."

"Well, thanks again. We'll be in touch. Enjoy your evening." King rose and started to turn away. He looked over at Joan, her drink and cigarette in hand, and he froze.

Paint thinner?

He whirled back around. "Millie, can you show me Bill's special stash of Scotch?"

41

It was the Scotch, or at least Bill Martin's secret cache, that Mildred Martin had never bothered to tell the police or FBI about. A relatively simple test at the police lab showed the bottle had been doctored with methanol.

King and Joan sat at the police station while Mildred was thoroughly interrogated.

Joan looked at King. "You're lucky she poured yours out from her regular stock."

King shook his head. "How'd the poisoned bottle get into the house?"

A man in a brown suit walked up to them. "I think we found that out."

He was one of the FBI agents assigned to the case. Joan knew him well.

"Hello, Don," said Joan. "This is Sean King. Don Reynolds."

The men shook hands. "We owe you guys on this one," said Reynolds. "Never would have guessed the Scotch, although she didn't tell us about her husband's secret cache. We had the other stuff tested previously."

"It was Sean's catch actually. Though I hate to admit it," she added, smiling. "You said you know how the doctored Scotch got there?"

"A couple of months ago the Martins hired a woman to help around the house. To assist with Bill Martin, who was basically an invalid."

"Mildred never mentioned that either?" King said incredulously.

"She said she didn't think it was important. She said the woman never gave Bill any medication or anything, though she said she was licensed to. Mildred liked to do that herself. And the woman left long before Martin died, so Mildred didn't think it was relevant."

"Where'd the woman come from?"

"That was the thing. She just showed up one day, said she understood that they might need some help because of Bill's condition, that she was a professional caregiver and was willing to come cheap because she needed the work. She had papers and stuff to show who she was."

"And now where is this very accommodating lady?"

"She said she'd gotten a permanent job in another town, and that was it. Hasn't been back."

"Obviously she did come back," said Joan.

Reynolds nodded. "Our theory is the woman came back to the house the day before Martin died and doctored the bottle, to make sure his next drink would be his last. The bottle of Scotch we found was loaded with methanol. Now, methanol is slow to metabolize into toxic levels. You're looking at twelve to twenty-four hours. If he'd been young and healthy and been found immediately, maybe Martin could have made it to a hospital and survived. But he wasn't young or healthy; he was terminal, in fact. And the Martins also didn't sleep together. After Mildred gave her husband the last pop through his G-tube, the pain probably would have hit him very soon. And he only weighed about ninety pounds. Normally you'd need one hundred to two hundred milliliters of methanol to kill an adult. I doubt they needed anywhere near that to kill Martin."

Reynolds shook his head and smiled wearily. "It's ironic they put it in the Scotch. Scotch contains ethanol, which is an antidote to methanol, because they both seek the same enzyme. However, there was so much methanol in the bottle the ethanol couldn't have countered it. Martin might have called out in agony, but Mildred never heard him, or so she says. So he might have lain there all night until he finally died. It's not like he could get out of bed for help. He was a complete invalid by that time."

"Mildred was probably passed out on gin. She likes her libations too," said King.

Joan added, "And this nurse obviously had learned the routine of the house, that both of them drank and didn't sleep together. Once she learned he was a Scotch drinker and had his own stash, and also that Mildred never touched the stuff, she had her method of murder. She'd appear to be long gone before the deed was done."

Reynolds nodded. "He could have been killed any number of ways, but it had to be in a manner that wouldn't require an autopsy, because that would have messed up the timing. Martin had to die in his bed. So he did, and Mildred found him there and assumed he died naturally, although the docs tell me death by methanol is by no means peaceful. And methanol metabolizes into formaldehyde, which is toxic, but then it's oxidized into formic acid. That's six times more lethal than methanol."

"So Martin was basically pickled before he got to the funeral home," said King.

"That's right. According to Bruno's staff, their boss was scheduled to be in the area that day and the next at a number of events. The procedure at the funeral home was for a body to lie in the viewing area for a couple of days. Martin died on a Monday, and he went to the funeral home Monday night. His body was laid out on Wednesday and Thursday, with burial scheduled for Friday. Bruno came by on Thursday."

"Still tight timing," said Joan.

Reynolds shrugged. "Probably the best they could do. Otherwise, how else could they get him to the funeral home? They couldn't very well invite him to Martin's house. It was probably the funeral home or nothing. Sure it was risky but it worked."

"And none of the woman's background checked out, right?" said Joan.

Reynolds nodded. "To use a cliché, she's completely disappeared without a trace."

"Description?"

"Older woman, at least fifty, medium height, a little stout. She had mousy brown hair with some gray in it, though that could have been dyed. And get this: she told Mildred her name was Elizabeth Borden."

King exclaimed, "Elizabeth Borden, as in Lizzie Borden who gave her mother forty whacks?"

"And when she saw what she had done, she gave her father forty-one," added Joan.

"So we have some people with a real warped, macabre sense of humor," said Reynolds.

Joan eyed him intently. "Okay, they're intelligent killers who read their criminal history. They're still killers."

"Well, thanks again for your help. I don't know where this leads us, but it's more than we had before."

"What's going to happen to Mildred?" asked King.

Reynolds shrugged. "You can't arrest someone for being stupid; otherwise, you'd lock up at least half the population. Unless we dig up something incriminating, nothing will happen to her. But if she *was* in on it, seems like she'd have gotten rid of the Scotch." He turned to Joan. "I heard you were investigating Bruno's disappearance on behalf of the family. That's cool. I know you won't do anything stupid, and you've already found something we missed, so if you need something, just let me know."

"Funny you should mention that – I have a list right here," replied Joan.

As Joan and Reynolds talked business, King watched Mildred Martin emerge from the interrogation room. She didn't look like the same woman. Gregarious, salty, full of punch when he first met her, she now looked like she'd soon be joining her dead husband.

After Reynolds walked off, Sean looked at Joan. "Now where?" he asked.

"We go to the funeral home."

"The feds already picked that field clean."

"Yeah, just like they did with Mildred Martin. Besides, I like funeral homes. You hear the most delicious gossip about the dearly departed, usually from their *friends*."

"Joan, you really are a cynic."

"Admit it. It's one of my most attractive qualities."

42

The police dropped off Mildred Martin at her house and then left. Down the street, at the end of the block, a black sedan melded into the darkness, a pair of alert FBI agents inside.

The old woman staggered into the house and locked the door behind her. She needed a drink so badly. Why had she done what she'd done? It was all so perfect, and she'd gone and messed it up, but then she'd recovered. Yes, she had. Everything was okay. She reached for the gin and filled her tumbler, using barely any tonic.

She drank down half the glass; her nerves began to steady. It would be okay; everything was fine. She was old, what could the FBI really do to her? They had nothing really; she was going to be okay.

"Mildred, how are you?"

She dropped her tumbler and let out a shriek.

"Who's there?" She backed up against the liquor cabinet.

The man came forward a little but remained in the shadows.

"It's your old friend."

She squinted at him. "I don't know you."

"Of course you do. I'm the man who helped you kill your husband."

She lifted up her chin. "I did *not* kill Bill."

"Well, Mildred, the methanol you put in his body certainly did. And you made the phone call to Bruno, just like I asked you to."

She looked more closely. "That . . . that was you?"

He moved forward some more. "I let you get your revenge on John Bruno and become rich with life insurance in the bargain, and found a way for you to put your poor, sick husband out of his misery. And all I asked was for you to play by the rules. That was all I demanded and you've disappointed me."

"I don't know what you're talking about," she said in a quivering voice.

"The rules, Mildred. *My* rules. And those rules didn't include another trip to the police station and further interrogation by the FBI."

"It was those people who came here asking questions."

"Yes, King and Dillinger, I know. Go on," he said pleasantly.

"I . . . I was just talking to them. I told them what you said to say. About Bruno, I mean. Just like you said."

"You were obviously more than candid. Come now, Mildred, tell me everything."

The woman was shaking badly.

He said soothingly, "Calm down, pour yourself another drink."

She did so and downed it. "I . . . we were talking about Scotch. I told him Bill liked his Scotch, that's all. I swear."

"And you put the methanol in the bottle of Scotch?"

"Yes, in Bill's special Scotch. The Macallan's."

"Why did you do that, Mildred? We gave you the methanol. You were supposed to just put it in a syringe and shoot it into his feeding tube. Nice and simple. All you had to do was follow instructions."

"I know, but . . . I just couldn't do it that way. I couldn't. I wanted it to seem like I was just giving him his Scotch, just like regular. See? So I mixed it in the bottle and then put that into him."

"Fine, so afterwards why didn't you pour the Scotch down the sink, or throw out the bottle?"

"I was going to, but I was afraid somebody might

see me. I throw out lots of empty bottles of booze, but I also know some of my neighbors thought I'd killed Bill for the insurance money. They might go through my trash. And even if I washed out the bottle and even broke it into pieces the police can still find things from little bits of glass. I watch those TV forensic shows – I know! I figured it'd be better if I just left it where it was. And then I just didn't want to go near it. I . . . I was feeling guilty, about Bill." She started to quietly sob.

"But you mentioned it, and King and Dillinger put two and two together. Now, why couldn't you have just shown them the Scotch you have in that liquor cabinet there?"

"It wasn't Macallan's. I told that young man that Bill only drank Macallan's. I . . . I was scared. I told him I still had the bottle. It just slipped out. I mean, everything was going great and then he just yelled out, to show him the Scotch. I thought if I didn't show him the bottle, he might get suspicious."

"Undoubtedly they would have. My goodness, how very thorough you were in spilling everything to complete strangers."

"He was a real gentleman," she said defensively.

"I'm sure he was. So they took the bottle, and they analyzed it and found it was poisoned. What did you tell the police?"

Mildred looked pleased with herself. "I told them a woman, a nurse, came to the house, and I hired her to look after Bill. And that she was the one who put the poison in there. I even told them her name." She paused and added with a flourish, "Elizabeth Borden. Get it? Lizzie Borden." She cackled. "Smart, huh?"

"Amazing, and you thought of all this on the way to the police station?"

She gulped her drink, lit a cigarette and blew smoke out. "I've always been quick that way. I think I would have made a better lawyer than my husband."

"How did you say you paid for this woman's services?"

"Pay?"

"Yes, pay. You didn't tell them she worked for free, did you? One rarely finds such an accommodating soul in real life."

"Pay, oh, well, I told them . . . I mean, I was sort of vague on that."

"Really, and they didn't press the point?"

She flicked her ash onto the floor and shrugged. "No, they didn't. They believed what I said. I'm the old, grieving widow. So everything's just fine."

"Mildred, let me tell you what they're undoubtedly doing right now. They're accessing your bank records to determine how you paid 'Lizzie.' Your records won't reflect any such payments. Next they'll question your 'nosy' neighbors about this woman, and they'll say they never saw her, because she doesn't exist. And finally the FBI will be back to see you, and you can be certain that visit will be very unpleasant."

She looked worried. "You really think they'd check all that?"

"They're the FBI, Mildred. They're not stupid. Not stupid like you."

He stepped closer to her. She now saw what he was carrying: a metal pole.

She started to scream, but he lunged forward and stuffed a wad of cloth down her throat and wound duct tape around her mouth and hands. Gripping her by the hair, he pulled her down the hallway and pushed open a door. "I've taken the liberty of drawing a bath for you, Mildred. I want you nice and clean when you're found."

He dumped her in the full bathtub, and the water sloshed over the sides. She tried to pull herself out, but he pushed her back under with the pole. With the duct tape across her mouth, and her smoke-packed lungs, she lasted less than half the time Loretta Baldwin had. He grabbed a bottle of Scotch from the cabinet, poured the contents into the bath and then smashed it against her head. Lastly he ripped the tape off her mouth, opened it and stuffed it full of dollar bills he'd pulled from her purse.

Where does one have to go to get reliable help these days? Where!

He looked down at her and said, "Just be glad you're dead, Mildred. Just be glad you don't have to feel my rage right now, because it's right off the *scale!*"

When he made his plans, he had contemplated killing Mildred too but concluded it would have raised too much suspicion. That decision had come back to haunt him. Still, there was no way to track her culpability back to him. It would be clear, though, that the same hand had struck down both Loretta Baldwin and Mildred Martin. That would probably confuse the authorities more than it would assist them. He didn't like it yet it couldn't be helped now. He scornfully looked down at her. *Idiot woman!*

He left by the back door and looked toward the end of the street, where he knew the FBI was lurking. "Go get her, boys," he muttered. "She's all yours."

A few minutes later the old Buick started up and drifted down the road.

43

The private plane Joan had engaged was like an upscale club with wings and jet engines. It had mahogany paneling, leather seats, a TV, full galley, bar, accompanying steward and even a small bedroom, where Joan had gone to catch a nap. King remained in his seat, eventually dozing off. The funeral home had yielded nothing helpful. The plane was taking them to Washington, D.C. Joan had wanted to check some things at her office before heading out again.

As the plane began its final approach, Joan burst out of the bedroom. The steward called out to her, "Ma'am, you have to take your seat now—"

She gave him a withering look and kept running up the aisle.

She reached King, who was still asleep, and shook him.

"Sean, wake up. Now!"

He didn't budge. She straddled his legs, so that

she was on his lap face-to-face, and started to slap him. "Wake up, damn it!"

He finally came around, groggy. When he focused on her and saw she was sitting, barefoot, skirt hiked and thighs spread, across his lap, he said, "Christ, Joan, get off me. I'm not looking for membership in the mile-high club."

"You idiot. This is about Mildred Martin."

Sean sat up straight now, and she climbed off, taking a seat next to him and buckling up.

"So talk!" he demanded.

"You told me Mildred said that Bruno called recently to tell Bill Martin about his running for president? And that she talked to him too?"

"Right. So?"

"So you heard the woman's voice. It's like a foghorn. Are you telling me that if Bruno recently heard that voice that someone could have later called and impersonated her voice and he wouldn't have known the deception?"

King slapped his armrest. "That's right! I mean how do you do that voice unless you've been smoking and drinking for fifty years?"

"And have adenoids the size of golf balls."

"So she lied to us. She did call Bruno and asked him to come and see her at the funeral home."

Joan nodded. "And that's not all. I called Agent

Reynolds with the FBI. He wasn't exactly candid with us. They thought from the start that her story was phony. He's checking out something that will definitely tell us whether she was in on it or not. Now, the Martins didn't have a lot of money, so how could they afford a caregiver?"

"Well, I don't know. Maybe they could."

"Granted, they might have, but if they did, because of their age they're also entitled to some partial reimbursement under Medicare."

King quickly got it. "So Medicare would have a record of that. But if Mildred didn't file for that assistance, if she claimed she paid the woman out of her own pocket . . ."

She finished his thought. "Then her bank records will show that. That's what Reynolds is checking. When he asked her about payment to the woman to try to get an ID, Mildred waffled badly. He said nothing because he didn't want her to get suspicious. He has agents watching her street, far enough away so she won't get her radar up. He doesn't want her bugging out on us."

"So if all this is true, she may know who has Bruno."

As the plane landed and came to a stop, Joan's phone rang.

"Yes." She listened for a minute, said thank you,

clicked off and turned to King with a smile. "God, the FBI can work miracles sometimes. No Medicare filing, no checks to the caregiver and no cash withdrawals. And the kicker is, Bill Martin had a half-million-dollar life insurance policy. And Mildred is the sole beneficiary. Since Bill Martin had had the insurance policy for years, the FBI didn't think, by itself, it was a legitimate motive to kill him. After all, she just had to wait a few months and she'd get it anyway when he died. They're going to pick up Mildred. She made that call to Bruno, probably from a phone booth."

"I can't believe she'd kill her husband for money. She seemed so devoted to him."

"Sean, for all your intelligence and sophistication, sweetie, you really know shit about women."

———

44

When she reported to the Secret Service's field office in Washington, Michelle was told that she'd spend at least the next month chained to a desk.

"I have a couple of weeks of vacation accrued. I want to take it now, please," she told her superior. He shook his head.

"Why? It's not like I'm going to have any duties at the desk."

"Sorry, Mick, it's coming from higher up than me."

"Walter Bishop?"

"Sorry, can't say."

She went straight to Bishop's office to confront him. What did she have to lose?

His first words were not encouraging. "Get out!" he barked.

"Two weeks of vacation, Walter. I'm due it and I want to take it."

"You've got to be joking. I want you right here where I can keep an eye on you."

"I'm not a child. I don't need watching."

"Consider yourself lucky. And a piece of advice: stay away from Sean King."

"What, now you're picking my friends?"

"Friends? People keep dying around him. You almost got killed."

"So did he!"

"Really. That's not what I heard. He got a bump on the head. You almost got your neck wrung off."

"You're way off base, Walter."

"You know, when Ritter was killed, there were rumors King was paid off to look the other way."

"And then to kill the assassin. How does that make sense?"

"Who knows? But the fact is, look at his life now. He lives in some big house, making lots of money."

"Oh, yeah. What a brilliant plan of his to ruin his life."

."So maybe he ticked somebody off. Somebody he did a deal with eight years ago, and that person is exacting payment."

"That is so crazy."

"Is it? I think your judgment's been seriously clouded by a good-looking guy who's got all these bad things happening to him. Start thinking like a professional and maybe your vision will clear. In the meantime all you're going to be doing is getting splinters in your ass from sitting at a desk."

The phone rang and Bishop snatched it up.

"Yeah? What? Who did . . .?" Bishop's face turned very red. He slammed the phone down and didn't look at Michelle. "Go take your vacation," he said quietly.

"What? I don't understand."

"Join the club. And you can pick up your creds and gun on the way out. Now get the hell out of my office!"

Michelle left before the powers-that-be changed their minds.

In the same building that a puzzled Michelle was now leaving with her pistol and badge, a number of grim-looking men sat in a conference room. They collectively represented the Secret Service, FBI and U.S. Marshals Service. The man at the head of the table was putting down the phone.

"Okay, Maxwell is officially on vacation."

"Giving her enough rope to hang herself?" asked a man who was from the FBI.

"Maybe, maybe not." He looked at the other end of the table. "What's your take?"

Jefferson Parks put down his soda and thought about this question. "Well, let's look at what we have. Loretta Baldwin is maybe connected to Clyde Ritter's assassination. According to what King told the police, the gun he found in her backyard might have been one Loretta saw somebody hide in the supply closet at the Fairmount. She was blackmailing that person and he eventually killed her."

The man at the head of the table was the director of the Secret Service, and he didn't look happy with this theory. "That might mean Arnold Ramsey didn't act alone in killing Ritter."

The FBI agent said, "How about Sean King's being the guy who killed Loretta? She might have been blackmailing *him*. Then he finds out who she is from Maxwell and kills her. He digs up the gun and conveniently loses it."

Parks shook his head. "King has an alibi for when Loretta was killed. And why would he have needed to hide a gun in the closet of the hotel? He killed Arnold Ramsey. And when the gun was taken from him and Maxwell, he was injured and Maxwell was almost killed. And King's life has been pretty messed up by all this."

"So you think he's innocent?"

Parks sat up straight. He'd lost his laid-back, country-boy demeanor, and his voice was crisp.

"No, I don't necessarily think that. I've been doing this long enough to know when someone's not being straight with me. He's hiding something. I just don't know what it is. I do have one theory. Maybe he was involved in Ritter's assassination somehow and covered up his tracks by killing Ramsey."

Now the director shook his head. "How does that work exactly? What could Ramsey offer in the way of payment? He was a college professor at a second-rate school. And I'm assuming King wouldn't have turned traitor for free or on some political principle."

"Well, we don't really know King's political beliefs, do we? And all of you have seen the video. He wasn't even watching Ritter."

"He said he just zoned out."

Parks didn't look convinced. "He *says*. But what if he was intentionally distracted?"

"If he had been, he would have told us."

"Not if he was covering for someone, and not if he was involved from the get-go. And you want to talk payment, okay. How many enemies do you think Clyde Ritter had? How many powerful folks from the other parties would have loved to see him out of the race? You think they wouldn't have paid a few million to have King look the other way? So he takes the heat for a while for being 'distracted,' and then he goes off with his millions and lives the good life."

"Okay, but where are all these millions?"

"He lives in a big house, drives a nice car, has a nice comfy life," countered Parks.

"He won a libel settlement," said the director. "And it was for a nice chunk of change. And I couldn't blame the guy, for all the shit they were saying about him. It's not like he was some screwup. He'd won just about every award the Service has to give. He'd been wounded twice in the line of fire."

"Fine, he was a good agent. Good agents turn bad sometimes. But as for the money, he mixes the settlement money in with the money he was paid, and who's to know the difference? Have you audited his finances?"

The director sat back, not looking too confident now.

'And how exactly does this play out with the Bruno kidnapping?" asked the FBI agent. "Aren't you saying they're connected?"

"Well, for that matter," said Parks, "how does it tie into my guy Howard Jennings?"

"Let's not overcomplicate things. There may be no connection at all," said the FBI agent. "We might have three separate cases: Ritter, Bruno and your WITSEC murder."

"All I know is that King and Maxwell keep turning up in the middle of it all," said the director. "Look at it this way: eight years ago King either messed up or turned traitor, and we lost a presidential candidate. Now Maxwell screws up and the exact same result happens."

"Not exactly the same," Parks pointed out. "Ritter was shot on the spot, Bruno was kidnapped."

The director sat forward in his chair. "Well, the purpose of this hastily formed task force is to figure out this mess as quickly as possible and hope and pray it doesn't become some enormous scandal. And you, Parks, you're already in the loop with them, so just keep doing what you're doing."

"The other variable is Joan Dillinger," said Parks. "I can't read that woman."

The director smiled. "You're not the first person to say that."

"No, it's more than that. I had a recent conversation with her, and she was saying some strange things. Like she owed Sean King. For what, she wouldn't say. But she was working real hard to convince me he was innocent."

"Well, not so unusual – they were colleagues."

"Right, and maybe something more. And they were *both* on the Clyde Ritter detail, weren't they?" said Parks, letting the question hang out there.

The director's brow was now very furrowed. "Joan Dillinger was one of the best agents we've ever had."

"Right, and now she's with some big-shot private firm. And she's investigating the kidnapping of John Bruno, and if she finds him, I bet the lady gets an enormous payday. And I found out she's asked King to help her in the investigation, and I doubt he's doing it for free." He paused and then added, "Of course, it's easy to find someone if you already know where he is."

"Meaning what?" said the director sharply. "That two former Secret Service agents kidnapped a presidential candidate and are now looking to be paid a fortune to recover him?"

"Yeah, meaning that," said Parks bluntly. "I'm assuming I'm not here to sugarcoat things and tell you what you want to hear. I'm not real good at that. I can send you another marshal who can if you want."

"And you think Howard Jennings was killed by King?" said the director angrily.

"I really don't know. What I do know is, King's gun matched and he was in the vicinity with no real alibi."

"Pretty stupid for a man plotting murder."

"Or pretty smart, because maybe a judge and a

jury thinks the same thing and believes he was set up."

"And the motive for killing Jennings?"

"Well, if King and Dillinger plotted to kidnap Bruno, and Jennings stumbled on that plot while working for King, I think that might be a motive for murder."

The men were all silent for a few minutes until the director broke the quiet with a long sigh. "Well, we have them all on our radar now. King, Maxwell and Dillinger – a most unlikely triumvirate when you think about it. Get back out in the field and keep us informed."

Parks looked around at them. "All right, but don't expect results overnight. And don't expect only the results you may want."

"Right now," said the director, "I think we're just waiting for the other shoe to drop." As Parks turned to leave, the director added, "Marshal, when that other shoe does drop, just make sure you're not under it."

In the parking garage Parks saw the woman getting into her vehicle.

"Agent Maxwell," he said. Michelle stepped back

out of her truck. "I hear you're taking some much-needed vacation."

She looked at him strangely, and then realization spread across her features. "Did you have something to do with that?"

"Where are you headed? Wrightsburg?"

"Why do you want to know?"

"How's your neck?"

"Fine. I'll be able to scream in no time. You didn't answer my question. Are you the reason they let me walk?"

"Maybe, though I feel more like a pawn than a full-fledged reason. If you're going to Wrightsburg, I'd like to hitch a ride."

"Why?"

"You're a smart lady, I think you know the answer to that."

As they climbed into her truck, Parks said, "It looks like you and Sean King have really struck up a friendship."

"I like him and respect him."

"Almost got you killed, though."

"That was hardly his fault."

"Yeah, I suppose so."

The way he said it made Michelle glance sharply at him, but the lawman was already looking out the window.

45

Joan and King were staying at a hotel in Washington when Joan received the news about Mildred Martin's murder. She called King's room and told him.

"Damn it," he exclaimed. "There goes another potential witness."

"And you know what this means, Sean."

"Yes, whoever killed Loretta Baldwin killed Mildred Martin." He added sarcastically, "Unless you buy that two different killers would murder their victims in the exact same way."

"So it's confirmed. She *was* lying. She made the call to Bruno. She poisoned her husband, and the Lizzie Borden stuff was made up. So why kill her?"

Neither one of them had the answer to that.

It was late morning when they drove back to Wrightsburg. By prearrangement they met Parks and Michelle at King's house for lunch.

Michelle and Parks had brought carryout Chinese,

and they all gathered on the rear deck to eat and discuss the case.

"Figured you two would be really hungry from all your detective work," said Parks as he pushed sweet-and-sour chicken into his mouth. "Heard from the FBI that you been burning up the frequent flier mileage on this Bruno thing."

"A lot of miles and not a lot of results," answered King.

Joan took a few minutes to bring them up to date on their investigations and interviews with Mildred Martin and Catherine Bruno as well as their non-interview with Sidney Morse.

"Sounds like Peter Morse hit the jackpot," said Michelle. "I wonder where he is?"

"My bet wouldn't be Ohio," said King. "I'm thinking a tiny island in the sun."

"Sounds wonderful," said Joan. "I'd love to try it."

Parks looked at some notes and then said, "Okay, Michelle filled me in on your talks with Ramsey's buddy at Atticus College, Horst?"

"Jorst," corrected Michelle.

"Right. And it didn't look like he could shed much light on anything."

"Ramsey obviously had a problem with Clyde Ritter," said King.

"Just political," asked Parks, "or something more?"

King shrugged. "Ramsey was a Vietnam War protester, a Berkeley-educated turbocharged radical, at least in his youth. Ritter was a former TV preacher and as conservative as Ramsey was liberal. Hell, if Ritter had had a gun, he probably would have shot Ramsey first!"

"I believe Thornton Jorst is worth another look," said Michelle. "Everything he told us made sense — too much sense, as though he were filling in the numbers for us, telling us exactly what he thought we came to hear. And there was something about his demeanor that wasn't quite right."

"Interesting," said Joan as she sipped her tea.

"And we're going to follow up with Kate Ramsey as soon as she gets back to Richmond," Michelle added.

"What happened to your reassignment?" asked King.

"They turned it into vacation instead."

Joan said, "My, I don't remember the Service being that accommodating."

"I think the good marshal here had something to do with it."

They all stared at a very uncomfortable-looking Parks.

He put down his chopsticks and took a swig of wine. "Good stuff."

"It should be," said King.

"Expensive?"

"Price often has little to do with how good a wine is. That bottle is maybe twenty-five dollars, and you'd be hard put to find a better Bordeaux at three times the price."

"You really have to educate me on this, Sean. It's so impressive," said Joan before her gaze fell fully upon Parks. "So, Jefferson, this rescue of Agent Maxwell you orchestrated. To what do we owe this magnanimous gesture?"

Parks cleared his throat. "Okay, I'll just lay it out for you. How's that? I'm not much into covert shit."

"Sounds yummy," she said. "I'm all ears."

"Joan, give it a rest," said King. "Go ahead," he told Parks.

"There's been a task force formed among the FBI, Secret Service and the Marshals. Its purpose is to figure out what the hell is going on with the Bruno disappearance, the murder of Howard Jennings, Susan Whitehead, Loretta Baldwin and most recently Mildred Martin. From the deaths of

Baldwin and Martin we know they were killed by the same person or persons."

Michelle said, "Right, this is Logic 101. Baldwin goes with Ritter, and Martin goes with Bruno. Therefore, if Baldwin and the Martins' deaths are connected somehow, Ritter and Bruno must be connected too."

"Maybe," said Parks warily. "I'm not running to any conclusions right now."

King left for a minute. When he returned, he handed Parks a piece of paper. It was the copy of the message he'd found pinned to Susan Whitehead's body. King glanced over at Joan, who flinched and then immediately rose and proceeded to read the note over Parks's shoulder.

Parks finished and looked up. "I heard about this note from the fibbies. So what's your take?"

"That maybe I'm at the center of all this somehow," King said.

"Pushing a post and giving feet?" said Parks.

"Secret Service parlance," said Michelle.

"It sounds like a revenge note to me," concluded Parks.

"And it concerns the Ritter assassination," said Joan.

"Ramsey hit his target. And Sean killed Ramsey,"

said Parks. "So who's left to take out revenge?" he added suspiciously.

"Keep in mind the gun in Loretta's backyard," said King. "Maybe there were two assassins there that day. I killed one of them, and the other one got away until Loretta started blackmailing him. If I'm reading the tea leaves right, the guy is on the scene now, and Loretta paid the ultimate price for her scheme. As did Mildred Martin when she messed up on the Bruno end of things."

Parks shook his head. "So that guy's coming after you? Why now? And why involve Bruno and the Martins? That's going to a lot of trouble. Don't take this the wrong way, but if this psycho wanted to pay you back, he could have killed you the other night when Michelle almost had her neck snapped."

"I don't think they wanted Sean to die that night," said Joan. She looked at Michelle. "They clearly didn't feel the same about you."

One of Michelle's hands went to her throat. "That's comforting."

"I'm not in the habit of making people comfortable," said Joan. "It's usually such a waste of time."

Parks sat back in his chair. "Okay, let's just suppose that Bruno and Ritter are somehow tied together. That accounts for the Martin murders and Loretta Baldwin too. Susan Whitehead's murder might have just been a way for the killer to put an exclamation point on the note left with you, Sean. But how does Howard Jennings tie into all this?"

"He worked for me," said King, putting aside for now his gut instinct that Parks's agenda was broader than merely finding Jennings's killer. "Maybe that's enough. I think Susan Whitehead was killed merely because the killer spotted her with me, maybe on the morning I discovered Jennings's body. He wanted to leave me that note, and decided to include a body with it as a sick way of making a point."

"I'd buy that if Jennings were just one of your neighbors. But he was a WITSEC."

King said, "Okay, how about this? Jennings goes into my office late that night for some reason, to catch up on some work, and he stumbles on this maniac going through my office. And he gets popped for his troubles."

Parks rubbed his chin and looked unconvinced while Joan nodded thoughtfully.

"That's plausible," she said. "But let's get back to the revenge angle. Revenge against Sean for what? Allowing Ritter to die?"

"Maybe our killer is some nut from Ritter's political party," said Michelle.

"Well, if so, he's held a long grudge," said King.

"Think, Sean, there must be someone," urged Joan.

"I didn't really know many of the Ritter people. Just Sidney Morse, Doug Denby – and maybe a couple of others."

"Morse is institutionalized," said Joan. "We saw that for ourselves. He catches tennis balls. He couldn't mastermind something like this."

"And besides," said King, "if the person we're after is the same guy who hid the gun in the supply closet and then was blackmailed by Loretta and then killed her, that person couldn't be someone backing Ritter's candidacy."

"You mean he would have been killing his own golden goose?" said Parks.

"Right. That's why we can rule out Sidney Morse even if he weren't a vegetable, and Doug Denby too. They'd have no motive."

Michelle suddenly looked excited. "What about Bob Scott, the detail leader?"

"But that doesn't make any sense either," said King. "Scott wouldn't have had to hide his gun. No one would have searched him. And even if they did, it would have been strange finding him not armed."

Michelle shook her head. "No, I meant his career, like yours, was ruined when Ritter died. That could

370

be a motive for revenge. Does anybody even know where he is?"

"We can find out," said Joan.

King scowled. "But that doesn't explain the gun I found and why Loretta was killed. She was killed because she was blackmailing someone. And that someone couldn't have been Bobby Scott because he'd have no reason to hide a gun."

Parks said, "Okay, Scott looks to be a strikeout. But let's go back to this Denby guy. Who was he?"

Joan said, "Clyde Ritter's chief of staff."

"Any idea where he is now?" asked Parks.

"No," said Joan. She looked at King. "How about you?"

"I haven't seen Denby since Ritter died. He pretty much dropped off the planet. It wasn't like any of the major parties would be picking him up. I imagine he was pretty much a pariah after partnering with Ritter."

"I know it seems highly unlikely given their respective ideologies, but could Denby and Arnold Ramsey have known each other?" wondered Michelle.

"Well, it's something we should check out," voiced Parks.

"Our suspect list is growing exponentially,"

commented Joan. "And we're not even sure if these multiple lines of investigation are even connected."

King nodded. "There are a lot of possibilities. If we're going to crack this thing, we have to work together. I think I can speak for the marshal and Michelle, but are you in?" he asked Joan.

She smiled demurely. "Of course. So long as everyone clearly understands that my participation is a paid engagement."

46

They laid the wires out in precise lengths and then connected them to the explosives, all of which were located at load-bearing points. They worked slowly and methodically, for at this juncture there was no room for error.

"Wireless detonators are a lot easier to work with," said "Officer Simmons" to the other man. "And we wouldn't have to carry all this damn cable."

The Buick Man stopped what he was doing and turned to look at him. They each wore battery-powered lights attached to plastic helmets, since the darkness here was complete. They could have been far underground where no light ever reached.

"And like cell phones versus hard line, they are unreliable, particularly as the signals would have to penetrate thousands of tons of concrete. Just do what you're told."

"Just voicing an opinion," said Simmons.

"I don't need any more opinions, especially from

you. You've been more than enough trouble. I thought you were a professional."

"I *am* a professional."

"Then start acting like one! I've had enough of amateurs running around not following my instructions."

"Well, Mildred Martin won't be doing any more running. You saw to that."

"Yes, and let that be a lesson to you."

The heavy-duty portable generator was set up in the corner, and Buick Man started going over its controls, lines and fuel tanks.

Simmons said, "You sure that'll give us all the power we need? I mean for everything you've got planned? That'll take a lot of juice."

Buick Man didn't even bother to look at him. "More than enough. Unlike you, I know exactly what I'm doing." He pointed with a wrench to a large coil of electrical wire. "Just make sure the lines are strung properly. To every location I gave you."

"And you'll double-check my work, of course."

"Of course," he replied tersely.

Simmons looked at the elaborate control board that was set up in the far corner of the room. "This is some nice stuff. The best, in fact."

"Just wire it the way I told you," Buick Man said curtly.

"What's a party without lights and sound, right?"

They started wheeling in the heavy boxes on hand trucks, unpacking these containers and stacking the contents neatly in another corner of the cavernous space.

The younger man looked at one of the items from the boxes. "You did a good job on these."

"They needed to be as accurate as possible. I don't like imprecision."

"Yeah, don't I know that."

While lifting a container Simmons suddenly grimaced and clutched at his side.

The Buick Man observed this and said, "That's what you get for trying to strangle Maxwell instead of simply shooting her. Didn't you ever consider that a Secret Service agent might be armed?"

"I like my victims to know my presence. It's just *my* way."

"While working for me you'll subvert your ways to mine. You're lucky the bullet just nicked you."

"I suppose you would have just left me to die if the bullet had done serious damage?"

"No. I would have shot you and put you out of your misery."

Simmons stared at his companion for a long moment. "I bet you would have."

"Yes, I would have."

"Well, we got the gun back, that's the important thing."

Buick Man stopped working and looked at him steadily. "Maxwell frightens you, doesn't she?"

"I'm not afraid of any man, much less a woman."

"She almost killed you. In fact, it's only by sheer luck that you escaped."

"I won't miss next time."

"See that you don't. Because if you do miss, I certainly won't miss you."

47

The following morning the group split up. Joan went off to Dobson, Tyler, the Philadelphia law firm where Bruno had worked, and also to interview Bruno's political staff. Parks set off too, though he didn't tell the others he was going to report in to the task force back in Washington.

Before they all parted, Michelle pulled Joan aside.

"You were part of Ritter's detail. What do you recall about Scott?"

"Not much. I was a recent transfer to Ritter's detail. I didn't know him all that well. And after the assassination we were all reassigned pretty much immediately."

"Recent transfer? Did you ask for it?" She stared pointedly at the other woman.

"Most things in life worth having are rarely handed to you. You have to go after them." Michelle involuntarily glanced at King, who was talking to Parks. Joan smiled. "I see you follow my logic precisely. One piece of advice while you're out sleuthing with Sean: he has a terrific nose for investigative work but can be impetuous at times. Follow his lead but watch over him too."

"Not to worry," said Michelle, and she started to walk away.

"Oh, and Michelle, I was very serious when I implied these people we're looking for don't care whether you live or die. So while you're covering Sean's back, don't forget to watch your own. I wouldn't want anything to happen to you. I can see that Sean is quite fond of having you around."

Michelle turned back around. "Well, some of us are lucky, aren't we?"

As Joan was driving off in her car, she placed a call to her office staff.

"I need all the background on and present whereabouts of Robert C. Scott, former Secret Service agent and detail leader for Clyde Ritter in 1996, and also on a man named Doug Denby, who was Ritter's chief of staff. And I need it ASAP."

King and Maxwell drove to Richmond to see Kate Ramsey, who'd returned to VCU and agreed to meet with them. The Center for Public Policy was on Franklin Street in the heart of Virginia Commonwealth University's downtown campus. The center was located in a beautifully refurbished brownstone. The street was filled with such houses, which represented the old wealth of a bygone era in Virginia's capital city.

Kate Ramsey met them in the reception area and led them back to a private office that was filled with books and papers, posters detailing various protests and other activities as well as music posters and assorted sports equipment befitting a youthful scholar.

Looking at the clutter, King whispered to Michelle that she must be feeling right at home and caught an elbow in the ribs.

Kate Ramsey was of medium height and had the build of a runner, with tight, lean muscles. Four different pairs of jogging shoes in the corner of her office confirmed this observation. Her hair was blond and tied back in a ponytail. Her clothes were college standard issue: faded jeans, sneakers and an Abercrombie & Fitch short-sleeved shirt. She seemed poised beyond her years and regarded them both with a very frank expression as she sat across from them at her desk.

"Okay, Thornton already called me, so you can just ditch the story about doing a documentary on political assassins."

"We weren't very good at that anyway," said Michelle. "And the truth is just a lot easier, isn't it?" she bluntly shot back.

Kate's gaze shifted to King, who looked back at her nervously. He had, after all, killed the woman's father. What was he supposed to say? *I'm sorry?*

The young woman said, "You've aged pretty well. Looks like the years have been good to you."

"Not recently. That's why we're here, Kate. I can call you Kate, can't I?"

The young woman sat back. "It *is* my name, *Sean.*"

"I know this is incredibly awkward."

She cut in. "My father made choices. He killed the man you were guarding. *You* really had no choice." She paused and drew a long breath. "It's been eight years. I won't lie to you and say I didn't hate you back then. I was a girl of fourteen, and you'd taken my father away."

"But now," said Michelle.

Kate's gaze remained on King. "Now I'm a grown woman and things are a lot clearer. You did what you had to do. And so have I."

"I guess you didn't have much choice in the matter either," commented King.

She leaned forward and started moving things around on her desk. King noted that she placed the pieces – a pencil, a ruler and other objects – at ninety-degree angles, then started over again. Her hands just kept moving, even as her gaze remained on King and Michelle.

"Thornton said there was new evidence indicating my father hadn't acted alone. What new evidence?"

"We can't tell you," said Michelle.

"Oh, that's great. You can't tell me, but you expect me to talk to you."

"If there was someone else involved that day, Kate, it's important we know who it was," said King. "I'd think you'd want that too."

"Why? It's not like it'll change the facts. My father shot Clyde Ritter. There were a hundred eyewitnesses."

"That's true," said Michelle, "but now we believe there's more to it."

Kate leaned back in her chair. "So what exactly do you want from me?"

"Anything you can tell us about the events leading up to your father's assassinating Clyde Ritter," said Michelle.

"He didn't suddenly come in one day and announce he was going to become a killer, if that's what you're wondering. I was only a kid at the time, but I still would have called someone about that."

"Would you?" said King.

"What's that supposed to mean?"

King shrugged. "He was your father. Dr. Jorst said you loved him. Maybe you wouldn't have called anybody."

"Maybe I wouldn't have," Kate said casually, then started shifting the pencil and ruler around again.

"Okay, let's assume he didn't announce his intentions. How about anything else? Did your father say anything that seemed suspicious or out of the ordinary?"

"My father had the veneer of a brilliant college professor but underneath was an unreformed radical still living in the sixties."

"Meaning what exactly?"

"That he was prone to saying outrageous things that could be construed as suspicious."

"Okay, let's get down to something more tangible. Any idea where he got the gun he used to shoot Ritter with? That was never traced."

"I was asked all that years ago. I didn't know then and I don't know now."

"All right," said Michelle. "How about anybody coming around in the weeks leading up to the Ritter shooting? Anybody you didn't know?"

"Arnold had few friends."

King cocked his head at her. "He's *Arnold* now?"

"I think I have the right to call him whatever I want."

"So he had few friends. Any potential assassins lurking in there?" asked Michelle.

"That's hard to say, since I didn't know Arnold was one. Assassins don't tend to broadcast their intent, do they?"

"Sometimes they do," responded King. "Dr. Jorst said that your father would come in and rant and rave to him about Clyde Ritter and how he was destroying the country. Did he ever do that around you?"

In response Kate stood and went to the window that looked out on Franklin Street, where cars and bikes drifted by and students sat on the steps of the building.

"What does it all matter now? One assassin, two, three, a hundred! Who gives a shit?" She turned and stared at them, her arms stubbornly folded over her bosom.

"Maybe you're right," said King. "Then again, it might explain why your father did what he did."

"He did what he did because he hated Clyde Ritter and everything he stood for," she said vehemently. "He never quite lost that drive to rock the establishment."

Michelle looked at some of the political posters

on her walls. "Professor Jorst told us you're following in your father's footsteps as far as 'rocking the establishment.' "

"Lots of things my father did were good and worthy. And what reasonable person wouldn't detest a man like Clyde Ritter?"

"Unfortunately you'd be surprised," said King.

"I read all the reports and stories that came out afterwards. I'm surprised no one did a TV movie about it. I guess it wasn't important enough."

King said, "A man can hate someone and not choose to kill him. By all accounts your father was a passionate man who firmly believed in certain causes, and yet he'd never engaged in any violent act before." At this Kate Ramsey seemed to twitch slightly. King noticed but continued his line of thought. "Even during the Vietnam War when he was young and angry and might have picked up a gun and shot someone, Arnold Ramsey chose not to. So given that history, your *father*, a tenured professor in middle age with a daughter he loved, could plausibly have made the choice not to violently act on his hatred of Ritter. But he might have if another factor was involved."

"Like what?" Kate asked sharply.

"Like someone else, someone he respected, asking him to. Asking him to join in killing Ritter, in fact."

"That's impossible. My father was the only one who shot Ritter."

"What if the other person got cold feet and didn't shoot?"

Kate sat down at her desk, her nimble fingers once more playing their geometric games with the pencil and ruler.

"You have evidence of that?" she asked without looking up.

"What if we did? Would it jog your memory? Does it bring anyone to mind?"

Kate started to say something, then stopped and shook her head.

King glanced at a photo on the shelf and went over and picked it up. It was of Kate and her mother, Regina. It must have been a more recent picture than the one they'd seen in Jorst's office, since Kate looked to be about nineteen or twenty. Regina was still a very lovely woman, but there was something in her eyes, a weariness that probably symbolized her life's tragic circumstances.

"I take it you miss your mother."

"Of course, I do. What sort of question is that?" Kate reached over and took the photo from him and put it back on the shelf.

"I understand they were separated at the time of his death?"

"Yeah, so? Lots of marriages break up."

"Any ideas why your parents' did?" asked Michelle.

"Maybe they'd grown apart. My dad was a borderline socialist. My mom was a Republican. Maybe that was it."

"Yet that was nothing new, was it?" said King.

"Who knows for sure? They didn't really talk about it that much. In her youth my mother was apparently some fabulous actress with a wonderful future. She gave up that dream to marry my dad and support his career. Maybe she came to regret that decision. Maybe she thought she'd wasted her life. I don't really know, and at this point I don't really care."

"Well, I guess she was depressed about Arnold's death. Maybe that's why she committed suicide."

"Well, if that was the reason, she waited years to get around to doing it."

"So you think it was something else?" asked King.

"I really haven't given it much thought, okay!"

"I don't believe that. I'm betting you think about it all the time, Kate."

One of her hands flew to her eyes. "The interview is over. Get out!"

As they walked down Franklin Street to Michelle's truck, King said, "She knows something."

"Yes, she does," agreed Michelle. "The question is, how do we get it out of her?"

"She's pretty mature for her age. But she's also got a lot wrapped up in that head of hers."

"I wonder how close Thornton Jorst and Kate are? He gave her the heads-up about us pretty fast."

"I was wondering that myself. I'm not thinking a romantic relationship."

"More like a surrogate father?" she suggested.

"Maybe. And dads will do a lot to protect their daughters."

"So what do we do now?" asked Michelle.

"We've clearly shaken up Kate Ramsey. Let's see where she might lead us."

48

Joan learned some interesting things about John Bruno from the support staff at his Philadelphia law firm. None of them had much good to say about Catherine Bruno.

"Nose stuck so far up in the air it's a wonder she doesn't drown when it rains," said one secretary about the blue-blooded Mrs. Bruno.

Joan cornered another woman at the law firm who'd also worked with Bruno during his stint as a prosecutor in Washington. The woman remembered Bill and Mildred Martin and had read of their deaths.

"An unlikely person to be murdered," said the woman with a frightened expression. "Bill was so sweet and trusting."

Joan pounced on this. "Trusting, yes, he was trusting. Even when he shouldn't have been perhaps."

"Well, I don't like telling tales outside of school."

"We're both grown; we can tell tales wherever

and whenever we want," Joan prompted. "Especially if it helps in the cause of justice and other things."

The woman remained silent.

"So you actually worked for both Bill Martin and Bruno at the U.S. Attorney's Office in Washington?"

"Yes. Yes, I did."

"And what was your impression of them?"

"Bill was too nice for his position. We all said that, never to his face, of course. As for Bruno, his personality fit his job perfectly, if you ask me."

"Tough, ruthless. Not above bending the rules to get results?"

The woman shook her head. "No, I wouldn't say that. He was tough, but I never knew him to cross the line."

"And yet I read that there were a lot of problems in the U.S. Attorney's Office back then."

"There were. Like I said, Bill Martin was too nice sometimes. Some of the prosecutors did cross the line. But let me tell you, a lot of the police officers back then were doing it. There were shakedowns all the time. During the protests in the late sixties and early seventies, I recall dozens of cases of officers fabricating evidence, making arrests for nonexistent crimes, intimidating people, blackmailing them. It was bad, real bad. A disgrace."

"And yet you're saying Bruno didn't participate in any of that?"

"Well, if he did, I certainly didn't know about it."

"Did you know Bill Martin's wife, Mildred?"

"A piece of work, that one. Always wanted to live beyond her means. She wasn't a fan of Bruno's, I can tell you that."

"So I gathered. Then it wouldn't surprise you if she bad-mouthed Bruno, made up lies about him?"

"Not at all. She was like that. She wanted her husband to be this hard-charging man of justice, secretly hoping it would take him, and her, to the big time, meaning big money. Now, Bill wasn't like that. Bruno *was*. I think she was jealous."

Joan sat back and digested this new information slowly. She studied the woman closely. She appeared to be telling the truth. If she was, this changed things.

"Would it surprise you if Mildred was involved somehow in either her husband's death or perhaps Bruno's disappearance?"

"It would about Bill. I really think she loved him. But about Bruno?" She shrugged. "Mildred could be vindictive as hell."

"Meaning what exactly?"

"That given the opportunity, she might have shot him and not thought twice about it."

Joan flew back to Virginia and picked up her car. As she was about to head out of the airport, her phone rang. It was her office, reporting back on her inquiry about the whereabouts of Bob Scott and Doug Denby. The report was startling. The magnificent Agency, with all its expensive resources and high-level contacts, couldn't find Bob Scott. About a year ago the former Secret Service agent had seemingly dropped off the planet. They'd traced him to Montana, where he'd apparently been living off the land. After that, nothing had been heard of him. He'd been divorced for years, was childless, and his ex-wife was remarried and knew nothing about her former husband's whereabouts. The Agency had also checked with sources at the Secret Service, but even they could offer no help. The pension payment checks sent to the Montana address had been returned over the past year.

Doug Denby had been easier to track. He'd returned to his native Mississippi after inheriting considerable property and money and was currently enjoying life as a country squire far from the bare-knuckled sphere of politics. He clearly wasn't running around killing people.

Joan clicked off her phone and was about to pull out onto the highway when the phone rang again. It was Jefferson Parks.

"Let me tell you," said the deputy marshal, "you still got a lot of admirers at the Secret Service. All I heard was how great you are. Made me want to puke."

Joan laughed. "I have that effect on lots of men."

"So any luck?"

"None so far. Bruno's law and campaign offices were pretty much dead ends."

"What are you going to do now?"

"I'm not sure. I've had no luck tracking down Bob Scott. There's been no trace of the guy from about a year ago."

"Okay, look, I know we're just a little old under-funded federal law enforcement agency, and we don't have the fancy stuff you folks have in the private sector, but how about I try to track down this guy from my end."

"Whatever you do will be very appreciated," remarked Joan pleasantly.

"But King doesn't seem to think this guy could be involved. Sure, Scott might be ticked at King for what happened. But he had no reason to kill Ritter and ruin his career. And then there's the gun thing."

"I've been thinking about that. Sean told me that the gun he found in Loretta's backyard was a snub-nose .38 revolver."

"So?"

"That's not Secret Service standard issue. So while it might not be suspicious for Scott to be armed, it *would* be suspicious if he was carrying *two* weapons, particularly a snub-nose, in case someone did check."

Parks wasn't convinced. "But why have two guns? If his plan was to shoot Ritter too, he could have used his own gun."

"What if another would-be assassin, Ramsey's partner, got cold feet, didn't fire and slipped the gun to the inside man, Bob Scott, to get rid of, thinking no one would suspect him. Then maybe Scott became nervous because he now had *two* guns, hid it in the closet, and that's when Loretta saw him."

"And Loretta started her blackmail scheme. Okay, that would give Scott the incentive to kill her. But Ritter's death wiped out Scott's career. Why would he do it?"

Joan sighed. "Why do anything? Money! And the fact that he's disappeared doesn't exactly reinforce his innocence."

"What more do you know about him?"

"Vietnam vet before he joined the Service. Maybe he was carrying some baggage from that. He was sort of gun-happy too. He might have flipped to the dark side. See, that was never fully explored. It was officially concluded Ramsey acted alone. We're the first people to really look at all the angles."

"Well, I guess it's about damn time. I'll call you if I hear anything. You going back to King's place?"

"Yes, or at the inn where I'm staying near there, the Cedars."

"Catch you later," said Parks.

Joan drove off, very much lost in thought.

So much lost in thought that Joan didn't notice the car following her, or the driver whose gaze was locked intently on her.

49

Dressed in a warm-up suit, Kate Ramsey finally left her office in the late afternoon, climbed into a VW bug and drove off. Michelle and King followed at a discreet distance as the VW drove to Bryan Park, on the outskirts of Richmond. Once there, Kate climbed out, stripped off her warm-up suit, revealing shorts and a long-sleeved T-shirt underneath. She did some quick stretching and took off running.

"Great," said King. "She could be meeting somebody, and we won't be able to see a damn thing."

"Yes, we will." Michelle climbed into the backseat of the truck.

King looked at her. "What are you doing?"

She grabbed his shoulder and turned him back around. "Just keep your eyes to the front, mister."

She started undressing. "I keep running stuff in a bag under the backseat. Never know when the urge might hit."

King's gaze flitted to the rearview mirror, where

one long bare leg and foot and then another
appeared as pants came down and shorts were slid
over muscled calves and sculpted thighs.

"Yeah," he said as he looked away when she
started taking off her shirt, "you just never know
about that old urge thing." He glanced outside and
watched as Kate Ramsey's efficient strides ate up
chunks of distance. She was almost out of sight.

"Michelle, you better hurry up or you'll never
catch—"

He stopped when the truck door opened and
closed and he saw Michelle, in a jogging bra, shorts
and track shoes, streak across the grass, her long legs
pumping and her muscled arms churning. He could
only stare in amazement as she effortlessly burned
up the distance between her and Kate.

"Friggin' Olympians," he muttered.

At first Michelle kept well out of sight of Kate, until
it appeared clear the young woman was out simply
to run. Then Michelle changed tactics. Instead of
shadowing Kate, she decided to take another shot at
talking to her. When she pulled up beside her, Kate
looked over, scowled and immediately picked up her
pace. Michelle quickly matched her stride for stride.

When Kate started to sprint and Michelle effortlessly kept pace with her, Kate slowed down.

"What do you want?" Kate said in a very tight voice.

"To talk."

"Where's your friend?"

"He's not much into running."

"I told you everything I know."

"Did you, Kate? Look, I just want to try to understand you. I want to help."

"Don't try to be my buddy, okay! This isn't some lame TV cop show where we're all of a sudden going to bond."

"You're right, this is real life, and a number of people have lost their lives or been kidnapped. We're trying to figure out what the hell is going on because we want to stop whoever's doing this, and I think you can help."

"I can't help you or anyone else."

"I don't think you've even tried."

Kate pulled up, hands on hips, sucking in quick breaths, and looked angrily at Michelle. "What the hell do you know about anything? You know nothing about me."

"That's why I'm here. I want to know more. I want to know as much as you're willing to tell."

"You just don't get it, do you? I've put this all

behind me. I don't want to relive that part of my life." They started to run again. "And besides, I don't know anything."

"How do you know you don't? Have you gone through every little detail, been asked every possible question, run down every line of possible inquiry?"

"Look, I try not to think about the past, okay?"

"So I take that as a no."

"Would you think about it much if he were *your* dad?"

"What I wouldn't do, Kate, is try to hide from the truth. Have you ever really talked about any of this? If you haven't, I'm here to listen. I really am."

As tears started to trickle down the other woman's cheeks, Michelle put a hand on Kate's shoulder and they both stopped jogging. She led Kate over to a bench, and they sat down.

Kate wiped her eyes with her hand and glared stubbornly at nothing. Michelle sat there patiently waiting.

Kate started off hesitantly and in a small voice. "I was in algebra class when they came and got me. One minute I'm doing x plus y problems, and the next minute my dad is national news. Do you know what that feels like?"

"Like your whole world is ending?"

"Yes," Kate said quietly.

"Were you able to talk to your mother about it?"

Kate waved her hand dismissively. "What was there to talk about? She'd already abandoned my father. That was her choice."

"Is that how you saw it?"

"How else could I see it?"

"You must have some idea why they separated beyond what you told us earlier."

"It wasn't my father's doing, I can tell you that."

"So it was your mother's choice, and you're saying you don't know why – other than maybe feeling she'd wasted her life with your father?"

"I do know that when my mother walked out, *his* life was basically over. He worshiped her. It wouldn't have surprised me if he'd committed suicide."

"Well, maybe he did."

Kate stared at her. "And what, took Clyde Ritter with him?"

"Two birds with one stone."

Kate studied her hands. "It started out like a fairy tale. My father was an activist in college. Civil rights marches, war protests, sit-ins, the whole works. My mother was the beautiful actress poised for stardom. But they fell in love. My father was tall and hand-some and smarter than everybody, and he wanted to do all this good. He was noble, he really was. He had great substance. All the people my mother knew were actors; people from the stage, basically all fluff. My father was something totally different. He didn't just act the part, he went out and risked his life to make the world better."

"Pretty hard for a lady to resist," Michelle said quietly.

"I know my mom loved him. What I just told you are things I learned from her and some of her friends. And I also found some of her diaries from when she was in college. They really did love each other. So I don't know why it didn't work out. Maybe it lasted longer than it should have considering how different they were. But maybe if she hadn't left, he wouldn't have done what he did."

"But maybe he didn't do it alone, Kate. That's what we're trying to get at."

"Your new evidence that you can't tell me," she said scornfully.

"A gun," said Michelle firmly. Kate looked startled but said nothing. "A gun that we found and that we believe was hidden in the Fairmount Hotel on the day Ritter was killed. We think there was a second assassin in the building, but that person didn't fire."

"Why not?"

"We don't know. Maybe he lost his nerve. Maybe

he and your father had a pact to do it together, and then he didn't, leaving your dad with the full responsibility." Michelle paused and then added quietly, "And maybe it was that person who talked your dad into doing what he did in the first place. And if he did, maybe you saw or overheard something that can help us."

Kate looked down at her hands and nervously picked at her nails. "My dad didn't have many visitors and not any real friends."

"So if somebody did come to see him, you probably would have noticed," Michelle suggested.

Kate remained silent for so long that Michelle almost rose to leave.

"It was about a month or so before Ritter was killed."

Michelle froze. "What was?"

"It must have been two o'clock in the morning, I mean some crazy hour. I was asleep but some noise woke me. I slept upstairs when I was with my father. He could be up at all hours, and at first I thought it was my dad talking, but then the voice was different. I crept to the top of the stairs. I could see a light on in my dad's study. I heard him talking to someone, or rather this person was talking and my dad was mostly listening."

"What was he saying? This other person? Wait, was it a man?"

"Yes."

"What did he say?"

"I couldn't make out much of it. I heard my mother's name used. 'What would Regina think?' Something like that. And then my father answered that times were different. That people changed. And then the other person said something I couldn't hear."

"Did you get a look at him?"

"No. My father's study had a door to the outside. He must have left that way."

"What else did you hear?"

"Nothing. They started speaking in lower voices. Probably realized they might wake me up. I thought about going downstairs and seeing who it was, but I was scared."

"Did your father ever mention who the visitor was, anything about it at all?"

"No. I was afraid to let him know I'd overheard, so I never brought it up."

"Could it have been someone who worked at the college?"

"No, I think I would have recognized his voice." There was something in her manner, a furtiveness, that Michelle didn't like, but she chose not to push it.

"Did you ever hear the name Ritter mentioned by the man? Anything like that?"

"No! That's why I never talked to the police about this. I . . . I was scared to. My father was dead, and I didn't know if anyone else was involved, and I just didn't want to drag anything up."

"And the person had mentioned your mother, and you thought it might reflect badly on her somehow."

Kate looked at her with hurt, swollen eyes. "People can write and say anything they want. They can destroy people."

Michelle took her hand. "I'll do everything I can to solve this case without doing any further harm. You have my word."

Kate squeezed Michelle's hand. "I don't know why I should, but I believe you. Do you really think you can find out the truth, after all these years?"

"I'll give it my best shot."

As Michelle rose to leave, Kate said, "I did love my father. I *still* love my father. He was a *good* man. His life shouldn't have ended that way. That it did makes you feel like there's no hope for the rest of us."

To Michelle, Kate sounded almost suicidal. She sat back down and put her arm around her. "Listen to me. Your father's life was his to do what he wanted with. Your life is exactly the same. You've endured so much, accomplished so much, you should have more hope than anyone. I'm not just saying that, Kate, I mean it."

Kate finally let out a tiny smile. "Thanks."

Michelle jogged back to the truck and climbed in. While King drove she filled him in on her conversation with Kate.

King slapped the steering wheel. "Damn, so there *was* someone. The guy who was talking to her father could have been the man with the gun in the closet."

"Okay, let's break this down. There were two assassins but only one followed through. Intentional or not? Cold feet, or was it all about setting up Ramsey?"

King shook his head. "If intentional and you know you're not going to use your gun, why even bring it to the hotel?"

"Maybe he and Ramsey met beforehand, and the other guy had to at least make a pretense of intending to carry it off. Otherwise, maybe Ramsey gets suspicious."

"Right, that could be. Okay, now we need to take a really hard look at Ramsey's background, probably back to college. If the man knew Regina

Ramsey, and Arnold Ramsey talked about times changing, the answer might lie in the past."

"And it also might explain why a Berkeley superstar was teaching at a little college in the middle of nowhere."

Michelle once again slid into the backseat. "You drive while I change back into my clothes."

King focused on the road as his ears picked up the sounds of garments being pulled off and on. "By the way, do you often strip to your birthday suit in the company of strange men?"

"You're not *that* strange. And, Sean, I'm really flattered."

"Flattered? About what?"

"You snuck a peek."

50

The four met back at King's house late that afternoon. Parks placed a large file box on the kitchen table. "That's the result of our search on Bob Scott," he told Joan.

"That was pretty fast," she commented.

"Hey, who you think you're dealing with, some Mickey Mouse outfit?"

King looked at her. "Checking out Scott? I told you he couldn't have been involved."

Joan eyed him intently. "I like to verify things independently. It's not like any of us are infallible."

"Unfortunately the reason it came so fast," said Parks a little sheepishly, "is because those dummies crammed practically everything in they could find about people named Bob Scott. So a lot of the paper is probably worthless. But there it is." He put on his hat. "I'm heading back out. I'll call if anything clicks, and I expect you to do the same."

After he left, the three had a quick dinner out on

the rear deck. Joan told them about her check on Doug Denby.

"So he's out of the loop," said Michelle.

Apparently."

King looked puzzled. "So according to the woman you spoke with at the law firm in Philly, Bruno didn't cheat when he was a U.S. attorney in D.C.?"

"If we can believe her. I tend to think she was telling the truth."

"So maybe Mildred was feeding us a pack of lies about Bruno."

"Now, *that* I can believe," commented Joan. She glanced inside to where the box Parks had left was sitting on the table. "We'll have to go through the files Parks brought."

"I can start on it," said Michelle. "Since I didn't know him, I might not skim over stuff that the two of you might." She excused herself and went inside.

Joan looked out over the water. "It is really beautiful here, Sean. You picked a nice spot to start fresh."

King finished his beer and sat back. "Well, I might have to pick another spot."

Joan glanced over at him. "Let's hope not. A person shouldn't have to re-create himself more than once in a lifetime."

"How about you? You said you wanted out."

"To go to some island with my millions?" She smiled in a resigned way. "Dreams more often than not don't come true. Particularly at my stage of life."

"But if you find Bruno, you get the big payoff."

"The money was only part of the dream."

When King shot her a glance, she quickly looked away.

"Do you sail much?" she asked.

"In the fall when the powerboats are gone and the winds pick up."

"Well, it *is* the fall. So maybe now would be a good time."

King looked at the clear sky and felt the nice breeze against his skin. They had a couple hours of daylight left. He stared at Joan intently for a few moments. "Yeah, now would be a good time."

King showed Joan how to manage the sailboat's tiller. He'd attached a five-horsepower motor on the stern just in case the wind died down. They steered a course out into the main channel and then drifted.

Joan admired the spread of mountains encircling the lake, the green still vibrant, although the nip of fall was clearly in the air.

"Did you ever think you'd end up in a place like

this after all those years of hotels and airplanes and pushing till dawn?" she asked.

King shrugged. "To tell the truth, no. I never thought that far ahead. I was always more of a live-in-the-present sort of person." He added thought-fully, "I'm more of a long-range thinker now."

"And where do your long-range thoughts lead you?"

"Nowhere until this mystery is cleared up. The problem is, even if we solve this thing, the damage has been done. I really might have to move from here."

"Running away? That doesn't sound like you, Sean."

"Sometimes it's just best to strike the tent poles and move on. You sort of get tired of fighting, Joan."

He sat next to her and took over the tiller. "Wind's changing. I'm going to tack back into it. The boom's going to come across. I'll tell you when to duck."

After he completed this maneuver, he let her take the tiller back, but he stayed next to her. She wore a pantsuit but had taken off her shoes and rolled her pant legs over her knees. Her feet were small and her toenails were painted red.

"You favored purple toenail polish eight years ago, didn't you?"

She laughed. "Red is always in but purple may mount a comeback. I'm actually flattered you remembered."

"Purple toenails and packing a .357."

"Come on, fess up, it was a wicked, irresistible combination."

He sat back and gazed off.

They were silent for some minutes, Joan looking at him nervously and King doing his best to avoid eye contact. "Did you ever think about asking me to marry you?" she asked.

He glanced at her with an astonished expression. "I was married back then, Joan."

"I know that. But you were separated and your marriage was really over."

He looked down. "Okay, maybe I did know my marriage was over, but I wasn't sure I wanted to attempt another one. And I guess I never really believed two Secret Service agents could ever make a marriage work. That life is just too crazy."

"I thought about asking you."

"Asking me what?"

"To marry me."

"You really are amazing. You were going to ask me to marry you?"

"Is there a rule somewhere that says the man has to propose?"

"Well, if there is, I'm sure you'd have no problem smashing it to pieces."

"I'm serious, Sean. I was in love with you. So much so that I'd wake up in the middle of the night with the shakes, terrified it would somehow all go away, that you and your wife would get back together."

"I didn't know that," he said quietly.

"How did you feel about me? I mean really feel about me?"

He looked uncomfortable. "Honestly? I was amazed you'd let me have you. You were on this pedestal, professionally and personally."

"So I was what, a trophy to be mounted on the wall?"

"No, I actually thought I was."

"I didn't sleep around, Sean. I didn't have that reputation."

"No, you didn't. Your reputation was the iron lady. There wasn't one agent I knew who wasn't intimidated by you. You scared the shit out of a lot of tough guys."

Joan looked down. "Didn't you know, prom queens tend to be very lonely creatures. When I joined the Service, women were still an anomaly. To succeed, I had to be more 'guy' than all the other guys. I had to make the rules up as I went along.

It's a little different now, but back then I really didn't have a choice."

He touched her cheek and turned her face to his. "So why didn't you?"

"Why didn't I what?"

"Ask me to marry you?"

"I was planning to but something happened."

"What was that?"

"Clyde Ritter's getting killed."

Now King looked away. "Damaged goods?"

She touched his arm. "I guess you really don't know me very well. It was a lot more than that."

He looked back at her. "What do you mean by that?"

Joan looked more nervous than King could ever remember. Except on that morning, at 10:32, when Ritter had died. She slowly reached into her pocket and pulled out a piece of paper.

King unfolded the paper and read the words there.

Last night was wonderful. Now surprise me, wicked lady. On the elevator. Around 10:30. Love, Sean

It was written on the stationery of the Fairmount Hotel.

He looked up to see her staring at him.

"Where did this come from?"

"It was slipped under the door to my room at the Fairmount at nine o'clock that morning."

He stared at her blankly. "The morning Ritter was killed?" She nodded. "You thought I wrote this?" She nodded again. "All these years you thought maybe I was involved in Ritter's death?"

"Sean, you have to understand, I didn't know what to think."

"And you never told anyone?"

She shook her head. "Just like you never told anyone about me on that elevator." She added quietly, "You thought I was involved in Ritter's death too, didn't you?"

He licked his lips and glanced away, his features angry. "They screwed us both, didn't they?"

"I saw the note that was on the body found in your house. It clearly implied the person was behind the Ritter assassination. As soon as I read it, I just knew we'd *both* been used. Whoever wrote the note that was slipped under my hotel room door pitted us against each other in a way that guaranteed our silence. Or at the very least would have cast suspicion on one or both of us. But there was a difference. I couldn't reveal the truth because then I'd have to tell what I was doing on that elevator. And once I did, my career was over. My motive was selfish. You, on the other hand, kept silent for another reason." She placed a hand on his sleeve. "Tell me, Sean, why did you? You must have suspected I was paid off to distract you. And yet you took the full blame. You could have told them I was on that elevator. Why didn't you?" She took a long, anxious breath. "I really need to know."

The jarring sound of the cell phone startled them both badly.

King answered it. It was Michelle calling from the house.

"Kate Ramsey phoned. She has something important to tell us. But she wants to do it in person. She'll meet us halfway, in Charlottesville."

"Okay, we're coming in now." He clicked off, took the tiller and silently steered the boat back. He didn't look at Joan, who, for once in her life, had nothing to say.

51

They met Kate Ramsey at Greenberry's coffee shop in the Barracks Road Shopping Center in Charlottesville. The three bought large cups of coffee and took a table near the back of the room, which only had a few patrons in it this time of night.

Kate's eyes were puffy, her manner subdued, even deferential. She fingered her coffee cup nervously, her gaze downcast. She looked up in surprise, however, when King pushed a couple of straws toward her.

"Go ahead and make your right angles. It'll calm you down," he said with a kindly smile.

Kate's expression softened and she took the straws. "I've been doing that since I was a little girl. I guess it's better than lighting up a cigarette."

"So you had something important to tell us," said Michelle.

Kate looked around. The person closest to them

was reading a book and scribbling some notes, obviously a student on a deadline.

She said in a low voice, "It's about the meeting my father had that night, what I was telling Michelle," she explained with a glance at King.

"It's okay, she filled me in," he said. "Go ahead."

"Well, there was something else he said that I caught. I mean I guess I should have told you before, but I really believed I must have misheard. But maybe I didn't."

"What was it?" asked King eagerly.

"It was a name. A name I recognized."

King and Michelle exchanged glances.

"Why didn't you tell us that before?" asked Michelle.

"Like I said, because I couldn't believe I'd heard right. I didn't want to get him in any trouble. And my father secretly meeting with a stranger late at night and his name coming up – well, to a fourteen-year-old girl it seemed bad. But I knew he'd never do something illegal."

"Whose name was mentioned?" asked King.

Kate took a very deep breath. King noted that she was now bending the straws into knots.

"The name I heard the man say was Thornton Jorst."

Michelle and King once more exchanged a significant glance.

"You're sure," said Michelle. "You heard him say Thornton Jorst?"

"I'm not one hundred percent certain, no, but what else could it have been? It's not exactly a name like John Smith. It sure sounded like Thornton Jorst."

"What was your father's reaction to that name?"

"I couldn't hear that clearly. But he said something like it was risky, very risky. For both of them."

King thought about this. "So the other man wasn't Thornton Jorst – that seems clear – but they were talking about him." He touched Kate on the shoulder.

"Tell us about Jorst's relationship with your father."

"They were friends and colleagues."

"Had they known each other before coming to work at Atticus?" asked Michelle.

Kate shook her head. "I don't think so, no. If they did, they certainly never mentioned it. But they were both in college in the sixties. People went all over the country doing insane things. It's funny, though."

"What is?" asked King.

"Well, sometimes it seemed to me that Thornton

knew my mother better than he knew my father. Like they'd met before."

"Did your mother ever mention that they had?"

"No. Thornton came to Atticus after my parents did. He was a bachelor, never really dated that I could tell. My parents were very friendly with him. I think my mother felt sorry for him. She would bake him little things and take them over to him. They were good friends. I really liked him. He was almost like an uncle to me."

Michelle said slowly, "Kate, do you think your mother—"

Kate interrupted her. "No, they weren't having an affair. I know I was very young back then, but still I would have known."

King didn't look convinced but said, "The man who met with your father, he mentioned your mother, Regina?"

"Yes. I'm assuming he must have known one or both of my parents. But look, I really can't believe Thornton is mixed up in any of this. He's just not the type to run around with guns plotting to kill people. He didn't have my father's genius or his academic credentials, but he's a good professor."

King nodded. "Right, he didn't have your father's brains or Berkeley Ph.D. background, and yet they ended up at the same college. Any idea why?"

"Why what?" Kate had assumed a defensive tone.

Michelle said, "Why your father wasn't teaching at, say, Harvard or Yale. In addition to his Berkeley career, he authored four books that I was told were easily in the top ten in their field. He was a serious scholar, a real heavyweight."

"Maybe he simply chose to go to a smaller college," said Kate.

"Or maybe there was something in his past that precluded him from being called up to the academic big leagues," remarked King.

"I don't think so," said Kate. "Otherwise, everybody would know."

"Not necessarily. Not if it had been expunged from his official record, but certain people in the very cliquish world of academics were aware. And they might have held it against him. So he ended up at Atticus, which probably felt lucky to have him, warts and all."

"Any thoughts on what those warts might be?" asked Michelle.

Kate said nothing.

King said, "Look, the last thing we're aiming to do is drag up any more dirt on your father. I say, let him rest in peace. But if the man who talked to your father was responsible for his shooting Ritter, I don't see any reason why the man shouldn't suffer for it.

And understanding your dad's past may help us find him. Because if I'm reading this right, this guy knew your father from the old days, and if he did, then he'd probably know what incident had tainted him enough to cut your dad off from the Harvards of the world, if indeed that was the case."

Michelle said, "Kate, you're the only hope we have with this. Unless you tell us what you know, it's going to be very tough for us to learn the truth. And I think you want to know the truth; otherwise, you wouldn't have called us."

Kate finally sighed and said, "Okay, okay, there were some things my mother said not too long before she killed herself."

"What were they, Kate?" Michelle prompted gently.

"She said my father was arrested during a demonstration. I think it was against the Vietnam War."

"What, for disorderly conduct or something?" asked King.

"No, for killing someone."

King leaned in close. "Who and how, Kate?" he said. "Everything you can remember."

"This is only from what my mother said, and she wasn't really all that clear about it. She was drinking heavily near the end of her life." Kate took out a tissue and dabbed at her eyes.

"I know this is hard, Kate, but it might help to get it out in the open," said King.

"From what I could gather it was a police officer or someone official like that. He was killed during this war protest that got way out of hand. In L.A., I think she said. My father was arrested for it. It actually looked really bad for him, and then something happened. My mother said some lawyers got involved on my dad's behalf, and the charges were dropped. And my mom said the police had trumped up the charges anyway. That they were just looking for a scapegoat, and my father was it. She was sure Dad hadn't done anything."

"But there must have been stories in the paper, or some scuttlebutt," commented Michelle.

"I don't know if it made the papers, but I guess there was a record of it somewhere because it obviously did hurt my dad's career. I checked into my mom's story. I confirmed that Berkeley let my dad graduate with his Ph.D. but did so very reluctantly. I guess they didn't have much choice; he'd already completed all the course work and his dissertation. The incident happened shortly before he graduated. But from what I could gather word spread in academic circles, and the places he applied to teach at after he graduated shut their doors on him. My mom said Dad bumped around here and there, scraping by before he got the job at Atticus. Of course, during those years he'd written all those books that were very well received in the academic community. Looking back, I think my dad was so bitter about being kept out of the top schools that even if any of them had come calling, he would have stayed at Atticus. He was a very loyal person, and Atticus had given him a shot."

King asked, "Any idea how your parents survived during the lean years? Did your mom work?"

"Here and there some, but nothing permanent. She helped my dad write his books, with research and such. I'm not really sure how they got by." She rubbed her eyes. "Why, what are you getting at?"

"I was just wondering," he said, "who these lawyers were who came in to represent your dad. Did your father come from money?"

Kate looked bewildered. "No, my father grew up on a dairy farm in Wisconsin. My mother was from Florida originally. They were both pretty poor."

"So it becomes even more puzzling. Why the lawyers coming to the rescue? And I wonder if your parents were getting by on money from an unknown source during the tough times."

"I guess it's possible," said Kate, "but I don't know where from."

Michelle looked at King. "Are you thinking the

person who talked to Ramsey in his study that night might be connected to the L.A. incident?"

"Look at it this way. This thing happens in L.A. and Arnold Ramsey gets nailed. But what if he wasn't alone in it? What if some person who was well connected was also at fault? That would explain some fancy lawyers swooping in. I know lawyers – they don't usually work for free."

Michelle was nodding. "That might explain why the man mentioned Regina Ramsey. Maybe he was recalling the past fights against authority in getting Ramsey to pick up a gun and rejoin the struggle."

"God, this is all too much," said Kate. She looked like she might start crying. "My father was brilliant. He should have been teaching at Harvard or Yale or Berkeley. And then the police lie and his life is over. It's no wonder he rebelled against authority. Where's the justice in that?"

"There isn't any," answered King.

"I can still remember so vividly when I heard the news."

"You said you were in algebra class," said Michelle.

She nodded. "I went out in the hallway, and there was Thornton and my mother. I knew something bad had happened."

King looked startled. "Thornton Jorst was there with your mother? Why?"

"He was the one who told my mother. Didn't he tell you that?"

"No, he didn't," said Michelle adamantly.

"Why would he have known before your mother?" asked King quizzically.

Kate looked at him, puzzled. "I don't know. I assumed he heard about it on TV."

"What time did they come and get you out of class?" asked King.

"What time? I . . . I don't know. It was years ago."

"Think, Kate, it's really important."

She was silent for a minute and then said, "Well, it was in the morning, well before lunch, I know that. Say eleven o'clock or so."

"Ritter was killed at 10:32. There is no way the TV stations could have run a story with full particulars, including the identity of the assassin, barely thirty minutes later."

"And Jorst also had time to pick up your mother?" asked Michelle.

"Well, she wasn't living that far from where I went to school. You have to understand, Atticus isn't that far from Bowlington, about half an hour by car. And my mom lived on the way."

Michelle and King exchanged anxious glances.

"It couldn't be possible, could it?" said Michelle.

"What? What are you talking about?" asked Kate. King rose without answering.

"Where are you going?" asked Kate.

"To pay Dr. Jorst a visit," he said. "I think there's a lot he hasn't told us."

"Well, if he didn't tell you about coming to see me at the school that day, maybe he didn't tell you about him and my mother."

King stared at her. "What about them?"

"Before she died she and Thornton were seeing each other."

"Seeing each other?" asked King. "But you said your mother loved your father."

"By then Arnold had been dead almost seven years. Thornton and my mother's friendship had endured and had turned into something else."

"Something else? Like what?" he asked.

"Like they were getting married."

52

Michelle had gotten only halfway through the Bob Scott file when she received the call from Kate. Since Michelle obviously wouldn't be getting back to it for a while, Joan had taken the box with her to the inn where she was staying and continued to go through it. After her last conversation with King, she needed something to take her mind off that very painful encounter.

When she opened the box and started sifting through its contents, she realized that Parks hadn't been joking: it was a mess. However, she dutifully turned every page, reading each document until it became clear it was not the right Bob Scott. After a couple of hours she called room service for a snack and a pot of coffee. She was going to be here a while, and she had no idea when King and Maxwell would be returning. She started to phone King but then decided against it.

She was nearing the bottom of the box when her

scrutiny intensified. She pulled out the sheaf of papers and spread them out on her bed. They appeared to be a warrant for the arrest of one Robert C. Scott. The address where the warrant was to be served was in Tennessee somewhere, although Joan didn't recognize the town's name. From what she could tell, it had to do with a weapons charge. This Bob Scott had some guns he shouldn't have. Whether it was the Bob Scott she was looking for or not, she couldn't tell yet. However, the Bob Scott she knew had loved his guns.

As she read further, it became even more intriguing. The Marshals Service had been engaged, as they often were, to serve the warrant on behalf of the Bureau of Alcohol, Tobacco and Firearms, or ATF. That was probably why Parks had been able to get his hands on this document. Bob Scott might have ties to this current case, but it would have to be from the Ritter angle. And yet they had all speculated that Bruno and Ritter might be connected somehow. They had the murders of Loretta Baldwin and Mildred Martin to show that connection. And yet how could such two very different cases involve all the same parties? What was the common denominator? What! It was driving her mad that the answer might be staring them all in the face and they still couldn't see it.

Her cell phone rang. It was Parks.

"Where are you now?" he asked.

"I'm at the Cedars. I've been going over that box you left. And I think I might have hit on something." She told him about the warrant.

"Damn, was it served on Scott?"

"I don't know. Presumably not, since if he'd been arrested, it would have shown up somewhere and we'd know about it."

"If the guy's got warrants issued against him for gun violations, maybe he's the wacko behind all this."

"But how do we tie him to everything? It doesn't make sense."

"Agreed," he said wearily. "Where are King and Maxwell?"

"They went to talk to Kate Ramsey. She called and said she had some more information for them. They were meeting in Charlottesville."

"Well, if her father wasn't working alone, the guy she overheard might have been Bob Scott. He would have been in the perfect inside place to set up the hit. A Trojan horse if ever there was one."

"How do you want to proceed on what I discovered?"

"I say we take a bunch of guys and go check it

out. Nice find, Joan. Maybe you're as good as everybody says you are."

"Actually, Marshal, I'm better."

As soon as Joan hung up, she jumped as though
she'd been electrocuted. "Oh my God," she
exclaimed, staring at her phone. "It can't be." She
said the next two words very slowly. "Trojan horse."

There was a knock at the door. She opened it,
and the attendant carried the tray.

"Over here okay, ma'am?"

"Yes," said Joan absently. Her mind was truly
whirling over this new development. "That's fine."

"Would you like me to pour out the coffee?"

"No, that's fine." She signed the check and turned
away. "Thank you."

Joan was about to make a phone call when she
felt the presence behind her. She turned, but didn't
even have time to cry out before everything went
dark. The young woman stood over Joan, who now
lay on the floor. Tasha bent down and went to work.

53

It was late at night when King and Michelle arrived at Atticus College. The building housing Thornton Jorst's office was locked. At the administration building Michelle persuaded a young intern on duty there to give her Jorst's home address. It was about a mile off campus on a tree-shaded avenue of brick homes, where a number of other professors lived. There was no car in Jorst's driveway as King pulled his Lexus to the curb, and no lights were on. They went up the drive to the front door and knocked, but no one answered. They looked around at the small backyard, but that was empty too.

"I can't believe it, but Jorst must have been at the Fairmount Hotel when Ritter was killed," said Michelle. "There's no other explanation unless somebody called him from the hotel and told him what had happened."

"Well, we'll ask him that. But if he was there, he must have hightailed it out before the area was sealed off. That's the only way he could have gotten to Regina and Kate with the news that fast."

"Think he'll admit being at the hotel?"

"I guess we'll find out, because I intend on asking him. And I'd also like to ask about Regina Ramsey."

"You'd think he would have mentioned they were talking marriage when we first spoke to him."

"Not if he didn't want us to know. Which makes me even more suspicious." King looked at Michelle. "Are you armed?"

"Guns and creds, the whole power pack, why?"

"Just checking. I wonder if people lock their doors around here?"

"You're not thinking of going in? That's breaking and entering in the nighttime."

"Not if you don't break when you enter," he said.

"Oh, really? Where'd you get your law degree? The University of Stupid?"

"All I'm saying is, it would be nice to have a peek with Jorst not around."

"But he might be. He might be in there sleeping. Or he might come back while we're inside."

"Not we, just me. You're a sworn law enforcement officer."

"You're a member of the bar. Technically that makes you an officer of the court."

"Yeah, but us lawyers can always get around

technicalities. It's our specialty, or don't you watch TV?" He went back to his car and got a flashlight. When he rejoined Michelle, she grabbed his arm. "Sean, this is crazy. What if a neighbor sees you and calls the cops?"

"Then we tell them we thought we heard someone calling out for help."

"That is so unbelievably lame."

King had already eased over to the back door and tried the knob. "Damn."

Michelle breathed a sigh of relief. "It's locked? Thank God!"

King swung the door open with a mischievous look. "Just kidding. I'll only be a minute. Keep a sharp lookout."

"Sean, don't—"

He slipped inside before she could finish. Michelle started wandering around, hands in her pockets, trying to look like she hadn't a care in the world while the acid ate away the lining of her stomach. She even attempted to whistle, but found she couldn't because her lips were too dry from her sudden anxiety attack.

"Damn you, Sean King," she muttered.

★

Inside, King found himself in the kitchen. As he swung his light around, the room was revealed as small and looked unused. Jorst seemed more of an eat-out kind of guy. He moved through to a living room that was very plainly furnished and neat. Bookcases lined the room and were, not surprisingly, full of tomes by Goethe, Francis Bacon, John Locke and the perennially popular Machiavelli.

Jorst's home office was off the living room, and this space was more reflective of the man. The desk was piled high with books and papers, the floor cluttered, the small leather sofa similarly stacked with objects. The place smelled strongly of both cigarette and cigar smoke, and King noted an ashtray on the floor that was filled with butts. The walls were covered with cheap bookshelves, and they sagged under the weight of the books resting there. King poked around the desk, opened drawers and looked for secret hiding places yet found nothing of the sort. He doubted that if he pulled out one of the books a hidden passageway would be revealed, but he dutifully slipped out a couple of volumes just in case. Nothing happened.

Jorst was working on a book, he'd said, and the condition of his study seemed to confirm this, since notes, drafts and outlines were piled everywhere. Organization was evidently not the man's strong suit, and King looked around in disgust at the mess. He couldn't live ten minutes like this, although in his youth his apartment had looked even worse. At least he'd grown out of his pigsty; Jorst apparently never had. King fleetingly contemplated inviting Michelle in so she could get a quick hit of clutter. It would probably make her feel better.

Digging under the piles on the desk, he found an appointment book, but it was singularly uninformative. He next moved upstairs. There were two bedrooms there, and only one was ostensibly in use. Here Jorst was neater. His clothes were arranged nicely in his small closet, his shoes stacked on a cedar rack. King looked under the bed and was greeted only by dust balls. The adjoining bathroom revealed only a damp towel on the floor and some toiletries stacked on the sink. He went across to the other bedroom, obviously a guest room. There was a small adjoining bath here too, but there were no towels or toiletries. There was a shelf against one wall that held no books, but did have some photos on it. He shined the light on them one by one. They were of Jorst with various people, none of whom King recognized until he looked at the last face.

The voice calling from below startled him. "Sean, get your butt down here. Jorst is back."

He looked out the window in time to see Jorst pulling his massive old car into the driveway. He turned off the light, put the photo in his pocket and carefully but quickly made his way down the steps and back toward the kitchen where Michelle was waiting. They exited via the back door, came around the side of the house, waited for Jorst to go inside and then knocked on the front door.

The professor came to the door, flinched when he saw them and cast a suspicious glance over their shoulders. "Is that your Lexus at the curb?" King nodded. "I didn't see anyone in it when I passed by. And I didn't see either of you on the sidewalk."

"Well, I was stretched out in the backseat waiting for you to come home," said King. "And Michelle had gone to one of your neighbors' homes to see if they knew when you'd be back."

Jorst didn't look like he believed the story, but he ushered them in, and they settled in the living room.

"So you talked to Kate?" he asked.

"Yeah, she said you gave her the heads-up about us."

"Did you expect that I wouldn't?"

"I'm sure you two are very close."

Jorst stared intently at King. "She was a colleague's daughter, and then she was a student of mine. Implying anything else would be a mistake."

"Well, considering that you and her mother were talking about getting married, you'd at least be her stepfather," said King. "And here we didn't even know you were dating."

Jorst looked very uncomfortable. "And why should you, since it's none of your business. Now, if you'll excuse me, I'm rather busy."

"Right, the book you're writing. What's it about, by the way?"

"You're interested in political science, Mr. King?"

"I'm interested in lots of things."

"I see. Well, if you have to know, it's a study of voting patterns in the South, post-World War II to the present, and their impact on national elections. My theory is that the South today is no longer the 'Old South.' That, in fact, it's one of the most heterogeneous, teeming pools of immigrants this country has seen since the turn of the last century. I won't say that it's quite yet a bastion of liberalism or even radical thought, but it's not the South depicted in *Gone with The Wind*, or even in *To Kill a Mockingbird*. In fact, the fastest-growing population element in Georgia right now is Middle Eastern."

"I can see how the Hindus and Muslims co-existing with the bubbas and the Baptists must be fascinating," opined King.

"That's good," said Jorst. "Bubbas and Baptists.

Mind if I use that line for one of my chapter headings?"

"Feel free. You didn't know the Ramseys before Atticus, did you?"

"No, I didn't. Arnold Ramsey was at Atticus about two years before I arrived. I'd been a professor at a college in Kentucky before coming here."

"When I said the Ramseys, I meant both Arnold and Regina."

"My answer is the same. I didn't know either until I came here. Why, did Kate say otherwise?"

"No," Michelle said quickly. "She did tell us that her mother was good friends with you."

"They *both* were friends of mine. I think Regina saw me as a hopeless bachelor and took it upon herself to make me feel welcome and comfortable. She was a truly remarkable woman. She worked with the drama class at the college and even performed in some of the productions. She was an astonishing actress, she really was. I'd heard Arnold talk about her talents, especially when she was younger, and assumed he was merely exaggerating. But when you saw her up there onstage, she was mesmerizing. And she was as kind and as good as she was talented. She was loved by many people."

"I'm sure she was," said King. "And after Arnold died, the two of you—"

"It wasn't like that," Jorst interrupted. "Arnold had been dead a very long time before we started seeing each other as anything more than friends."

"And it got to the point where you were talking marriage."

"I'd proposed and she'd accepted," he said coldly.

"And then she died?"

Jorst's features became pained. "Yes."

"In fact, she committed suicide?"

"So they say."

Michelle said quickly, "You don't think so?"

"She was happy. She'd accepted my proposal of marriage. Now, I don't think I'm vain in saying that it seems pretty far-fetched that the thought of being married to me would have driven her to suicide."

"So you're thinking she was murdered?"

"You tell me!" he snapped. "You're the ones running around investigating. You figure it out. That's not my area of expertise."

"How did Kate take the news of your upcoming nuptials?"

"All right. She loved her father. She liked me. She knew I wasn't looking to replace him. I truly believe she wanted her mother to be happy."

"Were you a Vietnam War protester?"

Jorst seemed to take this abrupt change in direction smoothly. "Yes, along with millions of other people."

"In California ever?"

"Where exactly is this all going?"

King said, "What would you say if we told you a man came to visit Arnold Ramsey for the purpose of enlisting his aid in killing Clyde Ritter and that this person mentioned your name?"

Jorst looked at him coolly. "I'd say whoever told you that was seriously mistaken. But then again, if it's true, I can't control other people using my name in conversation, can I?"

"Fair enough. Do you believe that Arnold Ramsey acted alone?"

"Until I'm presented with credible evidence to the contrary."

"By all accounts he wasn't a violent man, yet he performed the most violent act of all, murder."

Jorst shrugged. "Who knows what beats deeply within the hearts of people?"

"That's true. And Arnold Ramsey was involved in some serious protests in his youth. Perhaps one of which led to someone's violent death."

Jorst looked at him sharply. "What are you talking about?"

King had revealed that piece of information solely to gauge Jorst's reaction to it. "One more thing. Did you drive separately or with Arnold Ramsey to the Fairmount Hotel on the morning he killed Ritter?"

To his credit Jorst didn't show any reaction. His features were impassive. "You're saying I was at the Fairmount that morning?"

King stared right at the man. "You're saying you weren't?"

He thought about this for a moment. "All right, I *was* there. With hundreds of other people. So what?"

"So what? Along with dating Regina Ramsey, that's a pretty significant detail you forgot to mention."

"Why should I have? I did nothing wrong. And in answer to your question, I drove separately."

"And you must have run out of the place the very second after Ramsey fired, or else you wouldn't have had time to pick up Regina and go and tell Kate in the middle of algebra."

Jorst looked stonily at them; however, several beads of perspiration had appeared on his broad forehead. "There were lots of people running all over the place. I was as terrified as anyone else. I saw what happened. And I didn't want Regina and Kate finding out on the news. So I drove as fast as I could to tell them myself. I thought I was being considerate. And I don't appreciate how you seem to be drawing a negative conclusion from what I thought was a selfless act."

King drew very close to the man. "Why did you go to the hotel that morning? Did you have a beef with Ritter too?"

"No, of course not."

"So why, then?" persisted King.

"He was a presidential candidate. We don't get many of those down here. I wanted to see for myself. It's my field, after all."

"What if I say that's complete bullshit?" said King.

"I don't owe you an explanation," Jorst shot back.

King shrugged. "You're right. We'll send the FBI and the Secret Service down, and you can tell them. You have a phone we can use?"

"Wait a minute, just wait a minute." King and Michelle looked at him expectantly. "All right, all right," Jorst said quickly. He swallowed nervously, looking back and forth at them. "Look, I was worried about Arnold. He'd been so enraged about Ritter. I was afraid he might do something dumb. Please believe me that never for one second did I think that his plan was to kill the man. I never knew he had a gun until he fired it. I swear."

"Go on," said King.

"He didn't know I was there. I followed him over. The night before, he told me he'd be attending the event. I stayed in the back. The crowd was so big that he never noticed me. He stayed far away from Ritter, and I started thinking that I'd just over-reacted. I thought about leaving. I moved toward the door. Unbeknownst to me, it was right about then that he started moving toward Ritter. I turned back once, when I was right at the door. Just in time to see Arnold pull his gun and fire. I saw Ritter fall, and then I saw you fire and kill Arnold. And then the whole place exploded. And I was running as fast as I could. I was able to get out so quickly because I was already by the door. I remember almost running over one of the hotel maids who was standing by the door too."

Michelle and King looked at each other: Loretta Baldwin.

Jorst continued, his face now ashen. "I couldn't believe that it had happened. It all seemed like a nightmare. I ran to my car and drove off as fast as I could. I wasn't the only one. Lots of people were fleeing that scene."

"You never told the police this?"

"What was there to tell? I was there, saw what happened and fled, just like hundreds of other people. It's not like the authorities needed my testimony or anything."

"And you went and got Regina and told her. Why?"

"Why! For God's sakes, her husband had just shot a presidential candidate. And then been killed himself. I had to tell her. Can't you understand that?"

King pulled the photo he'd taken from the upstairs bedroom out of his pocket and handed it to Jorst. Jorst accepted it with shaky hands and looked down at the smiling face of Regina Ramsey.

"I guess I can, particularly if you were in love with her back then too," said King quietly.

54

So what do you think?" asked Michelle as they were driving off. "He might have been telling the truth. And maybe he thought he'd be the first on the scene to comfort the poor widow. Capitalize on his friend's death at the same time he's playing Good Samaritan."

"So he's a creep. But maybe not a murderer."

"I don't know. He clearly bears watching. I don't like it that he withheld being at the Fairmount all these years and that he was planning to marry Regina. That alone puts him high up on my suspect list."

Michelle jumped as though she'd been stabbed. "Wait a minute. Sean, this may sound crazy, but hear me out." He looked at her expectantly. "Jorst admits to being at the Fairmount. He's in love with Regina Ramsey. What if he's the one who talked Ramsey into killing Ritter? He clearly knew that Ramsey hated Ritter. He was his friend and colleague. Ramsey would listen to him."

"But Kate said the man she overheard wasn't Jorst."

"But she couldn't be sure of that. Jorst might have changed his voice a little because he knew Kate was in the house. Okay, so Jorst is the one who makes a pact with Ramsey. They go to the hotel, each is armed."

King picked up the thread of her deductions. "And then Ramsey fires, but Jorst doesn't. He slips out, hides his gun in the supply closet, where Loretta sees him, and then races off to tell Regina and Kate."

"With the thought of marrying the widow at some point."

"Well, he waited a long time to ask her," commented King.

"No, he might have asked before and she might have said no. Or he wanted to wait a reasonable time so there'd be no suspicion. Or maybe it took that long for Jorst to make Regina fall in love with him." She looked at him anxiously. "So what do you think?"

"It makes sense, Michelle, it really does. But then Regina died. Jorst didn't end up with her."

"Do you really think Regina Ramsey was murdered?"

"Well, if Jorst is to be believed and they were getting married, why would she have killed herself?"

King said slowly, "And Kate knew they were talking marriage. And Jorst said that Kate seemed to be okay with it."

Michelle said, "But what if she wasn't?"

"What do you mean?"

"Kate loved her father. She told me that if her mother hadn't left him, he might not have killed Ritter. But he does and he's dead. Then her mother is going to marry a colleague of her father's. And then she dies."

"So you're saying Kate murdered her mother?"

Michelle put up her hands. "I'm just saying it's a possibility. I don't want to believe it. I like Kate."

He sighed. "It's like a balloon. You punch one side, and another bump pops out on another side." He glanced at her. "Did you put together those timelines I asked for?"

Michelle nodded and pulled a notepad out of her bag. "Arnold Ramsey was born in 1949. He graduated high school in 1967 and attended Berkeley from 1967 until he received his Ph.D. in 1974. Arnold and Regina Ramsey were married that year too, by the way. Then the two bumped along until he took the position at Atticus in 1982. Kate was about a year old then." She stopped and looked over at him. He had a confused look on his face. "What's bothering you?"

"Well, according to what Kate told us, Ramsey was supposed to have been involved in some war protest in which maybe a police officer died. That started all his problems. Now, she told us that Berkeley reluctantly let him graduate with his Ph.D. because he had completed all the work for it, including his dissertation. So the incident must have happened about the time he was actually graduating."

"That's right. So?"

"Well, if he received his Ph.D. in 1974, he wouldn't have been protesting the Vietnam War. Nixon signed the cease-fire in early 1973 and, though both sides sniped at each other about violations of the cease-fire pact, fighting didn't start up again until 1975. And if the incident with the police officer happened *before* Ramsey earned his Ph.D., I bet Berkeley would have just canned him."

Michelle sat back. "I guess that's right."

"And if Ramsey wasn't protesting the war in 1974 when the police officer was killed, what was he protesting?"

Michelle suddenly snapped her fingers. "Nineteen seventy-four? You mentioned Nixon. That was when Watergate was happening. Right?"

King nodded thoughtfully. "And it makes sense that Ramsey would be protesting against a guy like

Nixon, calling for his resignation, which he finally gave in August of that year."

"But Kate said it was a war protest in L.A."

"No, she said that's what her mother said. And she said Regina had been drinking heavily during that time. She easily might have gotten the date, event and even the place wrong."

"So the incident that involved the officer being killed might have been in Washington and not L.A. and was about Nixon and not Vietnam?"

"If so, we should be able to find out details about that."

"And the law firm that interceded on Ramsey's behalf. Do you think that's D.C.-based too?"

"I guess we'll find that out." King pulled out his phone and punched in some numbers. "I'll check in with Joan. She's great at digging up stuff." However, there was no answer and King left a message.

King continued, "If somebody got him off, and a law firm was involved, that's something tangible we should be able to track down."

"Not necessarily. You can't possibly account for the whereabouts of everybody back then. Hell, Jorst could have been throwing rocks at City Hall in L.A., and we'd never be able to prove it. And finding anybody to talk about it might well be impossible.

And if there's nothing in the public record, poof, that's it."

King nodded. "What you say is completely logical. But we still need to check it out. It'll cost us nothing but time."

"Yeah," said Michelle. "But I've got a bad feeling we're running out of that really fast."

55

King and Michelle slept over at a motel near Atticus and arrived back at Wrightsburg the next morning. Parks was waiting at King's house.

"Have you heard from Joan?" King asked him. "I tried last night but there was no answer."

"I talked to her yesterday evening. She found out something about Bob Scott from the stuff I brought." He told the pair about the warrant in Tennessee.

"If it's the same Bob Scott, then maybe he can lead us somewhere and get some of these questions answered," said King.

"Call Joan again, and we'll map out how we're going to play this."

King dialed Joan's number but there was still no answer. Then he called the main number for the inn where she was staying. As he listened to the front desk person, his face grew pale and he felt his knees weaken. He slammed down the phone and shouted, "Damn it!"

Parks and Michelle both stared at him.

"Sean, what is it?" she asked quietly.

King shook his head in disbelief. "It's Joan," he said. "She's been kidnapped."

Joan had been staying in a cottage set in the rear grounds of the Cedars Inn. Her purse and phone were on the floor of her room. The tray of food was untouched. The pair of shoes she'd been wearing the day before were lying on the floor; the heel of one of the shoes was broken off. The cottage had a rear door that opened to an area where a car could have been parked and Joan taken out without anyone seeing anything. When King, Michelle and Parks arrived, Chief Williams was there with some of his men, taking statements and collecting the scant evidence available.

The room attendant who'd set out to bring her food had been thoroughly questioned. He was a young man, employed at the inn for a couple of years, and was visibly shaken by what had happened. He explained that as he was bringing the food to Joan's cottage, a young woman approached him. After confirming that the food was for Joan, she identified herself as Joan's sister just arrived for a visit and said she wanted to surprise her sibling by delivering the food herself. It had all seemed innocent enough. And the girl was very pretty and had given him a twenty-dollar bill for his troubles. He'd turned over the tray and gone back to the inn. That was all he knew.

Chief Williams came up to them. "Damn it, I'm running all over the place with murders and kidnappings. This was a peaceful place not too long ago."

With the chief's permission they took the box of Bob Scott's materials Joan had been going through, and the three held a quick conference in the parking lot. Parks repeated verbatim the discussion he'd had with Joan.

"She must have been snatched pretty soon after I hung up with her. She filled me in on Bob Scott. I said Scott certainly could have turned traitor, and he would have been a perfect mole for anybody plotting to kill Ritter, although I know you're not convinced he did it. We were going to wait for you two to get back from your meeting with Kate Ramsey before planning our next steps."

King walked over and looked at Joan's BMW while Parks went inside to speak to Chief Williams. The police had already searched the car and found nothing.

Michelle walked over to him, put a hand on his shoulder. "Are you okay?"

"I should have seen this coming," he answered.

"How? You're not psychic."

"We'd talked to a lot of people. Mildred Martin was murdered right after we were with her. It's not a stretch that they'd go after Joan."

"Or *you*! And what were you supposed to do, baby-sit her? I don't know the woman all that well, but I don't think she would have stood for that."

"I didn't even try, Michelle. I wasn't concerned about her safety. And now . . .?"

"We still have a shot at finding her. Alive."

"No disrespect, but our track record for finding people alive isn't too good."

Parks returned. "Look, I'm going to get a fix on this Bob Scott in Tennessee, and if it's the same guy, we're going down there with a bunch of folks and have us a talk. You can join us if you want."

"We want," answered Michelle for them both.

56

While Parks went off to investigate Bob Scott, Michelle and King returned to King's home. Michelle made lunch for them both but then couldn't find him. She finally spotted him sitting on the dock and joined him there.

"I made some soup and sandwiches. I'm not a big domestic type, but they're edible."

"Thanks," he said absently. "I'll be up in a minute."

Michelle sat down next to him. "Still thinking about Joan?"

He looked over at her and then shrugged.

"I didn't think you two were really friends anymore."

"We're not!" He added more calmly, "We're not. But a long time ago we were more than friends."

"I know this is hard for you, Sean."

They sat there for a bit until King said, "She flashed me."

"What?" Michelle said sharply.

"On the elevator, she flashed me."

"Flashed you. How?"

"Trench coat and nothing much on underneath. Come on, admit it, you were probably thinking it was something like that after you found out about her panties on the ceiling."

"Okay, maybe I was. But why would she do that? You were on duty."

"Because she got a note she thought was from me asking her to surprise me, on the damn elevator. And after the night we spent together, I guess she assumed I meant a suitable follow-up to that show."

"If they wanted to set up a distraction with Joan, how would they know when she'd be coming down?"

"The meet-and-greet was from 10:00 to 10:35. She knew that. So at least whoever was plotting to kill Ritter would know the time window they were working with. The note said to come around 10:30. But even if she didn't do it, I'm sure they'd have still attempted to kill Ritter."

"That was pretty risky for Joan. It's not like she had to."

"Well, sometimes love makes you do crazy things."

"So you think that was it?"

"That's what she pretty much told me. All these years she suspected I was involved in Ritter's death somehow. She thought I'd set her up, again somehow. When she saw the note that was pinned to Susan Whitehead, she realized maybe we'd both been used. That note on Susan Whitehead clearly indicated the person was involved in Ritter's killing. The note slipped under Joan's door was designed to use her to distract me, under the pretense of being written by me. But she couldn't tell anyone about the note and what she'd done on the elevator because it would have wrecked her career." He paused. "She asked me why, if I suspected her and I was clean, I'd never told anyone what she'd done."

"And what did you tell her?"

"I didn't tell her. Maybe I don't know why."

"I think you never really believed she was guilty of anything other than bad judgment."

"I saw the look in her eyes when the shot was fired. I never saw anyone more shocked. No, she wasn't part of it." He shrugged. "But what the hell does it matter now?"

"Like you said, love can make you do strange things. And it looks like whoever was behind this knew how you felt about Joan. That you wouldn't betray her. In effect, both your hands and Joan's were tied." She looked at him questioningly. "It's not a crime to care about someone, Sean."

"Sometimes it feels like it is. It's a little unsettling to have someone come back into your life who you thought was gone forever."

"Especially if what you thought eight years ago turned out to be wrong."

"I'm not in love with Joan," said King. "But I do care what happens to her. I want her back safe."

"We'll do all we can do."

"That still might not be enough," he said grimly, and then rose and headed up to the house.

As they were finishing up lunch, King's phone rang. When he answered, he looked puzzled and then said to Michelle, "It's for you. He says he's your father."

"Thanks. I gave him this number. I hope you don't mind. The cell reception is a little spotty around here."

"No problem." He handed the phone across to her.

Michelle and her father spoke for about five minutes. She wrote some information down on a sheet of paper, thanked her dad and hung up.

King was rinsing out the lunch dishes and stacking

them in the dishwasher. "So what was that all about?"

"I told you most of my male family members are police officers. My father, the Nashville police chief, belongs to all the national fraternal police organizations, and is high up in a lot of them. I asked him to do a little digging on this D.C. incident. To see if he could find out anything about an officer being killed around 1974 during a protest."

King wiped his hands dry on a towel and came and stood next to her. "So what'd he come up with?"

"A name. Only one name, but it might lead us somewhere." She glanced at her notes. "Paul Summers was on the D.C. police force back then. He's retired now but lives in Manassas. My dad knows him, and he's willing to talk to us. Dad says Summers could have some information for us."

King pulled on his jacket. "Let's go."

As they were heading out, Michelle said, "Sean, I don't agree with your keeping what Joan did secret all these years, but I admire you for doing it. There's something to be said for loyalty."

"Really? I'm not sure I agree. In fact, sometimes loyalty really sucks."

57

Paul Summers lived in a thirty-year-old split-level rancher in Manassas, Virginia, that was being infringed on all sides by new housing developments. Summers answered the door dressed in jeans and a burgundy Redskins football T-shirt. They sat in the small living room. He offered them something to drink, but they declined. Summers looked to be around sixty-five or so, with fine white hair, a wide smile, freckled skin, big forearms and a bigger stomach.

"Damn, so you're Frank Maxwell's girl," he said to Michelle. "If I told you how much your father bragged about you at the national conventions, it'd make you blush redder than this T-shirt I'm wearing."

Michelle smiled. "Daddy's little girl. It does get embarrassing sometimes."

"But, hell, how many dads have a daughter like you? I'd be bragging too."

"She does make you feel kind of inferior," said King with an impish glance at Michelle. "But then you get to know her and realize she's actually human."

Summers took on a somber expression. "I been following this stuff about Bruno. It stinks. I worked with Secret Service before, lots of times. And the stories I heard about protectees doing crazy stuff and leaving the Service boys high and dry. You got screwed, Michelle, plain and simple."

"Thanks for saying that. My dad mentioned you might have some information that could help us?"

"That's right. I was sort of the unofficial police historian when I was on the force, and let me tell you, those were some exciting times. People think America's gone to hell these days? They should check out the sixties and seventies." As he was talking, he pulled out a file. "I got some stuff here I think might help." He put on a pair of reading glasses.

"In 1974 Watergate was tearing the country apart. Folks were going after Nixon with a vengeance."

"I guess some of those events got a little out of control," said King.

"Oh, yeah. The D.C. police force was pretty used to large-scale demonstrations by that time, but still you never know." He adjusted his glasses and read over his notes for a few moments. "The break-in at the Watergate happened in the summer of 1972. It was about a year later that the country found out about Nixon's tapes. He claimed executive privilege and wouldn't release them. After he fired the special prosecutor in October of 1973, things really started to snowball and folks started talking impeachment. In July of 1974 the Supreme Court ruled against Nixon with regard to the tapes and he resigned in August. But before the Court handed down its opinion – it was around May of '74 – things got really hot in D.C. There was a huge protest planned along Pennsylvania Avenue with thousands of marchers.

"We had riot squads out, dozens of officers on horseback, the National Guard, hundreds of Secret Service agents, SWAT teams, even a damn tank; you know, the works. I'd been on the force ten years, had seen my share of riots, and I remember still being scared. I felt like I was in some third-world country and not the U.S. of A."

"And a police officer died?" said Michelle.

"No, a national guardsman," said Summers. "Found him in an alley with his head bashed in."

"And someone was arrested for it," said King. "But how could they have known for sure who did it? It sounded like chaos out there."

"Well, they did make an arrest and they were going to prosecute, but then everything just went away. I don't know why. I mean the National Guard kid was dead, no doubt about that, and somebody had killed him. The story made the papers, but then the Supreme Court ruled against the president and Nixon resigned in August of '74, and that dominated everything from that point on. People seemed to forget about the death of the national guardsman. The whole thing just faded away. After RFK and Martin Luther King, Nam and Watergate, I think the country was tired of it all."

King leaned forward. "Do you have the names of the people charged, arresting officers, prosecutors?"

"No, I'm sorry I don't. You're talking thirty years ago. And I wasn't involved in the case at all. I just heard about it afterwards. So I wouldn't recognize any names you might have in mind."

"How about the papers? You said there were stories?"

"Yeah, but I don't believe any of them named the parties charged. There was definitely something weird going on there. To tell the truth, the media didn't trust the government back then. Lot of unethical stuff going on. And I hate to say it, since I was a member of the force, but some of the men in blue did some stuff they shouldn't back then. They crossed the line sometimes, especially with the longhaired hippies coming to town. Some of my brethren didn't have a lot of patience for that. It was a real 'us against them' mentality."

"And maybe something like that happened here; you said the charges just went away," said Michelle. "Maybe they'd been trumped up."

"Maybe. But I really don't know for sure."

"Okay," said King. "We appreciate your help."

Summers smiled. "You're about to appreciate it a little more." He held up a piece of paper. "I do have one name for you. Donald Holmgren."

"Who's that?" asked Michelle.

"Public defender back then. A lot of the protesters that day were really young, and half of them were spaced-out on stuff. It was like all the war protesters – hippies and people like that – had switched their focus to Nixon. So I'm thinking the odds are good that whoever got charged was one of them. If they had no money for a lawyer, they'd be initially re-presented by the P.D. office. Holmgren might be able to tell you some more. He's retired now too but he's living in Maryland. I haven't talked to him, but if you approach it right, he might open up to you."

"Thanks, Paul," said Michelle. "We owe you." She gave him a hug.

"Hey, tell your old man everything he said about you was true. Wish my kids had turned out half as well."

58

Donald Holmgren lived in a townhouse on the out-skirts of Rockville, Maryland. His house was filled with books, magazines and cats. A widower now, he was about seventy and had a full head of gray hair and was dressed in a light sweater and slacks. He cleaned some cats and books off his living room sofa, and King and Michelle sat down.

"We appreciate your seeing us on such short notice," said King.

"No problem. My days aren't that busy anymore."

"I'm sure they were much busier when you were at P.D.," commented Michelle

"Oh, you can say that again. My tenure covered some interesting times."

"As I mentioned on the phone," began King, "the incident we're investigating is the death of the national guardsman around May of 1974."

"Right, I remember that case well. It's not like national guardsmen get killed every day, and thank

God for that. But that was some day. I was arguing a case in federal court when the demonstration started. They stopped the court proceeding, and everybody went to the TV sets and watched. Never seen anything like it before and hope I never do again. I thought I was in the middle of the storming of the Bastille."

"We understand that initially a person was charged with the crime."

"That's right. Started at first-degree murder, but as details followed, we were looking at getting it knocked down."

"So you know who handled the case?"

"I did," was his surprising reply. Michelle and King exchanged a look. Holmgren explained, "I'd been at the Public Defender's Service about sixteen years, started back when it was just the Legal Aid Agency. And I'd defended some high-profile cases too. But to tell the truth I don't think anybody else wanted it."

"You mean the evidence was so strong against the accused," said Michelle.

"No, the evidence wasn't overwhelming by any means. If I remember correctly, the person charged was arrested because he was coming out of the alley where the crime took place. Dead body, particularly one in uniform, and a bunch of hippies running

around throwing rocks, well, that's a recipe for disaster. I think they arrested the first person they saw.
You have to understand that the city was under siege,
and nerves were frayed to the breaking point. If I
remember correctly, the defendant was some college
kid. I didn't necessarily believe he'd done it, or if he
had, that he'd meant to. Maybe there was a scuffle,
and the soldier fell and hit his head. Of course, the
prosecutor's office back then had a reputation for
trumping up cases. Hell, we had police officers lying
under oath, writing up false charges, creating evidence, the works."

"Do you remember the name of the defendant?"

"I've tried to think of it since you called, but I
can't. It was a young man, smart, that I do remember.
Sorry, I've handled thousands of cases since then,
and I didn't work on that one very long. I remember
legal charges and defenses better than I recall names.
And it's been thirty years."

King decided to take a shot. "Was his name
Arnold Ramsey?"

Holmgren's lips parted. "Why, I couldn't swear to
it but I think that's right. How'd you know?"

"It would take too long to explain. That same
Arnold Ramsey, eight years ago, shot and killed
Clyde Ritter."

Holmgren's mouth gaped. "That was the same guy?"

"Yep."

"Well, now maybe I'm sorry he got off."

"But you weren't sorry back then?"

"No, I wasn't. As I mentioned, back then certain people weren't so much concerned with the truth as they were with getting convictions any way they could."

"But they didn't get one in the Ramsey case?"

"No. While I believed the case was only marginal, I still had to work with the facts I had, and they weren't great. And the government was playing real hardball. Wanting to make a statement, not that I totally blame them, I guess. And then I got taken off the case."

"Why?"

"The defendant got other counsel. Some firm out west, I think. I guess that was where Ramsey, if it was him, was from. I assumed his family had found out what happened and were coming to the rescue."

"Do you remember the name of the firm?" asked Michelle.

He thought for a bit. "No. Too many years and cases in the interim."

"And this firm somehow got the charges dropped?"

"Not only that, I heard they got the record of the arrest expunged, all the details. They must have been really good. In my dealings with the government back then, that rarely happened."

"Well, you said some of the government prosecutors were pretty unethical. Maybe people got paid off," suggested King. "Lawyers and cops."

"I guess that might have happened," said Holmgren. "I mean, if you're going to trump up cases, I suppose you'd be willing to take a bribe to make a case go away. The government lawyer on the case was young, ambitious as hell, and always struck me as being way too slick. But he was good at playing the game, looking to jump to bigger and better things. I never saw him cross the line, though others in the office did. I do know that I felt sorry for his boss, who took a lot of the heat when all the crap in that office hit the fan years later. Billy Martin was a good guy. He didn't deserve that."

King and Michelle looked at the man, utterly stunned. King finally found his voice. "And the name of the government lawyer who prosecuted Arnold Ramsey?"

"Oh, that one I'll never forget. It was the fellow who was running for president and then got kidnapped. John Bruno."

59

King and Michelle went straight from Holmgren's to VCU in Richmond. Kate Ramsey wasn't at the Center for Public Policy. They were able to talk the receptionist into giving them Kate's home phone number. They called, but the woman who answered was Kate's roommate. She didn't know where Kate was. She hadn't seen her since that morning. When Michelle asked if they could come to see her, she hesitantly agreed.

On the way over, Michelle asked, "Do you think Kate knows about Bruno and her father? Please don't tell me that. She can't."

"I have a sinking feeling you're wrong."

They drove to Kate's apartment and spoke with the roommate, whose name was Sharon. At first Sharon was reluctant to talk, but when Michelle flashed her badge, she became far more cooperative. With her permission they looked around Kate's small bedroom but found nothing that was helpful. Kate was a serious reader, and her room was stacked with works that would have taxed most academicians. Then King found the box on the top shelf of the closet. It held a gun-cleaning kit and a box of nine-millimeter shells. He looked ominously at Michelle, who shook her head sadly.

"Do you know why Kate carries a gun?" King asked Sharon.

"She was mugged. At least that's what she told me. She bought it about seven or eight months ago. I hate having the thing around, but she has a license for it and all. And she goes to shooting ranges to practice. She's a good shot."

"That's comforting. Did she have it with her when she left this morning?" he asked.

"I don't know."

"Has there been anybody coming to see Kate, other than school-related? A man, for instance?"

"As far as I know she doesn't even date. She's always out at some rally or march or attending council meetings to protest something. She makes me dizzy sometimes with all that goes on inside her head. I can barely make it to class and keep my boyfriend happy much less worry about the shape the world's in, you know."

"Yeah, I know. But I meant an older guy, maybe

in his fifties." He described Thornton Jorst but Sharon shook her head.

"I don't think so. Although a couple of times I saw her get out of a car in front of the apartment building. I couldn't see who was driving, but I think it was a guy. When I asked her about it, she became pretty evasive."

"Can you describe the vehicle?"

"Mercedes, a big one."

"So a rich guy. When was the first time you saw that?" Michelle said.

"Maybe about nine or ten months ago. I remember because Kate had recently started her postgraduate work here. She doesn't have many friends. If she was meeting anyone, she didn't do it here. But she's hardly ever here."

As they were talking, Michelle held the cleaning kit up to her ear and shook it. There was a small sound. She dug her fingers under the lining and pulled it out. Her fingers locked around a small key. She showed it to Sharon. "Any idea what this is to? Looks like maybe a storage locker."

"There are some of those in the basement," Sharon answered. "I didn't know Kate had one."

Michelle and King descended to the basement, found the storage closet, matched the number with the one on the key and opened it. King turned on a light, and they looked around at the stacks of boxes.

King drew a deep breath and said, "Okay, this will either be a bust or a gold mine."

Four boxes later they had their answer: neatly organized scrapbooks detailing two separate things. One was the Ritter assassination. King and Michelle looked at dozens of articles and photos of the event, including several of King, two of a much younger Kate Ramsey looking sad and alone and even one of Regina Ramsey. The text on the pages was heavily underscored with pen. "Not so strange for her to have collected these," said Michelle. "It was her father, after all."

However, the other subject cataloged here was far more chilling. It was all about John Bruno, from his early days as a prosecutor to his presidential candidacy. King spotted two yellowed newspaper articles describing investigations into corruption in the D.C. United States Attorney's Office. Bill Martin's name was prominently mentioned, but Bruno's wasn't. However, Kate had written at the top of each page: "John Bruno."

"Oh, shit," said King. "Our little political activist is involved in some serious stuff here. And regardless of whether Bruno deserved it or not, she's tagged him as a crooked prosecutor who ruined her father's life."

"What I don't get," said Michelle, "is that these stories were printed before Kate was even born. Where did she get them?"

"The man in the Mercedes. The guy making her hate Bruno for what he did to her father. Or didn't do." King added, "And maybe she blames Bruno for her father's death, reasoning if he'd been at Harvard or Stanford, he would've been happy and his wife wouldn't have left him and he never would have gone gunning for somebody like Ritter."

"But all that for what purpose?"

"Revenge? For Kate, for somebody else."

"How does that tie into Ritter and Loretta Baldwin and all the rest?"

King threw up his hands in frustration. "Damn it, I wish I knew. But I do know this: Kate is only the tip of the iceberg. And now something else makes sense." She looked at him. "Kate wanted to meet so she could tell us about this suddenly new revelation about Thornton Jorst."

"You think she was prompted to do that? To throw us off track?"

"Maybe. Or maybe she did it on her own, for another reason."

"Or maybe she's telling the truth," offered Michelle.

"Are you kidding? Nobody has so far. Why should the rules change now?"

"Well, I have to say, Kate Ramsey is a world-class actress. I never pegged her being involved."

"Well, her mother was supposed to be a superstar in that regard. Maybe she inherited those genes." King looked thoughtful for a moment and then said, "Get Parks on the horn and see what he's come up with on Bob Scott. I'm suddenly very interested in my ex-detail leader."

As it turned out, Parks had been very busy in the last several hours. He'd confirmed the address in Tennessee for Bob Scott and told Michelle that it had several intriguing attributes. It was a thirty-acre parcel in the mountainous rural eastern part of the state. The property had also been part of an army encampment during World War II and for twenty years thereafter, before it was sold to private owners. Since then it had changed hands several times.

Parks told Michelle, "When I found out it was once owned by the United States Army, I started wondering why Scott might want to own a spread like that. He'd been living in Montana for a while, real militia person, I guess, so why the move? Well, I've been poring over maps, blueprints and diagrams, and I found out the damn property has an underground bunker built into a hillside. The government and military had thousands of them constructed during the Cold War, from small and simple to the gargantuan one at the Greenbrier Resort in West Virginia to house the United States Congress in the event of nuclear war. The one Scott owns is pretty elaborate, with bunk rooms, a galley, bathrooms, shooting range, water and air filtration facilities. Hell, the army probably forgot it was even there when the property was sold. One other interesting thing: it has cells for housing prisoners of war, in case of invasion, I guess."

"A prison," said Michelle. "Pretty handy for holding kidnapped presidential candidates."

"That's what I'm thinking. And on top of that, this place in Tennessee is barely two hours by car from where both Ritter was killed and Bruno was kidnapped. Those three places roughly form a tri-angular shape."

"And you're sure it's the same Bob Scott?" asked Michelle.

"Pretty damn sure. But for this old warrant, it would have been tough to track him down; he's gone pretty far underground."

"Are you still planning to go down there?" asked Michelle.

"We found a friendly Tennessee judge who issued us a search warrant. We're going to pay that place a visit, but under a pretense because I don't want anyone getting shot. And once inside, we see what we see. It's a little dicey from a legal point of view, but I figure if we can get Bruno out before something happens to him, and bag Scott, then it's worth it. We'll let the lawyers figure it all out later."

"When are you leaving?"

"It'll take us a while to get everything set, and we'll want to do it in broad daylight. I don't want this Scott wacko to open fire on what he thinks are trespassers. It's about a four- or five-hour drive, so really early tomorrow morning. You still want to go?"

"We do," said Michelle with a glance at King. "And we may find somebody else there."

"Who's that?" asked Parks.

"A graduate student holding a long grudge." She clicked off and filled in King on the events. Then she pulled out a sheet of paper and started scribbling out some bullet points.

"Okay, here's my brilliant theory number two, which assumes that Jorst is not involved. Let's take it point by point," she began. "Scott sets up the

Ritter killing with Ramsey; he's the inside guy. For what motivation I don't know, maybe money, maybe he had some secret vendetta against Ritter." She snapped her fingers. "Wait a minute. I know it sounds crazy, but maybe Scott's parents gave all their money to Ritter when he was a preacher? You remember what Jorst said about that? And when I was doing background on Ritter, I confirmed he was a very rich man, basically because of these 'donations' to his church, a church he was somehow sole beneficiary of."

"I thought about that too. But unfortunately that theory doesn't fit the facts. I worked with Scott for years and know his history. His parents died when he was a kid. And they didn't have any money to leave him anyway."

She sat back with a frustrated look. "Too bad. That would have been a good incentive. Hey, what about Sidney Morse? His parents were wealthy. Maybe they gave their money to Ritter. Then maybe Morse was involved in Ritter's death."

"No. She gave her money to Morse when she died. I remember hearing about it when Morse came onto the campaign, because she passed away during that time. And in any event, we know the Ritter and Bruno cases are somehow connected. Even if Sidney had something to do with Ritter's death, he couldn't have been involved with Bruno's kidnapping. Not unless he knocked him out with a tennis ball."

"Okay, that's true. All right, let's still assume Bob Scott was behind it. That's the first part. Let's just say he was paid off to help orchestrate the assassination. It costs him his career, but so be it. He goes off and lives in the wilds of Montana."

"But what about Bruno? What connection could Scott have to the man?"

"Well, what if when he set up Ritter he did it because he and Ramsey were friends somehow, way back when? I know it seems crazy. Scott fought in Vietnam and Ramsey protested against it, but stranger things have happened. Maybe they met at some protest. You know, Scott was sick of the war and jumped to Ramsey's way of thinking. So maybe if he helped set up the assassination of Ritter with Arnold Ramsey, he also knows Kate Ramsey. And then he's also aware that Bruno ruined her father's career with trumped-up charges, and he told Kate that. Now Kate grows up hating Bruno, and Scott comes back in the picture somehow, and they team up to kidnap him and make him pay for what he did. That would pretty much explain it all."

"And the man who visited Arnold Ramsey, the

one Kate overheard saying Thornton Jorst's name – you're saying that was Scott?"

"Well, if Kate is really involved, she could have just lied about that to throw us off the truth, like we talked about. So what do you think?"

"Those are pretty good deductions."

"Well, I think we make a pretty good team."

King drew a deep breath. "Now I guess we wait and see what tomorrow brings."

60

The next morning they left at the crack of dawn in three vehicles. Parks drove with King and Michelle, and two Suburbans carrying grim-looking, armor-wearing federal agents followed them.

King and Michelle had filled in Parks on the developments with Kate Ramsey and Michelle's theory on how all the dots connected, however precariously.

Parks did not look convinced. "With the way things have been going in this case, I'm just waiting for another damn curveball."

On the way down over coffee and Krispy Kremes, Parks went over the attack plan: "We're going to send one of the trucks down to the house after we disguise it as a county survey vehicle. One of our guys goes up to the door with his clipboard while another pulls out the survey equipment. Some of our men will be inside the truck. The others will have surrounded the place and set up a perimeter.

Our guy knocks on the door, and when someone opens it, everyone pops out loaded for bear and we go in hard and heavy. If nobody's home, we go in clean and execute on our search warrant. With any luck no shots are fired, and we all go home happy and alive."

King was riding in the backseat. He reached over and touched Parks on the shoulder. "You know Bob Scott is a weapons freak, but he's also an expert in hand-to-hand. That's how he escaped from the Viet Cong. Story goes he spent six months filing a metal buckle down to a razor's edge and then cut the throats of his two captors with it. Not a guy you want to slip up with."

"I hear you. We go in with surprise and over-whelming force. Textbook. That's the best way I know how to do it." Parks then said, "You really think we'll find Bruno and maybe Joan there?"

"Maybe," said King, "but I don't know if they'll be breathing."

Buick Man and Simmons were completing their preparations. The generators were in place and fully operational. The wires had been laid, the explosives set, the detonators readied. The items that Buick Man had so diligently created were also in place and ready for the big moment. All equipment had been tested and checked a dozen times. All it had to do was work perfectly the thirteenth go-round, and victory was theirs.

As Buick Man surveyed his handiwork representing so much planning and work, he didn't even allow himself a look of satisfaction. Simmons noted this and put aside the box he was rechecking.

"Well, it's almost show time. Looks like we're actually going to pull it off. You ought to feel good about that."

"Go check on them," Buick Man ordered crisply, and then sat in a chair and went over every detail again in his head.

Simmons made his way to the prisoners and eyed them through the separate doors of the rooms they were being held in. Unconscious for now – their food had been drugged – they'd be awake soon enough. And if all went according to plan, he'd be on his way out of the country with enough money to last him several lifetimes. He returned to where Buick Man still sat, eyes closed, head lowered.

"How long before you think they come calling here?" Simmons asked, breaking the silence hesitantly, for he knew how the man craved quiet.

Buick Man answered, "Soon. They should be hitting the Tennessee bunker any time now."

"They'll be surprised."

Buick Man looked at him disdainfully. "That's the general idea. Do you have any comprehension of the thought and planning that's gone into this? Do you think this is all simply for your amusement?"

Simmons looked down nervously. "So when will she be getting back?"

"She'll be here in time. She wouldn't want to miss the next part. I'm actually looking forward to it myself." Now he looked at his companion. "Are *you* ready?"

Simmons squared his shoulders and assumed a confident look. "I was born ready for this stuff."

Buick Man stared at him intently for a moment or so and then lowered his head and closed his eyes once more.

61

Using binoculars, Michelle and King watched safely from the truck as a Suburban with a half dozen of Parks's men inside rolled down the dirt road toward the house, or more aptly, the cabin. Looking around, King thought that the area could not be any more remote. They were on the spine of a ridge of the Great Smoky Mountains, and the tricky topography had pushed the truck's four-wheel-drive power to its limits. Pine, ash and oak rose on all sides around them, forming a wall that would bring darkness there about two hours earlier than normal. Even now, at eleven o'clock in the morning, dusk seemed to be gathering, and there was a damp cold in the air that seemed to eat right through them, even inside the truck.

King and Michelle watched as the Suburban stopped in front of the cabin and the driver got out. There were no other vehicles visible; no smoke curled from the cabin's chimney, and not even a dog, cat or chicken graced the dirt front yard. Inside the truck the heavily armed federal agents were invisible behind the tinted glass. Well, King thought, the Trojan horse tactic had worked for thousands of years, and he hoped it continued its win streak here. As he sat there visualizing the agents lying in wait, another thought dimly took shape in his head: *Trojan horse?* He pushed it away for now and refocused on the coming siege.

The cabin was surrounded by the other agents, who lay in the dirt and grass and behind rock out-cropping on all sides, their rifles pointed at precise locations along the target: the doors, windows and other prime kill zones. King thought whoever was in the cabin would need to be a magician to escape this net. And yet the underground bunker was prob-lematic. He and Parks had discussed this. The blueprints the marshal had been able to obtain were missing one critical element: the location of the bunker's exterior doors and/or air vents, which it had to have. To guard against escape through these exits, Parks had posted men at points where it seemed logical the bunker would have outside access.

One of the agents walked up to the front door as another emerged from the truck and pulled out a surveyor's tripod. County public works insignia had been hung on the sides of the door. Underneath the men's bulky jackets was body armor, and their pistols rode on belt clips, ready to be pulled. The other men in the truck had enough firepower to take on an army regiment.

King and Michelle held their breaths as the agent knocked on the door. Thirty seconds went by and then a minute. He knocked again, called out. Another minute went by. He walked around the side of the cabin and reappeared on the other end about a minute later. As he walked back to the truck, he seemed to be talking to himself. He was, King knew, getting authority from Parks to hit the target. That authority must have been granted, because the doors to the Suburban burst open and the men piled out and flew toward the door that was blown open by a shotgun blast wielded by the point man. Seven men burst through this opening and disappeared inside. King and Michelle watched as men emerged from the woods on all sides of the cabin and moved toward it, rifles pointed and ready to fire.

All were waiting tensely for gunfire to signal that the enemy was there and prepared to go down in glorious flames. Yet all they heard was the breeze rustling the leaves and the occasional bird chirping. Thirty minutes later the all-clear was sounded, and

Michelle and King drove down and joined Parks and the other hunters.

The cabin was small and contained only a few pieces of rustic furniture, an empty fireplace, stale food in the cabinets and a mostly empty fridge. They had found the entrance to the bunker through a door in the basement.

The bunker was many times the size of the cabin. It was well lighted and clean and had been used very recently. There were storage rooms with shelves that were empty, but the dust patterns showed that things had been stacked there not long ago. There was a shooting range that, from the smell, had also seen activity. When they came to the prison cells, Parks nodded at King and Michelle, and they followed him down the corridor to one of the cells where the door was ajar. Parks used his foot to shove it fully open.

It was empty.

"They're all empty," grumbled Parks. "This was one big strikeout. But the place *was* occupied recently, and we'll go over it with a fine-tooth comb."

He stalked off to arrange for tech teams to scour the place. King stared at the inside of the cell and then shone his light into each crevice, flinching when something glinted back at him. He went inside, looked under the small cot and then said to Michelle, "Do you have a handkerchief?"

She handed him one, and he used it to pull the shiny object out. It was an earring.

Michelle examined it. "It's one of Joan's."

King looked at her skeptically. "How do you know that? It looks like any earring."

"To a man, yes. Women notice clothes, hair, jewelry, nails and shoes, just about anything another woman has on her body. Men only notice boobs and butts, usually in that order, and sometimes hair color. It's Joan's; she had it on the last time I saw her."

"So she was here."

"But she's not now, which means the odds are good she's still alive," commented Michelle.

"She might have dropped it on purpose," said King.

"Right. To let us know she was here."

While Michelle went to give the earring to Parks, King went into the next cell and shone his light around. He went grid by grid but saw nothing of any relevance. He checked under the bed and bumped his head as he was sliding back out. He stood, rubbed his noggin and noticed that he'd dislodged the small mattress. He bent over to set it straight before he was slapped on the hand for disturbing a crime scene.

That's when he saw it. The inscription was right at the edge of the wall where the mattress had covered it. He stooped and directed his light there. It must have been tough going, etching this into the concrete, probably using a fingernail.

As he read it, something clicked in his head, and he cast his mind back to the truck rolling down toward the cabin. Something Kate had told them was finally beginning to make sense. If it was true, how wrong they'd all been.

"What are you doing?"

He whirled around and saw Michelle standing there staring at him.

"Pretending I'm Sherlock Holmes and failing," he said with a sheepish look. He glanced over her shoulder. "How's it going out there?"

"The tech teams are gearing up to come in. I don't think they'll appreciate our presence."

"I hear you. Why don't you go tell Parks we're going to drive back to Wrightsburg? He can meet us back at my house."

Michelle looked around. "I was really hoping that today would answer all our questions. Now we just have more."

After Michelle left, King turned back to the wall

and again read over what was there, memorizing it. He debated whether to tell the others, but decided to let them find it on their own, if they did. If he was right, this changed everything.

62

On the drive back to Wrightsburg King was moodily silent. So much so that Michelle finally gave up any attempt to rouse him from his funk. She dropped him at his house

"I'm going to head back to the inn for a while," she said, "and check out a few things. I guess I should call into the Service. I'm still employed there, after all."

"Fine, good idea," King said absently, averting his gaze.

"If you don't want to give me your thoughts for a penny, I'll go as high as a nickel." She smiled and touched him lightly on the arm. "Come on, Sean, give it up."

"I'm not sure my thoughts right now are even worth a nickel."

"You saw something back there, didn't you?"

"Not now, Michelle. I need to think some things through."

"Okay, but I thought we were partners," she said, obviously hurt he wasn't interested in her assistance.

"Wait a minute," he said. "There is something you can do for me. You still have access to the Secret Service database?"

"I think so. I had a friend of mine slow-walk my admin leave papers. Actually, after they let me take my vacation time, I'm not sure what my status is. But I can find out quickly enough. I have my laptop back at the inn; I'll log on and check it out. What do you need to know?" When he told her, she looked very surprised. "What does that have to do with anything?"

"Maybe nothing, but maybe everything."

"Well, I'm doubtful that'll be on the Service's database."

"Then find it somewhere else. You're a pretty good detective."

"I'm not sure you really believe that," she said. "So far all my grand theories haven't really held up."

"If you find out that answer for me, there will be no doubt left in my mind."

She climbed into the truck. "By the way, do you have a gun?"

He shook his head. "They never gave it back to me."

She pulled her pistol out of its holster and handed it to him. "Here. If I were you, I'd sleep with it."

"What about you?"

"Secret Service agents always keep a spare. You know that."

Twenty minutes after Michelle left, King climbed into his Lexus and drove to his law office. He'd gone there at least five days a week for years until Howard Jennings had been found dead on the carpet. Now it seemed like a foreign land he was entering for the very first time. The place was cold and dark. He turned on lights and cranked up the heat and looked around at the familiar surroundings. They were a measure of how far he'd pulled himself out of the abyss created by the Ritter assassination. And yet as he admired a tasteful oil painting on the wall, ran his hand along the fine mahogany paneling, looked at the order and calm of the place which reflected that of his beautiful home, he didn't feel the usual sense of accomplishment and peace. Rather, he felt a kind of emptiness. What had Michelle said? That his home was cold, even a sham? Had he changed that much? Well, he told himself, he'd been forced to. You took the curves life threw, and you either adapted or got left by the side of the road, a self-pitying wreck.

He trudged to the small room in the lower level housing his law library. Though most research materials were now available on CD, King still liked to see the actual books on the shelves. He went to his Martindale Hubbell directory, which listed every licensed attorney in the country, separated by state. He pulled the volume for California, which, unfortunately, had the largest bar membership in the country. He didn't find what he was looking for but suddenly realized why. His edition of Martindale was the most recent. Maybe the name he was seeking would be listed in one of the older editions. He had a particular date in mind, but where could he find this listing? In an instant he had answered his own question.

Thirty-five minutes later he was pulling into a visitor's parking space at the University of Virginia's very impressive School of Law, situated on the north campus. He went directly to the law library and found the librarian he'd worked with in the past when he needed resource materials that were beyond the space and monetary limits of a small law practice. When he told her what he needed, she nodded. "Oh, yes, they're all on disk, but now we subscribe to the on-line service they offer. Let me sign you on. I can just bill it to your account here if that's all right, Sean."

"That'll be fine. Thanks."

She led him to a small room off the main library floor. They passed students sitting at small tables with laptops in front of them dutifully learning that the law can be equal parts exhilarating and stupefying.

"Sometimes I wish I were a student here again," King said.

"You're not the first to say that. If being a law student paid anything, we'd have lots of permanent ones."

The librarian logged him on the system and departed. King settled in front of the PC terminal and went to work. The speed of the computer and ease of the on-line service made his search much easier than the manual one at his office, and it wasn't long before he found what he was looking for: the name of a certain lawyer in California. After several false hits he was almost sure he'd found the one he was looking for. The lawyer was now deceased. That was why he hadn't been listed in King's current directory. But in the 1974 edition the man was front and center.

The only problem now was to verify that it was indeed the man he was seeking, and such verification couldn't be found on this database. Fortunately he thought he knew a way to get that confirmation. He called Donald Holmgren, the retired P.D. lawyer who'd initially handled Arnold Ramsey's defense. When King mentioned the name of the firm and the lawyer, and the other man gasped, he wanted to let out a victorious scream.

"I'm sure that was it," said Holmgren. "That's the man who handled Arnold Ramsey's defense. He was the one who cut that great deal."

As King clicked off his cell phone, so many things began to make sense. And yet there were many places where he was still in the dark.

If only Michelle would report back to him with the answer he'd been looking for. The answer that would match what had been scratched on the wall of that prison cell. If she did, he might actually find the truth in all this. And if he was right? The thought actually sent chills down his neck, because the logical conclusion to all this was that at some point they'd be coming for *him*.

63

When she got back to the inn where she was staying, Michelle eyed the box in the back of her truck. It contained the files on Bob Scott they'd retrieved from Joan's room at the Cedars. She carried it up to her room thinking she might go through it again in case Joan had missed something. As she sorted through it, she discovered that Joan's notes were in the box as well.

The weather had seesawed back to chilly again, so she stacked pieces of wood and kindling in the fireplace and ignited them with matches and rolled-up newspaper. She ordered some hot tea and food from the inn's kitchen. After what had happened to Joan, when the tray arrived, Michelle kept a sharp eye on the server and one hand on her pistol until the person left. The room was large and furnished in a graceful yet sumptuous style that would have made Thomas Jefferson smile. The cheery fire enhanced the serene atmosphere; all in all it was a cozy place. However, despite its amenities, the room's steep cost would have forced her to check out by now had not the Service offered to pick up the tab for her meals and lodging at least for a few days. She was certain they expected a substantial quid pro quo – namely, a reasonable solution to this jagged and maddening case. And they were no doubt aware that she – along with King – had helped develop most of the promising leads so far. Yet she was not so naive that she didn't realize that paying her lodging bills was a good way for the Service to keep tabs on her.

She sat cross-legged on the floor, hooked up her computer to the very new-looking data phone line in the wall behind the reproduction eighteenth-century writing desk and went to work on King's unusual request. As she'd predicted, the answer to his query wasn't on the Secret Service's database. She started making calls to Service colleagues. On the fifth try she found someone who could help. She gave the man the information King had given her.

"Hell yes," said the agent. "I know because my cousin was in the same damn prison camp, and he came out a skeleton."

Michelle thanked him and hung up. She immediately dialed King, who was home by this time.

"Okay," she said, barely containing her glee, "first you have to anoint me as the most brilliant detective since Jane Marple."

"Marple? I thought you'd say Holmes or Hercule Poirot," he shot back.

"They were all right, for men, but Jane stands alone."

"Okay, consider yourself so anointed, Miss Smart-ass. What do you have?"

"You were right. The name you gave me was the name of the village in Vietnam where he was held prisoner and then escaped from. Now, can you tell me what's going on? Where did you get that name from?"

King hesitated but then said, "It was scratched on the wall of the prison cell in the Tennessee bunker."

"My God, Sean, does that mean what I think?"

"There was also a Roman numeral two scratched in after the name. Sort of makes sense. It was his second POW camp; I guess that's the way he was looking at it. First Vietnam, now Tennessee."

"So Bob Scott was the prisoner in that cell, and he left the inscription as a way to say so?"

"Maybe. Don't forget, Michelle, it could have been left as misdirection, a clue we were meant to find."

"But it's such an obscure one."

"True. And there's the other thing."

"What?" she said quickly.

"The 'Sir Kingman' note that was pinned to Susan Whitehead's body."

"You don't think Scott could have written it? Why?"

"A number of reasons, but I still can't be sure."

"But assuming Scott isn't involved, who the hell else is out there?"

"I'm working on it."

"What have you been up to?"

"I had some legal research to do at the UVA law library."

"Did you find what you were looking for?"

"Yes."

"Care to fill me in?"

"Not yet. I need to think about it some more. But thanks for verifying that info. I'll talk to you soon . . . Miss Marple." He clicked off and Michelle put down her phone, not very pleased with his declining yet again to take her into his confidence.

"You help a guy out, and you think he'll return the favor, but nooo!" she complained to the empty room.

She threw some more wood on the fire and

started rummaging through the box of files and Joan's notes.

It felt a little awkward reading over the woman's personal comments on the case, considering she might be dead. Yet Michelle had to admit Joan kept meticulous notes. As she worked through them, she began to have a greater appreciation for the woman's skill and professionalism as an investigator. Michelle thought about what King had told her about the note Joan received on the morning of Ritter's murder. The guilt she must have carried all these years, though, seeing a man she cared for being destroyed while her own career rocketed onward and upward. And yet how much could she have really loved him if she chose not to speak up, in effect picking her career over her feelings for Sean King. And how must King have felt?

What was it with men anyway? Did they have this dominant gene that made them have to act noble when it came to suffering, however stupidly, as some woman walked all over them? Certainly a woman could pine over a guy just as hopelessly. And too often members of her gender fell for the bad boy who would break their hearts and even sometimes their heads. Yet a woman would have just cut her losses and moved on. Not the boys, though. They had to keep ramming their big pigheaded selves into a wall no matter how cold the heart lurking underneath the blouse and breasts. God, it was so frustrating that a man like King could be taken in by a woman like Joan.

Then she caught herself and wondered why it mattered so much. They were working a case together, that was all. And it wasn't like King was perfect. Yes, he was intelligent, sophisticated, good-looking, and had a witty sense of humor. But he was also more than a decade her senior. And on the negative side he was moody, aloof, occasionally rude and at times condescending. And he was so damn neat! To think that she'd actually cleaned out her truck to please—

She suddenly blushed at this frank admission and quickly refocused on the papers in front of her. She studied the warrant filed against Bob Scott that Joan had found and was the only reason they'd discovered the cabin and empty bunker. Yet from what King had just told her, the conclusion that Scott was behind all of this had become a lot more tenuous.

And still, it was *his* cabin, and the arrest warrant had been issued against him for a weapons violation. She looked at the document more closely. What exactly was the weapons violation? And why had the service of the warrant failed? Those answers unfortunately weren't apparent in the documents.

She gave up in frustration and continued perusing Joan's notes. She came across another name that gave her pause. For her, the fact that Joan had drawn a line across the man's name, ostensibly writing him off as a suspect, wasn't in itself conclusive. For though she probably wouldn't admit it to anyone, she was as confident about her investigative abilities as King was about his.

She said the name slowly, drawing out the two syllables of the last name. "Doug Denby." Ritter's chief of staff. Joan's notes said that after Ritter's death, Denby's life had actually taken a turn for the better with his inheriting land and money in Mississippi. Because of that, Joan had concluded he couldn't be their man. But Michelle wasn't that confident. Were some phone calls and general background information undertaken by Joan's people enough? Joan hadn't gone down to Mississippi to see for herself. She'd never laid eyes on Doug Denby. Was he really in Mississippi playing the country squire? Might he be instead around here somewhere, waiting to kill or kidnap his next victim? King said that Denby had been thoroughly upstaged by Sidney Morse on the Ritter campaign and come to resent him deeply. Maybe Denby had come to hate Clyde Ritter as well. What connection might he have had to Arnold Ramsey, if any? Or Kate Ramsey? Had he used his wealth to orchestrate some sort of revenge-filled campaign? So far Joan's inquiries hadn't answered those questions.

Michelle took a pen and wrote Denby's name under the one Joan had scratched out. She pondered whether to call King and ask him what he remembered about the man. Maybe she should take these notes over there and force him to sit down and work through them with her. She sighed. Maybe she just wanted to be around him. She was pouring another cup of tea and looking out the window, where it was clouding over and looking like rain, when her phone rang.

It was Parks reporting in. "I'm still in Tennessee," he said. He didn't sound happy.

"Anything new?"

"We've talked to some folks who have homes nearby, but they were no help. Didn't know Bob Scott, never seen him, that sort of thing. Hell, I think half these people are felons on the lam themselves. The place did belong to Bob Scott. He bought it from the estate of an old fellow who lived there about five years but, according to this fellow's family, didn't even know the bunker was there. And the place was wiped clean. No clues other than that earring you two found."

"Sean found it, not me." She hesitated and then

said, "Look, he found something else." She told him about the name of the village in Vietnam that had been scratched on the wall of the other prison cell.

Parks was furious. "Why the hell didn't he tell me that while he was down here?"

"I don't know," she answered, then thought about King's withdrawal from her. "Maybe he's not into trusting anyone right now."

"So you've confirmed Scott was a POW there during Nam?"

"Yes, I talked to an agent who knew the whole story."

"Are you telling me somebody came down here, took it over and made him a prisoner in his own home?"

"Sean said it might have been a trick, to throw us off."

"Where is our brilliant detective?"

"At his house. He's following up some other lines of inquiry. He's not really communicative right now. Apparently he wants to be alone."

Parks shouted, "Who cares what he wants? He might have cracked this whole case by now but isn't telling us squat!"

"Look, Jefferson, he's doing his best to find out the truth. He just has his own way of doing it."

"Well, his way of doing it is really starting to piss me off."

"I'll talk to him. Maybe we can meet later."

"I don't know how much longer I'm going to be down here. Probably won't be done until tomorrow. You just talk to King and make him see the error of holding out on us. I don't want to find out he's got some other evidence I don't know about. If he does, I'm going to slap him in a cell that looks a lot like the ones you two saw today. You understand?"

"Perfectly."

Michelle clicked off and pulled the phone line from her laptop out of the wall, winding it back up and putting it in her case. She stood and went over to the other side of the room to get something from her knapsack. So preoccupied was she that she didn't see it until it was too late. She tripped and fell. Rising back up, she looked at the oar with an angry expression. It was half under the bed, along with all the other junk from her truck. So stuffed was the underside of the bed that her possessions kept falling out, turning her bedroom into an obstacle course. This was the third time she'd tripped over something. She decided to do something about it.

As Michelle waged war against her junk, she didn't know that her entire conversation with Jefferson Parks had been captured by a tiny mass of circuits and wires. Inside the housing for her phone lines lurked another device very recently added and of which the owners of the inn were unaware. It was a state-of-the-art wireless surveillance device, so extraordinarily sensitive that it could capture not only conversations in the room or while Michelle was on the phone but anything spoken by the other party to the phone conversation.

A half mile away from the inn a paneled van was parked along the side of the road. Inside, Buick Man listened to the conversation for the third time and then shut off the tape. He picked up his phone and made the call, talking for some minutes and then ending with, "I can't tell you how disappointed I am."

These words sent a chill down the spine of the person to whom he was speaking.

"Do it," he said. "Do it tonight."

He hung up and looked in the direction of the inn. Michelle Maxwell had finally made it to the top of his list. He quietly congratulated her.

64

With everything else going on, King had somehow found the time to set up an appointment with a security company based in Lynchburg. He watched from the front window as the van emblazoned with "A-1 Security" pulled up.

He met the sales representative at the front door and told him what he wanted. The man looked around the house, then eyed King. "You look familiar. Aren't you the guy who found a dead body?"

"That's right. I think you'd agree I need a security system more than most."

"Okay, but just so we're straight, our warranty doesn't cover stuff like that. I mean, if another dead body turns up, you don't get a refund or anything like that. That's like an act of God, okay?"

"Fine."

They agreed on what was to be done.

"When can you get to it?" King asked.

"Well, we're kind of backed up. If somebody

cancels on us, we can pop you up higher on the list. I'll give you a call."

King signed the paperwork, they shook on it and the man left.

As night came, King thought about calling Michelle and having her come over. He'd kept her in the dark pretty long, and she'd been a trooper about it. Yet that was just his way. He always played things close to the vest, particularly when he was uncertain of the correct answer. Well, he felt more certain.

He called Kate Ramsey's apartment in Richmond. Sharon, the roommate, answered; Kate still hadn't turned up.

He told her, "Sit tight, and I'll let you know if she turns up. You do the same."

He hung up and stared out the big window at the lake. Normally when in a funk, he'd go out on the boat and think, but it was too chilly and windy for that. He turned on the gas fireplace, sat down in front of it and ate a simple meal. By the time he'd convinced himself to call Michelle he figured the hour was too late.

He thought about John Bruno's kidnapping. It was clear to King now that the man had been abducted because he had *supposedly* destroyed Arnold

Ramsey's life with falsified homicide charges. Those charges had been dropped only after the intervention of a lawyer whose identity King now knew. He wanted very much to share this information with Michelle, and even glanced at the phone, thinking he might call her despite the lateness of the hour. It could wait, he decided. Next King thought about what Kate told them she had overheard. Or thought she had overheard. The name Thornton Jorst, supposedly uttered by the mystery man to her father. But King was convinced that what the man had actually said was not Thornton Jorst, but "Trojan horse."

And something else Kate said was troubling him. According to her, Regina Ramsey said a police officer was killed during a war protest, and implied that the incident damaged Arnold Ramsey's academic career. But Kate also told them the University of Berkeley let her father receive his Ph.D. because he'd *already* earned it. Kate had to know they could easily discern that 1974 was when Ramsey received his Ph.D. and easily conclude that the protest wasn't about the war. Why had she done that? No answer to that question came to mind.

He looked at his watch and was surprised to find it was after midnight. After making sure all the doors and windows were secured he carried the gun

Michelle had given him upstairs. He locked his bedroom door, then slid a bureau across it for added security. He checked to make sure the gun was fully loaded and that a round was in the chamber. He undressed and crawled into bed. The gun on the nightstand beside him, he soon fell asleep.

65

It was 2:00 a.m., and the person at the window raised a gun, took aim at the bulky figure lying in the bed and shot through the window, the glass tinkling as it broke. The slugs tore into the bed, blowing feathers into the air from the down comforter.

Roused from sleep by the shots, Michelle fell off the couch and onto the floor. She'd dozed off while going through Joan's notes, yet was now instantly alert. Realizing someone had just tried to kill her, she pulled her gun and fired back at the window. She heard footsteps racing away and crawled toward the window, listening intently as she did so. She reached the wall and cautiously peered over the windowsill. She could still hear the strides of the person running away, and he also seemed to be wheezing. To her expert ears, his strides were curious, as though the runner was wounded or injured in some way. Whatever the cause, they weren't normal. They were more like disjointed lunges, and her mind played with the idea that either she'd hit the would-be assassin or he'd already been wounded when he came to kill her tonight. Could it be the man she'd shot in her truck, the one who'd done his best to wring her neck? Perhaps the man who called himself Simmons?

She heard a vehicle start up and didn't even try to race to her truck and follow it. She had no idea if anyone else was out there waiting. She and King had run into one ambush that way. She had no desire to repeat the mistake.

She went over to the bed and looked down at the mess. She'd taken a nap there earlier, and the covers and thick pillows had gotten balled together. To the shooter it must have looked like her sleeping there.

Yet why try to kill her now? Were they getting too close? She hadn't done all that much. Sean certainly had found out more than—

She froze. King! She grabbed her phone and dialed his number. It rang and rang but there was no answer. Should she call the police? Parks? It could be that King was just sleeping hard. No, her gut told her otherwise. She ran for her truck.

★

The alarm woke King. Groggy for a moment, he quickly became alert and sat straight up. There was smoke everywhere. He jumped up, then fell to the floor trying to breathe. He made it to the bathroom, soaked a washcloth and draped it over his face. He crawled back out, braced his back against the wall and, using his legs, levered the bureau away from the door. He touched the door to make sure it wasn't hot and then cautiously opened it.

The outside hallway was full of smoke, and the smoke alarm continued to shriek. Unfortunately it wasn't connected to a central monitoring station, and the single volunteer fire department station that serviced the area was many miles away. And his house was so remotely situated no one may have noticed it was on fire. He crawled back inside his bedroom with the idea of getting to the phone, but the room was so smoky he lost his bearings and was afraid to venture farther in. He slithered back out into the hallway and along the catwalk. He could see sparks and red flames down below, and he prayed the stairs were passable. Otherwise, he'd have to jump, possibly into an inferno, and that wasn't a very appealing idea.

He heard sounds coming from down below. He was coughing from smoke inhalation and desperately wanted to get out of the house, but he was still aware this could be a trap. He clenched the gun and shouted out, "Who's down there? I'm armed and I'll shoot."

There was no answer, which fueled his suspicions even more until he looked out the big front window as he lay on the catwalk. He saw the flashing red lights in his front yard, and he could hear the sirens of other fire trucks coming. Okay, help was here, after all. He reached the stairs and looked down. Through the smoke he could make out firefighters in bulky overcoats and helmets, with tanks strapped to their backs and masks covering their faces.

"I'm up here," he shouted. "Up here!"

"Can you make your way down?" called out one fireman.

"I don't think so, it's a wall of smoke up here."

"Okay, just stay there. We'll come for you. Just stay there and stay down! We're bringing the hoses in now. This whole place is on fire."

He heard the whoosh of spray from fire extinguishers as the men charged up the stairs. King was sick to his stomach and nearly blind from the smoke in his eyes. He felt himself being picked up and hauled swiftly down the stairs. In another minute he was outside and sensed people hovering over him.

"Are you okay?" one of them said.

"Get him some damn oxygen," said another. "He's breathed in a ton of carbon monoxide."

King felt the oxygen mask being placed over his face, and then he had the sensation of being lifted into the ambulance. For a moment he thought he could hear Michelle calling out to him. And then everything went black.

The sirens, flashing lights, radio staccato and other "sound effects" immediately stopped as the fireman hit the master switch on the control box with one hand and took the gun from King with the other. Everything became quiet once more. The fireman turned away and went back to the house, where the smoke was already starting to peter out. It had been a very carefully controlled "fire," with all the elements of the inferno artificially created. He went inside the basement, set the ignition switch on the small device next to the gas lines and left the house. He climbed into the back of the van, and it immediately drove away. The van reached the main road and accelerated, heading south. Two minutes later the small explosive device went off in King's basement, setting off the gas lines, and the resulting explosion ripped Sean King's beautiful home apart for real.

The fireman pulled off his helmet and mask and wiped his face.

Buick Man looked down at the unconscious King. The "oxygen" he'd been given included a sedative.

"It's good finally to see you, Agent King. I've waited a long time for this."

The van sped on into the darkness.

66

Michelle had just turned off onto King's long drive when the explosion rocked the night. She floored the truck and kicked gravel and dirt all the way up. She slid the truck to a stop as boards, glass and other parts of the destroyed house blocked her way. She jumped out, dialing 911 on her phone as she did so and screaming to the dispatcher what had happened, telling the woman to send everything she could.

Michelle raced through the wreckage, dodging flames and smoke and screaming out his name. "Sean! *Sean!*"

She went back to her truck, grabbed a blanket, covered herself with it and hurtled through the front door, or where the front door had been. The wall of smoke that met her was overwhelming, and she staggered back out, gagging and dropping to her knees. She sucked in some fresh air and this time entered through a gaping hole in what was left of the structure. Inside she crawled forward, calling out every few seconds for him. She started for the stairs, thinking he might be in his bedroom, only the stairs weren't there anymore. Her lungs heaving, she had to go back out to get some untainted air.

Another explosion rocked the structure, and she jumped off the front porch a few seconds before it came tumbling down. The concussive force of a second explosion knocked her through the air, and she landed hard, all the breath squeezed from her. She felt all sorts of heavy things hitting all around her, like mortar fire. She lay there in the dirt, her head cut, her lungs drowning in lethal fumes, her legs and arms bruised and battered. The next thing she knew sirens were everywhere and the sounds of heavy equipment surrounded her. A man in bulky clothing knelt down next to her, gave her oxygen, asked if she was okay.

She couldn't say anything as more trucks and cars lumbered up the drive and teams of volunteer firefighters attacked the inferno. As she lay there, the remaining parts of Sean King's house collapsed and fell in. Only the stone chimney remained standing. With that searing image in her mind Michelle blacked out.

★

When Michelle awoke, it took her a few minutes to realize she was lying in a hospital bed. A man appeared next to her, holding a cup of coffee and wearing a relieved expression.

Jefferson Parks said, "Damn, we almost lost you. The firemen said a thousand-pound steel beam that got blown off the house was lying six inches from your head."

She tried to sit up, but he put a hand on her shoulder and held her down.

"Will you just take it easy? You got the shit kicked out of you. You can't just get up and waltz away after something like that."

She looked around frantically. "Sean, where's Sean?" Parks didn't answer right away, and Michelle felt tears rushing to her eyes. "Please, Jefferson, please don't tell me . . ." Her voice broke.

"I can't tell you anything because I don't know. Nobody does. They haven't found any bodies, Michelle. No indication Sean was even there. But they haven't finished searching. It's, well, it was a bad fire and there were gas explosions. I guess what I'm trying to say is there might not be much to find."

"I called his house last night, there was no answer. So maybe he wasn't home."

"Or maybe it had already blown."

521

"No, I heard the explosion when I was driving up to his house."

Parks pulled the chair up next to the bed and sat down. "Okay, tell me exactly what happened."

She did, with as much detail as she could remember. And then she recalled what else had happened, an event that had gotten pushed to the back of her thoughts by what had occurred at King's house.

"Someone tried to kill me at the inn last night, right before I went to Sean's. They fired through my window and into my bed. Luckily I'd fallen asleep on the couch."

Parks's face turned red. "Why the hell didn't you call me last night? No, instead you go running into a building that's exploding. Do you have a death wish?"

She sat back and pulled at the corners of her sheet. Her head was hurting, and she noticed for the first time that there were bandages on her arms.

"Did I get burned?" she asked wearily.

"No, just cuts and bruises, nothing that won't heal. I don't know about your head. You'll probably just keep doing stupid things until your luck runs out and you lose that."

"I just wanted to make sure Sean was okay. I thought if they went after me, they'd go after him too. And I was right. That explosion was no accident, was it?"

"No. They found the device that was used. Said it was pretty sophisticated stuff. It was set right next to the gas piping in the basement. Blew the place sky-high."

"But why? Especially if Sean wasn't even there?"

"I wish I could answer that, but I can't."

"You have people looking for him?"

"Everybody and everywhere we can think of. The FBI's in the loop, the Marshals Service, Secret Service, Virginia State Police, locals; nothing's turned up yet, though."

"Anything else? Any leads on Joan? Isn't there anything?"

"No," Parks said in a discouraged tone. "Nothing."

"Well, I'm going to get out of here and get to work." She started to rise again.

"What you're going to do is lie there and get some rest."

"You're asking the impossible!" she exclaimed angrily.

"I'm asking the reasonable. You fly out of here all banged up and disoriented and maybe black out in your truck and kill yourself and someone else, well, I don't see how that can be a positive thing.

And remember, this is your second stint in the hospital within a few days. The third time might be the morgue."

Michelle looked ready to erupt again, but then she just lay back. "Okay, you win for now. But the minute something happens you call me. If you don't, I'll track you down and it won't be pretty."

Parks held up his hands in mock protest. "Okay, okay, I'm not looking to make any more enemies, I got enough already." He went to the door, then turned back. "I'm not going to give you any false hopes. The chances we're going to see Sean King again are pretty remote. But while there's still a chance, I won't sleep."

She managed a smile. "Okay. Thank you."

Five minutes after he left, she hurriedly threw on her clothes, dodged the nurses on duty and escaped the hospital by a rear exit.

67

King awoke to total darkness. It was also chilly wherever he was, although he had a growing suspicion of where that might be. He took a deep breath and tried to sit up. It was as he'd thought. He couldn't. He was restrained. Leather bindings, by the feel of it. He turned his head, letting his eyes adjust to the blackness, but there was no ambient light here; he could make out nothing. He could be floating in the middle of the ocean for all he knew. He stiffened as he heard murmuring from somewhere; so low were the noises he couldn't tell if they were human. Then he heard footsteps coming toward him. And a few seconds later he felt the presence of someone next to him. Then this person touched him on the shoulder, gently, not threatening at all. And then the touch became a clench. As more pressure was exerted and then something pricked his skin, King bit his lip, determined not to cry out at the pain.

Finally he managed to say in a very calm tone,

"Look, you're not going to crush me to death with your hands, so just back the hell off!"

The pressure immediately ceased and the footsteps moved away. King felt the sweat on his brow. Then he became chilled and felt sick to his stomach. They must have shot him up with something, he decided. He turned his head to the side and vomited.

At least being able to retch made him feel alive. "Sorry about the rug," he muttered. He closed his eyes and slowly dozed off.

Michelle's first stop was King's ruined home. As she walked through the rubble, firefighters, police deputies and others were inspecting the damage and putting out small blazes. She spoke with some of them, and they confirmed no human remains had been found. As her gaze ran over the rubble of what had been Sean King's "perfect" home, Michelle grew increasingly despondent. There was nothing she could learn from this. She went down to the dock and sat on King's sailboat for a while, gazing out at the calm lake, trying to draw some strength and inspiration from being at least close to things the man so dearly loved.

Two items were bothering her greatly: the warrant for Bob Scott, and verifying the whereabouts of Doug Denby. She decided to do something about both. She drove back to the inn, calling her father along the way. As a very well-respected chief of police, Frank Maxwell knew everybody in Tennessee worth knowing. She told her father what she needed.

"Is everything all right? You don't sound too good."

"I guess you haven't heard, Dad. They blew up Sean King's house last night, and now he's missing."

"My God, are *you* okay?"

"I'm fine." She said nothing about the attempt on her life. Years ago she'd decided not to confide too much to her father about her professional side. His sons could walk into danger, and their father would consider it simply part of the job. However, he'd not take it well that his only daughter had almost been killed. "Dad, I need that info just as fast as you can get it."

"I hear you. It won't take long." He hung up.

She arrived at the inn, grabbed Joan's notes from her room and made a series of phone calls concerning Doug Denby, the last to Denby's home in Jackson, Mississippi. The woman who answered would give her no information about Denby, not even confirming that he lived there. That wasn't so odd, since Michelle was a stranger. And yet if Denby had money and no obligation to show up at a job every day, he could be anywhere. And no one she'd talked to could provide Denby with alibis for any of the critical times in question. His position in the Ritter campaign definitely made him a suspect, yet what would be his motivation?

The ringing phone startled her. She snatched it up. It was her father. He spoke succinctly as she wrote down the information.

"Dad, you're the best. I love you."

"Well, it would be nice if you visited more often. It's your *mother* who keeps asking," he added quickly.

"Deal. When this is all wrapped up, I'm heading home."

She dialed the number her father had given her. It was the law office that had handled the sale of the property in Tennessee to Bob Scott. Her father had already called the lawyer and told him Michelle would be calling.

"I don't know your father, but I've heard wonderful things about him from mutual acquaintances," the attorney said. "Now, I understand this has to do with a sale of land."

"That's right. You handled the closing of that property from a decedent's estate to a Robert Scott, I believe."

"Yes, your father mentioned that in his call. I

pulled the file. Robert Scott was the purchaser. He paid in cash; it wasn't that much actually. It was just an old cabin, and while there's substantial acreage it's all woods and ridges and very remote."

"I understand the previous owner didn't know there was a bunker on the property."

"Your father mentioned the bunker. I have to admit I didn't know either. It wasn't in the title search. And I had no reason to suspect there was one. If I had, I suppose I would have gone to the army. I really don't know. I mean what do you do with a bunker?"

"Have you actually been to the property?"

"No."

"I have. The bunker was accessed through a door in the basement."

"That's impossible!"

"Why?"

"There was no basement. I have the floor plan for the cabin in front of me."

"Well, there might not have been a basement when your client owned it, but there is now. Perhaps this Bob Scott knew of the bunker and built the basement to have access to it."

"I suppose that's possible. I was looking back through the chain of title, and there have been multiple owners since the army. In fact, when the army owned it, there was no cabin. One of the subsequent owners built it."

"You wouldn't happen to have any photos of Bob Scott, would you? It's really important," she added.

"Well, we normally make a copy of the party's driver's license when we do a real estate closing – you know, to verify identities since they're signing legal documents for recordation."

Michelle almost jumped in her excitement. "Can you send me that picture by fax, like right now?"

"No, I can't."

"But it's not privileged information."

"No. That's not it." He sighed and said, "Look, when I opened the file this morning, it was the first time I'd looked at it since the transaction closed. And, well, I didn't find the copy of Mr. Scott's driver's license."

"Maybe you forgot to make a copy."

"My secretary has been with me thirty years, and she's never forgotten before."

"So maybe someone took the copy out of the file."

"I don't know what to think. It's just not here."

"Do you remember what Bob Scott looked like?"

"I really only saw him once, for a few minutes, at the closing. And I do hundreds of those a year."

"Would you take a minute and think about it and try to describe him to me?"

The lawyer did so, and Michelle thanked him and hung up.

The description the lawyer had given was too vague for her to know if it was Bob Scott. And in eight years people can change a great deal, particularly those who've fallen out of the mainstream, like Scott. And she had no idea what Denby even looked like. God, she was going around in circles. She took several deep breaths to calm herself. Panicking was not going to help Sean.

Unable to move forward on any of her lines of inquiry, she started wondering about King's. He said he was working on something – something that required extra research. What had he said? He'd gone somewhere. She racked her tired mind trying to think of it.

And then she had it. She grabbed her keys and ran for her truck.

68

Michelle walked quickly into the UVA law library and up to the service desk. The woman who was there wasn't the one who'd helped King, but after Michelle asked, she was directed to the librarian who had.

Michelle flashed her Secret Service badge and told the woman she needed to see what King had been researching.

"I heard on the news about his home burning down. Is he all right? They didn't say."

"Well, we just don't know right now. That's why I need your help."

The woman told Michelle what King had asked for, then took her to the same room and logged her onto the system.

"It was the Martindale Hubbell directory," the woman said.

"I'm sorry, I'm not a lawyer. What exactly is Martindale Hubbell?"

"It's a directory of all licensed lawyers across the U.S. Sean has a set at his office, but it was the most recent one. He needed a directory that went back some time."

"Did he mention how far back?"

"Early seventies."

"Did he mention anything else? Anything that would narrow it down more?" Michelle didn't know exactly how many lawyers were licensed in the U.S., but she figured there were far more than she had time to look at.

The woman shook her head. "I'm sorry, that's all I know."

She left, and Michelle looked at the screen with a discouraged expression when she saw that the directory contained well over one million names. *There are over a million lawyers in the United States? No wonder things are so screwed up.*

Not really knowing where to start, she ran her gaze over the home page and noticed a drop-down screen that made her sit up very straight. It was entitled "Recent Searches." It listed the last few documents the user from this remote location had been working on.

She clicked on the first item there. When she saw the name of the lawyer listed, and where he was from, she leaped up and sprinted through the library, causing many aspiring attorneys to stare.

She was on her phone before she even got to her truck. Her mind was racing so fast, filling in the blanks at such a fierce rate, that the person she called said hello three times before she even realized it.

"Parks," she yelled into the phone, "it's Michelle Maxwell. I think I know where Sean is. And I know who the hell is behind this."

"Whoa, just slow down. What are you talking about?"

"Meet me in front of Greenberry's coffee shop at the Barracks Road Shopping Center just as fast as you can. And call up the cavalry. We've got to move fast."

"Meet you at Barracks Road? Aren't you in the hospital?"

She clicked off without answering.

As she sped off, she prayed they wouldn't be too late.

Parks met her in front of the coffee shop. He was alone, and not looking happy. "What the hell are you doing out of the hospital?"

"Where are your men?" she asked.

The marshal looked to be in a foul temper.

"What, do you think me and the cavalry just sit around the campfire waiting for you to blow the bugle? You call and scream in my ear and don't tell me a damn thing, and you expect me to conjure up some army and I don't even know where the hell we're supposed to be going. I work for the federal government, lady, just like you, with limited budgets and manpower. I'm not James Bond!"

"Okay, okay, I'm sorry. I was just really excited. And we don't have much time."

"I want you to take a deep breath, collect your thoughts and tell me what's going on. And if you've really cracked this thing and we need the manpower, we'll get it. It'll only take a phone call. Okay?" He looked at her with equal parts hope and skepticism.

She took a long breath and forced herself to calm down. "Sean went to the law library and looked up some information on a lawyer who I think represented Arnold Ramsey when he was arrested back in the seventies."

"Ramsey was arrested? Where did this angle come from?"

"Something Sean and I just stumbled on."

Parks looked at her curiously. "What was the lawyer's name?"

"Roland Morse, a lawyer from California. I'm certain he's Sidney Morse's father. Sidney Morse must have known Arnold Ramsey way back when, maybe in college. But that's beside the point. Jefferson, it's not Sidney, of course; it's Peter Morse, the younger brother. He's behind all this. I know it sounds like a stretch, but I'm almost positive it's him. Sean looked away for an instant, and Clyde Ritter was killed and his brother's life was ruined. He's got the money and the criminal background to put this all together. He's avenging his brother, who's sitting in a mental hospital catching tennis balls. And we never even had him on our list of suspects. He's got Sean and Joan and Bruno. And I know where." When she told him, Parks said, "Well, what the hell are we waiting for? Let's go!" They jumped into her truck, and she laid rubber off both rear tires getting out of the parking lot. While she was doing that, Parks got on his phone and commenced summoning the cavalry. Michelle prayed they were not too late.

69

When King woke up, he was so thickheaded he was sure he'd been drugged. His head slowly cleared, and it was then he realized he could move his arms and his legs. He gingerly felt around him. There were no restraints. Ever so slowly he rose, at the same time preparing for an attack. He edged his foot down until it found the floor. Then he stood. There was something in his ear and something rubbing at the back of his neck, and he felt the bulge at his waist.

Then the lights came on, and he found himself staring at his image in a large mirror on the opposite wall. He was dressed in a dark suit and patterned tie, and on his feet were black rubber-soled dress shoes. And his probing hand had just pulled out a .357 from his shoulder holster. Even his hair was combed differently. Just like he'd styled it back in . . . Damn! Even his graying temples had been darkened. He tried to check the gun's magazine, but it had been sealed in such a way that it wouldn't come open. He could tell by the weapon's weight that the mag was loaded. Yet he was betting that the ammo in there was blanks. It was the exact model he had carried back in 1996. He put the gun back in his belt holster and looked in the mirror at a man who seemed *exactly* eight years younger. As he drew nearer to the mirror, he noted the object on his lapel. It was his Secret Service lapel pin, red, the color he wore on the morning of September 26, 1996. A pair of sunglasses were in his jacket breast pocket.

As he turned his head, he saw the curly cord of the ear receiver in his left ear. It was undeniable: he was Secret Service agent Sean Ignatius King once more. It was amazing that all of this had started with the murder of Howard Jennings in his office. The sheer coinci— He stared at his stunned reflection in the mirror. The trumped-up charges against Ramsey, it hadn't been Bruno at all. The last piece finally clicked into place. And now there wasn't a damn thing he could do about it. Actually the odds were he'd never have the chance to right it.

He suddenly heard it, off in the distance somewhere, the low murmurings of what seemed to be hundreds of muffled voices. The door at the other end of the room stood open. He hesitated and then walked through it. Passing down the hall, he felt a little like a rat in a maze. Actually the farther he went, the more he felt that way. It wasn't a comforting thought, but what choice did he have? At the end of the corridor something slid open, and through this portal bright light was revealed along with the amplified sounds of the murmuring voices. He squared his shoulders and walked through.

The Stonewall Jackson Room of the Fairmount Hotel looked far different from the way it had looked the last time King was there. Yet it still felt intimately familiar. The room was brightly lit, the velvet rope and stanchions exactly where they were eight years ago. The crowd – represented by hundreds of carefully painted cardboard characters inserted on metal stands and holding "Elect Clyde Ritter" pennants and signs – stood behind the barrier. The din of their simulated voices emanated from hidden speakers. It was quite a production.

As he looked around, the memories came flooding back. He saw painted cardboard faces of his Secret Service colleagues positioned exactly where they stood all those years ago, badly positioned as it turned out. There were other faces he recognized. Some of the painted crowd held infants to be kissed, others pads and pens for autographs, still others nothing except broad smiles. On the back of the wall the large clock had been rehung. According to that timepiece, it was about 10:15. If this was what he thought it was, he had about seventeen minutes to go.

He glanced over at the elevator banks, and his gaze became a deep frown. How exactly was that going to play out? They couldn't do it the same because the surprise was no longer there. Yet they'd taken Joan for some reason. He felt his pulse quicken, and his hands started to shake a little. It was a long time since he'd been with the Service. In the intervening years he'd done nothing more strenuous than lift some heavy verbiage in thousands of boring, if creative, legal documents. And yet in sixteen more minutes he sensed he was going to have to perform just like the experienced agent he'd once been. Observing the lifeless figures arrayed behind the purple line, he wondered where among them would emerge the real, red-blooded assassin.

The lights dimmed and the sounds of the crowd ceased, and then footsteps approached. The man looked so different that if King hadn't been expecting to see him, he probably wouldn't have recognized him.

"Good morning, Agent King," said Buick Man. "I hope you're ready for your big day."

70

When they had arrived, Parks and Michelle spoke
with the officer who was heading up the local contingent of police that Parks had summoned. He had
called in marshals and other law enforcement from
the North Carolina area. "They'll get there before
we do," Parks had told Michelle on the way down.
She had said, "Tell them to form a perimeter around
the hotel: They can be right on the tree line and
still remain hidden."

Michelle and Parks knelt along the tree line
behind the Fairmount Hotel. A police cruiser was
blocking off the road leading to the hotel, but still
out of sight of the place. Michelle spotted a sniper
up a tree, his rifle with long-range scope aimed at
the front door of the hotel.

"You sure you have enough people here?" she
asked Parks.

He pointed toward other places in the darkness,
indicating where other lawmen were positioned.

Michelle couldn't see them but sensed their comforting presence.

"We have more than enough to do the job," he said. "The question is, can we find Sean and the others alive?" Parks laid down his shotgun and picked up his walkie-talkie. "Okay, you've been in that hotel and know the layout. What's the best way for us to hit it?"

"The last time we were here, when we nabbed the convicts, Sean and I managed to make a gap in the security fence as we were leaving. It was easier than climbing over. We can go in that way. The front doors are chained shut, but a large window about thirty feet from the front has been busted. We can go in there and be in the lobby within seconds."

"It's a big place. Any idea where they might be?"

"I have a guess, but it's a pretty educated one. The Stonewall Jackson Room. It's an interior room right off the lobby. There's one door going in and a set of elevators inside."

"Why are you so sure they're in this Stonewall Jackson Room?"

"This is an old hotel, and there are lots of creaks and groans and rats and creepy things. But when I was in that room and the door was closed, I didn't hear anything. It was quiet, too quiet. But when the door was open, you could hear all the normal sounds."

"I'm not getting your point."

"I think the room's been soundproofed, Jefferson."

He stared at her. "I'm starting to see where you're going with this."

"Are your men in position?" He nodded. Michelle checked her watch. "It's almost midnight but there's a full moon. There's an open stretch of ground we have to cover before we reach the fence. If we can direct the main attack from inside, we might have a better chance of not losing anybody."

"Sounds like a plan. But you lead the way. I don't know the lay of this land." Parks spoke into his walkie-talkie and ordered his men to move their perimeter closer in.

Michelle started to sprint off but he grabbed her arm.

"Michelle, I was a pretty good athlete when I was younger, but I was no Olympian. And now my knees are shot, so could you just slow down enough so I can keep you in sight?"

She smiled. "Not to worry, you're in good hands."

They darted through the trees until they came to the open ground they had to cross to get to the fence. They paused there, and Michelle looked at the hard-breathing Parks.

"You ready?" He nodded and gave a thumbs-up.

She jumped out and ran for the fence. Behind her Parks did the same. As she hustled along, Michelle focused at first on what was in front of her. And then her attention moved to what was behind. And what was there was suddenly chilling.

Those weren't the sounds of normal strides; they were the same disjointed lunges she'd heard outside her bedroom window at the inn – the ones made by the person who'd tried to kill her. She'd been wrong. It wasn't the painful jogging of a wounded man. It was the arthritic loping of a man with ruined knees. And he was now wheezing too.

She jumped behind a fallen tree a split second after the shotgun was racked, and the blast hit right where she'd been. She rolled, pulled her weapon and fired back, scattering shots in a wide, lethal arc.

Parks cursed at his miss and threw himself down, barely avoiding her fire. He fired again.

"Damn you, girl," he yelled. "You're too quick for your own good."

"You bastard!" Michelle screamed back as she scanned the area both for an exit and any accomplices Parks might have. She aimed two shots at Parks that blew chips off the large rock he was hunched behind.

He returned the favor with two blasts from his shotgun. "Sorry, but I had no choice."

She eyed the line of thick woods directly behind her and wondered how she could make it there without dying. "Oh, thanks. That makes me feel a lot better. What, doesn't the Marshals Service pay good enough for you?"

"As a matter of fact, they don't. But I made a big mistake a long time ago when I was a cop in D.C., and it's come back to haunt me."

"Care to enlighten me before you kill me?" Keep him talking, Michelle told herself. Maybe she could figure a way out of this.

Parks hesitated and then said, "Nineteen seventy-four ring a bell?"

"The Nixon protest?" Michelle racked her brains, then she seized upon it. "When you were a D.C. cop, you arrested Arnold Ramsey." Parks said nothing. "But he was innocent. He didn't kill that national guards—" The truth hit her in a blinding flash. "*You* killed the guardsman and pinned it on Ramsey. And you were paid to do it."

"Crazy times back then. I was a different person, I guess. And it wasn't supposed to be that way. I guess I hit the kid too hard. Yeah, I was paid off all right, and as it turns out, I wasn't paid nearly enough."

"And whoever you were working for back then is blackmailing you to do all this?"

"Like I said, it's cost me big. No statute of limitations on murder, Michelle."

She wasn't listening now. It had occurred to her that he was employing the same strategy she was. Keep her talking while they outflanked her. Now she was trying to recall the exact model of shotgun Parks was carrying. Okay, she had it. Five-shot Remington. Or at least she hoped. He'd fired four times, and it was so quiet out here she was sure she would have heard him reload.

"Hey, Michelle, you still there?"

In answer she fired three rounds at the rock and received a shotgun blast in return. As soon as the buckshot sped by, she leaped to her feet and raced to the woods.

Parks jammed fresh shells in, cursing the whole time. But by the time he took aim she was too far away for his buckshot to do any damage, and accelerating fast. He yelled into his walkie-talkie.

Michelle saw him coming. She cut to the left, hurdled a log and went flat to the ground just before the slug slammed into the bark.

The man she thought was a police sniper up

the tree was now also gunning for her. She placed several shots in his direction and then slithered on her belly for about ten yards before leaping to her feet.

How could she have been so damn blind? Another shot slammed into a tree near her head, and she hit the ground again. As she sucked in air, she assessed her abysmal options. There really weren't any that didn't involve her violent death. They could track her grid by grid, and there wasn't much she could do about it. Wait, her phone! She grabbed for it only to find it had fallen off her belt clip. Now she was cut off from all help and had at least two killers stalking her in dark woods in the middle of nowhere. Okay, this beat the hell out of the worst nightmares she'd ever had as a child.

She sprayed a few more shots in the direction she thought they were coming from, then leaped up and sprinted hard. The full moon was both a blessing and a curse. It enabled her to see where she was going, but it also allowed her pursuers to spot her as well.

She broke free from the woods, then pulled up just barely in time.

She was right at the edge of the embankment of the river she'd observed on her first visit here. A long drop awaited her if she took another step. The problem was that Parks and his partner were right behind her. She checked her mag: there were five rounds left, and she had one spare mag on her. Okay, in another few seconds they'd break free of the trees and have an unobstructed shot at her unless she could find somewhere to hide and nail them first. Still, even if she got one of the shooters, that would reveal her position, and the other shooter would probably bring her down. She looked around, seeking a solution with higher odds of survival. Then she checked out once more the long drop and the fast-moving river. Her plan came together in seconds. While some might call it foolish, most would term it suicidal. But what the hell, she'd always loved the extremes in life. She holstered her weapon, took a deep breath and waited.

As soon as she heard them make the clearing, she screamed and jumped. She had picked her spot carefully. About twenty feet down, there was a small rock ledge. She hit it and splayed out, grabbing for anything she could. Still, she almost slipped off and came within two frantically curled fingers of plunging into the river.

She glanced up and saw Parks and the other man peer down, looking for her. Because of where she'd landed, a chunk of jutting rock to the left of her blocked their view of her location. And the moon was behind them, silhouetting both men beautifully. She could have picked them both off with no problem, and was really tempted to do so. But she was thinking big picture here, and she had another plan. She put her shoe against the small tree trunk that had caught on the ledge she was on. That and its natural cover was why she'd picked this landing place. She pushed against the tree trunk until it was right at the edge of the precipice. She looked up at Parks. They were shining lights around, looking for her and pointing. As soon as they were both looking the other way, she gave the trunk one huge push, and it plunged downward. At the same time, she let out the loudest scream she could manage.

She watched as the trunk hit the river's surface, then glanced up at the men as they shone their lights at that spot. Michelle held her breath, praying they'd believe that she'd plunged to her death in the river. As seconds went by and they didn't leave, Michelle began to think that she'd indeed have to attempt to shoot them both. Moments later, though, they apparently made up their minds she was dead, turned and went back into the woods.

Michelle waited for about ten minutes, to make sure they were really gone. And then she grasped a rock jutting out of the side of the embankment and began to climb up. If Parks and the other man could have seen the expression on the woman's face as she pulled herself from oblivion, they would have been, despite their weapons and superior number, in very real fear for their lives.

71

You've changed a lot, *Sidney*," said King. "Lost weight. I hardly recognized you. You look good, though. Your brother hasn't aged nearly as well."

Sidney Morse, Clyde Ritter's brilliant campaign manager who was supposed to be sitting in a mental hospital in Ohio, looked at King with an amused expression. He also held a pistol that was pointed at King's chest. Dressed in an expensive suit, his face clean-shaven, graying hair thin but nicely styled, Morse was a slender, distinguished-looking man.

"I'm impressed. What led you to think someone other than the unfortunate Mr. Scott was behind this?"

"That note you left on my bathroom door. A real Secret Service agent would never have used the phrase 'pushing a post'; he would've just written 'pushing.' And Bob Scott was ex-military and always used the twenty-four-hour clock. He wouldn't have used '*a.m.*' And then I started thinking, why

Bowlington? Why the Fairmount Hotel in the first place? Because it was thirty minutes from Arnold Ramsey, that's why. As campaign manager you could have easily arranged that."

"But so could several others, including Doug Denby and Ritter himself. And to the world I'm a zombie in Ohio."

"Not to a Secret Service agent. I admit, it took me some time but I finally got it." He nodded at the gun Sidney held. "You're left-handed, I finally remembered that. Munching your candy bars. We in the Service tend to focus on the small details. And yet the 'zombie' in Ohio catches tennis balls in his right hand. And in a photo at the hospital Peter Morse was holding a baseball bat in his right hand, so I had confirmation of that."

"My dear brother. He was never good for much."

"Well, he was an integral part of your plan," King said in a prompting manner.

Morse smiled. "I see you haven't the brains to really figure all this out, that you just want me to lay it out for you. All right, I really don't see you testifying about it later. I got the sanitized guns Arnold and I had at the Fairmount from my criminally inclined brother."

"And you hid your gun in the supply closet after Ritter was killed."

"And that maid person saw me and spent the next seven years blackmailing me, only stopping when she believed I'd been committed. Your friend Maxwell unwittingly revealed the blackmailer's identity to me. And I paid her back. With interest."

"Just like you did Mildred Martin."

"She couldn't follow directions. I don't tolerate stupid people."

"I guess that included your brother."

"It was probably a mistake to involve him, but he was family, after all, and quite willing to help. However, as time went by and my poor brother continued to abuse drugs, I was afraid he'd talk. I also had all the family money, and there was always the possibility of blackmail. The best place to keep one's 'problems' is in plain sight, so I kept him around, supported him. When the time came, I switched identities with him and had him committed."

"But why switch identities at all?"

"It ensured that the world thought I was somewhere else while I put this little plan together. Otherwise, people might start nosing around." Morse stretched his arms out. "Think about it. Several of the players in the Ritter imbroglio brought together on an elaborate set like this? People inevitably would start thinking about me. Being

553

institutionalized was better than even being dead. People can fake their deaths. I was confident no one would be able to find out I had committed Peter rather than the other way around." Morse smiled. "And why do it if you're not going to do it with panache?"

King shook his head. He figured he'd buy as much time as possible by keeping Morse talking. The man obviously wanted to brag about his grand plan, and King could use the extra time to work out a strategy. "I would have done it differently. Commit him, then kill him. That way, you're assured people think you're dead."

"But killing him could lead to an autopsy, and that might show he wasn't me if they got old medical and dental records to compare against. If he dies naturally, all is fine. Besides, we looked enough alike, and the other little touches I devised were enough to fool anyone. My genius is in the details. For example, this room is soundproofed. Why bother in a deserted hotel? Because you just never know about sound: it carries in strange, unpredictable ways, and I really can't have any interruptions. It would ruin the whole performance, and I've never disappointed an audience yet. I also like to bring things off with a certain flair. Like the note you mentioned. I could have just slipped it in your mailbox. But a body hanging on the door, it's classic. And blowing up your house. It's just the way I do things."

"But why involve Bob Scott? Like you said, no one would suspect you."

"Think, Agent King, think. Every drama needs a villain. Besides, Agent Scott never accorded me the respect I deserved when I was with Ritter. He lived to regret that."

"Okay, so you fried your brother's brain, mutilated his face to further disguise his identity, fattened him up while you slimmed down, moved to Ohio, where no one would know either of you, and established the identity switch. That's quite a production. Just like the Ritter campaign."

"Clyde Ritter was simply a means to an end."

"Right. This had nothing to do with Clyde Ritter and everything to do with Arnold Ramsey. He had something you wanted. You wanted it so badly you led him to his death so you could take it."

"I did him a favor. I knew Arnold hated Ritter. His academic career had peaked long ago. He was at rock bottom and ripe for the offer I made him. I let him relive his past glory as a radical protester. I let him go down in history as the assassin of an immoral, disgusting man, a martyr for the ages. What could be better?"

"You walking off with the real prize. The prize

you tried to get thirty years ago when you set up Ramsey for killing a national guardsman. But that attempt failed and so did the Ritter plan. Even though Arnold was gone, you still weren't going to win."

Morse looked amused. "Go on, you're doing very well. What didn't I win?"

"The woman you loved, Regina Ramsey, the actress with a huge future. I'm betting she starred in some of your productions way back when. And it wasn't just business. You loved her. Only she loved Arnold Ramsey."

"Ironically I introduced them to each other. I'd met Arnold when I was doing a play having to do with the civil rights protests and needed some research. I never imagined two people so totally opposite . . . Well, he didn't deserve her, of course. Regina and I *were* a team, a truly great one with the whole world waiting. We were poised to hit the big time. The dominating presence she had onstage, she would have been a Broadway star, one of the greatest."

"And made you a star too."

"Every great impresario needs a muse. And don't be fooled, I brought out the best in her. We would have been unstoppable. Instead, my artistic power disappeared when she married him. So my career was destroyed even as Arnold wasted her life in his pathetic little academic world at a third-rate college."

"Well, that was your doing. You ruined *his* career."

"You've asked a lot of questions, let me ask one. What really turned your attention to me?"

"Something I heard pointed me in your direction. So I started digging into your family. I found out your father was the attorney who got Ramsey off the murder charge in D.C. I guess your plan was to make Ramsey appear guilty so Regina would stop loving him, then you'd swoop in as the white knight, save Arnold and take Regina as your prize. That's right out of a movie script."

Morse pursed his lips. "Only the script didn't work."

"Right, but then you waited until another opportunity came along."

Morse nodded and smiled. "I'm a very patient man. When Ritter announced his candidacy, I knew that opportunity had come."

"Why not just kill your romantic rival?"

"What's the fun in that? Where's the drama? I told you it's just not how I do things. And besides, if I'd simply done that, she would have loved him all the more. Yes, I had to kill Arnold Ramsey, but I didn't want her to mourn for him. I wanted her to loathe him. Then we could be a team again. Of course, Regina was older then, but the talent she had – that never goes away. We could still make the magic happen again. I just knew it."

"And so the Ritter assassination was your next major production."

"It was actually very easy to convince Arnold to do it. Regina and he had finally separated, but I knew she still loved him. Now was the time to show him as an unhinged killer, not the noble, brilliant activist she'd married. I secretly met with Arnold numerous times. I'd helped support them through the lean times. He saw me as a friend. I reminded him of his younger days looking to change the world. I challenged him to be a hero again. And then when I told him I was willing to join him, that Regina would be so proud, I knew I had him. And the plan worked beautifully."

"Except that the grieving widow rejected you once more. And this time it was far more devastating, because the reason was she didn't love you."

"That actually wasn't the whole story, which is why we're here today."

King looked at him quizzically. "And then later she committed suicide. Or did she?"

"She was getting remarried. To a man remarkably similar to Arnold Ramsey."

"Thornton Jorst."

"She must have had a defective gene for such people. I began to see that my 'star' wasn't so perfect. But after all these years if I couldn't have her, no one else could either."

"So you killed her too."

"Let's put it this way: I let her join her miserable husband."

"And now we come to Bruno."

"You see, Agent King, every great play has at least three acts. The first was the national guardsman, the middle act was Ritter."

"And all this is the closing curtain. Bruno and me. But why? Regina is dead. What do you gain by doing all this now?"

"Agent King, you lack the vision to see what I've created here."

"Sorry, Sid, I'm more of a down-to-earth guy. And I'm not in the Secret Service anymore, so you can just drop the 'agent.' "

"No, today you're a Secret Service agent," Morse said firmly.

"Right. And you're a psychopath. And when this is over, I'll make sure you're reunited with your brother. You can throw the tennis ball to him."

Sidney Morse pointed his gun at King's head. "Let me tell you exactly what you're going to do.

When the clock reaches 10:30 a.m., you will take up your position behind the rope. All the rest is taken care of. You have a very important role in this play. I'm certain you know what it is. I wish you luck in carrying it out. Bad luck, of course."

"So will this be an exact replay of 1996?"

"Well, not exactly. I don't want it to be boring for you."

"Hey, maybe I'll have some surprises of my own."

Morse chuckled. "You're not in my league, Agent King. Now remember, this isn't a dress rehearsal. It's the real thing, so hit your marks. And just so you know, this play will have only a one-night run."

Morse disappeared into the shadows, and King sucked in a long breath. Morse was every bit as intimidating and masterful as before. King's nerves were close to running away from him. It was him against who knew how many. He had one gun, and he didn't for a second believe his ammo was anything other than blanks. He eyed the clock. Ten minutes until it started. He looked at his own watch. It read almost 12:30. He didn't know whether that was a.m. or p.m. Morse, of course, could have set his clock for any time he wanted.

He looked around, trying to find something, anything, that might help him survive. All he saw was a replay of a horrific event that he'd never wanted to think about, much less relive.

And then it struck him: who was going to play the role of Arnold Ramsey? The answer came to him in a flash. Like father, like daughter! That son of a bitch. He really was going to do it again.

Michelle flitted along the trees, keeping a close eye out for anyone near the hotel. As she did so, she saw Jefferson Parks climb into a truck, its wheels kicking up dirt as he raced off. Okay, one less opponent to worry about, she thought. Satisfied it was safe to try it, she bent low and crab-walked to the fence. She was about to start climbing but then drew back. The low hum had puzzled her, and then she saw the wire running to the fence. She stepped back, picked up a stick and tossed it against the chain link. It hit and was immediately fried. Great, the fence was electrified. She couldn't use the gap in the fence because she'd told Parks about it, and they might be watching for her there, not convinced of her death by drowning. And the gap was so small she couldn't have avoided touching the fence anyway.

She moved back into the woods and thought through the dilemma. Finally she remembered what she'd seen on her first visit here and realized it might be her only way in. She ran to the back of the building where the slope of the land running up to the fence formed a perfect launch site of sorts. She'd been a champion long and high jumper in high school, but that had been a while ago. She measured off the distances, did a few practice jogs, eyed the height of the fence in relation to where she'd be jumping from. She removed her low-heeled shoes, tossed them over the fence, took up her starting position, said a silent prayer, drew in a long breath and took off at a dead run. She counted off her steps, just as she'd been coached. She came within a few seconds of aborting the whole thing as the electrified fence drew closer and closer. If she failed here, the defeat would not consist merely of a few tears at being beaten in a track meet. This one was for keeps.

She lifted off, her legs, arms and back working in unison, her muscle memory returning just in time as she twisted her body, arched her back and cleared the top of the fence by six inches. There was no soft foam to break her fall, and she slowly rose, aching all over, and put her shoes back on. Threading her way to the building, she found another broken window and slipped inside.

72

As the time moved to 10:26, a man appeared from the same doorway King had come through. John Bruno looked confused, frightened and ready to vomit. King could relate; he wanted to throw up too. He and Bruno were the Christians awaiting the lions as the bloodthirsty crowd eagerly anticipated the coming slaughter. When King approached him, Bruno instantly recoiled. "Please, please don't hurt me."

"I'm not going to hurt you. I'm here to help."

Bruno looked at him with a bewildered expression. "Who are you?"

King started to say something and then stopped. How exactly could he explain this? "I'm your Secret Service agent," he finally said.

Surprisingly Bruno seemed to accept this without question. "What's going on?" asked Bruno. "Where are we?"

"We're in a hotel. And something is about to happen. I'm not exactly sure what."

"Where's the rest of your men?"

King looked at him blankly. "I wish I knew . . . sir." This was all beyond insane, but what else was he supposed to do? And he had to admit, his demeanor as an agent had come back more easily than he would have thought.

Bruno saw the room's exit door. "Can't we just leave?"

"Uh, no, that wouldn't be a good idea." King was watching the clock as it moved to 10:29. Eight years ago Ritter was in front of him, dealing with the adoring crowd. King wasn't going to make that mistake with Bruno. He led him over to the rope. "I want you to stand behind me. Whatever happens, just keep behind me."

"Yes, absolutely."

Actually King wanted to get behind him. After all these years here he was: a damn human shield again.

He pulled the gun from his pocket. If the bullets weren't real, he had no chance. He eyed the velvet rope. He took a step forward. He was within an inch of it now, ironically almost in the exact same spot Ritter was in when Ramsey shot him. As the hand moved to 10:30, King chambered a round.

"Well, bring on the fat babies to kiss," mumbled King. "Just bring it on."

As Michelle peered around the corner, she saw the man standing outside the door to the Stonewall Jackson Room. He was armed with a pistol and rifle and looked to be the man who'd impersonated the police sniper in the tree before joining Parks in trying to kill her. She couldn't see his face clearly, but she suspected this man was Simmons. If so, she had an advantage. Should she jump out and tell him to freeze? He might get a shot off and be lucky enough to hit her. And then she looked up and saw the sentry glance at his watch and smile. That could only mean . . .

She rolled out, her pistol aimed at his chest. She did tell him to freeze, but she modified that approach somewhat by firing at the same time as she cried out. The slugs hit him right in the pecs; he yelled out and dropped. Michelle ran forward, reached the fallen man, kicked his weapons away, knelt down and checked his pulse. The booted foot came up and caught her on the shoulder, and Michelle tumbled back and lost her gun.

The man staggered up, grasping at his chest. How could that be? She'd nailed him squarely in the upper torso. She answered her question almost immediately as she struggled to her feet. Body armor. She lunged for her gun but so did he. They crashed into each other, and he got a stranglehold around her neck.

"This time," he hissed in her ear, "you're going to die, bitch." It was the man who'd tried to kill her in her truck.

She couldn't match him in strength, so she decided to use her advantage. She jammed her elbow into his left side, right where she believed she'd shot him that night. He moaned and his grip broke and he went to his knees. She kicked away from him, slid across the floor and fumbled for her gun. As her hands closed around it, she turned and saw Simmons rise up and pull a knife from his belt.

She aimed and fired, and the round hit him in the dead center of the forehead. She dragged herself over to him. As she stared down at his body, she had an idea. It just might work.

73

At precisely 10:31 King realized he had a major problem, or at least another major problem to join all the others. He glanced at the elevator. If the present held to the past, something was going to happen with that elevator. The problem was, if those doors somehow opened and King didn't look away to see what it was, he and Bruno might be attacked from that direction. Yet if he did look to see what it was, as he had eight years ago, that momentary distraction could spell doom for them both. He envisioned Sidney Morse watching him ponder this dilemma and laughing his butt off.

As the clock moved to the fateful minute, King reached back and grabbed hold of Bruno. "When I tell you to go down," he whispered urgently, "you go down!"

It was as though King could see every sliver of the clock's movement as the hand moved to 10:32. He readied his pistol. He thought about firing a round, to see if his ammo was live, but Morse could very well have only given him one real bullet, and he would have wasted it. Morse had probably figured that one too.

He made sweeping arcs with his gun, and his grip on Bruno's coat grew tighter. The candidate's breathing was accelerating so fast King was afraid he might just faint. He thought he could hear the smacks of Bruno's heart and then realized they were his own. Okay, he was as ready as he was going to be.

The clock hit 10:32, and the arc of King's gun became faster as he tried to cover every inch of the room. The lights went out, and they were plunged into total darkness. And then the room erupted in kaleidoscope lights that would have done any disco proud. They swept around the room like a flash fire, and the voices started up on high volume. It was deafening and blinding, and King had to shield his eyes. Then he remembered and reached in his pocket and put on his sunglasses. Score one for the guys in shades.

Then the *ding* of the elevator came.

"Damn you, Morse!" King called out.

The doors slid open, or was it just a trick? Indecision was tearing King apart. Should he look over or not?

"Hit the floor!" he told Bruno, and the man dropped instantly. King turned his head, determined only to look for a split second. He never made it that far.

Joan Dillinger was right in front of him. Hanging less than ten feet away, suspended from the ceiling, it appeared. It was as though she were on a cross, spread-eagle, her face pale and her eyes closed. King didn't know if she was real or not. He took a couple steps forward and reached out his hand, and it went right through her. Stunned, he jerked his head in the direction of the elevator. There was Joan, trussed up and suspended by wire. Her image had been projected by some mechanical means. She appeared dead.

Looking at the woman, he felt an immense rage. And that was probably what Morse was counting on. That realization alone served to calm King down.

As he turned back, he stiffened. Standing directly in front of him, between two of the cardboard characters, was Kate Ramsey, her pistol pointed at his chest. "Put down the gun," she ordered.

King hesitated, then laid down his gun. The lights returned to normal and the special effect sounds stopped.

"Get up," she told Bruno. "Stand up, you bastard," she screamed.

Bruno rose on shaky legs, but King kept between the candidate and his would-be assassin.

"Listen to me, Kate. You don't want to do this."

A voice boomed out from somewhere. It was Morse, playing the role of the director, calling out his next "shot."

"Go ahead, Kate. I've delivered them both to you, just as I promised: the man who ruined your father's career, and the man who took his life. Your bullets are steel-jacketed. One shot and you can kill them both. Do it. Do it for your poor father. These men destroyed him."

Kate's finger tightened on the trigger.

"Don't listen to him, Kate," said King. "He's the one who set up your father. He was the one who got him to kill Ritter. Bruno had nothing to do with any of it."

"You're lying," she said.

"The man you overheard talking to your father that night. It was Sidney Morse."

"You're wrong. The only name I heard was Thornton Jorst."

"You didn't hear his name, Kate, you only thought you did. What you heard wasn't 'Thornton Jorst.' What you heard was *Trojan horse*."

Kate didn't look as confident now.

King pressed this small advantage. "I'm sure

Morse told you everything to say to us. But that part you told us was true, only you didn't realize its significance." Kate's expression became confused, and her finger relaxed ever so slightly against the trigger.

King continued, talking fast. "Morse was the Trojan horse, the inside man on the Ritter campaign. That's how he explained it to your father. Morse knew Arnold hated what Ritter was doing to the country. But Morse didn't care about Ritter's politics. So why did he join the campaign? Because Morse loved your mother. She was his Broadway-star-to-be. With your father out of the way, she'd be his. And when that failed, he killed your mother. And now he's using you just like he used your father."

"That's crazy. If what you say is true, why is he doing all of this now?"

"I don't know. He's insane. Who else would put something like this together?"

"He's lying about all of it, Kate," boomed out Morse. "I'm doing this all for you. To give you justice. Now shoot them!"

King held Kate's gaze. "Your father killed, but he did so in what he believed was a noble cause. That man" – King pointed in the direction of Morse's voice – "that man is a cold-blooded murderer, and he did it out of sheer jealousy."

"You killed my father," she said bluntly.

"I was doing my job. I had no choice. You didn't see your father's expression that day. But I did. You know what he looked like? Do you really want to know?"

She looked at him, tears in her eyes, and slowly nodded.

"He looked surprised, Kate. Surprised. At first I thought it was the shock of actually killing someone. But then I realized he was surprised because Morse hadn't pulled his gun and fired. Morse was standing right near me. They'd made a pact. Your father was actually looking at him. It was right then he knew he'd been deceived."

Morse called out, "Last chance, Kate. Either shoot them or I will."

King looked at her with pleading eyes. "Kate, you can't do it. You can't. I'm telling you the truth. You *know* I am. Whatever lies he's fed to you, you're not a killer, and he can't make you be one."

"*Now!*" screamed Morse.

Instead, Kate started to lower her gun. Suddenly the door to the room crashed open. This distracted Kate for a moment, and King grabbed the velvet rope, swung it up and knocked the gun out of her hands. She screamed and fell back.

King shouted at Bruno, "Run! Out the door!"

Bruno turned and raced toward the exit where Michelle was just coming through.

The lights came fully on and blinded them all momentarily. Michelle saw it before anyone else did. She screamed and launched herself. "Bruno, down!" she yelled.

The gun fired. Michelle lunged in front of the candidate, and the slug hit her in the chest.

King pointed his pistol in the direction of the shot and fired. That's when he discovered Morse had never intended on giving him a chance. His gun was loaded with blanks.

King screamed out, "Michelle!"

She wasn't moving, even as Bruno fled out the door. And then the lights went out again, pitching them into darkness.

74

King crouched in the dark, frantically searching for something. Then the lights came back on, although at a lower level of brightness. He sensed something behind him and whirled. Sidney Morse was standing there pointing his gun.

"I knew she didn't have the guts for it," said Morse, flicking his pistol in Kate's direction where the young woman still lay on the floor. "Not like your *father*!" He swept his hand around the room. "I gave you a grand stage on which to perform, Kate. I scripted you perfectly; this was the great finale. Your mother would have given a dazzling performance. You failed miserably."

King helped Kate up and then stood between her and Morse.

"A human shield again, Sean, eh," said Morse, smiling. "It seems to be your miserable lot in life."

"Bruno got away, and so help me I'll kill you for shooting Michelle."

Morse eyed him confidently. "Bruno will never leave the Fairmount alive. As for Maxwell, her luck ran out. At least she went down in the line of fire. What more could a Secret Service agent ask for?"

He turned his attention to Kate. "Now, you asked a question. Why all this now? I'll tell you. This is no more about John Bruno than it was about Clyde Ritter." He pointed his gun at Kate. "Eight years ago it was about your father. Today it's all about you, dear, sweet Kate."

Her chest heaving and tears streaming down her face, she said, "Me?"

Morse laughed. "You really are a fool, just like your father." He eyed King. "You said that Regina rejected me because she didn't love me, she didn't want the magic. That was only partially true. I believe that she did love me, but she couldn't go back onstage after Arnold died, she couldn't become my star once more, because someone else needed her more." He looked back at Kate. "You. Your mother couldn't leave *you*. You needed her, she told me. You were her life. How incredibly wrong she was. What was a single, pathetic teenager to a legendary career on Broadway, a life with *me*?"

"That's because a man like you can't understand real love," said King. "And how can you blame Kate for that? She knew nothing about it."

575

"I can blame her for any reason I want!" Morse screamed. "And on top of that, when Regina wanted to marry this Jorst idiot, Kate was all for it. Oh, yes, I had my spies. She wanted a man just like her father. That alone is enough to justify her death. But there's more. I've followed your career, Kate. And you grew up just like your miserable father with all your pathetic protesting, marching and being such a noble do-gooder. It was déjà vu. I had killed Arnold, but there he was again: come back to life like the Hydra." Morse's eyes narrowed as he looked at the young woman. He said more calmly, "Your father ruined my life by keeping the woman I needed, the woman I *deserved*, away from me. And then you took up the banner after he died. But for you, Regina would have been mine."

"I can't believe my mother ever would have loved someone like you," Kate said defiantly. "I can't believe I ever trusted you."

"Well, I'm quite an actor myself, dear Kate. And you were so gullible. When Bruno announced his candidacy, I immediately thought of you. What a stroke of good fortune. Here was the very man who'd prosecuted your father for a crime I'd set him up for, running for the same office as the man your father had gunned down. It was perfect. The idea for the entire reenactment came to me instantly. And so I came to you, gave you the whole sad story about your poor father, and you bought every syllable of it."

Kate started toward him but King held her back.

She cried out, "You told me you were their friend. That you helped my father when he was arrested for murder and that John Bruno had destroyed his career." She looked at King. "He brought me all these news clippings. He said he knew my parents and helped them, long before I was born. They never mentioned him to me, though. But he said he was at the Fairmount that day and that you didn't have to shoot my father; that he was putting his gun down when you fired. He said you were really a murderer." She looked back at Morse. "It was all lies."

Morse shook his head. "Of course, it was. It was part of the play."

"It's a dangerous thing to believe a madman, Kate," said King.

"Not a madman, Agent King. A visionary. But I'll grant you, there's a fine line between the two. And now," said Morse with a dramatic sweep of his hand, "comes the third and final act. The tragic death of Kate Ramsey as, aided and abetted by the poor, demented former Secret Service agent Bob Scott, she avenges her beloved father, taking with

577

her John Bruno and Sean King – with, of course, all supporting evidence being found later courtesy of me. When you think about it, the symmetry really is breathtaking: father and daughter, the assassins of two presidential candidates perishing on the exact same spot. It's really one of the best pieces I've ever written."

"And you really are insane," said King.

"The mediocre always throw stones at the brilliant," Morse said smugly. "And now the last member of the Ramsey family – the sweet, loving Ramsey family – will finally disappear from this earth. I'm sure you'll die beautifully, Kate. And then I can go on with my life. My artistic power has been completely restored now. Another new identity and Europe beckons. The possibilities are limitless, even without your *mother*." He pointed his pistol at Kate.

King raised his gun too. "Actually, Sid, I've pared down your options to one."

"It only fires blanks," said Morse. "You found that out a few minutes ago."

"Which is why I knocked Kate's gun out of her hand and picked it up when the lights went out."

"You're bluffing."

"Am I? My gun's on the floor. But if you try to check, I'll shoot you. Sort of like the trick you used with the elevator. And the two guns look exactly the same anyway. It'll be impossible to tell. But go on and take a peek. Then when my bullet slams into your head, you'll know you were wrong. You screwed up, Sid. On a set you never lose track of the gun props. A *brilliant* director like you should know that."

Morse suddenly didn't look as confident.

King pressed his advantage. "What's the matter, Sid? A little nervous? It doesn't take courage to shoot an unarmed man or drown old ladies in bathtubs. But now we can see how brave you really are because you're not safely behind the scenes anymore. You're the star of the show, front and center, and your audience is waiting."

"You're a lousy actor. Your bravado is hardly convincing," replied Morse, but there was tension in his voice.

"You're right, I'm no actor, but I don't have to be, because this isn't make-believe. The bullets are real, and at least one of us is going to die, and we won't be getting back up for an encore. I tell you what, duels make for great theater, so let's have one, Sid. Just you and me." King put his finger on the trigger. "On the count of three."

His gaze bored into Morse, who was now pale, his breathing accelerated.

"Come on now, don't freak out on me. I'm just

an ex–Secret Service agent. Sure, I've gunned down guys who were shooting at me, but how good can I really be? Like you said, I can't possibly be in your league." King paused and then started to count. "One . . ."

Morse's hand started to tremble and he took a step back.

King squeezed the pistol grip tightly. "I haven't fired a gun in eight years. You remember the last time I did, right? I'm so rusty. In this light even at this close range, I can probably only hit your torso. But it'll still kill you."

Morse's breathing accelerated even more and he took another step back.

"Two." King's gaze never left Morse's face. "Make sure you hit your marks, Sid, and don't forget to take a bow as you're falling to the floor with a big hole in your chest. Don't worry, though, death will be instantaneous."

As King started to count "Three," Morse screamed. The lights went out, and King ducked down as the shot sailed over his head. He breathed a sigh of relief. His ruse had worked.

A minute later the woman who'd shot Michelle moved through the darkness past mounted figures on her way toward King. As soon as the lights had gone out, Tasha slipped on a pair of night-vision goggles and could see things clearly, whereas King could see nothing. She passed the fallen Michelle, then ducked in-between two of the wooden frames. King had retreated with Kate to a corner, but from here Tasha had a clean shot. The orders she had just been given were clear. Regardless of what else happened, Sean King and Kate Ramsey had to die.

Tasha took aim, smiling as she did so. Killing people, that's what she did. And now she was about to add two more to her hit list.

The slight noise behind her caused her to whirl around. The beam of light from the flashlight hit her right in the eyes, blinding her, and a far harder object followed. As the bullet slammed into Tasha's head, her homicidal career came to an abrupt end.

Michelle rose on shaky legs. She rubbed her chest where the bullet had ripped into the body armor she'd taken off Simmons. The impact had actually knocked her out. It stung like hell but she was alive. Luckily she'd come to just in time.

Using her flashlight, she found King and Kate. "Sorry, I had a little problem, or I would've been backing you up sooner. Are you all right?"

He nodded. "Did you see Sidney Morse?"

"Sidney, he's behind this?" King nodded. She looked puzzled. "I thought it was Peter Morse."

"I just recently figured it all out myself. Do you have a knife?"

She handed him one. "I pulled it off Simmons along with this flashlight. What are you going to do?"

"Just wait for me outside the room. And take Kate with you."

Michelle and Kate headed to the door. King made his way over to the elevator where Joan was still strung up. He checked her pulse. She was alive. He cut her down, lifted her over his shoulder and met Michelle and Kate outside.

Suddenly he put Joan down, leaned over and sucked in long breaths. The effect of his risky face-off with Morse was now hitting him.

"What's the matter?" said Michelle.

"I think I'm going to be sick," he snapped. "That's what."

Kate spoke up. "You were bluffing about the gun, weren't you? It wasn't mine. You just had blanks."

"I was bluffing about the gun, yes," he said between gritted teeth.

Michelle put a hand on his back. "You'll be okay."

"I'm too old for this macho *crap*." He took a few

last deep breaths and straightened up. "Do you smell smoke?" he asked.

They ran toward the exit and were met by a horrified-looking Bruno. He pointed down the hall where the flames were already impenetrable. Another wall of flames blocked the passageway to the upper floors.

Michelle spotted a black cable on the floor. She pointed it out to King.

"Is that what I think it is?"

He examined it. When he looked up, his face was pale. "He's wired the building with explosives." He glanced around. "Okay, we can't go out and we can't go up." He eyed the other way down the hall. "And if I remember correctly, that goes to the basement. And there's no exit from there."

"Wait a minute," said Michelle. "We *can* get out through the basement."

75

They reached the lower level as smoke from the growing inferno followed them. The lights were on down here, so they could see reasonably well.

"Okay, now what?" said King as he looked at the long hallway that was blocked by debris about midway down. "I told you there were no exits down here. We checked that out when Ritter was here."

"No, over here," said Michelle. She opened the door on the large dumbwaiter. "We'll take this up to the third floor."

"The third floor!" exclaimed Bruno angrily. "And then what, we jump? That's brilliant, Agent Maxwell, just brilliant!"

Hands on hips, Michelle stood right in front of Bruno. "This time you're going to do exactly what I tell you, so just shut up and get in . . . *sir*." She pushed Bruno into the dumbwaiter and then turned to Kate.

King stepped forward. "You go up with Bruno,

then send it back down. I'll follow with Joan and Kate."

Michelle nodded, then handed him her pistol. "Real bullets. Just watch yourself."

She climbed into the dumbwaiter, and she and Bruno started pulling on the ropes, propelling themselves upward.

As King tried to revive Joan, Kate slumped to the floor.

"You can just leave me. I don't want to live," she said.

He knelt beside her. "Morse played with your head and your heart, and that's a hard combo to beat. Still, with all that, you couldn't pull the trigger."

"I feel like such a fool. I just want to die."

"No, you don't. You have a long life ahead of you."

"Right. For what, prison?"

"What exactly have you done wrong? You haven't killed anybody. As far as I know, Morse kidnapped you too and held you here."

She looked at him. "Why are you doing this for me?"

He hesitated, then said, "Because I did take your father away from you. I was only doing my job, but when you take someone else's life, doing your job doesn't seem a good enough explanation." He paused. "And you did try to help us. You knew the story you told us about the 1974 war protest wouldn't wash, didn't you? You knew you were way in over your head in something really bad. I'm right, aren't I?"

"Yes," she said quietly.

They heard the dumbwaiter coming back down.

"Okay, let's get out of here," said King.

As he helped her up, Kate's scream made him whip around.

Coming at them out of the smoke was Sidney Morse. He swung his metal pole at King; however, King threw himself to the floor, and Morse missed.

King pulled Michelle's gun and pointed it at Morse.

"No more bluffs," Morse said with a sneer.

"No more bluffs," answered King.

The bullet hit Morse in the chest. Looking astonished, Morse dropped to his knees and let the pole fall from his hands. He glanced down, touched the blood streaming out of the wound, then stared dully back up at King.

King rose slowly, pointing his gun squarely at the man's heart. "The first shot was for me. This one's for Arnold Ramsey." King fired and Morse fell backward, dead.

"And you really should have had more respect for

the Secret Service," said King quietly as he stood over the body.

When King saw the blood on the end of the metal pole, he froze for an instant, then turned and stared in disbelief. Kate lay against the wall, the side of her head crushed in. Morse had missed him and hit her. The young woman's lifeless eyes stared at him. Morse had killed both the father and the daughter. King knelt down and gently closed her eyes.

He could hear Michelle screaming for him through the dumbwaiter shaft.

He looked at the dead woman for a long moment. "I'm so sorry, Kate. I'm so damn sorry."

King picked up Joan and placed her in the dumbwaiter, then got inside and pulled the rope with all his strength.

Inside a room off the basement corridor, the detonation timer that Morse had engaged before his murderous attack clicked to thirty seconds and counting.

On the third floor King lifted Joan out of the dumbwaiter and explained to Michelle what had happened with Kate and Morse.

"We're wasting time," said Bruno, who obviously couldn't have cared less about the young woman's death. "How do we get out of here?"

"This way," said Michelle as she ran down the hall. They reached the end, and she pointed to the garbage chute attached to the window opening. "There's a Dumpster at the end of the chute."

"I'm not jumping into a garbage bin," said Bruno indignantly.

Michelle said, "Yes, you are."

Bruno seemed about to explode in anger before he noted the deadly serious look in her eyes. He climbed into the chute and with a shove from Michelle rocketed down, screaming all the way.

"You're next, Michelle," said King.

She climbed into the chute and disappeared.

As King, carrying Joan, climbed into the chute, the detonation timer clicked to five seconds.

The Fairmount Hotel started to implode right as King and Joan landed in the Dumpster. The force of the hotel's disintegration knocked the Dumpster over, which was probably a good thing because the metal bottom shielded them from the brunt of the concussive force, smoke and debris. In fact, it pushed the heavy container a good ten feet across the pavement where it came to a stop a few feet from the electrified fence.

After the dust cleared, they climbed out and looked at the pile of rubble that used to be the Fairmount Hotel. Gone were the ghosts of Arnold

Ramsey and Clyde Ritter, as well as the specter of guilt that had haunted King all these years.

King glanced over as Joan groaned, then slowly sat up and looked around, her eyes finally focusing. She saw John Bruno and snapped back. She swung around and spotted King, her expression one of complete astonishment.

He shrugged and said, "Better start taking catamaran lessons."

He looked over at Michelle. She smiled weakly and said, "It's over, Sean."

He gazed at the rubble once more and said, "Yeah, maybe it finally is."

Epilogue

A few days later Sean King sat on a charred hunk of wood that had been part of his beautiful kitchen as he surveyed the spot where his home had been. He turned when he heard the car pulling up.

Joan got out of her BMW.

"You look fully recovered," he said.

"I'm not sure I ever will be." She sat next to him. "Look, Sean, why won't you take the money? A deal is a deal. You earned it."

"With all you went through you deserve it more than me."

"All *I* went through! My God, I was drugged. You went through a nightmare fully awake."

"Just take the money and enjoy life, Joan," he said.

She took one of his hands. "Well, will you come with me? At least that way I can support you in the lifestyle you've grown accustomed to." She attempted a brave smile.

"Thanks, but I think I'll stay here."

She looked around at the devastation. "Here? What's here, Sean?"

"Well, it's my life," he said, and slowly removed his hand from hers.

She rose, looking embarrassed. "For a moment there I thought the fairy-tale ending would actually happen."

"We'd fight all the time."

"And that's a bad thing?"

"Let me know how you're doing," he said quietly. "I do want to know."

She took a long breath, dabbed at her eyes, then looked at the mountain vistas. "I don't think I thanked you for saving my life."

"Yes, you did. And you would have done the same for me."

"Yes, I would have," she said earnestly. She turned away, looking so miserable that King rose and held her. She kissed him on the cheek.

"Take care of yourself," she said. "Be as happy as you can be." She started to walk away.

"Joan?" She turned back. "I didn't say anything about you being on that elevator, because I cared for you. I cared for you a lot."

★

King was alone for a while until Michelle drove up and joined him.

She said, "I'd ask how's it going, but I guess I know the answer to that." She picked up a hunk of drywall. "You can rebuild, Sean, better than before."

"Yeah, only it'll be smaller. I'm in a downsizing phase of life. Clean, simple lines, maybe even a little clutter here and there."

"Now, don't go crazy on me. But where are you going to stay for now?"

"I'm thinking about renting a houseboat from the lake marina and docking it here. Spend the winter and maybe the spring on the water while I rebuild."

"Sounds like a plan." She glanced at him nervously. "So how's Joan?"

"She's off with her new life."

"And her new millions. So why didn't you take your cut?"

"Indentured servitude isn't all it's cracked up to be." He shrugged. "She's actually a good person, if you look behind the titanium exterior. And I think she really loves me. Under different circumstances maybe it could have worked."

Michelle looked as though she wanted to know what circumstances had prevented such a result but decided it was best not to ask.

"So where have you come from? D.C.?" asked King.

"Yes, closing out a few things. Bruno withdrew from the election, luckily for America. They caught up to Jefferson Parks at the Canadian border, by the way. So you suspected him?"

"Right near the end. This whole thing started when Howard Jennings was relocated to Wrightsburg and came to work for me. Parks was his handler. He was the only one who could have arranged that."

"Well, that one was staring me in the face, and I never even saw it." She shook her head and continued, "Parks recruited Simmons and Tasha Reed, the woman I shot at the hotel; they were both formerly in witness protection. Morse paid them all to help. The warrant for Bob Scott was a phony. Parks stashed it in the box he gave Joan so we'd be led to the bunker that Morse bought in Scott's name. They found Scott's body in the rubble."

"All in the name of love," said King wearily.

"Yeah, Sidney Morse's sick, twisted version of it anyway." Michelle sat down next to him. "So what's next for you?"

"What else? Back to being a lawyer."

"Are you telling me that after all this excitement you want to go back to drafting leases and wills?"

"It's a living."

"Yeah, but it's not really *living*, is it?"

"Well, what about you? I guess you've been reinstated at the Service."

"Actually I resigned this morning. That's what I really went to D.C. for."

"Michelle, are you crazy? You just threw away years of your life."

"No, I saved myself from more years of doing something I really didn't want to do." She rubbed her chest where the slug meant for Bruno had hit her. "I've been a human shield. Not the healthiest way to spend one's time. I think I bruised a lung."

"So what are you going to do?"

"Well, I have a proposition for you."

"Another proposition from a lovely lady. What did I do to deserve this?"

Before Michelle could answer, another truck pulled up. It was an A-1 Security van. Two men clad in work clothes and tool belts climbed out.

"Jesus, Mary and Joseph," said the older of the pair as he looked around at where the house had been. "What happened here?"

"Really bad timing on my part, getting that A-1 system," said King.

"I'll say. I guess you won't be needing us today."

"No, but when I have another house, you'll be the first person I call."

"Was it a fire in the kitchen?"

"No, a bomb in the basement."

The older man just stared at King, then nervously motioned for his helper to jump back in the van. They kicked up gravel in their flight.

King nodded at Michelle. "Okay, your proposition?"

"All right, here it is." She paused and then announced in a dramatic tone, "We start a private investigation firm."

King stared dumbly at her. "You want to hit me with that one more time?"

"We start our own P.I. firm, Sean."

"We're not detectives."

"Sure we are. We just solved a huge, complicated mystery."

"We don't have any clients."

"We will. My phone's already been ringing off the hook with offers. Even Joan's old firm called; they wanted me to take her position. But I say, screw that, let's go into business for ourselves."

"You're serious about this, aren't you?"

"Serious enough that I already put a deposit down on a little cottage about a mile from here. It has lakefront. I can do sculling, and I'm also thinking about getting a boat and a wave runner. Maybe I'll invite you over. We can race."

He looked at her and shook his head in amazement. "Do you always move at the speed of light?"

"I figure if you think too much about things, life sometimes just passes you by. And my best decisions always have been made on the fly. So what do you say?" She put out her hand. "Is it a deal?"

"You want an answer right now?"

"Now's as good a time as any."

"Well, if you want an answer right now, it's going to have to be . . ." He looked at her smiling face, and that little spark she always carried in her eyes, and then he actually thought about spending the next thirty years of his life crafting brain-numbing legalese while earning his living in quarter-hour increments. He shrugged and said, "Then I guess it's going to have to be yes." They shook hands.

"Okay," she said excitedly, "sit tight, we have to do this right."

She ran to her truck, opened the door, and a pair of ski poles and a snowboard promptly fell out.

"I hope your office will be neater than your truck," said King.

"Oh, it will be, Sean. I'm really very organized in my professional life."

"Uh-huh," he said doubtfully.

She jammed the stuff back in and returned with a bottle of champagne and two glasses.

"I'll let you do the honors," she said, handing him the bottle.

He looked at the label, then popped the cork. "Nice choice."

"It should be for what I paid for it."

"So what do we call this fledgling agency?" he asked as he poured out the champagne.

"I was thinking . . . King and Maxwell."

King smiled. "Age before beauty?"

"Something like that," she answered.

He handed her a glass of the bubbly.

"To King and Maxwell," said Michelle.

And they officially clinked glasses on it.

Acknowledgments

To Michelle, my number one fan, best friend and love of my life. I wouldn't be here without you.

To Rick Horgan, for another great editing job. I think we each owe the other a beer.

To Maureen, Jamie, and Larry, for all your help and support.

To Tina, Martha, Bob, Tom, Conan, Judy, Jackie, Emi, Jerry, Karen, Katharine, Michele, Candace, and all the rest of the Warner Books family, for always going the extra mile for me.

To Aaron Priest, my guiding light in more ways than one.

To Maria Rejt, for her insightful comments.

To Lucy Childs and Lisa Erbach Vance, for all you do behind the scenes.

To Donna, Robert, Ike, Bob, and Rick, for all your help and invaluable input.

To Neal Schiff, for your added wisdom and help.

To Dr. Monica Smiddy, for all your thoughts and

specialized knowledge. Your overwhelming enthusiasm was much appreciated.

To Dr. Marina Stajic, for all your help. It was fascinating talking with you.

To Jennifer Steinberg, for once again finding lots of answers.

To my wonderful friend Dr. Catherine Broome, for patiently answering all my questions.

To Bob Schule, for being such a great friend and first-class consultant, for reading the early drafts and giving me lots of good advice.

To Lynette and Deborah, for keeping the "enterprise" straight on course.

And lastly, my apologies to any passengers on the Amtrak Acela train who overheard me discussing with various experts poisoning techniques for the story line and were probably scared out of their wits with my seemingly diabolical intent.

extracts reading groups
competitions books new
discounts extracts events
competitions reading groups
new extracts discounts
books events books
reading groups new titles reading groups
interviews books
new books extracts events new
discounts discounts
new books events books
events new
discounts extracts discounts
www.panmacmillan.com
extracts events reading groups
competitions books extracts new